Glowing praise for
Captives of the Night

"If you enjoy the lushness of complex characterizations and verbal interplay that is, by turns, seductive, yearning, and satirical, if you're seeking a love story that is tenderly sensual and compellingly romantic, take a look at *Captives of the Night*. And prepare to be wowed."
—*All About Romance*

"Loretta Chase, truly a gifted author, brings a brilliant life to these two strong characters. Their tender love story is one that should not be missed."
—*Gothic Journal*

"The stunning talent of Loretta Chase soars to new heights of glory in this love story of shattering intensity and incandescent brilliance."
—*Romantic Times*

Fabulous reviews for
The Lion's Daughter

"A writer of exceptional expertise, Ms. Chase leaves an indelible mark on the romance genre. Sure to become a cherished classic and all-time reader favorite, this dazzling foray into high adventure and romance will steal your heart completely away."
—*Romantic Times*

"A stirring portrayal of sexual awakening and love in a colorful, faraway land . . . I didn't want it to end."
—*Rendezvous*

"Loretta Chase makes a masterly historical romance debut . . . a keeper."
—*Mary Jo Putney

continued . . .

CAPTIVES of the NIGHT

LORETTA CHASE

BERKLEY SENSATION, NEW YORK

THE BERKLEY PUBLISHING GROUP
Published by the Penguin Group
Penguin Group (USA) Inc.
375 Hudson Street, New York, New York 10014, USA
Penguin Group (Canada), 90 Eglinton Avenue East, Suite 700, Toronto, Ontario M4P 2Y3, Canada
(a division of Pearson Penguin Canada Inc.)
Penguin Books Ltd., 80 Strand, London WC2R 0RL, England
Penguin Group Ireland, 25 St. Stephen's Green, Dublin 2, Ireland (a division of Penguin Books Ltd.)
Penguin Group (Australia), 250 Camberwell Road, Camberwell, Victoria 3124, Australia
(a division of Pearson Australia Group Pty. Ltd.)
Penguin Books India Pvt. Ltd., 11 Community Centre, Panchsheel Park, New Delhi—110 017, India
Penguin Group (NZ), Cnr. Airborne and Rosedale Roads, Albany, Auckland 1310, New Zealand
(a division of Pearson New Zealand Ltd.)
Penguin Books (South Africa) (Pty.) Ltd., 24 Sturdee Avenue, Rosebank, Johannesburg 2196,
South Africa

Penguin Books Ltd., Registered Offices: 80 Strand, London WC2R 0RL, England

CAPTIVES OF THE NIGHT

A Berkley Sensation Book / published by arrangement with the author

PRINTING HISTORY
Avon Books edition / February 1994
Berkley Sensation edition / May 2006

ISBN: 0-425-20965-2

BERKLEY SENSATION®
Berkley Sensation Books are published by The Berkley Publishing Group,
a division of Penguin Group (USA) Inc.,
375 Hudson Street, New York, New York 10014.
BERKLEY SENSATION is a registered trademark of Penguin Group (USA) Inc.
The "B" design is a trademark belonging to Penguin Group (USA) Inc.

PRINTED IN THE UNITED STATES OF AMERICA

10 9 8 7 6 5 4 3 2 1

Acknowledgments

Several themes in the story, both artistic and detective, are based on my undergraduate studio art courses with Professor Donald Krueger, who also provided some of the most useful historical resources for Regency-era crime and justice, and numerous details on artistic methods and materials of the period. Lesli Cohen, administrative assistant in the same Clark University academic department, provided additional technical guidance, as well as her usual generous and enthusiastic moral support. Both, however, must be absolved of blame for errors, excesses, and/or inadequacies, factual or fictional.

Prologue

January 1819

TWILIGHT HAD FALLEN OVER VENICE, TO plunge the marble corridors of the palazzo into gloom. The sound of unfamiliar masculine voices made seventeen-year-old Leila pause at the top of the stairs. There were three men, and though she couldn't make out the words, the rhythms of their low-pitched speech told her they weren't English.

She peered down over the elaborately carved balustrade. As her father emerged from his study, one of the men moved toward him. From her lofty vantage point, Leila could see only the top of the stranger's head, shimmering gold in the light of the open study doorway. His voice was an easy, friendly murmur, smooth and soft as silk. But Papa's wasn't smooth. The edginess she heard in his tones made her anxious. Hastily she retreated round the corner and hurried back down the hall to her sitting room.

With shaking hands she took out her sketchbook and forced herself to focus on copying the intricate woodwork of the writing desk. It was the only way to take her mind off whatever was happening on the floor below. She certainly couldn't help her father—if he needed help, and perhaps he didn't. He might simply be vexed by the interruption at teatime. In any case, she knew very well she was supposed to keep out of sight. Papa's work for the government was difficult enough. The last thing he needed was to be worrying about her.

And so, left to her usual companions—her sketchbook and pencil—Leila Bridgeburton awaited the arrival of the tea tray, sadly aware that today, just like yesterday and the day before, it would contain only service for one.

THE MAN WITH the shimmering gold hair was Ismal Delvina, twenty-two years old. He had recently arrived in Venice after a most unpleasant voyage from Albania. Since he'd spent most of that journey recovering from poisoning, he was not in particularly good humor. His angelic countenance, however, evinced only the sweetest amiability.

He hadn't noticed the girl above, but his servant, Risto, had heard the swish of skirts and looked up an instant before the girl retreated.

As they followed Jonas Bridgeburton into the study, Risto softly mentioned the discovery to his master. The master's infallible instincts did the rest.

Ismal smiled at his unwilling host. "Shall I send my servant upstairs to ascertain the girl's identity?" he asked, making Bridgeburton start. "Or would you be so kind as to spare him the trouble?"

"I haven't the least idea—"

"I pray you will not tax our patience by pretending there is no girl, or that she's merely a servant," Ismal smoothly interrupted. "When my men become impatient, they forget their manners, which are not so elegant in the first place."

Bridgeburton glanced from the huge Mehmet, leering down from his six-and-a-half-foot height, to the dark-featured countenance of the smaller but more openly hostile Risto. The color draining from his face, the Englishman turned back to their master. "For God's sake," he croaked, "she's only a child. You can't—you won't—"

"In short, she is *your* child," said Ismal. With a sigh, he dropped into the chair behind Bridgeburton's untidy desk. "A most unwise father. Given your activities, you should have kept the girl as far from you as possible."

"I did—she was—but the money ran out. I had to take her out of school. You don't understand. She doesn't know anything. She thinks—" Bridgeburton's panicked gaze shot round the study, from one pitiless countenance to the next. He glared at Ismal. "Damn you, she thinks I'm a government agent—a hero. She's no good to you. If you let these filthy bastards near her, I'll tell you nothing."

Ismal merely flicked a glance at Risto. As the latter moved to the door, Bridgeburton lunged at him—but Mehmet moved in the same instant and dragged the Englishman back.

Ismal took up a letter from the heap on Bridgeburton's desk. "You will not alarm yourself," he said. "Risto goes to administer laudanum, that is all—merely to ensure there will be no interruptions while we complete our business. You will not make any unpleasantness, I hope. I prefer not to make you childless, or the little girl an orphan—but Risto and Mehmet—" He gave another sigh. "They are barbarians, I regret to say. If you find it difficult to cooperate quickly and fully, I fear it will prove impossible to soothe their turbulent spirits."

Still perusing the letter, Ismal sadly shook his head. "Daughters can be so very troublesome. Yet so valuable, are they not?"

LEILA REMEMBERED WAKING—or dreaming she was waking—and the prompt onset of sickness. There was movement, and a man's voice. It was reassuring, but it wasn't Papa's. And it couldn't calm her churning stomach. That was why, in the night of the dream or the actual night, the carriage had stopped and she had stumbled out and fallen to her knees. Then, even after the retching stopped, she had not wanted to get up again. She had wanted only to stay there and die.

She didn't remember climbing back into the carriage, but she must have returned to it somehow, because when she woke again, it was to the same bone and belly-wrenching bump and rattle. She began to believe she was truly conscious, because she was thinking: Italy's roads were nothing like the smooth, macadamized roads of England, and the carriage wheels were surely made of stone or iron, and the Venetians had not yet invented carriage springs.

Leila smiled weakly because maybe all this was funny. She heard an answering chuckle, as though she'd told a joke. Then the masculine voice said, "Coming back at last, are we?"

Her cheek was pressed to wool. When she opened her eyes she saw it wasn't a blanket, but a man's cloak. She looked up, and even that slight motion made her so dizzy that she clutched at the cloak to keep from falling. Belatedly she realized she couldn't possibly fall. She sat on the man's lap, securely cradled in his arms.

She was vaguely aware that it wasn't right to be there, but everything in the whole world was wrong. Since she had no idea what else to do, Leila began to cry.

He pushed a large, crisp handkerchief into her shaking hands. "Laudanum can be very sick-making if you're not used to it."

Between sobs, she managed to choke out an apology.

He pressed her closer and patted her back and let her sob until she was done with it. By that time, it was too late to feel afraid, even if he was a stranger.

"L-laudanum," she stammered when she found her voice again. "B-but I d-didn't t-take any. I n-never—"

"It doesn't last forever, I assure you." He smoothed her damp hair back from her face. "In a very short while, we'll stop at an inn, and you'll wash your face and have some tea, and feel more yourself again."

She didn't want to ask the question. She was afraid of the answer. But she reminded herself that being afraid didn't help or change anything.

"Wh-where is P-Papa?"

His smile faded. "I fear your father got himself into serious trouble."

She wanted to close her eyes and lay her head on his shoulder again and pretend it was a bad dream. But the dizziness was subsiding, and her mind painted chilling recollections: the three foreigners in the hall below . . . her father's edgy voice . . . the little maid trembling as she carried in the tea tray . . . the odd taste of the tea. Then dizziness . . . and falling.

And she understood, without having to be told. Those men had killed Papa. Why else would she be in this fast-moving carriage with an Englishman she'd never seen before?

But he was holding her hand and urging her to be brave. Leila made herself listen while he explained.

He'd come to deliver a friend's note to Papa and arrived just as a badly beaten servant had staggered out of the palazzo. The servant had hardly finished explaining how foreigners had invaded the house and killed the master when he spotted one of the villains returning.

"We managed to take the brute by surprise," the man went on, "and learned he'd been sent back for you."

"Because I saw them." Leila's heart thudded. They'd come back to kill her.

He squeezed her hand. "It's all right now. We're going away. They'll never find you."

"But the police—someone must—"

"Best not."

The sharpness in his tone made her look up.

"I scarcely knew your father," he said. "But from the looks of things, it's plain he'd got himself involved with some very dangerous people. I strongly doubt the Venetian police would trouble themselves with protecting a young English female." He paused. "I was told you had no other connections in Venice."

She swallowed. "Or anywhere. There was only . . . Papa." Her voice broke.

He was dead, killed in the line of duty, just as she'd dreaded ever since he'd told her about his secret work for

England. She wanted to be brave, and proud of him, for he'd died in a noble cause, but the tears fell anyway. She couldn't help grieving, and she couldn't help feeling utterly, hopelessly alone. She had no one now.

"Don't worry," the man said. "I'll take care of you." Tilting her chin up, he gazed into her tear-stained face. "How would you like to go to Paris?"

The carriage's interior was gloomy, but there was light enough to make out his face. He was younger than she'd assumed at first, and very handsome, and his gleaming dark eyes made her feel hot and muddled. She hoped she wasn't going to be sick again.

"P-Paris," she echoed. "N-now? W-why?"

"Not exactly *now*, but in a few weeks—because you'll be safe there."

"Safe. Oh." She eased her chin away from his smooth fingers. "Why? Why are you doing this?"

"Because you're a damsel in distress." His mouth wasn't smiling, but she heard a smile in his voice. "Francis Beaumont would never abandon a damsel in distress. Especially such a pretty one."

"Francis Beaumont," she repeated, wiping her eyes.

"Yes. And I shall never abandon you. Rely upon it."

She had no one and nothing else to rely upon. She could only hope he meant it.

NOT UNTIL THEY reached Paris did Francis Beaumont reveal the rest of what the servant had told him: that the father she idolized was a criminal who trafficked in stolen weaponry and had apparently been killed by displeased customers. Leila screamed that the servant was a liar and wept hysterically in her rescuer's arms.

But weeks later, Andrew Herriard, a solicitor, arrived, and she couldn't deny the facts then. He was, according to the will he showed her, her guardian. He also had her father's private papers, along with copies of police documents, which more than confirmed what the servant had told Mr. Beaumont. The Venetian police had blamed

Leila's disappearance on her father's killers. In the circumstances, Mr. Herriard felt it was safer not to correct that impression. There was nothing to object to in his wise and gentle counsel, even if she'd had the heart. But she hadn't. She listened and agreed, her head bowed, her face hot with shame, all the while aware she was worse than alone. She was an outcast.

But Mr. Herriard promptly set about giving her a new identity and rebuilding her life, and Mr. Beaumont—though under no similar legal obligation—helped arrange for her studies with a Parisian art master. Though she was the daughter of a traitor, the two men stood by her and looked after her. In return, she gave them all the gratitude of her young heart.

And in time, innocent that she was, she gave Francis Beaumont a great deal more.

Chapter 1

"I DON'T WANT TO MEET HIM." LEILA JERKED her arm from her husband's grasp. "I have a painting to finish, and no time to make idle chit-chat with another dissolute aristocrat while you get drunk."

Francis shrugged. "Surely Madame Vraisses' portrait can wait a few minutes. The Comte d'Esmond is perishing to meet you, my precious. He admires your work." He took her hand. "Come, don't be cross. Just ten minutes. Then you can run away and hide in your studio."

She stared coldly at the hand grasping hers. With a short laugh, Francis withdrew it.

Turning away from his dissolute face, she moved to the hall mirror—and frowned at her reflection. She had been planning to work in the studio, which meant that her thick, gold-streaked hair was merely dragged back from her face and tied behind with a ragged ribbon.

"If you want me to make a good impression, I'd better tidy myself up," she said. But when she started toward the stairs, Francis blocked her way.

"You're beautiful," he said. "You don't need to tidy anything. I like you mussed."

"Because you're thoroughly undiscriminating."

"No, because it makes you look like what you are. Tempestuous. Passionate." His voice was taunting. His gaze trailed over her ample bosom to linger on her—regrettably—equally lavish hips. "One of these nights—maybe tonight, my love—I'll remind you."

She crushed a surge of revulsion and a fear she told herself was irrational. She hadn't let him touch her in years. The last time he'd tried to wrestle her into an embrace, she'd broken his favorite oriental urn over his head. She would fight him to the death—and he knew it—rather than submit, ever again, to the body he'd shared with countless women, and to the humiliation he called *love-making*.

"You wouldn't live to tell of it." Pushing a stray lock of hair behind her ear, she gave him a cold smile. "Do you know, Francis, how sympathetic French juries are to any reasonably attractive murderess?"

He only grinned. "What a hard creature you've turned out. And such a sweet kitten you were once. But you're hard to everyone, aren't you? If they get in your way, you just walk over them. Best that way, I agree. Still, it's a pity. You're such a lovely baggage." He leaned toward her.

The door knocker sounded.

With an oath, Francis drew back. Shoving a loose hairpin back into place, Leila hurried to the parlor, her husband close behind. By the time their visitor was announced, they were perfectly composed, the model of a proper British couple: Leila, her posture straight, upon a chair, with Francis standing dutifully at her side.

Their guest was ushered in.

And Leila forgot everything, including breathing.

The Comte d'Esmond was the most beautiful man she had ever seen. In real life, that is. She'd encountered his like in paintings, but even Botticelli would have wept to behold such a model.

Greetings were exchanged over her head, whose internal mechanisms had temporarily ceased functioning.

"Madame."

Francis' nudge brought her back to the moment. Leila numbly offered her hand. "Monsieur."

The count bowed low over her hand. His lips just brushed her knuckles.

His hair was pale, silken gold, a fraction longer than fashion decreed.

He also held her hand rather longer than etiquette decreed—long enough to draw her gaze to his and rivet all her consciousness there.

His eyes were deep sapphire blue, burningly intense. He released her hand, but not her gaze. "This is the greatest of honors, Madame Beaumont. I saw your work in Russia—a portrait of the Princess Lieven's cousin. I tried to purchase it, but the owner knew what he had, and would not sell. 'You must go to Paris,' he told me, 'and get one of your own.' And so I have come."

"From Russia?" Leila resisted the urge to press her hand to her pounding heart. Good grief. He'd come all the way from Russia—this man who probably couldn't cross a street in St. Petersburg without having to fight off a hundred desperate painters. Artists would sell their firstborn for a chance to paint this face. "Not merely for a portrait, surely."

His sensuous mouth eased into a lazy smile. "Ah, well, I had some business in Paris. You must not think it is mere vanity which brings me. Yet it is only human nature to wish for permanence. One seeks out the artist as one might seek out the gods, and all to the same purpose: immortality."

"How true," said Francis. "At this very moment, we are all slowly decaying. One moment, the mirror reflects a well-looking man in his prime. In the next, he's a mottled old toad."

Leila was aware of the faint antagonism in her husband's voice, but it was the count who held her attention. She saw something flash in his fiercely blue eyes, and that brief glitter changed not only his face but the atmosphere of the room itself. For one queer instant the face of an angel became its opposite, his soft chuckle the Devil's own laughter.

"And in the next moment," Esmond said, releasing Leila's gaze to turn to Francis, "he's a banquet for worms."

He was still smiling, his eyes genuinely amused, the devilish expression utterly vanished. Yet the tension in the room increased another notch.

"Even portraits can't last forever," she said. "Since few materials are permanently stable, there's bound to be decay."

"There are paintings in Egyptian tombs, thousands of years old," he said. "But it hardly matters. We shall not have the opportunity to discover how many centuries your works endure. For us, it is the present that matters, and I hope, madame, you will find time in this so-fleeting present to accommodate me."

"I'm afraid you'll want some patience," Francis said as he moved to the table bearing a tray of decanters. "Leila is just completing one commission, and she's engaged for two more."

"I am known for my patience," the count answered. "The tsar declared me the most patient man he'd ever met."

There was a clink of crystal striking crystal and a pause before Francis responded. "You travel in exalted circles, monsieur. An intimate of Tsar Nicholas, are you?"

"We spoke on occasion. That is not intimacy." The potent blue gaze settled again upon Leila. "My definition of intimacy is most precise and particular."

The room's temperature seemed to be climbing rapidly. Leila decided it was time to leave, whether her allotted ten minutes had passed or not. As the count accepted a wineglass from Francis, she rose. "I had better get back to work," she said.

"Certainly, my love," said Francis. "I'm sure the count understands."

"I understand, and yet I must regret the loss." This time Esmond's intent blue gaze swept her from head to toe.

Leila had endured far too many such surveys to mistake the meaning. For the first time, however, she felt that meaning in every muscle of her body. Worse, she felt the pull of attraction, dragging at her will.

But she reacted outwardly in the usual way, her countenance becoming more frigidly polite, her posture more arrogantly defiant. "Unfortunately, Madame Vraisses will regret even more the delay of her portrait," she said. "And she is one of the *least* patient women in the world."

"And you, I suspect, are another." He stepped closer, making her pulse race. He was taller and more powerfully built than she'd thought at first. "You have the eyes of a tigress, madame. Most unusual—and I do not mean the golden color alone. But you are an artist, and so you see more than others can."

"I do believe my wife sees plainly enough that you're flirting with her," said Francis, moving to her side.

"But of course. What other polite homage may a man pay another man's wife? You are not offended, I hope." The count treated Francis to an expression of limpid innocence.

"No one is in the least offended," Leila said briskly. "We may be English, but we have lived in Paris nearly nine years. Still, I am a working woman, monsieur—"

"Esmond," he corrected.

"*Monsieur,*" she said firmly. "And so, I must excuse myself and return to work." She did not offer her hand this time. Instead, she swept him her haughtiest curtsy.

He answered with a graceful bow.

As she headed for the door a tightly smiling Francis hurried to open for her, Esmond's voice came from behind her. "Until next we meet, Madame Beaumont," he said softly.

Something echoed in the back of her mind, making her pause on the threshold. A memory. A voice. But no. If she'd met him before, she would have remembered. Such a man would be impossible to forget. She gave the faintest of nods and continued on.

AT FOUR O'CLOCK in the morning, the unforgettable blue-eyed gentleman relaxed in a semirecumbent position upon the richly brocaded sofa of his own parlor. Very much in the same manner, many years before, had he often reclined upon his divan, to plot against his wily cousin, Ali Pasha. In those days, the gentleman was called Ismal Delvina. Nowadays, he was called whatever was most convenient to his purposes.

At present he was the Comte d'Esmond.

His British employers, with the aid of their French associates, had thoroughly documented his bloodline and title. Ismal's French was flawless, as were most of the other eleven languages he spoke. To speak English with a French accent presented no difficulty. Speech, in any form, was one of his many gifts.

Apart from his native Albanian, Ismal preferred English. It was an unsystematic language, but marvelously flexible. He liked playing with its words. He had very much liked playing with "intimacy." Madame Beaumont had become wonderfully incensed.

Smiling at the recollection of their too brief encounter, Ismal sampled the thick Turkish coffee his servant, Nick, had prepared.

"Perfect," he told Nick.

"Of course it's perfect. I've had practice enough, haven't I?"

Nonetheless, Nick visibly relaxed. Though he'd served Ismal six years, the younger man had not lost his determination to please. Twenty-one-year-old Nick was a trifle short on patience, and he was not very respectful, except in public. But then, he was half-English, and in any case, Ismal had had his fill of obsequious menials.

"Practice you've surely had," Ismal said. "Even so, I am impressed. You've endured a long and tedious night following me and my new friend from one Parisian den to the next."

Nick shrugged. "As long as it was worth your while."

"It was. I believe we shall have disposed of Beaumont in a month. Were the matter less urgent, I should allow Nature to take her course, for Monsieur is well on the way to disposing of himself. This night he consumed opium enough to kill three men his size."

Nick's dark eyes glinted. "Does he eat it or smoke it?"

"Both."

"That does make it easier. You've only to add a few

grains of strychnine or prussic acid—gad, you could do it
with ground up peach pits or apricots or apples or—"

"I could, but it is not necessary. I have an unconquerable aversion to killing unless it is absolutely necessary.
Even then, I dislike it excessively. Also, I have a particular
aversion to poison. The method is not sportsmanlike."

"He's hardly been sportsmanlike himself, has he? Besides, it would get rid of him without a lot of fuss."

"I want him to suffer."

"Well, that's different, then."

Ismal held out his cup, which Nick dutifully refilled.

"It has taken many months to track down this one man,"
Ismal said. "Now that his greed puts him in the palm of my
hand, I wish to play with him for a while."

It had begun in Russia. Ismal had been pursuing another inquiry when the tsar had thrust a more disturbing
problem into his hands. Peace negotiations between Russia and Turkey were threatened because the sultan had obtained some letters that didn't belong to him. The tsar
wanted to know how and why those letters had ended up in
Constantinople.

Ismal was well aware that throughout the Ottoman Empire, spies routinely intercepted correspondence. Yet these
letters had not been anywhere in the sultan's domains, but
in Paris, safely locked in a British diplomat's dispatch box.
One of the diplomat's aides had shot himself before he
could be questioned.

In the following months, traveling between London and
Paris, Ismal had heard a number of other stories—of similar thefts, inexplicable bankruptcies, and other abrupt, major losses.

As it turned out, the events were connected. Those involved had one thing in common: all had, at one time or
another, been regular visitors to an unprepossessing building in a quiet corner of Paris.

The place was known simply as *Vingt-Huit*—number
twenty-eight. Within its walls one might, for a price, enjoy any of the full range of human vices, from the most
mundane to the most highly imaginative. There were

some people, Ismal well understood, who would do anything for a price—and others desperate or corrupt enough
to pay it.

It was Francis Beaumont they paid.

They didn't know this, of course, and Ismal himself
hadn't a solid piece of proof. Nothing he could use in a
court of law, that is. But Francis Beaumont could not be
brought to a court of law, because none of his victims
could be brought to the witness stand. Each and every one,
like the young aide, would choose suicide rather than submit their sordid secrets to public scrutiny.

Consequently, it was left to Ismal to deal with
Beaumont—quietly, as he'd dealt with so many other
matters troubling King George IV, his ministers, and his
allies.

Nick's voice broke in on his master's meditations.
"How do you mean to play this time?" he asked.

Ismal studied the contents of the delicately painted cup.
"The wife is faithful."

"Discreet, you mean. She'd have to be crazy to be faithful to that corrupt swine."

"I think perhaps she is a little crazy." Ismal looked up.
"But she possesses a great artistic gift, and genius is not always fully rational. Beaumont has been fortunate in her
artistic dedication. Her work occupies nearly all her mind
and time. As a result, she scarcely notices the many men
seeking her attention."

Nick's eyes widened. "You don't mean to tell me she
didn't notice *you*?"

Ismal's soft chuckle was rueful. "I was obliged to exert
myself."

"Well, I'll be hanged. I'd have given anything to see
that."

"It was most disconcerting. I might have been a marble
statue, or an oil portrait. Form, line, color." Ismal made a
sweeping gesture. "I look into her beautiful face and all I
discern is lust—the lust of an *artist*. She makes me an object. It is insupportable. And so I am a bit . . . indiscreet."

Nick shook his head. "You're never indiscreet—not

without a purpose. I'll lay odds your purpose wasn't just to make her pay proper attention."

"I believe you mean 'improper attention.' The lady is wed, recollect, and the husband was present. And so when I obtained a reaction not altogether artistic, I also obtained a reaction from him. He is vain as well as possessive. Consequently, he was displeased."

"He's got a lot of nerve. The goat's bedded at least half the married women of Paris."

Ismal waved this aside. "What interested me was that he was surprised, even by my very small success with his wife. It seems he is unaccustomed to worrying about her. Now, however, I have planted the seed of doubt, which I shall cultivate. That is but one of the ways I shall make his days and nights unquiet."

Nick grinned. "No harm in mixing some pleasure with business."

Ismal set down his cup and, closing his eyes, leaned back against the plump cushions. "I believe I shall leave the greater part of the business to you. There are persons at the upper levels of Parisian authority in Beaumont's pay. You will arrange a series of incidents which will require him to pay more for protection. The incidents will also frighten away some of the more vulnerable clients. They pay a great deal for secrecy. If they feel unsafe, they will cease patronizing *Vingt-Huit*. I have some other ideas, which we will discuss tomorrow."

"I see. I'm to do the dirty work while you amuse yourself with the lady artist."

"But of course. I cannot leave Madame to you. You are half English. You have no comprehension of violent-tempered women, and so, no appreciation. You would not have the least idea what to do with her. Even if you did, you haven't the necessary patience. I, however, am the most patient man in the world. Even the tsar admits this." Ismal opened his eyes. "Did I tell you that Beaumont nearly dropped a decanter when I mentioned the tsar? It was then I knew beyond doubt I'd found my man."

"No, you didn't mention it. Not that I'm surprised. If I

didn't know you better, I'd think the only one you were interested in was the woman."

"That, I hope, is precisely what Monsieur Beaumont will think," Ismal murmured as he closed his eyes once more.

FIONA, THE VISCOUNTESS Carroll, was intrigued. "Esmond—a bad influence? Are you serious, Leila?" The raven-haired widow turned to study the count, who stood talking with a small group of guests by the recently unveiled portrait of Madame Vraisses. "That's quite impossible to believe."

"I'm sure Lucifer and his followers were beautiful, too," said Leila. "They had all been angels, recall."

"I've always pictured Lucifer as dark—rather more in Francis' style." Her green eyes gleaming, Fiona turned back to her friend. "He's looking especially dark this evening. I do believe he's aged ten years since the last time I was in Paris."

"He's aged ten years in three weeks," Leila said tightly. "I didn't think it was possible, but since the Comte d'Esmond became his bosom bow, Francis has taken a decided turn for the worse. He hasn't slept at home for nearly a week. He came in—or rather, was carried in—this morning at four o'clock. He was still in bed at seven o'clock this evening, and I was half inclined to attend the party without him."

"I wonder why you didn't."

Because she didn't dare. But this Leila would not confide, even to her one woman friend. Ignoring the question, she went on detachedly, "It took another twenty minutes to rouse him and make him take a bath. I do wonder how his tarts can bear it. The combination of opium, liquor, and perfume was overpowering. And of course he notices nothing."

"I can't think why you don't throw him out," said Fiona. "It's not as though you're financially dependent on him. You haven't any children he could threaten to take away. And he's too lazy for violence."

There were worse consequences than violence, Leila could have told her. "Don't be absurd," she said, taking a glass of champagne from a passing servant. She usually waited until later in the evening to enjoy her single glass of wine, but tonight she was tense. "The last thing I need is to live separately from my husband. The men plague me enough as it is. If Francis were not about, playing the possessive spouse, I should have to fight them off myself. Then I'd never get any work done."

Fiona laughed. She was not, strictly speaking, beautiful, but she seemed so when she laughed, partly because everything about her seemed to gleam: the even white teeth, the sparkling green eyes, the ivory oval face framed by sleek black curls. "Most women would rather a complaisant husband," she said, "especially in Paris. Especially when someone like the Comte d'Esmond appears on the scene. I'm not sure I'd mind his exerting his bad influence on me. But I should want to observe him at close range first."

The mischievous spark in her eyes intensified. "Shall I catch his attention?"

Leila's heart gave a sharp thump. "Certainly not."

But Fiona was already looking toward him again, her fan poised.

"Fiona, you must not—really, I shall leave you here—"

Esmond turned at that instant and must have caught Fiona's eye, for she beckoned with the fan. Without hesitation, he began crossing the room to them.

Leila rarely blushed. Her face felt warmer than it should, however. "You're shockingly forward," she told her friend as she started to move away.

Fiona caught her arm. "I shall seem a great deal more brazen if I'm obliged to introduce myself. Don't run away, Leila. It's not Beelzebub, you know—at least not on the outside." Her voice dropped as the count neared. "Lud, he's *stunning*. I do believe I shall faint."

Well aware that Fiona was no more likely to swoon than to stand on her head, Leila set her jaw, and with rigid politeness, introduced the Comte d'Esmond to her incorrigible friend.

Not ten minutes later, Leila was waltzing with him. Meanwhile, Fiona—who'd been so determined to study Esmond closely—was dancing with a laughing Francis.

Leila was still trying to figure out just who had engineered this arrangement when the count's soft voice came from above her head.

"Jasmine," he said. "And something else. Unexpected. Ah, yes—myrrh. An intriguing combination, madame. You blend scents in the same distinctive way you mix colors."

Leila used a light hand with perfume, and she'd put it on hours ago. He should have needed to be much closer to identify it, but he held her nearly a foot away. It was a fraction too near for English propriety, though well within Gallic bounds. All the same, he seemed far too close. In their many encounters since their first meeting, he had never touched her except to kiss her knuckles. Now she was tautly aware of the warm hand clasping her waist, the faint friction of glove against silk as he gracefully guided her round the ballroom.

"With scent at least I need only please myself," she said.

"And your husband, of course."

"That would be pointless. Francis has almost no sense of smell."

"In certain circumstances, that may be a gift—when, for instance, one walks the streets of Paris on a hot summer day. But in other circumstances, the loss must be a profound one. He misses so much."

The words were harmless enough. The tone was another matter. The last and only time Esmond had flirted openly with her was the day she'd met him. Leila wasn't certain he'd flirted covertly since then, either. Maybe the tone she heard as seductive wasn't meant to be. But intended or not, she felt the inner hurry his soft voice had triggered time and time again, even during the briefest of encounters. In its wake came the usual flutter of anxiety.

"I'm not sure how profound it is," she said coolly, "but it does affect his appetite. It seems to be getting worse. I believe he's lost a stone in the last month."

"So I have observed."

She looked up, then wished she hadn't. She had looked up into those eyes a score of times by now, yet every time they caught and held her fascinated. It was the rare color, she told herself. The blue was too deep to be human. When—if—she painted those eyes, anyone who hadn't met him would believe she'd exaggerated the color.

He smiled. "You are transparent. Almost I can see you selecting and mixing your oils."

She looked away. "I've told you I'm a working woman."

"Do you think of nothing else?"

"A woman artist must work twice as hard as a man to achieve half his success," she said. "If I weren't single-minded, I wouldn't have stood a chance of painting Madame Vraisses' portrait. At tonight's unveiling, they would have been applauding a male artist instead."

"The world is stupid, I agree. And I, perhaps, am also a little stupid."

She was, too, to look up into those eyes again. She was already short of breath and dizzy—from trying to talk and waltz simultaneously. "You don't think women should be artists?" she asked.

"Alas, I can think only one stupid thing: that I dance with a beautiful woman who cannot distinguish a man from an easel."

Before she could retort, he swept her into a turn—so swiftly that she missed a step and tripped over his foot. Almost in the same heartbeat, an arm like a whipcord lashed round her waist and hauled her up hard against a mainmast of solid, male muscle.

It was over in an instant. The count scarcely missed a beat, but went on easily guiding her through the crowd of dancers quite as though nothing had happened.

Meanwhile, a fine stream of sweat trickled between Leila's breasts, and her heart hammered so loudly that she couldn't hear the music. Not that she needed to hear it or think about what she was doing. Her partner was fully in control, as poised and sure of himself as he'd been at the start.

He was also several inches closer than he'd been before, she belatedly discovered.

Her swimming mind cleared and the haze of swirling colors about her resolved into individuals. She saw that Francis was staring at her, and he wasn't laughing any more. He wasn't even smiling.

Leila became aware of a faint pressure at her waist, urging her a fraction nearer. Now she realized she'd felt it before and must have responded mindlessly—just like a well-trained horse answering the smallest tension of the reins, the lightest pressure of knee to flanks.

Heat swam up her neck. She was not a damned *mare*. She tried to draw back, but the hand clasping her waist didn't respond. "Monsieur," she said.

"Madame?"

"I am no longer in danger of falling."

"I am relieved to hear it. For a moment, I feared we were not well-suited as partners. But that, as you have discovered, is absurd. We are perfectly suited."

"I should be better suited at a greater distance."

"Undoubtedly, for then you should be at liberty to think of your greens and indigos and raw umber. Later, you may reflect upon them to your heart's content."

Her gaze, incredulous, shot up to his.

"Ah, at last I have your undivided attention," he said.

THAT NIGHT, FRANCIS did not go out with the Comte d'Esmond, but accompanied Leila home and to her bedroom. He stood on the threshold for a moment, as though making up his mind about something, then entered the room and sat on the edge of the mattress.

"You're not staying in here," she said as she hung her evening cape in the wardrobe. "And if you've come to read me a lecture—"

"I knew he wanted you," he said. "He pretends he doesn't, but I knew—from that very first day. Gad, that innocent face of his. I've seen and dealt with them all, but he—Christ, sometimes I wonder if he's human."

"You're drunk," she said.

"Poison," he said. "Do you understand, my love? He's

poison. He's like—" He made a vague gesture. "Like human laudanum. It's so pleasant . . . so sweet . . . no
cares . . . just pleasure. If you take the right dosage. But
with him, you don't know what the right dosage is—and
when it's wrong, it's poison. Remember how sick you were
all those years ago, that night when we left Venice? That's
how I feel . . . inside, outside."

Francis hadn't mentioned Venice in years. She eyed him
uneasily. He had come home delirious before, but never in
this wretched state. Usually, he was in a fantasy world of
his own. He'd ramble on incoherently, but the sound was
happy. Pleasure, as he'd said. Now he was miserable and
maudlin and ill. His cheeks were grey and sunken, his
bloodshot eyes swollen. He looked sixty, not forty. He had
been so handsome once, she thought, sickened.

She didn't love him. She'd recovered from her girlish
infatuation years ago, and it hadn't taken him much longer
to kill even the mild affection that remained. Yet she could
remember what he'd been once and imagine what he might
have become, and so she could grieve for the waste and the
weakness that had brought him to this, and pity him. But
for the grace of God, she might have sunk with him. Providence, however, had given her talent and the will to pursue
it. She'd also been blessed with a wise and patient
guardian. If not for Andrew Herriard, she might be
pitiable, too, despite talent and will.

Leila moved to him and brushed the damp hair back
from his forehead. "Wash your face," she said. "I'll make
you some tea."

He took her hand and pressed it to his forehead. He was
feverish. "Not Esmond, Leila. For God's sake, anyone but
him."

He didn't know what he was saying. She would not let
him upset her. "Francis, there isn't anyone," she said patiently, as to a child. "No lovers, not even a flirt. I won't be
anyone's whore—not even yours." She took her hand
away. "So don't talk rot."

He shook his head. "You don't understand and there's
no point in explaining it because you won't believe me. I'm

not sure even I believe it—but that doesn't matter. One thing's clear enough: we're getting out of Paris."

She was moving away, intending to fill the washbasin for him. Now she turned back, her heart thudding. "Leave Paris? Because you took more intoxicants tonight than was good for you? Really, Francis—"

"You can stay if you like, but I won't. Think of that, my sweet, if nothing else. I won't be around to keep your admirers out of your hair—which I know is about all I'm good for these days—a bloody bodyguard. But maybe you've decided you don't want one any more. You didn't want one tonight, obviously. Talk of whores," he muttered. "That's just what you'd be. One of hundreds. You should see the tarts when they get a glimpse of the beautiful Comte d'Esmond. Like maggots swarming over a ripe cheese. Anything, anyone he wants—as many as he wants—and it never costs him a sou. Even you, precious." He looked up at her. "You'd do his portrait for free, wouldn't you?"

The picture Francis painted was disgusting. It was also, Leila had no doubt, accurate. So, too, was his assessment of her. Francis was not a stupid man, and he knew her very well. She met his gaze. "You can't truly believe I'm in danger."

"I *know* it. But I don't expect you to see how dangerous he is—or admit it if you did." He rose. "It's your choice. I can't force you to do anything. I'm leaving for London. I want you to come with me." He gave her a bitter smile. "I wish I knew why. Maybe you're my poison, too."

Leila wished she knew why, too, but she'd given up trying to understand her husband years ago. She'd made a mistake in marrying him and found a way to live with it. Her life could have been better, but it also could have been far worse. A great deal worse could have befallen her had Francis not come to her rescue in Venice. At present, thanks to Andrew Herriard, she was financially secure. Despite her gender, she was gaining respect as an artist. She had a friend in Fiona. When she was working, she was happy. In general, she was happier than most of the women she knew, though her husband was a hopeless profligate. And he . . . well, he was as good to her as he was capable of being.

In any case, she dared not stay in Paris or anywhere else without a husband. And he, she knew, would never let her remain here without him, whatever he claimed.

"If you're truly determined to go," she said carefully, "of course I'll go with you."

His smile softened. "It isn't a whim, you know. I mean it. London. By the end of the week."

She bit back a cry. The end of the week—three commissions abandoned . . . But she'd get others, she told herself.

There wouldn't be another Comte d'Esmond. There would never be another face like that. Still, it was only that—a subject for painting. She doubted she could ever do it justice anyhow.

She thought perhaps it was safer not to try.

"Do you need longer?" Francis asked.

She shook her head. "I can pack up the studio in two days," she said. "One, if you help."

"Then I'll help," he said. "The sooner we're gone, the better."

Chapter 2

London, 1828

AS IT TURNED OUT, FRENCH ARISTOCRATS weren't the only ones wanting their countenances immortalized. A week after settling into the modest townhouse in Queen's Square, Leila was at work, and through spring, summer, and autumn, the commissions came thick and fast. The work left her no time for social life, but she doubted she could have had one anyhow. Her London clients and acquaintances moved in more exclusive circles than her Parisian ones. Here, the position of a bourgeois female artist was far more tenuous, and Francis' increasing profligacy wasn't calculated to strengthen it.

He had plenty of friends. The English upper classes, too, bred debauchees in abundance. But they were increasingly disinclined to invite him to their homes and respectable assembly halls to dine and dance with their womenfolk. Since Society would not invite the husband, it could not, with very rare exceptions, invite the wife.

Leila was too busy, though, to feel lonely, and it was futile to fret about Francis' worsening behavior. In any case, being shut away from the world made it easier to disassociate herself from his vices and villainies.

Or so she thought until a week before Christmas, when the Earl of Sherburne—one of Francis' constant companions and husband of her latest portrait subject—entered the studio.

The portrait of Lady Sherburne wasn't yet dry. Leila had finished it only that morning. Nonetheless, he insisted on paying for it then—and in gold. Then it was his, to do with as he wished. And so, Leila could only watch in numb horror while he took a stickpin to his wife's image and, with cold, furious strokes, mutilated it.

Leila's brain wasn't numb, though. She understood he wasn't attacking her work, but his evidently unfaithful wife. Leila had no trouble deducing that Francis had cuckolded him, and she needed no details of the affair to realize that this time Francis had crossed some dangerous line.

She also saw, with devastating clarity, that the wall between her life and her husband's had been breached as well. In alienating Sherburne, Francis had put her in peril . . . and she was trapped. If she remained with him, his scandals would jeopardize her career; but if she ran away, he could destroy it utterly. He need only reveal the truth about her father, and she'd be ruined.

He'd never threatened her openly. He didn't need to. Leila understood *his* rules well enough. He wouldn't force her to sleep with him because it was too damned much of a nuisance to fight with her. All the same, she was his exclusive property; she wasn't to sleep with anyone else, and she wasn't to leave.

All she could do was retreat as far as possible.

She said nothing of the incident, hoping Sherburne's pride would keep him silent as well.

She ceased painting portraits, claiming she was overworked and needed a rest.

Francis, lost in his own drink- and opiate-clouded world, never noticed.

For Christmas, he gave her a pair of ruby and diamond eardrops, which she dutifully donned for the hour he remained at home, then threw into her jewel box with the

previous nine years' accumulation of expensively mean-
ingless trinkets.

She spent New Year's Eve with Fiona at the Kent estate
of Philip Woodleigh, one of Fiona's ten siblings.

Upon returning home on New Year's Day, Leila heard
Francis angrily shouting for servants who'd been given the
day off. When she went up to his room to remind him, she
discovered, with no great surprise, that he'd had his own
New Year's Eve celebration—mainly in that room, judging
by the stench of stale perfume, smoke, and wine that assaulted her when she reached the threshold.

Sickened, she left the house and took a walk, down
Great Ormond Street, onto Conduit Street, and on past the
Foundling Hospital. Behind its large garden two burial
grounds lay side by side, allotted respectively to the
parishes of St. George the Martyr and St. George, Blooms-
bury. She knew not a soul interred in either. That was why
she came. These London residents couldn't disturb her,
even with a memory. She'd escaped here many times in recent months.

She had wandered restlessly among the tombstones for
an hour or more when David found her. David Ives, Marquess of Avory, was the Duke of Langford's heir. David
was four and twenty, handsome, wealthy, intelligent and, to
her exasperation, one of Francis' most devoted followers.

"I hope you don't mind," he said after they'd exchanged
polite greetings. "When Francis said you'd gone for a
walk, I guessed you'd come here. It was you I wanted to
see." His grey gaze shifted away. "To apologize. I'd promised to go to Philip Woodleigh's, I know."

She knew she'd been a fool to believe the worthless
promise, to hope he'd start the New Year fresh, among decent people . . . perhaps meet a suitable young lady, or at
least less dissolute male friends.

"I wasn't surprised you failed to appear," she said stiffly.
"The entertainment was tame, by your standards."

"I was . . . unwell," he said. "I spent the evening at
home."

She told herself not to waste sympathy on an idle young

fool bent on self-destruction, but her heart softened anyhow, and with it, her manner.

"I'm sorry you were ill," she said. "On the other hand, I did get my wish: for once, at least, you didn't spend the night with Francis."

"You'd rather I were ill more often, then. I must speak to my cook and insist upon indigestible meals."

She moved on a few paces, shaking her head. "You're a great vexation to me, David. You awaken my maternal instincts, and I've always prided myself on not having any."

"Call them 'fraternal,' then." Smiling, he rejoined her. "I'd much prefer it. Less wounding to one's manly pride, you know."

"That depends on your point of view," she said. "I've never seen Fiona, for instance, show any regard for her brothers' manly pride. She leads them all about by the nose—even Lord Norbury, the eldest—whereas their mother can do nothing with them." She shot David a reproving look. "Mine is more like the mama's case, obviously."

His smile slipped. "The Woodleighs are not an example, but the exception. Everyone knows Lady Carroll is the true head of the family."

"And you're too male to approve that state of affairs."

"Not at all." He gave a short laugh. "All I disapprove is your talking of the Woodleighs when you should be flirting with me. Here we are in a graveyard. What could be more morbidly romantic?"

He was one of the few men she would flirt with, because he was safe. Never once had she glimpsed the smallest hint of lust in that handsome young face.

"You ought to know by now that artists are the least romantic people in the world," she said. "You mustn't confuse the creators with the creations."

"I see. I must turn into a blob of paint—or better yet, a blank canvas. Then you might make anything of me you wish."

I dance with a beautiful woman who cannot distinguish a man from an easel.

She tensed, remembering: the low, insinuating voice, the force of collision, the shattering awareness of masculine strength . . . overpowering . . . the heat.

"Mrs. Beaumont?" came David's worried voice. "Are you unwell?"

She pushed the memory away. "No, no, of course not. Merely cold. I hadn't realized how late it was. I had better go home."

Surrey, England, mid-January 1829

Ismal paused in the doorway of Lord Norbury's crowded ballroom only for a moment. It was all he needed. He wanted but one swift glance to locate his prey. Leila Beaumont stood near the terrace doors.

She wore a rust-colored gown trimmed in midnight blue. Her gold-streaked hair was piled carelessly atop her head—and doubtless coming undone.

Ismal wondered if she still wore the same scent or had mixed a new one.

He wasn't sure which he would prefer. His mind was not settled about her, and this irritated him.

At least the repellent husband wasn't here. Beaumont was probably writhing in the arms of some overpainted, overperfumed trollop—or lost in opium dreams in some London sinkhole. According to recent reports, his tastes, along with his body and intellect, had rapidly deteriorated upon his removal to London.

This was just as Ismal had expected. Cut loose from his sordid little empire, Beaumont was rapidly sinking. He no longer possessed the wit or will to build another enterprise like *Vingt-Huit*. Not from scratch—which, thanks to Ismal, was the only way it could be done.

Ismal had quietly and thoroughly disassembled the Paris organization Beaumont had so hastily abandoned. The various governments were no longer troubled by that knotty problem, and Beaumont could do nothing now but rot to death.

Considering the lives Beaumont had destroyed, the suffering and fear he'd caused, Ismal considered it fitting that the swine die slowly and painfully. Also fitting that he die in the way he'd ruined so many others—of vice and its diseases, of the poisons relentlessly eroding mind and body.

The wife was another matter. Ismal hadn't expected her to leave Paris with her husband. The marriage, after all, was merely a formality. Beaumont himself had admitted he hadn't slept with his wife in five years. She became violent, he said, if he touched her. She'd even threatened to kill him. He treated the matter as a joke, saying that if a man couldn't have one woman in bed, he'd only to find another.

True enough, Ismal thought, if one referred to the common run of women. But Leila Beaumont was . . . ah, well, a problem.

While he pondered the problem, Ismal let his host lead him from one group of guests to the next. After he had met what seemed like several hundred people, Ismal permitted himself another glance toward the terrace doors. He caught a glimpse of russet, but could no longer see Madame Beaumont properly. She was surrounded by men. As usual.

The only woman he'd ever seen linger at her side was Lady Carroll, and she, according to Lord Norbury, had not yet arrived from London. Leila Beaumont had come yesterday with one of Lady Carroll's cousins.

Ismal wondered whether Madame had spied him yet. But no. A great crow-haired oaf stood in the way.

Even as Ismal was wishing him to Hades, the large man turned aside to speak to a friend, and in that moment Leila Beaumont's glance drifted round the ballroom, past Ismal . . . and back . . . and her posture stiffened.

Ismal didn't smile. He couldn't have done so if his life depended on it. He was too aware of her, of the shocked recognition he could feel across half a room's length, and of the tumult that recognition stirred inside him.

He left his own group so smoothly that they scarcely noticed he was gone. He dealt with the men about her just as adroitly. He ingratiated himself without having to think about it, chatted idly with this one and that until he'd made his way to the center of the group, where Leila Beaumont stood, spine straight, chin high.

He bowed. "Madame."

She gave him a quick, furious curtsy. "Monsieur."

Her voice throbbed with suppressed emotion as she introduced him to those nearest her. Her lush bosom began to throb, too, when one by one her admirers began to drift away. She was not permitted to escape, however. Ismal held her with social inanities until at last he had her to himself.

"I hope I have not driven your friends away," he said, looking about him in feigned surprise. "Sometimes I may offend without intending to do so. It is my deplorable English, perhaps."

"Is it?"

His gaze shot back to her. She was studying his face with a penetrating, painterly concentration.

He grew uneasy, which irritated him. He should not allow himself to feel so, but she had been irritating him for so long that his mind was raw from it. He returned the examination with a simmering one of his own.

A faint thread of pink appeared in her cheeks.

"Monsieur Beaumont is well, I trust?" he asked.

"Yes."

"And your work goes well, I hope?"

"Very well."

"You have accommodated yourself to London?"

"Yes."

The short, fierce syllables announced that he'd driven painting altogether from her mind. That was enough, he told himself. He smiled. "You wish me at the Devil, perhaps?"

The pink deepened. "Certainly not."

His glance trailed down to her gloved hands. The thumb of her right hand moved restlessly over the back of her left wrist.

She followed his gaze. Her hand instantly stilled.

"I think you have wished me at the Devil since our first encounter," he said. "I even wondered whether it was on my account you fled Paris."

"We didn't *flee*," she said.

"Yet I offended somehow, I am sure. You left without word—not even the simple adieu."

"There wasn't time to take leave of everybody. Francis was in a great—" Her eyes grew wary. "He had made up his mind to go, and when he makes up his mind, he can't bear delay."

"You had promised me a portrait," Ismal said softly. "My disappointment was great."

"I should think you'd have recovered by now."

He took a step nearer. She didn't move. He clasped his hands behind his back and bowed his head.

He was just close enough to detect her scent. It was the same. There was as well the same tension between them that he remembered: the pull . . . and the resistance.

"Yet the portrait is reason enough to come to England, I think," he said. "In any case, this is what I told your charming friend, Lady Carroll. And she took pity on me, as you see. Not only did she invite me to join her family and guests in this picturesque town, but she ordered one of her brothers to accompany me, lest I lose my way."

He raised his head. In her tawny eyes he saw a turmoil of emotion—anger, anxiety, doubt . . . and something else, not so easy to read.

"Yes. Well. It would appear that Fiona has lost hers. She should have been here hours ago."

"Indeed it is a pity, for she will miss the dancing. Already the music begins." He looked about. "I have expected to discover some English gentleman bearing down upon us, seeking his partner for the first dance. But no one comes this way." He turned back to her. "Surely someone has asked you?"

"I know my limits. If I begin now, I shan't last the evening. I've reserved four dances only."

"Five," he said, holding out his hand.

She stared at it. "Later . . . perhaps."

"Later you will put me off," he said. "Your feet will hurt. You will be fatigued. Also, I may become fatigued as well, and so I may . . . misstep. I did this once, I recall—and never danced with you again." He lowered his voice. "You will not make me coax, I hope?"

She took his hand.

"THIS MORNING?" FIONA repeated. "You can't be serious. You've been here hardly two days. And I've only just come."

"You should have come sooner." Leila shoved her russet gown into the valise.

They were in her assigned bedroom. It was only eight o'clock in the morning, and the party hadn't ended until nearly dawn, but Leila was well rested. She'd slept like the dead. That wasn't surprising. She had gone to bed feeling as though she'd just spent five years at hard labor—with Esmond as the ruthless overseer. The entire evening had been a battle. Actually, she would have preferred open warfare, with real weapons. How did one fight shadow, innuendo, hint? How could he seem to behave so properly yet make one feel so hotly improper?

Fiona sat on the bed. "You're running away from Esmond, aren't you?"

"As a matter of fact, yes."

"You're a fool."

"I cannot deal with him, Fiona. He is beyond me. He's beyond anything. Francis was quite right."

"Francis is a sodden degenerate."

Leila took up a petticoat, rolled it into a ball, and stuffed it into a corner of the valise. "He isn't stupid, especially about people."

"He's jealous because Esmond is everything he's not—or what Francis may have been once, but won't be ever again. That cur doesn't deserve you, never did. He certainly deserves no loyalty. You should have taken a lover long ago."

Leila shot her friend a look. "Have *you*?"

"No, but only because I haven't found just the right one. It's not on account of some idiotic *principle*."

"I won't be anybody's whore."

" 'Whore' is a man's word," Fiona said. "Reserved for women. A man is a rake, a libertine. How dashing it sounds. But a woman who behaves the same way is a whore, a tart, a trollop—gad, the list is endless. I counted up once. Do you know, English contains about ten times as many disagreeable terms for a pleasure-loving woman as it does for her male counterpart? It makes one think."

"I don't need to think about it. I don't wish to think about it. I don't care what the words are. I will not sink to Francis' level."

Fiona let out a sigh. "You haven't even got to the point of flirting with your lovely count," she said patiently. "And he's not going to drag you to bed forcibly, my dear. I assure you, my brother does run a respectable household, and you may stay out your week without the least fear of being sold into white slavery."

"*No*. It's . . . He's treacherous. I don't—oh, how am I to explain?" Leila pushed her hair back from her face. "Can't you see for yourself? Francis was right, as usual. Esmond does something to people. It's like—oh, I don't know. Mesmerism."

Fiona lifted her eyebrows.

Leila couldn't blame her. Of course it sounded insane. She sat down on the bed beside her friend. "I had resolved not to dance with him," she said. "It was the last thing in the world I wanted to do. Then—oh, I know it sounds laughable, but it wasn't. He threatened to—to *coax* me."

"Coax you," Fiona repeated expressionlessly.

Leila nodded. "And immediately, *that* became the last thing in the world I wanted." Looking down, she saw that she was rubbing her thumb over her wrist. She frowned. He'd noticed even that. He missed nothing, she was sure. The smallest self-betrayal. It had told him she was uneasy, and he used it. He'd threatened to coax her because he knew—the wretch *knew*—she was afraid he'd addle her even more than he'd already done.

"I don't think it's Esmond at all," Fiona said. "Your nerves are frayed, and that's Francis' doing, mostly—and overwork, as you admitted weeks ago."

"What Francis does is of no concern whatever to me. If I heeded his moods, I should go mad. But I know it's the opiates and the drink, and so I ignore it. He's the one with the frayed nerves. So long as he keeps out of my studio, he can tear the house to pieces for all I care. I scarcely see him anymore—and the servants are well-paid to clean up after him."

"Yet you prefer to go back to that? When you might have the Comte d'Esmond just by crooking your little finger?"

"I strongly doubt Monsieur comes at any woman's beckoning. Rather the other way about, I suspect. He does precisely as he pleases." Leila rose and resumed packing.

Despite Fiona's unceasing remonstrances, Leila was finished in another half hour. Very soon thereafter, she climbed into a hired carriage and headed for London.

She was home shortly after noon. She changed out of her traveling dress into an old day gown, donned her smock, and marched into her studio. Then and only then did she begin to release the turmoil that had been roiling inside her since the moment she'd spied Esmond in the ballroom at Norbury House.

Fortunately, she didn't have to decide what to do. She had assembled a still life before she'd left, and no one had touched it. The two daily servants never entered her studio to clean unless expressly told to do so.

The heap of bottles, jars, and glasses seemed merely a haphazard mess, but it presented an ideal painterly exercise. One had to *look*, concentrate totally, and paint only what one saw.

She looked, she concentrated, she mixed her colors, she painted . . . a face.

She paused, staring disbelievingly at the canvas. It was the face of the man she'd fled.

Her heart thudding, she scraped away the paint with her

palette knife, then began again. Once more she focused upon her subject, and once more the face appeared.

And she knew why. Esmond's countenance haunted her because he was an enigma. She could read faces intuitively but not his.

The mystery had plagued her in Paris. She hadn't seen him, refused to think of him, for ten months. Yet after less than ten minutes in his company, she'd been lost again in the puzzle. She couldn't stop herself from trying to understand what he did, how he did it—whether his eyes told the truth or lied, whether the sweet, lazy curve of his mouth was reality or illusion.

He had caught her, and understood what she was doing and didn't like it. She'd seen the anger: one evil spark in those fathomless blue depths, there and gone in the space of a heartbeat. He'd caught her trying to peer behind the mask and didn't like it. And so, he'd driven her off. He'd done that with his eyes alone, with one look of burning intensity . . . and she'd backed off, scorched.

Yet some dark part of her had wanted to be burned again.

Perhaps it was not entirely the artist in her, but this dark part that had kept her with him in the first place. She might have walked away any time, might have greeted him and gone, but she didn't. Couldn't. Wanted to, didn't want to.

She wasn't an indecisive or unsure woman. Yet she'd remained with him, all the while barely able to think, let alone speak, because she felt as though she were being torn in two. Yes. No. Go away. Stay.

Now, though he was miles away, she couldn't drive him out of her mind with work. Now he was *in* the work, and she couldn't get him out.

Concentration washed away, and anger flooded in. Her temples began to throb. She threw down the brush and hurled the palette at the canvas, knocked oils and solvents to the floor. Furious tears streaming down her face, she stormed from one end of the studio to the other, tearing it to pieces. She hardly knew what she was doing, didn't care. All she wanted was destruction. She was ripping the

drapes from the windows when she heard her husband's
voice.

"Dammit, Leila, they can hear you all the way to
Shoreditch."

She swung round. Francis stood in the doorway, clutching his forehead. His hair was matted, his jaw dark with
stubble.

"How the devil am I to sleep through this?" he demanded.

"I don't care how you sleep," she said, her voice
choked with tears. "I don't care about anything, especially
you."

"Gad, you picked a fine time for one of your fits. What
in blazes are you doing home, anyway? You were supposed
to be at Norbury House the week. Did you come back just
to have a tantrum?"

He entered the studio and looked about. "One of your
better ones, by the looks of it."

She pressed her fist to her pounding heart and looked
about at what she'd done. Another tantrum. God help her.

Then she saw him pick up the canvas. "Leave that
alone," she said too shrilly. "Put it down and get out."

He looked up at her. "So this is what it's all about. Pin-
ing for the pretty count, are you?" He tossed the canvas
aside. "Want to run back to Paris and be one of the maggots crawling over him, do you?"

The thunder in her head was abating, but the furious
frustration remained. She set her jaw. "Go away," she said.
"Leave me alone."

"I wonder how he'll like dealing with a temperamental
artiste. I wonder what he'll think of *Madame's* little rages.
I wonder what method he'd use to quiet you down. No
telling with him. Maybe he'll beat you. Would you like
that, my love? You might, you know. Some women do."

She felt sick. "Stop it. Leave me alone. Talk your filth to
one of your whores."

"You were one of my whores once." He eyed her up and
down. "Don't you remember? I do. You were so young and
sweet and so very eager to please. Insatiable, too, once you

got over your girlish shyness. But that was only to be expected, wasn't it? Like papa, like daughter."

A claw of ice fastened on her belly. Never, since the day he'd first broken the news, had Francis referred openly to her father.

"Ah, that gives you a turn, does it?" As his glance moved from the canvas back to her, his dissolute mouth twisted into a smirk. "What a fool I was not to have thought of it before. But then there was so little at stake in Paris. What do the French care what your papa did or was? The English, though—they're another matter, aren't they?"

"You bastard."

"You shouldn't have made me jealous, Leila. You shouldn't be painting the face of a man you haven't seen in nearly a year. Or has it been? Have you been seeing him on the sly? Was he at Norbury House? You might as well tell me. I can find out easily enough. Was he there?" he demanded.

"Yes, he was there!" she snapped. "And I left. So much for your disgusting suspicions. And if your cesspit mind isn't satisfied with that, ask your friends—ask anybody. He's only just arrived in England."

"How did he come to be at Norbury House?"

"How the devil should I know? He was invited. Why shouldn't he be? He's probably related to half the peerage. Most of the French nobility is."

The twisted smirk hardened. "Fiona invited him, I'll wager. Pandering for you, as usual—"

"How dare you—"

"Oh, I know what she's about. She'd love to help you make a cuckold of me, the black-haired she-wolf."

"A cuckold?" she echoed bitterly. "What does one call what you've made *me*? What name does one give the wife? Or maybe the title 'wife' is sufficient joke in the circumstances."

"What should you like to be instead? A divorcée?" He laughed. "Even if we could afford it, you wouldn't like that a bit, would you? Why not? The scandal might do wonders for your career."

"It would destroy my career, and you know it."

"Don't think I won't make a scandal if you attempt an affair." Kicking aside the canvas, Francis crossed the room to her. "Don't think I won't make you pay in private as well. Can you guess how you'll pay, my precious?"

He stood inches away. Revulsion churned inside her, but she refused to retreat. If she appeared to doubt her own strength and will, even for a moment, he'd doubt it, too. She lifted her chin and gazed coldly up at him.

"You're not to see him again," he said. "Or Fiona."

"You do not tell me who I may and may not see."

"I'll bloody well tell you what I like—and you'll obey!"

"And you can roast in hell! You don't dictate to me. I won't take orders from a whoremongering swine!"

"You viper-tongued little hypocrite! I let you go your way—let you deny me your bed—and this is what I get. You skip off to Surrey to wrap your legs about that—"

"Shut your filthy mouth!" Hot tears welled in her eyes. "Get out! Go drink yourself senseless, why don't you! Eat more of that poison you love so much! Intoxicate yourself to death! Only let me be!"

"By gad, if my head weren't pounding like a steam engine, I'd—" He raised his hand. He was just about furious enough to strike her, she knew. Yet she wouldn't shrink from him.

He only stared at his hand. "But of course I can't throttle you, can I? Because I adore you so." He chucked her under the chin. "Naughty baggage. We'll speak of this later, after you've calmed down. And you won't come in and knock me on the head with a blunt instrument, will you, love? We're not in France any more, recollect. English juries are not at all soft-hearted—or headed—about women. They've hanged plenty—even the pretty ones."

She made no answer, only stood rigid and silent, staring at the floor as he left the studio. She remained so while his footsteps faded down the hall. When, finally, she heard his bedroom door slam shut, she moved stiffly across the room and sat down on the sofa.

She wiped her eyes and blew her nose.

She was not afraid, she told herself. Any scandal Francis brought down on her must hurt him, too—as he'd realize when he recovered from last night's debauch. If he recovered. If the drink and opiates weren't destroying his reason.

In the ten months since they'd come to London, he'd grown steadily worse. Some days he didn't leave his bed until dinnertime. He took laudanum to sleep, and again when he woke, to relieve the pain of rising from his bed. Always, he needed something—drink or opiates to dull the restlessness or peevishness, the headache and other discomforts. Always he needed something to carry him through this demented existence he called living.

She should not have quarreled with him. His mind was diseased. She might as well try to argue a man out of cholera. She should not have let him upset her.

She rose from the sofa and picked up the offending canvas. She should not have taken a fit about *that*, certainly, she chided herself. It had happened only because she'd let Esmond upset her. What a fool she'd made of herself: running away from Norbury House, after babbling to Fiona about mesmerism, for heaven's sake.

"Gad, I shall become as deranged as Francis," she muttered. "Just from living with him, probably."

There was a thump and a crash from down the hall. "That's right, you poor sod," she said, glancing up from the smeared painting. "Knock over the furniture. Throw things about. Maybe that's from living with *me*."

She righted the easel, set the canvas back upon it, dug out fresh supplies of paint from the cupboard, retrieved her brushes from various parts of the room, and resolutely set to work.

Her mind—if not her heart—cleansed by the recent tempest, she eventually succeeded in obliterating every trace of the Comte d'Esmond's provoking countenance.

While she worked, she told herself she *could* leave Francis. She could go away from England and change her name. Again. She could paint anywhere. She was only seven and twenty. That wasn't too old to begin again. But she'd think it over later when she was calmer. She'd talk to Andrew. Though no longer her guardian, he was still her solicitor. He'd advise and help her.

Hand and mind occupied, she didn't notice the time passing. Not until she'd finished the painting and begun cleaning up did she glance at the clock on the mantel. Then she discovered it was past teatime. She'd been working for hours in rare, blessedly uninterrupted quiet. But where the devil was her tea?

She was about to yank the bell rope when Mrs. Dempton came to the open studio door bearing a heap of bed linens.

As the servant glanced into the wrecked studio, her jowly countenance tightened with disapproval.

Leila ignored it. Obviously, she and Francis were not ideal employers. They'd been through three different sets of servants in ten months. All had disapproved of her.

"When will tea be ready?" Leila asked.

"In a trice, mum. I was only hoping to get in to change Mr. Beaumont's bedding first—but the door's still shut tight."

And Mrs. Dempton knew better than to knock. When Francis' door was closed, he was not to be disturbed unless the house was on fire. Today Mrs. Dempton had surely heard for herself what had happened when the master's wife had troubled his rest.

"Then I suppose he'll have to wait until tomorrow for clean sheets," said Leila.

"Yes, mum, only he did ask particular, and told Mr. Dempton he'd have a bath, and now the water's near boiled away, because I told Mr. D. not to haul it up until that door was open. The last time—"

"Yes, Mrs. Dempton. I quite understand."

"And Mr. Beaumont asked for scones for his tea, which I was happy to make, I'm sure, as he don't eat enough to keep a mouse alive, but there they are, turning stone cold in the kitchen and the water boiled away and you looking for your tea, and the bedding not even changed." The disapproving expression sharpened into accusation.

She thought it was all Leila's fault, obviously. Leila had

quarreled with her husband and he'd locked himself in his room to sulk, inconveniencing the servants.

But surely he'd given the orders after the quarrel, and so he could not have been sulking then—or intending to sleep so long. Leila frowned. Laudanum, of course. He'd complained of a headache. He must have taken laudanum and fallen asleep. There was nothing new in that.

Nonetheless, she felt a prickle of uneasiness.

"I had better look in on him," she said. "He may have an engagement. He'll be vexed if he sleeps through it."

She left the studio and moved quickly down the hall to his bedroom. She rapped at the door. "Francis?" He didn't answer. She gave a harder rap and called to him more sharply. No response. "Francis!" she shouted, pounding on the door.

Silence.

Cautiously she opened the door and looked in.

Her heart skidded to a stop.

He lay on the carpet by the bed, his hand wrapped about the leg of the toppled nightstand.

"Francis!" Even as she cried out, she knew he couldn't hear her, couldn't be roused, ever again.

Mrs. Dempton came running at the sound, stopped short at the doorway, and let out an ear-splitting shriek.

"Murder!" she screamed, scuttling back from the door. "God help us! Oh, Tom, for the love of heaven! She's killed him!"

Leila didn't heed her. She moved stiffly to her husband's too-still form and, kneeling beside him, touched his wrist, his neck. His flesh was cool, too cool. No pulse. No breath. Nothing. Gone.

She heard Mrs. Dempton screeching in the hall, heard Tom's heavy footsteps as he hurried up the stairs, but it was mere noise in some other world far away.

Dazedly, Leila looked down.

Broken glass. Shards from the water glass, smooth and clear, and the etched glass of the laudanum bottle. Puzzle pieces of blue and white porcelain . . . the water pitcher.

"Missus?"

She looked up into Tom Dempton's narrow, leathery face. "He—he's . . . Please. Get the doctor. And—and Mr. Herriard. Quickly, please. Hurry, you must hurry."

He knelt beside her, checked for signs of life as she had, then shook his head. "Doctor won't do him no good, missus. I'm sorry. He's—"

"I know." She understood what had happened, though it didn't make sense, either. Yet the doctor had warned him. Francis himself knew. He'd told her: the wrong dosage was poison. She wanted to scream.

"You must go," she told Dempton. "The doctor must come and—and . . ."

Sign the death certificate. Papers. Life went away and left papers. Life went away and you put what was once alive into a box. Into the ground. Only a few hours ago he'd stood shouting at her.

She shuddered. "Get the doctor. And Mr. Herriard. I'll stay with—with my husband."

"You're all a-tremble," said Dempton. He offered his hand. "Best come away. Mrs. D. will stay with him."

She could hear Mrs. Dempton weeping loudly in the hall beyond. "Your wife is the one who needs looking after," Leila said, fighting to keep her voice level. "Try to calm her, please—but do fetch the doctor. And Mr. Herriard."

Reluctantly, Tom Dempton left. Leila heard his wife trailing after him down the stairs.

"She killed him, Tom," came the strident voice. "You heard her screaming at him, telling him to die. Told him to roast in hell, she did. I knew it would come to this."

Leila heard Dempton mutter some impatient response, then the slam of the door. Mrs. Dempton's cries subsided somewhat, but she didn't quiet altogether, and she didn't come back upstairs. Death was there, and she left Leila to look upon it alone.

"I'm here," she whispered. "Oh, Francis, you poor . . . Oh, God forgive you. Forgive me. You shouldn't have gone alone. I would have held your hand. I would. You were kind once. For that . . . Oh, you poor *fool*."

Tears trickling down her face, she bent to close his eyes. It was then she became aware of the odd scent. Odd . . . and wrong. She looked at the broken laudanum bottle, its contents soaking the carpet near his head. But it wasn't laudanum. This smelled like . . . ink.

She sniffed, and drew back, chilled. There was water and laudanum. Nothing else. No cologne. But she knew this odor.

She sat back on her heels, her eyes darting about the room. She'd heard the noise. The crash and the thump. He'd knocked over the nightstand, and pitcher bottle and drinking glass had crashed down with it. He'd fallen. But not another sound. No cry for help, no curses. Just the noise for an instant, then silence.

Had he died in that instant?

She made herself bend close and sniff again. It was on his breath and in the air about him. So very faint, but there: bitter almonds. Why had she thought of ink?

Her mind didn't want to think but she made it. Ink. The doctor. In Paris. Long ago, yes, telling her to keep the windows open. He'd taken up a bottle of blue ink. Prussian blue. Even the fumes could make her very ill, he'd told her. "Artists, they are so careless," he'd said. "Yet it is they who spend their lives amid poisons of the most deadly kind. Do you know what this is made of? Prussic acid, child."

Prussic acid. The symptoms began in seconds. It killed in minutes. The heart slowed . . . convulsions . . . asphyxiation. A teaspoon of the commercial variety could kill you. It was one of the deadliest of poisons, because it was so quick, the doctor had said. It was also hard to detect. But there was the bitter almonds odor.

That was what she smelled.

Someone had poisoned Francis with prussic acid.

She shut her eyes. Poisoned. Murdered. And she had been quarreling with him, loudly, bitterly.

She's killed him. You heard her . . . Told him to roast in hell.

English juries . . . they've hanged plenty—even the pretty ones.

A jury. A trial. They'd find out. About Papa.

Like papa, like daughter.

Her heart raced. She'd never have a chance. They'd all believe she was guilty, that evil was in her blood.

No. No, she would not hang.

She rose on shaky limbs. "It was an accident," she said under her breath. "God forgive me, but it must be an accident."

She had to think. Coldly. Calmly. Prussic acid. Bitter almonds. Yes. The ink.

She crept noiselessly from the room, looked down the stairs. She could hear Mrs. Dempton sobbing and talking to herself, but she was out of sight. Her voice was coming from the vestibule, where she was waiting for her husband to return with the doctor. They'd be here any moment.

Leila hurried to the studio, snatched up a bottle of Prussian blue and was back in Francis' bedroom in seconds.

Her hands trembling, she unstopped the bottle and laid it on its side amid the shards of the laudanum bottle. The ink trickled from the bottle onto the carpet, and the potent fumes rose.

The fumes. She must not remain here and inhale them. The doctor had said even that could make one ill.

She rose and retreated only as far as the threshold, though she wanted to run as fast and as far away as possible. She wanted to faint, to be sick, to be anything but fully conscious. She made herself stay. She mustn't run. She mustn't leave Francis alone, and she mustn't be sick or swoon. She must think, prepare herself.

She focused all her will on that. There were sounds below, but she shut them out. She must make herself very calm. No tears. She couldn't risk even that small loss of control. She needed all her will.

She heard the footsteps upon the stairs, but didn't look round. She couldn't. She wasn't ready. She couldn't command her muscles.

The footsteps neared. "Madame." It was a soft voice, a

whisper so low she wasn't sure she heard it. The entire house seemed to be whispering. Murder.

Like papa, like daughter.

Hang the pretty ones.

"Madame."

Her head turned slowly, jerkily . . . to inhumanly blue eyes and a crown of spun gold hair. She didn't understand why he was there. She wasn't sure he truly was there. She couldn't think about that or anything. Tears were burning her eyes and she mustn't cry, mustn't move. She would shatter like the glass, the bottle, the pitcher. Broken . . . puzzle pieces.

"I c-can't," she mumbled. "I must . . ."

"Yes, madame."

She swayed, and he caught her in his arms.

She shattered then and, pressing her face to his coat, she wept.

Chapter 3

IT WAS FATE THAT HAD DRIVEN HIM HERE, Ismal thought, and Fate that sent Leila Beaumont into his arms.

Fate, evidently, was in a vicious humor.

Ismal was aware of her soft, untidy hair tickling his chin and of the lush ripeness of the body pressed tautly to his. With the awareness came a hunger so fierce that it darkened his reason. But he dragged his mind back from the darkness to take in the room beyond, for he was all too aware of what lay there as well.

He'd turned her back to the scene when he caught her, and now he studied it over her head: the corpse, the overturned nightstand, the broken glass and crockery . . . and one unbroken bottle of ink. The hysterical woman servant below had babbled of murder. His instincts told him the same.

At the sound of footsteps, Ismal looked down to the landing, just as Nick appeared there, his upturned countenance politely blank.

Ismal nodded, and Nick hurried noiselessly up to him.

"Take her to one of the rooms below, and get her

brandy," Ismal told him in Greek, his voice a shade too harsh. "Do what you must to keep her there."

Nick gently disentangled her from his master and pushed a fresh handkerchief into her hands. "It'll be all right, madam," he said soothingly. "Don't you mind a thing. We'll see to it. I'll fix you some tea. You leave it to me," he continued as he guided her down the stairs. "Doctor's on his way. There, lean on me, that's right."

Leaving Mrs. Beaumont in his servant's capable hands, Ismal slipped into the master bedroom.

He studied Beaumont's blue-tinged countenance briefly, then lifted the eyelids. If he'd died of a laudanum overdose, the pupils would be narrowed to pinpricks. Instead, they were widely dilated.

Ismal sniffed cautiously, then drew back, his eyes on the ink bottle. The main odor was that of the ink, and it was not healthy, he knew. That, however, wasn't what had killed Francis Beaumont. Though the odor about the mouth and body was barely discernible, Ismal's sensitive nose recognized it. Beaumont had ingested prussic acid. Frowning, Ismal rose.

Allah grant him patience. To kill the man was understandable, but she might as well have killed herself, too, while she was about it, for she could not have devised a quicker route to the gallows. Motive, means, opportunity— all pointing to her.

But it was done, he told himself, and could not be done again more intelligently. At least she'd shown sense enough to spill the ink. That should confuse matters. He would take care of the rest. Lord Quentin, the man he'd secretly worked for this last decade, would insist upon it.

He would see, as quickly as Ismal had, that an inquest was unavoidable. Even if the physician failed to notice the odor of prussic acid, he'd be sure to observe the dilated pupils. He'd want an autopsy.

In any case, the death *was* suspicious, thanks to the curst Mrs. Dempton. Ismal had hardly entered the house before the demented female had not only repeated what she'd overheard of the quarrel, but reported that Mrs.

Beaumont had sent for her lawyer as well as the doctor. Mrs. Dempton would share these incriminating tidbits with everyone else who'd listen. The newspapers would be all too eager to listen.

Since, given these disagreeable circumstances, an inquest was inevitable, it had better be carefully managed. Only one verdict—accidental death—was acceptable. The alternative was a murder investigation and public trial. The *Vingt-Huit* matter might easily come to light, opening Pandora's box. News of the government's clandestine activities could set off a public outcry that could easily bring down the present ministry. Even if the government survived the uproar, countless people—not simply Beaumont's victims, but their innocent kin—would suffer public disgrace and humiliation. Whole families could be destroyed, here and abroad.

In short, one could either allow one woman to get away with murder or set off a cataclysmic scandal.

It was not a difficult choice, Ismal reflected as he left the master bedroom and shut the door behind him. For once, duty and inclination were in full agreement.

IN THOSE FIRST terrible moments in the master bedroom, Leila had forgotten that Andrew Herriard had already left for the Continent the previous day. Thanks to a storm in the Channel, her message was slow to reach him in Paris. Consequently, he didn't get back to London until the day before the inquest.

He came straight to the house, without stopping to change out of his traveling clothes. Still, not until Fiona had left them alone in the parlor did his calm amiability give way to frowning concern.

"My dear girl," he said, taking Leila's hands in his.

The gentle voice, the warm strength of his hands, drove back the demons of the last six days.

"I'm all right," she said. "It's a—an unpleasant business, but merely a formality, I'm sure."

"A terrible strain upon you, all the same." He led her to

the sofa and sat down with her. "Take your time and tell me as best you can, from the beginning."

She told him virtually the same story she'd told Lord Quentin three times, the magistrate twice, and Fiona once. It was the truth, but not all of it. Leila told Andrew a bit more about the quarrel, but not much more. She described it in general terms, letting him assume she couldn't remember the details clearly. She didn't mention the prussic acid odor or the ink she'd spilled.

Even with Andrew, whom she would trust with her life, there was only one route to take: the death was an accident.

She was guiltily aware that Andrew would be appalled at what she'd done. To shield a murderer was a criminal act, and he would not countenance it, regardless what was at stake.

She wasn't so noble. While Andrew might find some way to save her from the gallows, the truth about her father would surely come out and destroy her career. She would, as always, find some way to survive. But Andrew's career would be jeopardized as well. He had never told the authorities he'd found Jonas Bridgeburton's daughter alive, and he'd had to take some not strictly legal steps to give her a new identity.

The average lawyer's career might withstand a small, very old blot on his copybook. Andrew Herriard, however, was one of the most highly regarded solicitors in England, not simply because of his brilliant legal mind, but because of his unshakable integrity. He was being considered for a knighthood at least, possibly a peerage.

Leila wouldn't let his life be blighted because of her.

No matter what happened at tomorrow's inquest, no matter what the doctors found in Francis' body, she wouldn't be destroyed, and Andrew wouldn't be disgraced. She'd had six days to think and plan, and she'd found, as she always did, a way to manage matters. She hadn't let Francis victimize her. She wouldn't let a lot of law officers do it, either.

All she cared about now was Andrew, and her heart lightened when his worried expression began to abate. She had only to glance up into his gentle brown eyes to know he believed her innocent.

"It was simply an unlucky chain of circumstances," he said reassuringly. "Still, you were fortunate that particular client happened along. I understand Esmond is very well connected, here as well as abroad."

"Apparently he had only to snap his fingers and Lord Quentin came running."

"I couldn't ask for a better man than Quentin to oversee this farce of an inquiry. An unavoidable farce, thanks to Mrs. Dempton's unaccountable behavior. She will cost the Home Office much needless labor and expense." He searched her face. "But they're minor concerns at present. I'm sorry you've had to endure so much. At least I find you in good hands: Lady Carroll is devoted to you—and that young manservant seems a steady fellow."

"He's Esmond's servant," she said. "Nick is a sort of bodyguard. I was given a choice between him and one of Quentin's men. Someone was needed to keep out the curious." She explained that apart from her dressmaker, only David had been admitted. He'd called the day after Francis' death, and she'd asked him to discourage others from calling until after the inquest.

"Very wise." He smiled. "You've done everything just as I should have advised. It would seem I'm scarcely needed."

"I only wish you hadn't been needed," she said. "I'm sorry to bring so much trouble to you."

"Nonsense," he said briskly. "As usual, you leave me little to do. You've acted wisely and bravely, as you have for years. My only regret is that this marriage has demanded so very much wisdom and courage. Even in death, he's a trouble to you."

His sympathy set her conscience shrieking. "I'd have been in worse trouble if he *hadn't* married me," she said. "And I should be in far worse by now if you hadn't forgiven me and stood by me and—and helped me become better."

She would never forget the day, ten years ago, when

she'd had to explain why she must marry Francis Beaumont, though Andrew disapproved. She would never forget Andrew's grieved expression when she confessed she was no longer a virgin. His sorrow had been far more devastating than the anger and disgust she'd steeled herself for.

He'd gently explained that her father was a man of strong passions, which overcame his better nature because he let them rule him. When the baser passions ruled, the path from innocent pleasure to vice became treacherously steep, and it was all too easy to slip.

She had wept with shame, because she had slipped so easily, and because he was so very disappointed.

He had told her, then, that she wasn't altogether to blame, being young, with no one to protect and guide her. Francis Beaumont should not have taken advantage, but men generally did, given the smallest encouragement or opportunity.

Leila had wept the more then, aware that somehow she must have encouraged, provided the opportunity. Certainly she hadn't avoided Francis. She'd been infatuated with the handsome, sophisticated man who devoted so much time to a lonely young girl.

"Perhaps it's all for the best," Andrew had consoled her. "At least you'll have a husband to look after you. And now you've discovered how easy it is to slip, you'll be alert in the future, and take greater care."

Leila had tearfully promised she would. She knew she might have been abandoned to the streets, as other ruined girls were. Instead, Francis would wed her and Andrew had forgiven her. But she must never err again. She must prove she wouldn't follow her father's path, but would rule the wicked nature she'd inherited.

And she had.

Until now.

"It was all long ago," Andrew said, as though he saw the memory reflected in her eyes. "We shouldn't dwell upon that now—but death has a way of stirring up the past." He rose. "What we want is a piping hot pot of tea and a dose of Lady Carroll's lively conversation to lift our spirits. I shall give you proper legal advice, and she'll doubtless suggest a host of ways to shock the coroner out of his wits."

THE INQUIRY INTO the death of Francis Beaumont was one of the most splendidly orchestrated in recent British history, thanks to Ismal.

He had personally selected the medical experts, analyzed their postmortem reports, reviewed the numerous depositions, and decided the order in which witnesses would be called. Though the coroner and jurors didn't know it, the inquest was over as soon as the first witness, the Comte d'Esmond, had given his testimony.

Aware that not an iota of prussic acid had been found in the corpse, Ismal had only to demolish Mrs. Dempton's credibility to set events moving inexorably to a verdict of accidental death.

That was easy enough. He'd discovered her weaknesses when he'd listened to Quentin question her. All Ismal had to do was drop a few intriguing hints during his own testimony to guide the coroner's subsequent questioning of Mrs. Dempton.

Ismal exited immediately after testifying, to return soon thereafter disguised as a shabby country constable. He was in time to hear Mrs. Dempton characterize her late master as a saint and the mistress as a tool of Satan. Closely questioned, the servant tearfully and obstinately denied what all the world—including the coroner—knew to be true: that Beaumont spent most of his hours, waking and sleeping, intoxicated; that he was a habitual user of opiates, both in raw and laudanum form; and spent most of his time in brothels, gambling hells, and opium dens.

Mr. Dempton came next, with nothing significant to add but the fact that Mrs. Beaumont had sent for her solicitor as well as the physician.

Quentin, who came next, took care of the lawyer issue by mildly remarking that Mr. Herriard having been Mrs. Beaumont's guardian, she would naturally seek his assistance in her time of trouble.

The neighbors had seen and heard nothing.

Then the doctors—six of them—testified, one by one. They hadn't found prussic acid, Ismal knew, because it was nearly impossible to detect after the fact, even in the best of circumstances. In Beaumont's case, only a minute dose had been needed: both prussic acid and opiates produced similar cynanotic symptoms, and his internal organs were already irreparably damaged by years of abuse. It was this damage, and Beaumont's frequent headaches, that the medical experts used to explain the uncharacteristic dilation of the pupils. Two doctors even went so far as to assert that he'd died of natural causes; the laudanum dosage would not have proved fatal, they said, but for the degenerate state of the digestive organs.

Indeed, Madame had chosen her poison wisely. What Ismal couldn't understand was why she hadn't chosen her time wisely as well. He'd assumed she'd acted in the heat of the moment. Yet poisoning, especially this one, wanted forethought.

Beaumont had been dead for hours when he was found, which meant she must have poisoned the laudanum shortly after the quarrel. But how had she found the prussic acid so quickly? Had she kept it in the studio? Yet that would indicate planning, and surely she'd plan a safer time than right after a loud, bitter quarrel. The trouble was the timing. Tom Dempton, one floor below, had heard a noise from the master bedroom at the same time Madame claimed to have heard it: moments after Beaumont had reentered his room and shut the door.

How the devil had she done it?

Had she done it?

But she must have. There was the ink.

Yet nothing else fit.

The problem had plagued Ismal these last seven days. It had wanted all his will and pride to keep from going back to her and questioning, manipulating, using all of his vast store of tricks to extract the secret from her. But that would be as good as admitting he was stymied. Which he wasn't, he assured himself. Never in ten years had he encountered a problem he couldn't solve. He remained at this inquest, whose outcome was already decided, solely to study her and find, in a gesture, a turn of phrase, the clue he wanted. Her turn was coming soon. Then he'd have his answer.

He'd scarcely thought it when he became aware of a pulsing change in the atmosphere. He looked to the door just as Leila Beaumont entered, shrouded in black, like the night.

She strode down the narrow aisle between the benches, her gown rustling in the stunned silence. When she reached her place, she threw back her veil, swept the assembled onlookers one insolent glance, then fixed the coroner with a look that should have incinerated him.

About Ismal, males of assorted degrees, high and low, began to breathe again. Even he had been struck breathless for a moment. By Allah, but she was magnificent. Fire and ice at once.

Mine, the savage within him growled.

In time, his civilized self soothed. *Patience.*

LEILA'S ENTRANCE INTO the inquiry room caused a bit of a stir, which she had not only expected, but dressed for. Scorning to elicit pity, she had attired herself as dashingly as the unrelieved black of deep mourning allowed.

She wore an immense velvet bonnet, tilted back on her head at a fashionable angle, and trimmed with wide satin ribbons. Her black bombazine dress boasted wide shoulders and enormous sleeves, its high hem trimmed with two deep flounces that ended precisely at her ankles. Her elegant fur-lined boots proved a wise choice for a bitter cold day and this draughty chamber.

Since she had been kept out of the room while the coroner examined the other witnesses, she had no idea what had been said. Judging by Andrew's expression, however, matters mustn't be going very badly for her. He looked annoyed, but not worried.

Esmond wasn't here. She hadn't seen him since the day Francis had died. She didn't know for certain whether he believed her innocent or guilty, but his absence made her suspect the latter. He didn't want his noble name soiled by association with a murderess, no doubt. For all she knew, he hadn't testified at all, but had used his influence to get out of it.

No one, of course, had told her who would be called to testify. Despite the fact that one was, according to law, considered innocent until proven guilty and this was merely an inquest, not a trial, Leila had been treated as suspects generally were, i.e., kept utterly in the dark.

No one had given even Andrew information—because her own lawyer might be so audacious as to use it to *help* her, God forbid.

Secretive bastards.

She lifted her chin as she met the coroner's weary gaze.

In response to his questions, Leila gave him all the redundant information he sought: her name, place of residence, length of residence, et cetera. His clerk industriously wrote it all down, just as though no one in the world knew who she was until this moment.

After that, she was obliged to describe where she had been the night before her husband's death, the mode of transportation which had brought her home, and more et ceteras—all, in short, that she'd told Lord Quentin and the magistrate, repeatedly.

Only when the coroner asked why she'd cut short her stay at Norbury House did Leila allow a note of irritation to creep into her voice. "With all due respect, the information you seek is in my signed deposition," she said.

The coroner glanced down at a paper before him. "You said only that you had changed your mind. Would you care to elucidate for the jurors?"

"I had gone to the country to rest," she said, looking straight at the jurors. "The visit was not restful. There were many more houseguests than I had anticipated."

"And so you returned home and immediately went to work?" The coroner lifted an eyebrow. "Is this not odd in one who desired rest?"

"Since I wasn't going to get any, I thought I might as well try to be productive."

"Indeed. *Were* you—er—productive?"

Given at least half a dozen persons' description of the state of her studio—which the coroner had in writing in front of him—she wasn't surprised at the question.

Leila met his piercing gaze defiantly. "Not at first. As you have doubtless already learned, I had a quarrel with myself, and consequently took out my vexation on the objects in my studio. As you have also already learned, the disturbance woke my husband. Whereupon we argued."

"Would you describe the disagreement, madam?"

"Certainly," she said. The onlookers promptly came to attention, as one might expect. Until today, she had consistently refused to describe the quarrel, regardless of how much she'd been coaxed, prodded, and bullied. They were expecting revelations.

"Mr. Beaumont made several disagreeable remarks," she said. "I responded by bidding him to perdition."

Audience expectations sank several degrees.

"If you would be more specific, Mrs. Beaumont," the coroner said patiently.

"I would not," she said.

This elicited a low buzz of speculation. The coroner bestowed a cold stare upon the onlookers. The buzzing ceased.

Then, somewhat less patiently, he asked if she would do the jurors the courtesy of explaining why she chose to withhold vital information.

"My husband was evidently suffering the aftereffects of a night of entertainment," she said. "He was irate at being wakened and had a thundering headache besides. Had he not been in this state, he should not have been so disagreeable. Had I not already been vexed before he entered, I should not have even listened, let alone responded, to bad-tempered comments. To attempt to repeat the ill-chosen remarks of the moment is to give them an appearance of veracity and a permanence they do not merit. Even had we meant a fraction of what we said, I should not repeat it. I do not wash my linen in public."

Scattered whispers among the onlookers.

"I sympathize with the principle, Mrs. Beaumont," said the coroner. "However, you must be aware that your servant understood the exchange to be of a threatening nature."

"So far as I am aware, the servant you refer to was incapable of understanding," Leila said coldly. "She was of no assistance to me when I discovered Mr. Beaumont's body. On the contrary, she launched into an hysterical fit from which she did not recover until she had consumed a sizable portion of my late husband's best sherry."

There was a louder buzz and some laughter. The coroner uttered a sharp rebuke, and the room instantly hushed.

He turned back to her. "May I remind you, madam, that Mrs. Dempton overheard the quarrel hours before this—er—hysteria you diagnose."

"Then I cannot account for her attributing to me threats which I did not make," Leila replied. " 'Go to perdition,' is not, so far as I understand the English language, a threat, regardless how vulgar the specific terminology used. My own terminology was most unladylike, admittedly. I did not, however, threaten violence. I most certainly did not commit violence, except upon inanimate objects—my own belongings in my own studio."

"You have indicated that you were vexed," the coroner persisted. "To bid your husband to—er—perdition indicates a considerable anger."

"If I had been angry enough to do him injury," she said, "which I presume is what you are getting at, I should very much like to know why I didn't commit violence on the spot, while I was in this enraged state. Yet Mrs. Dempton saw him shortly after he left the studio. I'm sure she's told you he bore no marks of ill-usage."

There was more laughter and another reprimand from the coroner.

"We are inquiring, madam—as the law obliges us—into a death whose cause is questionable," he said quellingly.

"Surely it must have appeared so to you, since you agreed to summon the authorities."

Surely it must be plain to him that a guilty person wouldn't have agreed so readily or cooperated so fully. Leila had done both, as the coroner must be aware, for all his frowns.

"The cause did not appear questionable to me," she said. "I agreed because *others* appeared to have doubts, and I did not wish to stand in the way of their putting these doubts to rest in the way they thought proper. I thought then and still do, however, that the inquiry would prove a great waste of the government's resources."

"It would seem then that, at the time, you were the only one not in doubt regarding your husband's demise."

At the time. That was significant. Apparently, the autopsy had produced no clear evidence of foul play.

"It was not precisely unexpected," she said, her confidence soaring. "Mr. Beaumont took too much laudanum, despite warnings from his physician of the risk of overdose. It is called opiate poisoning, I understand. It was obvious to me that my husband had—as his physician had warned—accidentally poisoned himself."

That wasn't strictly perjury, she told her conscience. Francis certainly hadn't taken the poison on purpose.

"I see." The coroner looked down again at his notes. "According to Mrs. Dempton, you mentioned poison during the quarrel. You are telling us that the poison you referred to was the laudanum?"

"I referred to drink as well as opiates. I certainly was not expressing an intention of poisoning him myself—if that is what troubles you about Mrs. Dempton's statement."

"Yet you can understand, madam, how the words might be construed by another?"

"No, I cannot," she said firmly, "unless that other took me for an idiot. *Had* I threatened murder, I hope I would not be such a fool as to commit the act immediately thereafter, especially when it was more than likely the servants had overheard the alleged threat. To do so, I should have to be either an imbecile or a madwoman."

Leila paused to allow this to sink in while she swept the room a haughty glance, daring these men to believe her mad or imbecilic. There wasn't one woman here. Only men. Andrew was nodding sympathetically. Near him sat David's father, the Duke of Langford, his countenance a stony blank. There were the jurors, watching her avidly . . . Lord Quentin, his expression unreadable . . . several Bow Street officers she recognized . . . other representatives of authority . . . some appearing suspicious, some doubtful. Some had the grace to look abashed. They *had* thought she was stupid, every last one of . . .

Her glance shot back to a corner of the dingy room, where a particularly unkempt constable leaned against the wall. His greasy brown hair streaked with grey, he looked to be close to fifty. His grubby coat and stained waistcoat stretched over an unsightly paunch. He was studying the floor while absently scratching his head.

It was impossible, Leila told herself. She must have imagined that glint of unearthly blue. Even if the man had looked up, she couldn't have discerned the color of his eyes at this distance. Yet she was certain she'd felt their searing penetration.

She wrenched herself back to the moment. Whatever she'd felt or imagined, she could not afford to be distracted.

"Your sanity and intelligence are not being called into question, Mrs. Beaumont," the coroner was saying. "We are simply attempting to reconstruct a clear picture of the events preceding your husband's death."

"I have described them," she said. "After my husband left my studio, I did not see him alive again. I did not leave my studio at any time between his departure and my discovery of his body, when Mrs. Dempton was close behind me. I had remained in the studio, working—with the door open—until after teatime. I could not have done otherwise, as the painting must clearly demonstrate."

This time, the coroner didn't trouble to conceal his puzzled dismay. "I beg your pardon, madam. What painting? And what has it to say to anything?"

"Surely the Crown's officers observed the still-wet painting I had completed during those hours in the studio," she said. "Any artist could tell you that it had not been done in a state of agitation or haste. Had I interrupted my work to do away with my husband, I could not have produced that sort of technical study. It wants total concentration."

The coroner stared at her for a long moment, while the whispering rose to a low roar. He turned to his clerk. "We had better call in an artistic expert," he said.

Several jurors groaned. The coroner glared at them.

The glare moved to Leila. "I only wish, madam," he said, "that you had been more forthcoming previously regarding these matters. Surely you understood their importance. You might have spared the Crown precisely the waste of resources you mentioned earlier."

"I *thought* they were important," she said haughtily. "But no one else must have done, since I was never asked the relevant questions. While I am no expert in inquiries of this sort, I was puzzled why the focus of concern appeared to be my quarrel with Mr. Beaumont and Mrs. Dempton's hysteria. Though I did not understand why matters of hearsay took precedence over material facts, it was not my place to tell professionals how to do their business. I should not have taken the liberty of mentioning these matters today had it not appeared that they were likely to be overlooked altogether."

"I see," he said, his voice almost a growl. "Is there anything else you wish to *mention*, Mrs. Beaumont?"

SOME TIME LATER, Ismal climbed into the carriage seat opposite Lord Quentin.

"Well, it took long enough, but we got our verdict," said His Lordship. "Accidental death by laudanum overdose."

"Better the inquiry was lengthy," Ismal said. "The coroner is satisfied he's done his duty thoroughly."

He removed his greasy wig and studied it. Leila Beaumont had recognized him. Even Quentin hadn't, at first—

but she had, from across a large room . . . while she was being interrogated by an irritable coroner. Surely she was the Devil's own work.

"And the public will be satisfied, too, I hope." Quentin frowned. "I'm not, but that can't be helped. We couldn't afford a murder verdict."

"We did what was necessary," Ismal said.

"Maybe I'd have liked it better if she hadn't made us look a pack of fools."

Ismal smiled faintly. "The painting business, you mean."

Sir Gregory Williams, the artistic expert, had insisted the painting could not have been completed in less than two days and refused to believe it had been done by a woman. As a result, several officers had been ordered back to Madame's house to obtain other samples of her work. An hour after uttering his misogynistic remarks, Sir Gregory had been forced to gulp them back down.

"Sir Gregory appeared rather foolish," said Ismal. "Still, he had conscience enough to admit his mistake. Yes, the lady had undoubtedly painted the glassware study, he admitted, and yes, the treatment of the subject as well as the brushwork evidenced a serene state of mind."

Ismal, too, had been obliged to admit a mistake, inwardly at least. He hadn't considered the implications of the wet painting. In the studio, all his attention had been given to the devastation she had wrought. All his interest had focused on her temper . . . so much passion.

He'd let emotion taint his objectivity—an unforgivable sin. He was furious with himself, and with her, the cause. Nonetheless, his expression remained one of mild amusement.

"It was that dratted ink," Quentin said. "If she didn't kill him—"

"Obviously, she did not."

"You weren't so sure before."

"I did not need to be sure. Her guilt or innocence was irrelevant to my task."

"If she didn't spill that ink to protect herself, it could

have been to protect someone else," Quentin persisted. "Or
do you think the ink bottle *had* stood upon the nightstand,
where it had no business being? No diary in the drawer, no
paper, not even a pen. How do *you* explain it?"

"Beaumont may have set it down for a moment and forgotten it." Ismal shrugged. "There are a host of explana-
tions."

"Doesn't explain her. Quick-witted female like that."
Quentin's countenance grew thoughtful. "It does make one
wonder. Did she *really* think Beaumont's death was an accident? Did that clever woman miss what was obvious even
to me?"

"Does it matter?" Ismal dropped the wig onto the seat
beside him. "The matter is settled, our secrets are safe, and
none of your noble friends will be troubled by an embarrassing murder investigation."

"More than likely, it was one of those noble friends who
did it," Quentin said gloomily. "Even though my hands are
tied and justice seems to be out of the question, I should
like to know who killed him." He leaned forward, his hands
on his knees. "Don't *you* want to know who did it? Don't
you have a lengthy list of questions you'd like answered
about this plaguey business?"

Yes, Ismal thought. He'd like to know how the curst
woman had recognized him today. That was even more
troubling than his uncharacteristic leaping to a wrong con-
clusion. His civilized self told him she'd penetrated his disguise because she was an artist, more keenly observant
than others. The superstitious barbarian inside him believed this woman could see into a man's soul.

He told the barbarian that no human being, even he,
could read minds or hearts. He discovered secrets, yes, but
that was no magical power, merely a well-honed skill in
observing and translating the smallest clues of voice, face,
gesture. Accordingly, he never betrayed himself through
such inadvertent clues. Yet she must have discerned . . .
something. In some way, he'd betrayed himself to her, just
as in the last week he'd somehow let desire undermine his
intellect.

He didn't like "some ways" and "somehows" and the loss of control they implied. Once, a decade ago, a woman had weakened his will and reason, and he was still paying. He wouldn't risk destruction again. He would attend the funeral, for appearances' sake. Then, he would return to the Continent, and this time, forget her.

And so, aloud he said, "No, I am not curious. It is done, our problems are over, and I am content."

Chapter 4

FRANCIS' FUNERAL TOOK PLACE THE DAY AFTER the inquest. The Comte d'Esmond attended the services and came with the others to the house after. He expressed his condolences and courteously offered to let Nick remain with Leila until she'd found replacements for the Demptons.

She politely declined—to Esmond's relief, she was unhappily certain. His speech and manner were all that was correct—neither a degree too cool nor overwarm. But she could sense the chill in him as palpably as if a wall of ice stood between them.

Unfortunately, when she went on to explain that one of Mr. Herriard's staff would fill in temporarily, both David and Fiona insisted she borrow from their staffs instead. Fiona was growing rather sharp with David when the Duke of Langford, who'd been standing nearby talking to Quentin, took it upon himself to render a judgment.

"Esmond's servant has had a week to familiarize himself with your requirements," said His Grace. "His remaining would produce less disruption, on all sides. I should think you've had disruption enough, Mrs. Beaumont."

"Quite right," said Quentin. "Simplest solution, I should think."

Leila glimpsed a flash of something—rage, or perhaps disgust—in Esmond's eyes, but before she could respond, he did.

"*Certainement,*" he murmured. "I return to Paris soon, in any case, and so there is not the smallest inconvenience. Nick can follow me after your household affairs are settled."

She glanced at Andrew, who nodded agreement, naturally. One didn't contradict the Duke of Langford. David had turned away. Even Fiona, who habitually contradicted everybody, held her tongue.

Leila lifted her chin as she met Esmond's enigmatic blue gaze. "I seem to be outnumbered," she said. "All the same, I regret trespassing further on your generosity."

He responded with some chivalrous, typically Gallic nonsense and shortly thereafter took his leave.

He left the chill behind, and something terribly like despair. Not since that night long ago in Venice had Leila felt so bitterly, wretchedly alone.

By now she knew how much Esmond had helped her. After Andrew had provided a detailed report of the inquest, she'd perceived how very unpleasantly matters could have gone for her had anyone but Quentin supervised the case.

She'd meant to express her gratitude to Esmond. She'd even rehearsed a brief but neatly worded speech. The trouble was, the wall of ice had cut her off before she could begin. Now she suspected that he'd merely acted gallantly, as his nationality—and, no doubt, some sort of noblesse oblige—required. Having obliged, however, he refused to be further associated with her.

She should not be surprised, and she had no business feeling angry or hurt, she told herself. Langford was definitely no friendlier. It was clear he didn't want his son or Fiona—daughter of one of his dearest friends—associated with a bourgeois female artist whose poor taste in husbands and lack of breeding had resulted in scandal. He'd made it clear that even their servants were too good for the likes of Leila Beaumont—let the foreigner's menial look after her.

The irony was, Langford couldn't know how richly she deserved his censure. He couldn't know, either, the high price she was paying already. Frantic to save herself and shield Andrew, she'd never truly contemplated the consequences of concealing murder: the total isolation, the need to guard every word, gesture, expression, lest something slip—very possibly to the killer himself—and worst of all, the bitter pangs of conscience.

She couldn't look her friends in the eye, and she couldn't look at others without suspecting them. She couldn't wait for her visitors to leave, yet she dreaded being alone with her guilt and fears.

Her visitors did leave at last, and exhaustion got her through that first night. She was too tired even to dream.

But in the days after that, she knew no peace. She lost her appetite. She couldn't work, couldn't bear to take up a drawing pencil. Every time the door knocker sounded, every time a carriage clattered into the square, she thought it was Quentin, coming to arrest her, or the killer, coming to silence her forever.

She diagnosed herself as hysterical, yet the hysteria continued, exacerbated by nightmares that made her dread falling asleep.

Finally, a week after the inquest, she told Nick she was going to church—St. George the Martyr was but a few steps from the house—and set out for a brisk walk. She ended, as she had so many times before, in the burial ground.

Where Francis lay now.

The stone she'd ordered wasn't yet in place. There was only the newly dug earth, lightly dusted with snow, and a simple marker to show the place.

She couldn't mourn for him. That hypocrisy, at least, was beyond her. Grief wasn't what had drawn her here.

She stared down resentfully at the mound of earth.

Alive, he'd tormented her as much as she'd let him; dead, he contrived to torment her still. If not for him, she wouldn't be guilty and anxious and so miserably alone.

"Who was it," she demanded, under her breath. "Who was it had enough of you, Francis? He's going to get away with it, you know. Because I was so . . . oh, so damnably clever. A bit of ink, you see, to mask the . . . scent."

It was then she remembered.

Esmond . . . nearly a year ago . . . at the party, the unveiling of Madame Vraisses' portrait . . . the merest dab of perfume, put on hours before and all but evaporated . . . yet he'd accurately identified the ingredients.

Then she understood why the wall of ice had come between them.

"He smelled the poison," she murmured. "Not just the ink solution, but the poison, too, and he must have thought—" She looked about her. Heaven help her, she was reduced to this: talking to herself—in a graveyard.

What next, the ravings of a madwoman?

Was that what Esmond believed? That she was mad, a temperamental artist who'd killed her husband in a demented rage?

But Esmond had *helped* her, and she had thought . . .

No, she hadn't thought at all. She had collapsed in his arms and stopped thinking altogether.

Because he'd come, as she'd wanted, from the moment she left Norbury House. She'd fled, yes, and that was right, but her heart couldn't be made entirely right. The wicked part of her had wanted what was wrong. She'd wanted him to pursue her and destroy her will and . . . take her away with him.

She shuddered. Vile weakness, that's what it had been. In a moment of distress and confusion—and yes, relief at his coming—her control had crumbled, along with her reason.

Esmond, so acutely perceptive, would have had no trouble sensing her guilt and terror—and must have promptly concluded she'd done murder. He hadn't sent for Quentin as a favor to her, but most likely because, being a foreigner, Esmond didn't *know* anyone else connected with the Home Office. He hadn't been trying to help her at all.

Good God, how stupid she'd been. Yet it was hardly surprising she'd mistaken Esmond's motives, she reflected bitterly. She'd deluded herself from the start. In a mad panic, she'd concealed the worst of crimes to save her own skin. Not even that—to save her precious career. And as to nobly shielding Andrew—she *knew* justice was far more important to him than badges or titles.

In short, she had proved that Francis had been right: like papa, like daughter.

Ten years after that first shameful sin with Francis, she'd slipped again. Disastrously. And because she was weak by nature, she would continue to sink . . . to worse, and still worse—to the very depths of degradation.

That, she found, was more terrifying than the gallows.

And so she hurried from the burying ground out to the street, where she hailed a hackney and ordered the driver to take her to Whitehall.

"Be quick about it," she snapped—and added, under her breath, "before I weaken."

WHEN HE ENTERED Lord Quentin's office, Ismal's countenance was angelically serene. His gut, meanwhile, was twisting itself into knots. It was his own fault, he told himself, for dawdling in London another week. Had he left immediately after the inquest, he wouldn't have been forced today to race to Quentin's office in response to the terse note: "Mrs. Beaumont is here. You'd better come immediately."

Ismal bowed to Madame and politely greeted His Lordship. When they were done with the usual courtesies, Quentin waved Ismal to the chair next to her. Ismal moved to the window instead. Whatever was coming was going to be unpleasant. Every instinct told him so. The air about her hummed almost audibly with tension.

"I'm sorry to put you through this again, Mrs. Beaumont," said Quentin, "but it's best that Esmond hear the story from you." He looked to Ismal. "I've already explained to Mrs. Beaumont that you've assisted us on occasion and might be trusted implicitly."

The knots inside tightened. Ismal merely nodded.

Madame stared at a large green glass paperweight on Quentin's desk. "My husband was murdered," she said levelly. "And I've done something very wrong. I interfered with the evidence."

Ismal looked at Quentin. His Lordship nodded.

"Madame refers to the ink, I believe," Ismal said.

She didn't even blink, but remained fixed on the paperweight. "You knew all along," she said. "Yet you never said a word."

"Most persons do not keep bottles of ink upon the nightstand, but upon a desk," Ismal said. "Still, your husband might have been the exception."

"You *knew* I brought it there," she said. "And so you thought—" She broke off, flushing. "It doesn't matter. I brought the ink there." She bit off each word, and the ribbons of her black bonnet trembled with the emphasis. "To mask the odor. Of prussic acid. I knew he hadn't died of an overdose."

After a pause, she went on. "I know it was wrong, but I had to make Francis' death look like an accident. I didn't kill him. Yet I also couldn't see how anyone would believe that, once it was known he'd been murdered."

"You did not realize at the time that Mrs. Dempton was mentally unbalanced," said Ismal.

"She was the least of my problems," Madame answered impatiently. "I know the difference between an inquiry into a suspicious death and a full-fledged murder investigation. The Crown must look into everything, and I couldn't afford to let that happen."

She turned her gaze full upon him then. Against the unnatural pallor of her face, her golden eyes burned fever-bright.

"My maiden name is not Dupont," she said. "It was changed years ago. My father was Jonas Bridgeburton."

Those five words tore across the space between them with the force of a rifle shot. The room reeled about him, but Ismal didn't move. His face didn't change.

The girl. This was the girl Risto had spied upon the stairs that night so long ago. Ten years it had been, yet Ismal remembered.

He'd gone to Bridgeburton seeking revenge on another man. After that visit, Ismal had gone from one mad act to the next, to the very brink of death. The scar in his side bore testimony to that. It twinged now and then, when something occurred to remind him of those dark days.

Bridgeburton he'd scarcely thought of at all. The man had been merely a means to an end—a brief visit, a prompt departure, and it was over. But it wasn't. Nothing ever was.

Fate, Ismal thought. He said nothing. His body and countenance he could control. He was not sure he could trust his voice.

Unaware of the enormity of what she'd just revealed, Madame continued in the same bitingly precise tones. "You may not have heard of him. He was murdered ten years ago this week. His enemies spared the Crown the expense of trying and hanging him. He was a criminal, you see. He stole military supplies from his own government and sold them to the highest bidder. I was informed that the government had compiled a long list of his crimes. Blackmail and slave trading, as I recall, were only a few of his many other activities." Her gaze reverted to the paperweight.

"A rather large dossier was compiled," Quentin amplified, apparently for Ismal's benefit, though His Lordship knew perfectly well this wasn't news. "Our men, in conjunction with the Venetian police, were in the process of investigating Bridgeburton when he met with a fatal accident."

"They claimed it was an accident, but it was murder," she said. "The authorities must have agreed they were well rid of him. Doubtless they thought it a waste of time and money to find his killers."

Just as certain other authorities had seen no point in finding Francis Beaumont's killer, Ismal reflected. Yet according to the report, Bridgeburton had fallen into a canal, drunk on absinthe and wine. Surely he hadn't been murdered. Ismal had told Risto and Mehmet the man was not to be killed . . . though that didn't mean they'd followed orders, curse them.

"At any rate," she continued, "how Papa died isn't the issue, but what he was. I knew that if people learned my father was a criminal, I should be ruined—even if Francis hadn't been killed. As it was, I could hardly expect anyone to believe Jonas Bridgeburton's daughter hadn't followed in his footsteps."

Beyond doubt, in normal circumstances, she would have been ruined, if not hanged, Ismal reflected. The sins of the fathers all too often were visited upon the children, even in this enlightened country.

Yet she had come to Quentin and confessed all this damning truth. And Quentin—who had as much reason as she to support the accidental death verdict—hadn't tried to convince her she was mistaken about her husband's demise. On the contrary, Quentin had sent for his top agent.

"Why was I summoned?" Ismal asked, his voice very soft.

"Mrs. Beaumont wants her husband's death looked into," Quentin answered. "I agree with her."

She hadn't wanted Ismal here, though. He could feel it: the rage gathering and pulsing within her and rippling through the quiet chamber, like a dangerous undertow in a falsely still sea. "If you've sent for me, you cannot wish it looked into openly," he said.

"That's correct," said His Lordship. "I've explained that we generally call on you when we encounter problems of some delicacy. Mrs. Beaumont had already perceived the potential for embarrassment to certain parties." He smiled ruefully. "We haven't much choice, it appears."

Madame's chin went up, and the ribbons fluttered. "I

simply pointed out to Lord Quentin that my husband did not limit his debaucheries to the lower orders. He was a corrupting influence. He had a talent for attracting innocents. I am sure any number of husbands, wives, and parents wished him dead. Many of their names may be found in Debrett's Peerage. I saw that in the course of a murder investigation mine would not be the only name dragged through the mud. I felt Lord Quentin should be alerted to the problem."

"Most perceptive," Ismal said softly. "Yet do you also perceive the futility of a *covert* investigation? What is to be done if we discover the so-called murderer's identity? Are we also to try and hang him—or her—secretly?"

"I did not *demand* a covert investigation," she said. "I know that, in trying to save my own skin, I as much as helped my husband's killer get away scot-free. I have committed a wrong. I wish to make it right. It is up to Lord Quentin how to do it." The anger she so ferociously held in check throbbed in her voice now. "I did not send for you. He did. That makes him the one to ask, I should think."

Though he knew what the answer would be, Ismal dutifully turned to Quentin. "My lord?"

"Why don't we cross that bridge when we come to it?" Quentin said, as any fool might have predicted. "Will you take the case or not?"

As though he had any choice, Ismal thought angrily, while his impassive gaze moved from one to the other. She wished him at the opposite end of the earth, and he wished he could oblige her. But the investigation could be turned over to no one else. He was the only one who would not inadvertently stumble onto the matter of *Vingt-Huit*. Furthermore, as Quentin well knew, no man had more to lose by betraying Madame's origins than Ismal did. If that came out, so might the other scandal, closely connected—the one in which Ismal had figured prominently, and for which he ought to have been hanged.

But it was Fate, Ismal reminded himself. Fate had begun spinning this web ten years ago.

Bridgeburton's daughter, this woman in widow's black.

Bridgeburton's daughter, this woman who made his heart beat too fast, who made chaos of reason. It was on her account Ismal had come to England, on her account he'd lingered, against wisdom and caution. She had drawn him here, to this moment . . . and it was upon the web of her life that he was caught.

And so, there was no choice and only one answer to give them.

"Yes," Ismal said in his sweetest, most amiable tones. "I accept the case."

THOUGH UNDOUBTEDLY DISPLEASED with Quentin's choice of investigator, Madame was obliged to accept it. When Ismal told her to expect him at her house at eight o'clock that evening, she simply nodded. Then she took her leave of the two men with a politeness so glacial that Ismal was amazed the window didn't frost over.

He stared at the door after it had closed behind her.

"Couldn't be helped," said Quentin. "I couldn't take the chance. If I put her off, she might go to someone else, and then we'd be in the soup."

"I might have put her off," Ismal said. "But you tied my hands—because you are as much plagued by curiosity as she has been by her so-English conscience."

"Maybe it's my English conscience, too. I admit I wanted Beaumont dead, but I did decide against a summary execution. Otherwise I might have hired someone a deal less expensive than you to finish the business, mightn't I?"

Ismal moved to the desk and picked up the paperweight. "Did you know, when I told you Beaumont was the man behind *Vingt-Huit*, who his wife was?"

"Certainly. Didn't you?"

"Do you not think I would have mentioned it?"

Quentin shrugged. "No telling what goes on in that devious mind of yours. Bit of a shock, was it?"

"I do not care for surprises."

"You handled it well enough," was the unsympathetic

answer. "You always do. And you always know everything, don't you? And tell only what you choose. It was only reasonable to suppose you'd recognized her right off, back in Paris."

Ismal traced the contours of the paperweight with his fingers. "I never saw her in Venice," he said. "I knew only that there was a daughter—a child, I assumed. I left her to Risto. He gave her laudanum, and there was no trouble. The drug must have confused her mind, for her father was not murdered. When I left the house, he was drunk only. I departed before my servants did, yet I told them not to kill him." His gaze met Quentin's. "I did not kill that woman's father."

"I never said you did. Not that it makes any difference. You did enough. In the circumstances, I assumed you'd prefer to handle the present problem yourself."

Aye, he'd done enough, Ismal reflected. And he'd never be done paying for it, evidently.

Ten years ago he had plotted grand schemes of empire. Sir Gerald Brentmor, via his partner, Jonas Bridgeburton, had illegally supplied the weapons Ismal needed to overthrow Albania's ruler, Ali Pasha. But Sir Gerald had a brother, Jason, living in Albania, who was on Ali's side. Had he been his usual cautious self, Ismal would have dealt with the ensuing obstacles more wisely. But he became obsessed with Jason's daughter, and nothing—neither the daughter Esme's obvious hatred of him and clear preference for an English lord, nor Ali Pasha's wrath—could restore Ismal's reason.

Even after Lord Edenmont had taken Esme away and wed her, Ismal had persisted in mad schemes for revenge on everyone who'd thwarted him. He'd gone to Bridgeburton and forced him to betray all his partner's secrets. After that, the mad race to England . . . to blackmail Sir Gerald . . . and steal Esme . . . and then the bloody climax, when her family had rushed to her rescue. In the ensuing battle on a Newhaven wharf, Ismal had lost his two most devoted followers, Mehmet and Risto, and nearly been killed himself.

He had fully deserved to hang, on several counts. In the course of a few hours, he'd kidnapped a nobleman's wife, tried to kill her husband, and succeeded in killing her uncle. But the family couldn't prosecute him. A trial would have exposed Sir Gerald's crimes, and the taint of treason would have clung to his family, making them social outcasts.

For their sake, Ismal's infamies had been hushed up, and he was sent away on Captain Nolcott's ship, bound for New South Wales.

Quentin interrupted Ismal's grim recollections. "Mrs. Beaumont obviously didn't remember you."

"She could not have observed much before Risto spotted her," Ismal said. "As I recall, the hall was poorly lit, and I stood there but a few moments. The drug would have clouded her mind. And it was ten years ago. A long time." If she had remembered, he assured himself, he would have known, even if she held her tongue. He would have sensed it. All the same, he was uneasy.

"Still, she is intelligent and observant," he said. "It would be best to take no chances. The Brentmor family must be apprised of the situation. None of them knows I am here."

Except for Jason Brentmor, Ismal had not seen any of the Brentmor family since the day he'd been carried, nearly dead, onto the ship. Before he left, he'd made his peace with them all, according to the custom of his country. According to those rites, his soul was wiped clean of the shame. Yet his pride could not endure facing those who'd witnessed his humiliation.

"Lady Edenmont's expecting her fourth child any day now, so they're all at Mount Eden at present," said Quentin. "Except for Jason, who's in Turkey with his wife. I'll drive out and explain matters. I assume you prefer they keep away?"

"That would be wisest. I can watch my own tongue, control my own behavior. I cannot control everyone else's every word and gesture, however. We cannot afford to awaken the smallest suspicion."

Ismal crossed to the desk and returned the paperweight to its place. "That is why I have preferred to work outside England. A short visit is not so risky—but this . . ." He shook his head. "I might be here for weeks, months perhaps. The longer I remain, the greater the risk that I will be recognized."

"Apart from the Edenmonts and Brentmors, there's scarcely anyone left who'd remember you from a decade ago," Quentin said impatiently. "Who else saw you but the sailors—Nolcott's crew, mostly, and every last one of them drowned in the shipwreck a month later. Only three survivors—you, Nolcott, and that Albanian fellow who was guarding you. In the first place, neither's anywhere near England. In the second, they're not likely to betray the man who saved their lives."

The shipwreck had spared Ismal the degradation of New South Wales' convict settlements, and he'd aided his own cause by rescuing the two men most able to help him. Nolcott and Bajo had returned the favor by letting him escape and pretending he'd drowned with the others. But Fate had permitted Ismal only a few weeks' freedom before he collided with Quentin. Thanks to the detailed description Jason had previously provided, Quentin had recognized Ismal and promptly taken him into custody.

Ismal's smile was thin. "I only wish saving two lives had been amends enough for you, my lord."

Quentin leaned back in his chair. "Certainly not. Nothing less than a lifetime's servitude would do. For your own good, of course. Otherwise, there's no telling what sort of trouble you'd have got into by now." He smiled. "You represent a *philanthropic* effort, you know."

"I know well enough I was no charity case with you. Jason had told you I was clever and devious, and you saw a use for me."

"Just as you saw a use for me. Which is as it should be. Sentiment's not wise in our line of work. Still, you've done well enough with our bargain. You live like a prince and hobnob with royalty. Nothing to complain of, I hope?"

Only this accursed case, which would not end, whose

tangled threads led back a decade to the most shameful period of his life, Ismal thought. "No, my lord, nothing to complain of," he said.

"And nothing to worry about, either. Edenmont and his in-laws are bound to cooperate. After all, they have a great deal to lose if any of the truth gets out. Jason Brentmor took some pains to make sure no one would find out his brother was involved with Bridgeburton."

"We all have much to lose," Ismal said.

"Yes, well, I count on you to handle the matter with your usual discretion." Quentin paused. "It seems Mrs. Beaumont will require considerable diplomacy. She didn't seem at all pleased about my sending for you."

"I think she wished very much to hurl your handsome paperweight at . . . somebody," Ismal said. "I doubt she will give me a warm welcome this evening."

"Think she'll break furniture, do you? Over your head, perhaps?"

"Luckily, my skull is very hard. If Lord Edenmont could not break it, there is a reasonable chance Madame cannot, either."

"I hope not. That head of yours is very valuable to us, you know." Quentin threw him a shrewd glance. "Take care you don't lose it, my dear *count*."

Ismal's reply was an angelic smile.

"You understand me, I think?" Quentin persisted.

"Think what you like," Ismal said. With that and one graceful bow, he left the room.

DESPITE LEILA'S FERVENT prayers to the contrary, the Comte d'Esmond arrived precisely at eight o'clock that evening, as he'd appointed. Well aware that he hadn't been pleased with his assignment, she supposed he'd spent some time arguing with Lord Quentin after she left—to no avail, apparently.

She didn't understand how Quentin came to have the power to give the count orders of any kind. He'd told her Esmond was an agent of some sort, and totally trustworthy, but he hadn't explained the count's exact position with His Majesty's government. Given her previous experiences with Esmond, Leila had small hope of enlightenment.

By the time Nick had shown the count into the parlor, her nerves were wound taut as clocksprings.

Nick swiftly vanished again and, after a terse exchange of greetings, she offered wine, which Esmond declined.

"Nick tells me you have not yet interviewed new servants," he said.

"I had a great deal on my mind, as you are unfortunately now aware."

His mouth tightened. He moved to the window and looked out. "It is just as well," he said. "I shall send to Paris for a proper housekeeper and manservant."

"I am perfectly capable of hiring my own staff, monsieur," she told him frigidly.

He came away from the window, and her breath caught.

The candlelight drew streaks of molten gold in his silky hair and burnished the smooth contours of his perfectly sculpted face. His flawlessly cut coat of deep blue hugged his powerful shoulders and slim waist, and turned his sapphire eyes the color of a late night sky. She wished she had her weapons—a brush in her hand and a blank canvas before her—so that she could reduce him to color and line, two dimensions, aesthetics. But she was weaponless, trapped, in a room where there was suddenly far too much of him, demanding and fixing her attention, and stirring a host of unwanted memories: the heat of a rock-hard body pressed, for an instant, to hers . . . the scorching intensity of a piercing blue glance . . . and the scent, distinctively, dangerously, his.

He was all flawless elegance and aristocratic courtesy, detached, aloof . . . yet he dragged at her senses, insistently, and she couldn't break the pull for all her will. All she could do was fight to hold her ground, and so she clung to her anger as though it were a life rope.

Esmond met her icy stare with a small smile. "Madame, if we quarrel over every minor matter, we shall make the progress of snails. I am aware that you are vexed with Lord Quentin's choice of investigator."

"I'm aware you're vexed with it, too," she said.

His smile remained in place. "A fortnight has passed since your husband's death. Whatever trail might have existed is cold. No evidence of prussic acid was found anywhere—in your husband's body or in the house. Except for the ink, that is. But we now know the ink was not in the room until you put it there. There was no sign of forced entry or burglary. Our murderer did not leave behind so much as a piece of lint. No one saw anyone—including your husband—leave or enter the house during the previous evening. We cannot ask direct questions of anybody, lest the wrath of the English nobility fall upon us and crush us. In the circumstances, it seems next to impossible that we shall ever discover who killed Monsieur Beaumont. I shall spend the remainder of my life upon this case. Naturally, I am delighted."

If she'd had a fraction less control, she would have slapped him. As it was, she was so angry and mortified that tears stung her eyes. She blinked them back.

"If the task is too much for you," she choked out, "then tell Lord Quentin to find someone else. I didn't ask for you."

"There is no one else," he said. "The matter is exceedingly delicate, as you well know. I am the only one of Lord Quentin's associates who possesses the necessary discretion. I am also the only one who possesses the necessary patience. I have enough of that for both of us—which is fortunate, for I suspect you have very little. I have just pointed out only one small necessity—trustworthy servants—and already you wish to strike me."

Leila felt heat rising in her neck. Stiffly she turned away, moved to the sofa, sat down, and folded her hands in her lap. "Very well. Send for the damned servants," she said.

"It is for your protection." He walked to the fireplace and studied the grate. "It is also for discretion's sake. Since we have so little that is concrete, we must talk and reflect. I shall be forced to ask you endless questions, some of them impertinent."

"I'm prepared for that," she said. She wasn't. She could never be prepared for *him*.

"Based on what I learn from you, I shall go out and seek further enlightenment," he continued. "Then I must return again and again to ask more questions." He glanced over his shoulder at her. "Do you understand? It is a long process. Sometimes I may be here for hours. Since no one must know I am investigating the matter, my visits could arouse disagreeable gossip. If you do not wish such gossip, I must visit in secret, which means after dark. I must come and go unnoticed. Thus the necessity for servants of unquestionable discretion and loyalty."

Weeks, she thought. Weeks of his coming and going by night. Asking questions. Probing. Why oh why had she gone to Quentin?

Because the alternative was worse even than this, she reminded herself.

She stared at her folded hands. "I can't risk gossip. I shouldn't be allowed into respectable households to do portraits if people thought me . . . immoral."

"But of course. A woman of uncertain reputation is not permitted in many great houses. The English appear to believe that women's frailties are contagious, while men's are not." He wandered to the curio cabinet and studied the collection of oriental objects behind the glass. "This is why you never took lovers and why you continued to live with your husband."

In spite of her inner turmoil, she'd almost smiled at his apt assessment of the English double standard. The last sentence wiped her amusement away. "That's not the *only* reason," she indignantly told his back. "I do have morals— not that it's any of your affair."

"English morals," he said.

"Since I happen to be English, I don't see what other sort I ought to have."

"You might have the practical sort," he said. "But you possess the so-English conscience. Your husband is dead.

This is inconvenient, for it makes you a solitary woman who must step even more carefully to keep her reputation white. The practical course is to find a companion to see you through your interminable English mourning period, then acquire another husband."

Leila stifled a gasp.

"Instead," he went on, "you seek revenge—for a man who shamed and betrayed you repeatedly."

She could not believe her ears. She stared at him—or rather his back, for he'd moved on to the ornate table that bore a tray of decanters. This wasn't what she had expected, not of the man who'd withdrawn so coldly, believing her a murderess. But she should have known better than to *expect* anything. Esmond defied logic. She would not, however, let him put her on the defensive.

"It doesn't matter what sort of man Francis was," she said. "No one had the right to kill him—not in cold blood, in that despicably underhand way. Worse men than he have been murdered, and the judges have pointed out that the bad character of the victim doesn't mitigate the crime. I couldn't make myself believe it mitigated even what I had done—else I should never have gone to Quentin. I-I'm sorry it took so long for me to stop being a coward. I realize that's made everything harder for you."

"To me it seems you make everything harder for yourself," he answered. "What you perceive as cowardice to me seems sensible caution. I saw that you had a great deal to lose and nothing to gain by voicing your suspicions. That is simple enough to comprehend. But when these great abstractions enter the equation—justice, good and evil, courage and cowardice, truth—ah, then, everything changes."

Having apparently studied Francis' decanters to his satisfaction, Esmond returned to the window.

Leila tried to bring her focus back to her hands, or the table nearby—on anything but him. She couldn't. His prowling the perimeter of the room made her edgy. He moved with the fluid grace of a cat, and just as noiselessly.

Unless one watched, it was difficult to determine where he was and where he was going and what he would do. She was having enough trouble trying to make sense of his words and making the right replies.

"The authorities were 'sensible' and 'practical' about my father's death," she said. "Consequently, I'll never know who killed him. For all I know, I've seen his murderer, even spoken to him. It's not a pleasant idea to live with."

"I am sorry, madame."

She wasn't looking for pity, and wished she'd chosen her words more carefully. The compassion she heard in his voice hurt. "I know the chances of that are remote," she said. "With Francis, it's different. His killer could be one of scores of people I know. Someone I've served tea, or dined with. I've tried to be sensible about it, but everyone I see stirs up the same question. It makes me frantic, wondering, 'Is this the one?' "

He turned his head to meet her gaze . . . and hold it. "It is too much, I understand, for you to live with two unsolved mysteries. To me, most of life is unsolved mysteries. But our characters are different, are they not?"

His steady gaze made a flurry within her, as though her secrets were living creatures, scurrying to hide from that probing blue light.

"I don't think my character has much to do with the problem at hand," she said. "Unless you have any lingering suspicions that I killed Francis."

"From the beginning, that did not make sense to me. For some time now, I have considered it out of the question. The only puzzle was the ink—which you have explained."

Relief washed over her, so profound that she was embarrassed. His belief in her guilt or innocence should not have loomed so large. Yet it had haunted her . . . because *he* haunted her. Still. He saw too much, and she had too many secrets. She could only pray his penetrating eyes wouldn't uncover them.

"That does simplify matters," she said briskly. "You've eliminated one suspect."

He smiled. "Now only several hundred thousand remain. Shall we cross Lord Quentin off the list?"

She nodded. "If he had done it, he'd have tried to convince me I was mad—and probably would have had me carted off to Bedlam forthwith."

"We make progress. Two suspects eliminated. And myself, madame? Or perhaps I raced to and from Norbury House the previous night while everyone slept?"

"Don't be silly. You hadn't any mo—" She broke off, her face burning.

He came to the sofa, clasped his hands behind his back, and gazed down at her. Too close. The air grew heavier, overwarm and crackling with tension.

He let the silence lengthen, deliberately, she thought. The oppressive stillness made her all the more fiercely, inescapably aware of him.

"Desire," he said very softly.

The word whispered its wickedness in her heart, and echoed there. It seemed to echo through the entire room, a devil's whisper, taunting.

"Shall we pretend it was not so?" he asked. "Will you, so very observant, feign ignorance of the obvious?"

"It's pointless to discuss it," she said tautly. "I know perfectly well you didn't kill Francis."

"But I had so potent a motive. I had wicked designs upon his wife."

"You would never be that stupidly desperate," she said, scowling at her hands. "For anybody."

His soft chuckle made her look up. "I agree that killing your husband does not strike me as the wisest way to further my designs."

"Not to mention it's too curst *direct*."

His blue eyes glinted. "You would prefer I were more direct?"

"I prefer to discuss the *crime*," she said. "Which is what you were hired—assigned—whatever the devil it was—to do."

"I shall do so, I promise you."

"That is all I de—require."

"But of course," he amiably agreed.

"Very well, then." Her palms were damp. She pretended to smooth out a crease in her skirt. "I suppose you'd like to get started."

"Yes. In the bedroom."

Her hands stilled.

"The scene of the crime," he said. There was a tinge of amusement in his voice.

"I thought the officers had scoured every inch of the house," she said, fighting to keep her tones level. "Do you expect to find anything useful after a fortnight?"

"I am hoping you will find something for me. You lived with the victim, while I knew him only socially. It is you who can tell me most about your husband, his friends, his habits. Also, you are an artist. Your powers of observation make you a most useful partner in this enterprise."

For two weeks Leila's head had been churning with questions, speculations, theories. She had noticed a great deal, though those observations hadn't led to any satisfactory conclusions. She had prepared herself to cooperate fully and share her observations freely and frankly. She needn't be so reluctant to accompany an investigator to Francis' bedroom, she chided herself. It was business. Nothing more.

Esmond had moved to the door. He stood waiting.

Leila rose. "I trust no one saw you come?" Her voice was just a bit unsteady. "It wouldn't do, you know—"

"I am aware of the proprieties," he said. "With the English, appearance is everything."

She wanted to throttle him. "Appearance." She closed the distance between them in a few strides. "Is that sarcasm or innuendo? I've noticed you're very good at both. And at *appearances*."

She waited for him to open the door, but he only smiled down at her. "Now what appearance of mine do you take exception to, I wonder?" he asked softly. "The one in the inquiry room, as a constable?"

She blinked. "Good grief. How did you know I—"

"That is the same question I should ask *you*. Quentin

himself did not recognize me until I spoke to him—in my own voice."

"I didn't *know*," she said. "I merely . . . guessed."

"Sensed," he corrected. "There is a difference."

Her heart thudded. "I'm observant. You just said so."

"I was most disconcerted," he said.

"Well, you've returned the favor, monsieur. How in blazes did *you* know?"

He shrugged. "Perhaps I am a mind reader."

"There's no such thing."

"Then what was it, do you think?" His voice had dropped to a whisper.

Also, Leila belatedly noticed, he had somehow moved several inches nearer without appearing to move at all.

She reached for the door handle. "I think I am being led down a path I do *not* wish to follow," she muttered, jerking the door open.

She marched out and on toward the stairway.

Chapter 5

ISMAL WAS WELL AWARE THAT MADAME WAS trying very hard to believe his motives were purely professional. She wouldn't have to try so hard if he'd behaved himself, which he had more than ample reason to do.

In the first place, it was the height of folly to become entangled in any way with any participant, male or female, in an investigation.

In the second, according to his Albanian code of honor, he owed her amends for her father's death. Even if his men hadn't killed Bridgeburton, they *had* rendered the Venice household defenseless, making murder easy for someone else. To protect Madame during the present murder investigation and provide justice by finding her husband's killer constituted a form of amends for the injury Ismal had thoughtlessly done her a decade ago. To use her beautiful body to slake his lust, on the other hand, was to heap insult upon injury.

Last, but most significant, she was dangerous. She'd haunted him ceaselessly after he'd left Paris and drawn him here against his better judgment. She had then stirred his feelings so intensely that he'd made not merely a mistake, but an unbelievably stupid one. Worst of all, she saw through him—not everything, not even a fraction. Nonetheless, that she glimpsed anything at all of the truth clearly proved she was a serious problem.

Yet he wanted her still, more than ever.

And so, instead of behaving himself, he had deliberately cast sexual lures, testing his powers of attraction against her fierce resistance. Which demonstrated—as if one needed more evidence—just how dangerous she was to him.

Even now, as he followed her up the stairs, it wasn't crime scenes he contemplated, but her criminally tempting body.

Black became her far too well, and this gown in particular was fiendishly well-designed. Despite the fashionably exaggerated shoulders and sleeves, her form appeared in all its tantalizing lushness. The twilled fabric hugged her full, firm breasts and wrapped itself snugly about her small waist, then swelled lazily below with the curve of her hips.

Ismal had studied countless women clothed and unclothed, and not always with detachment. He was not immune to desire nor did he wish to be, for desire was the beckoning of pleasure.

In her case, it was an invitation to disaster. Yet the invitation, he silently admitted as they reached the top of the stairs, was well nigh irresistible.

A single oil lamp stood on the hall table near the master bedroom door. The soft light caught the golden threads in her hair and lit gold sparks in her eyes, but the rest was shadow. Such was desire: an uncertain light amid the darkness of unreason.

He took up the lamp, opened the door, and let her proceed him into the room.

"You can set it on the nightstand," she said. Her voice was brittle. "Not that there's much to see. Less than you did before, I'm sure."

"Let me see with your eyes," he said. He put the lamp down and moved away to stand by the fireplace, in the shadows. He knew how to make himself invisible. With her, this would be difficult, but after a few minutes, if he was careful, she would at least partially forget he was there. "Tell me what you noticed."

She stood silent for a moment or two, looking about her—and collecting her composure, no doubt. He wondered whether it was the room, where death had been, that troubled her most, or himself.

"The oddest part was the tidiness," she said finally. "Most of the house was so orderly that I felt certain Francis had hardly been home the entire two days I was away. The trouble is, two other circumstances contradict that notion. One, his clothes didn't reek, and they weren't nearly as rumpled and stained as they usually were after a night's entertainment. Two, there were so very many wine bottles in the kitchen." Already her voice was losing its edge, her posture easing. Ismal guessed that she had not only steeled herself to talk about this, but had organized her thoughts beforehand.

"Francis didn't like to drink alone," she explained. "All I can conclude is that whatever he did that night wasn't in character. Either he had company and didn't make a mess, or stayed home alone and didn't make a mess, or went out and behaved himself."

She strode purposefully to the foot of the bed. "I considered the possibility that he'd brought a woman home, and she may have been the sort who habitually cleans up after men. But there was no sign of that—none of the usual signs, that is. He'd brought tarts home before, when I was away. Yet he had the effrontery to complain about my refusing to share his bed." She paused but an instant, and her voice was cool when she continued. "There's no point pretending all the world doesn't know it, or that I minded his telling people. I had rather be deemed a callous wife than a loose-moraled one. As we've discussed, the latter reputation would injure my career. And I didn't object to his tarts, either. Better them than me, I felt."

"But it was not always so, was it?" Ismal asked. He'd meant to hold his tongue, but he needed to know. Her cool, cynical speech drove his mind back to Venice and the girl he'd left defenseless. She'd been married nearly ten years, which meant she'd wed soon after her father's death. In the intervening years, life had taught her to be cynical. Though this happened to everyone to some extent, he was troubled.

"No, of course it wasn't always that way," she said. "I was seventeen when I married Francis, and thoroughly infatuated. I do believe he was faithful for a time. I was twenty, the first time I noticed the perfume and rouge on his clothes. Even after that, it was a while before I comprehended the extent of his infidelities."

She turned to face him. "It's a question of degree. One is prepared for the occasional affair, the mistress. But Francis was a tomcat. It was the same as the drink, and later, the opium. He did nothing in moderation. There are limits—at least for me. Martyrdom isn't in my style."

"I have no patience with martyrs," he said.

This elicited a faint smile. "Nor do I. Still, some women haven't much choice. He never beat me, you know. I'm not sure what I would have done if he were that sort. But he wasn't. In any case, once I opened my eyes, it wasn't so very difficult to manage matters."

"Also, you had your work."

"Yes, which few other men would have tolerated, let alone encouraged. Francis had his good points, you see. But that's my view of him. I had certain . . . compensations. I daresay you'll get rather different portraits of him from others."

Ismal understood the portrait she drew well enough—but it was the portrait of her that intrigued and disturbed him. She'd given him insight, not so much into Beaumont's alleged "good points," as into the resourcefulness and resilience she'd needed to endure her marriage. Beaumont could have destroyed her, but she had not allowed it to happen. She'd even found a way to view the man with a degree of charity and mild affection he couldn't possibly deserve.

But then, she weighed and measured upon her own scales of justice. She even believed the bad character of the victim didn't mitigate the crime. Ismal thought it did, in this case—but she didn't seem to realize how evil Beaumont had been. Next to him Ali Pasha appeared almost saintly.

"But you must have been aware of his good points," she said. "You spent a great deal of time with him."

Ismal recognized a probe when he heard one. His instincts went on the alert. "A few weeks," he said carelessly. "He was an entertaining companion."

"I expect so. He did know Paris better than many Parisians did. I'm sure he could find every last brothel or opium den blindfolded."

"I believe he could. I hope the same cannot be said of London," Ismal added. "I shall be obliged to visit every single place he patronized, in hopes of obtaining information. However, I shall leave that task for later. Perhaps your help will lead me upon a different trail."

"I shouldn't think you'd mind that sort of job."

He smiled, though she couldn't see it. "But now it will be a *job*. I must observe everything objectively, ask the right questions, keep my wits about me at all times. There is a great difference, you see, between visiting a brothel to lose oneself in pleasure and going there to work. As any prostitute can tell you."

"I shall have to take your word for that." Her voice was crisp. "Though Francis brought his tarts home from time to time, we were never introduced, let alone on speaking terms."

"Certainly you would not know such women, and it was ill-mannered of me to mention the subject at all."

"Don't be ridiculous. I've just been talking about them, haven't I?"

There was a rustle of skirts as she moved to the other side of the bed, farther from the light. It was only a few steps, yet she stirred the air, making the lamplight tremble. Hers was not a quiet grace, but insolent, tempestuous. A passionate soul in a lavish body.

Ismal suppressed a sigh. The Devil had made her on purpose to test and torment him. It was *impossible* to be fully objective. It was close to impossible to think straight. Leaving the safety of the shadows, he took up the lamp.

"It may prove necessary to discuss these women later," he
said. "For now, however, we shall deal with the friends
with whom you were acquainted. If you are not too weary,
perhaps you will help me make a list."

"We're done in here, then?"

"For the present."

"I didn't tell you much." She headed for the door.

"More than I had hoped. Very little is clear, but now at
least there is one thing." He reached the door an instant too
late to open it for her, but his words made her pause on the
threshold.

"I gave you a clue?" she asked.

"Oh, yes. The tidiness. The behavior not in character.
Someone *influenced* that behavior, do you not think? Either
the murderer or an innocent companion. But an innocent
companion—then another to administer poison?" Ismal
shook his head. "That seems far-fetched. For the time being, I must give strong consideration to those able to influence his behavior."

She eyed him with some puzzlement. "That's a clue, is
it? You must have patience indeed, to begin with something
as small and vague as that."

"It is enough," he said. "The piece of lint. One must begin somewhere."

"I suppose." There was a dissatisfied note in her voice.
"Where next, then?"

"It does not matter. At present, we need only begin our
list of possible suspects. The studio, perhaps?"

She gave a small start. "Are you serious? It's a terrible
clutter even on my best days, and it smells of turps and oils
and—"

"I like the windows," he said. "They are the largest in
the house." He knew the studio was no larger than this
room, but it was airier, thanks to the draught from the tall
windows. He wanted more air. The tension between them
thickened an atmosphere already heavy with Beaumont's
secrets . . . with evil.

His reply elicited one sharp glance, but that was all. In
silence, Madame Beaumont led him to the studio.

* * *

WINDOWS, LEILA THOUGHT ruefully as she attacked the mess on the studio worktable. That was *her* piece of lint about him, her small, vague clue. The Comte d'Esmond liked big windows.

His presence in her sanctuary made her edgy. He prowled the space in the same way he had prowled the parlor, examining everything, though here he touched nothing. He was wandering the opposite end of the room, studying the bookshelf, the fireplace, the sofa, and the shabby rug on which it stood. As though every object hid a secret. Her secrets.

"There's another stool behind that stack of canvases in the corner," she said rather too sharply. "Just shove them out of the way."

Even as the words came out of her mouth she realized that the idea of Esmond "shoving" anything was ludicrously incongruous. Out of the corner of her eye she watched him gently stack the canvases, one by one, against the wall. You'd think they were Ming vases, the way he handled them.

She was already seated, a folded sheet of foolscap before her, when he brought the other stool to the table.

"Do you want to discuss them first, or shall I simply write down everyone I can think of?" she asked. "Or perhaps you'd rather write. My penmanship is not elegant."

She pushed the foolscap and pen toward him. She didn't have to push far. She'd shoved most of the extraneous materials to her right and left, to clear a space opposite hers. But he had placed his stool to her right, and sat before a heap of sketchbooks, brushes, pencils, bits of charcoal, and other artistic miscellany.

"No, you must write," he said. "I cannot read my own hand, and it vexes me. Write the names of all your husband's friends you can think of. Later, we can discuss."

"London friends?"

"*All.*"

"That could take all night," she said.

"Stop when you are weary."

Strangling an oath, Leila dipped her pen into the ink, bowed her head, and proceeded to write. It went quickly at first, with the obvious names, then more slowly as she strove to recall the host of men and women she'd met or heard mentioned, but rarely interacted with.

Absorbed in the task, she didn't notice the time passing. As much as half an hour may have gone by when she became aware that Esmond had not moved a muscle, scarcely seemed to be breathing . . . and that he was watching her.

She hadn't looked up. She didn't need to see it. The awareness was a troubling warmth upon her skin—her face, her neck, her hands—and a tingling in her scalp. It was something like a caress, but something more like the pull of the air just before the lightning crackles.

She had felt it too many times before—even at a distance, in the inquiry room, when she had recognized him . . . *sensed*, as he'd said.

She hadn't wanted to think about what he meant by "sensed," but she couldn't avoid it now. It was an animal awareness, elemental as scent.

Silence blanketed the room. She could hear her own breathing, and the hurry of it, in time with the hurried beat of her heart. Her hand stiffened, and the pen tore into the paper, spluttering ink. She set the pen down.

"You are weary," he said.

"My hands," she said, frowning at them as though they truly were the cause. "Sometimes I—there's a—a spasm. It'll go away in a minute." She spread her hands on the table, stretching the fingers. "It happens. The same muscles, you know, overused. Fiona says I should soak them several times a day in warm, scented water, but I haven't the time or patience."

"Let me see."

"There's nothing to see. It's muscles. You can't—"

She caught her breath as he took her hand.

He turned it palm up and pressed his thumb against the soft flesh. "The little muscles are in knots," he said.

"There, you see." He pressed, and Leila swallowed a moan. "And there."

"Oh." That at least was not a moan. More of a gasp, she consoled herself while the blood raced to her cheeks.

"I shall untie them," he said.

"That isn't neces—"

His fingers coiled with hers, and she couldn't speak or think past the surge of sensation.

Esmond had held her hand before—in greeting or farewell, or while dancing—and the contact had disturbed her. That was nothing to the pulsing intimacy of this: his fingers twined with hers while his thumb kneaded the muscles, warming, coaxing, and drawing out the tension like a thread.

She was aware of his voice telling her of bones and muscles and circulation, but she couldn't concentrate on the words. She was too conscious of his hands and what they were doing to her, mind and body.

As the muscles began to ease, the warmth he stirred became liquid pleasure, coiling through her blood.

It was intoxicating. Sinfully so. Her mind grew drunk with it, conjuring images of those devil's hands moving over her skin . . . everywhere. She could, almost, feel those caresses, and that "almost" made her yearn for what she imagined.

Her gaze lifted to his, to the blue enigma of his eyes and the unearthly beauty of his face, and she searched for some hint that he knew what he was doing to her. All she found was a quiet concentration, as detached as the words he uttered. No potter could have been more soberly focused upon his wheel. Her hand might have been a piece of clay.

His thumb slid to her wrist, to the hammering pulse, and paused.

"You have strong hands," he said softly. "Have you ever sculpted?"

She shook her head and wished she could shake it into sense. "I was happier with a brush." So weak and breathless her voice sounded. But she *was* weak. Even now, though he'd stopped, she couldn't find the will to free her hand. His were strong, too, and warm, and so sure. They possessed her, held her as his eyes could hold her. Perhaps he could do this so easily because she was *not* sure, because her outer assurance was a veneer, concealing the wanton within. She hadn't realized how thin that veneer was until she'd met him. Never before had it felt as fragile as it did now.

"I cannot sculpt or paint or draw," he said. "Even my penmanship is an abomination. Yet my hands are good." He released her and, edging a bit nearer, laid his left hand flat, palm down, upon the table.

It was perfectly proportioned and graceful, the fingers long, the nails smooth oblongs, neatly manicured. It told her nothing.

"You're right-handed," she said. "Show me that one."

"They match, madame."

"Any artist knows they never do exactly. Let me see."

His smoothly composed countenance tightened, but only for an instant, and the change was so subtle and fleeting that she might have believed it a trick of the light. Her intuition didn't believe that, however.

He set his right hand down next to its mate.

As she studied it, her brow wrinkled. Something was wrong . . . the wrist. She leaned closer, looking from one to the other. "That's odd," she murmured.

She stared at her own wrists, then his again. She moved his hands closer together, then traced the back of his wrist with her fingers.

"You broke it," she said. "Badly."

Very badly. She couldn't begin to imagine what it must have felt like, but it hurt just to look. The bones had been skillfully set, but the perfection could not be restored. A practiced eye could discern the distortion, the faint scars. Leila could feel the damage, too—the several places where the bones didn't meet perfectly. There was a spur at the base of his thumb, and that knuckle was uneven.

She had thought him a perfect work of art, but he was

not. A part of him had been broken. Though the mending was well done, it was there. It hurt to look at it, to touch it.

Something stirred her hair, a warmth on her scalp. Belatedly, Leila realized what she was doing—stroking his hand—and noticed that his head had bent nearer, and what she'd felt was his warm breath. And something else, sensed rather than felt: the fire she was playing with.

Sliding her hand away, she drew back. "I studied anatomy," she said. "I was . . . curious. How rude. I beg your pardon."

"It was broken," he said. He didn't draw back. "But it happened a long time ago, and my hand has fully recovered. I was fortunate in my physician."

"Oh. A boyhood injury."

"Yes. Boys are often foolish."

"It must have hurt like the very devil. You broke it in several places. You're very lucky it mended so well. You might have lost use of it entirely."

"Yes. It might have been much worse."

Something in his tone made her gaze lift again to his smoothly composed countenance. Faint lines had appeared at the corners of his eyes.

"Is that why you don't like to write?" she asked.

The lines tightened, and one fierce shaft of blue fire shot at her before his lashes lowered to veil his eyes. "No. My hand functions well enough. It is my laziness. To write clearly and beautifully was always too much work."

She couldn't imagine what there was to lie about, why he needed to. Yet she was sure he was lying. A part of her wanted to persist, to probe, but the searing blue flash warned her off. A moment ago she'd sensed danger. How many warnings did she need?

Francis had told her this man was irresistible—like a drug, and equally treacherous. She ought to know better than to venture too close.

She couldn't afford to let herself be drawn, even by curiosity. At heart, she wasn't so different from Francis. She'd taught herself to avoid temptation, because she

doubted her strength to resist it. From curiosity to fascination would be, for her, the first small step down a
treacherous slope to ruin. Already she'd let herself be
drawn too far.

"That's more honest than my own excuse," she said,
dropping her own gaze. "I claim that my thoughts go too
quickly for my hand." She picked up her pen and frowned
at the point she'd spoiled.

"You are weary," he said.

"It's been rather a long day."

"I should have considered," he said. "Not once, but
twice did you tell your painful story. I know it took great
courage to do so. I should have let you rest this night, and
begun our work tomorrow instead."

Leila wished the work had never begun. She had a dark
picture in her mind of how it might end. In heartbreak and
rage . . . the maddening frustration . . . and the shame.

"Confessing to Quentin wasn't nearly as difficult as I'd
imagined," she said. "But then, one always imagines the
worst. Anyhow, I'm used to hard work—hours of it. With
some of my patrons, every brushstroke is like lifting immense rocks, or tunneling a coal mine. That all happens in
my head," she added with a forced smile, "but it makes me
just as tired."

"I understand," he said. "This case, regrettably, will
prove much the same as a difficult patron. Tedious. Exasperating. And I shall be the most tedious and exasperating
of all, I fear. But no more tonight, madame."

He picked up the sheet of foolscap, folded it, and put it
in his breast pocket. "I shall have plenty to occupy me until tomorrow evening." He smiled. "Then, I shall be inconsiderate again. You would be wise to go to bed soon and
sleep late tomorrow. I shall tell Nick to encourage you to
rest."

ISMAL TOLD NICK nothing whatsoever, scarcely
glanced at his servant en route to the back door. Nick did

not spare his master more than a glance, either, but steadily continued rubbing the kitchen worktable with one of his special mixtures. It would be a waste of breath to tell him that when Eloise, the housekeeper, came, she would only rub it again with her own exotic preparation. If there was a piece of furniture about, Nick must treat it: clean it, massage it, work oils and herbs into its surface. No slave in a harem could have tended a concubine more lovingly than Nick would tend that scarred, worn table.

Madame's studio table was battered and worn, too, Ismal recalled as he slipped into the garden. His scarred hand had lain upon it, she couldn't know how unwillingly.

He'd realized it was futile to hope she wouldn't see. He should have distracted her. He had that skill. Yet he hadn't done it. He had submitted . . . and died ten small deaths of shame and another ten of pleasure.

The shame lay in the truth he didn't tell her: that it was Lord Edenmont who had broken his wrist when, like an animal, Ismal had fought for Esme—for a woman who would have cut her own throat before submitting to him. Yet he had wanted her, and at the time, he would have committed any barbarism to have her.

Now he wanted another woman, and once again his mind would not let it go. Leila Beaumont had only to touch his hand, and sorrow for him, and his mind turned dark and savage with desire.

He had even wanted, for one terrible moment, to tell her the truth—and worse, to *show* her what kind of man he truly was, in his soul. He'd wanted to sweep the artist's clutter from that battered table and have her there. Like the conscienceless barbarian he was.

He brooded on these mortifying truths until he'd reached his townhouse. Only then, after the door was closed and bolted and Leila Beaumont safely out of reach, did he allow himself to meditate on the pleasure.

He walked into the library, took off his coat, removed the paper from the pocket, unwrapped his neckcloth, and stretched out on the sofa to study her handwriting.

As she had told him, it was not elegant. It was angular, the bold strokes crushed together—a scrawl as insolent as the way she moved.

Ismal traced the strokes with his finger. Almost, he could feel her pulse beating, as it had under his thumb. He had made it beat so—rapidly, unevenly. He'd made love to her hand, and that was a little mad, but also . . . delicious. Her penetrating eyes had become enchantingly dazed, but not for long, not nearly long enough.

He'd watched her confusion soften to yearning and had known he might have gone further. He had wanted to, badly enough—to press his mouth to that hammering pulse—to touch his mouth to her flesh—her neck, her shoulders, her breast . . . He swore under his breath.

To want anything badly, especially a woman, was fatally unwise. He was thirty-two years old, and even in his youth he had not panted and salivated over women like a rutting mongrel. He was as calculating in seduction, as artfully manipulative in lovemaking, as in all else. Even in the throes of pleasure, he remained in control.

He could not control Leila Beaumont properly. One moment, she was clay in his hands. In the next, she slipped free somehow and . . . questioned. Everything.

More disquieting still, she seemed to sense every untrue answer. The falsehood about his broken hand hadn't satisfied her any more than those about his penmanship. He doubted she'd have been satisfied even if he could have overcome his innate caution so far as to put pen to paper.

That caution went far too deep to be overcome, though, because it had been bred into him early. In Albania, there was no such thing as *private* correspondence, thanks to Ali's spies. Very young, Ismal had understood that even the most harmless remarks could be fatally misconstrued by the periodically deranged vizier. Thus, what one wrote became part of the game of survival. On the rare occasions Ismal had put anything in writing, he'd taken care to employ another's style—sometimes to shield himself, more often to make trouble for the other.

It was beyond doubt a useful skill in his present profession. No one, for instance, would ever know who'd written the discreet warnings to *Vingt-Huit*'s most vulnerable patrons, or the complaints about the place to the Parisian police.

Assuredly, it would have been easy enough to forge another's handwriting for Madame's benefit, but that was still too risky. Undoubtedly, she'd notice something false or wrong, just as she had the instant she'd looked at his hands . . . and wrought so much havoc in the process.

The pitying way she had looked at them, and tenderly touched them, moving closer—too close—of her own volition, so that her scent coiled about him and stole into his blood . . . and her hair, so soft . . . her neck . . . the silken skin that made him so hungry.

And so he'd endured ten deaths fighting to keep his baser instincts under control.

"Fool," he reproached himself. "Imbecile."

He willed himself to focus on her list. She had made four and a half dense columns of names across the wide paper. He perused each column several times. Most of these people he had met. Several he eliminated as too stupid for the crime. None of the other names stirred his instincts—probably because they were obstinately fixed upon Leila Beaumont.

He considered the first column again, the names that had come quickest to her mind. Among them were Goodridge, Sherburne, Sellowby, Lackliffe, and Avory. . . .

Ismal frowned as he scanned the column again. In Quentin's office, she'd said Beaumont was a corrupting influence with a talent for attracting innocents. Yet precious few on her list qualified as such.

Tomorrow night, then, Ismal would pursue that question.

Tomorrow night, he thought, would be a long time in coming. He was impatient for it already—he, the most patient of all men.

He rose from the sofa and moved to the window, her list still in his hand. The gaslights winked in the mist-laden darkness. It was not so late. London was fully awake—most of it. The demimonde had only begun to play.

There would be diversion, certainly, at Helena Martin's cozy establishment this night. At present, she was the most fashionable of London's courtesans. Several of the men on Madame's list would undoubtedly be there. Yet a visit need not be all work. Helena had delivered her invitation personally, and another sort of invitation had glowed warmly in her dark eyes.

That would be best, Ismal decided. Just as Beaumont had told him: if a man couldn't have one woman in bed, he had only to find another.

Ironic that both men were obliged to seek substitutes for the same woman.

Ismal shrugged. Life was full of ironies.

Chapter 6

WITHIN TEN MINUTES OF JOINING THE THRONG
at Helena Martin's, Ismal located three of the men on the
list. Two—Malcolm Goodridge and the Earl of
Sherburne—were busy vying for Helena's attention. After
exchanging a few social pleasantries, Ismal decided he
would leave Helena to them. Though she was a beautiful,
vivacious woman, he saw in a moment that she wouldn't
make a satisfactory substitute.

With two possible suspects so intensely occupied, and
no other female in the vicinity promising sufficient distraction, Ismal focused on the third man on the list: Lord
Avory, the Duke of Langford's heir. Ismal noted that the
marquess was tall, fair, and aristocratically handsome—
and he didn't belong here.

Though he was trying to belong by flirting with a red-
haired ballet dancer, Ismal was certain His Lordship's
heart wasn't in it. A man bent on pleasure with an accommodating female would not have that hunted look in his
eyes.

Since they'd met at Beaumont's funeral, it was easy
enough for Ismal to strike up a conversation. And, since the

young man didn't want to be where he was, it was even easier to detach him from the redhead and extract him from the party altogether.

A half hour later, they were sharing a bottle of wine in a private room of a club on the fringes of St. James'. Ismal's admiration of the Canaletto landscape hanging over the mantel had led to a discussion of art and so, very soon to Leila Beaumont, whose talents Avory couldn't praise highly enough.

"It isn't simply that she makes excellent representations," the marquess was saying. "It's that the subject's character and personality truly *infuse* the work. One day, mark my words, her portraits will be priceless. I'd give anything to have one—of anybody."

"But surely you own one of yourself," Ismal said. "You are a good friend, after all."

Avory studied the contents of his glass. "She hadn't the time."

"I sympathize," Ismal said. "She had no time for me, either. I had almost lost hope until, at Norbury House, Lady Carroll told me that Madame had no new commissions."

"Mrs. Beaumont stopped accepting them after she finished Lady Sherburne's portrait. Near Christmas that was. She'd been working nonstop since moving to London and she wanted a good, long rest, she told me."

"I was unaware of this." Ismal wondered why neither the artist nor Lady Carroll had told *him*. "All I comprehended was that there might be time for me. But she had left Norbury House, and so, in the next moment, I was in my carriage, making for London, posthaste." He smiled ruefully. "Little did I know I would be obliged to admit this to a coroner and jury. Yet I cannot regret my action. If not for my vanity and greed for a portrait, I should not have arrived at the Beaumont house when someone, clearly, was needed."

"It must have been ghastly for her." The marquess turned the wineglass in his hands. "I didn't get word until late that night. I called first thing next morning, but Lady Carroll was there by then and—Well, I could only do Mrs.

Beaumont the kindness of keeping away, and urge every-one else to do likewise—as she asked. And they all obliged, though I'm sure they were dying of curiosity."

He looked up. "Odd, isn't it? Society is rarely so con-siderate, even of its own, and she's not—well, one of us, I suppose you'd say, though that sounds hideously snob-bish."

Ismal wondered just how many had kept away out of loyalty, and how many out of fear. Beaumont knew secrets. People might worry that his wife was privy to some of them. Ismal wondered whether Avory, for instance, had heard a request or a threat.

"It was good of her friends to respect her privacy," Is-mal said.

"Frankly, I was happy to keep away from the inquest. It would have made me wild to watch her being questioned." The glass turned round and round in the marquess' hands. "Father said you were one of the first to testify, and you left immediately after."

"I felt this would be wisest, in the circumstances," Ismal said. "All the men at the inquest, except for her respectable solicitor, were either elderly or plain. I was the only one of her admirers there. I wanted the jury to attend to the proceedings—not to speculate whether I was her lover. Be-cause you and the other fine gentlemen kept away, I was too . . . conspicuous."

Avory reached for the wine bottle. "I should think you'd be that regardless who was there. You're rather out of the common way."

Ismal knew perfectly well he was. He was also aware the remark was a probe and wondered what exactly Avory was looking for.

He said nothing. He waited.

The marquess refilled their glasses. When this was done and still Ismal didn't speak, a muscle began to work in the younger man's jaw.

"I didn't mean any offense," Avory said tightly. "Surely you've noticed the women swooning in your vicinity. Even if you've grown inured to that, you must have realized—"

He set down the wine bottle. "Well, I am putting my foot in it. As usual."

Ismal's expression was mildly curious, no more.

"I thought you realized you were the exception," Avory went on doggedly. "That is to say, Francis had never been jealous of anyone. He'd never worried about Mrs. Beaumont at all . . . until you came along. I thought you knew."

The marquess was mightily curious about Beaumont's jealousy. Perhaps Beaumont had dropped some hint of the true reason. He might have done, if he and Avory had been very intimate. That was a reasonable assumption, given Beaumont's attraction to both sexes and the marquess' apparent discomfort with courtesans. It would explain, too, his devotion to a man so much older, and so far beneath him in every way.

There was an easy way to find out.

"Beaumont was tiresome, and most unkind," Ismal said. "I should not say this of your friend, but in truth, he vexed me greatly."

"He could be . . . vexatious."

"Because he made such a show of jealousy, I could scarcely speak to his wife without stirring scandal," Ismal said. "This was not only inconsiderate of her reputation, but also unfair."

"He wasn't always . . . considerate."

"I am a reasonable man, I hope," Ismal went on. "If she does not wish the liaison, I must accede to her wishes and make do with whatever small privilege she bestows—a dance, conversation, flirtation. I contented myself accordingly. Why could he not do the same?"

"With Mrs. Beaumont, you mean? I'm afraid I don't—"

"*Non, non,*" Ismal said impatiently. "With me. Never before did I have this problem with another man. I was tactful, I thought. I told him I had no interest in him—in any man—in that way. I—"

"Good God." Avory sprang up from his chair, spilling wine in the process. He quickly—and shakily—set the glass upon the mantel.

One question answered. The marquess hadn't even

suspected Beaumont was infatuated with the Comte d'Esmond.

Ismal promptly assumed a deeply chagrined expression. "I beg you will excuse my indelicacy," he said. "In my vexation, I forgot myself and where I was. Such matters are not spoken of openly in your country."

"Not generally." The marquess raked his fingers through his hair. "At least not on such short acquaintance."

"Please forget I mentioned this thing," Ismal said contritely. "I would not dream of offending you—but you are too easy to talk to, and I let my thoughts go straight from my brain to my tongue without reflection."

"Oh, no, I'm not—well, not offended. It's flattering that you find me easy company." Avory tugged at his neckcloth. "I was merely . . . startled. That is, I knew you upset him. It never occurred to me that he was jealous in—in *that* way. Well."

He collected his wineglass and returned to his seat. "You'd think, after two years, I'd know better than to be shocked at anything to do with him. Yet he never—I hadn't an inkling."

"Ah, well, I am older—and French."

"I can hardly take it in." Avory drummed his fingers on the chair arm. "He—he mocked them, you see—men of that sort. He called them . . . 'mollying dogs' and—and 'bum boys'—and—well, I daresay you've heard the names."

Beyond doubt, the marquess couldn't have been Beaumont's lover. Why, then, the unsuitable friendship? Was it by choice, or because Beaumont knew something about him? That Avory was another man's lover, then? Unaware that Beaumont was guilty of the same so-called crime, Avory would have been vulnerable to blackmail. That was a good motive for murder, though by no means the only possible scenario.

Which was just as well, Ismal told himself. Pursuing the possibilities would keep his mind busy. Off Madame. For a while at least. "I know many names," he said amiably. "In twelve languages."

His companion snatched at the conversational escape route. "Twelve? Indeed. I'm impressed. And are you as fluent in the rest as you are in English?"

THOUGH HE HADN'T mentioned a time, Leila had assumed Esmond would appear at eight o'clock the following evening. Instead he turned up an hour earlier, unannounced, at her studio door—while she was bent over her sketchbook, wearing the same grubby gown and smock she'd donned after luncheon.

It could have been worse, she told herself. She might have been spattered with paint and stinking of oils and varnish. Not that that would have mattered, either. A man who intended to spend several hours a night plaguing an artist—and who, moreover, appeared without invitation or notice—had no right to expect fashionable perfection.

"I trust you sneaked in the back way," she said, snapping her sketchbook shut.

"Unobserved, I promise." He laid his hat on the empty stool opposite her. "Nonetheless, that task will be much easier when Eloise and Gaspard arrive."

"You mean the Parisian servants, I collect. The 'loyal and trustworthy' ones."

He moved a step nearer. "You have been working," he said, nodding at her sketchbook.

"Not really. Just sketching. Keeping myself busy." She set the sketchbook on top of another and neatly aligned the edges. "I shouldn't do even that during early mourning. It's disrespectful of the dear departed. On the other hand, Francis would find it hilarious that I kept idle out of grief for *him*."

"Lord Avory tells me that you ceased accepting portrait commissions more than a month ago. I did not know this was your own decision—that offers were made, but you rejected them."

"I wanted a rest," she said.

"So Lord Avory explained last night."

"Last night?" she echoed, a bit too shrilly. "You saw David last night? But I thought you were going to study my list."

"I did." He took up a pencil and studied it. "Then I went out, and happened to meet the marquess."

She had nothing to be dismayed about, Leila told herself. One could hardly expect the Comte d'Esmond to be innocently tucked into his bed before midnight. She wondered where he'd met David in the middle of the night. At a gambling hell, probably. Or a whorehouse. She shouldn't waste energy feeling disappointed in David. As to Esmond, a night's dissipation was in keeping with his character. Yet an image filled her mind of his devil's hands caressing . . . someone else . . . and her temples began to throb.

"He was on your list," said Esmond. "Yet you have some objection."

"Certainly not," she said. "One must assume you know what you're about."

"But you do not like it." He put down the pencil and strolled away to the sofa. Frowning, he sat down and appeared to give the shabby rug his deepest consideration. "Your countenance is all disapproval."

She hoped that was all he saw, though she hadn't any right to disapprove of his amusements. Her feelings about David, on the other hand, she needn't conceal from anybody.

"Oh, very well then," she said. She took up the pencil he'd handled and quickly set it down again. "I don't like it. I didn't like putting David on the list—but you said *all* of Francis' friends, and I could scarcely leave David off, when he was with Francis so often. But the idea of David as a murderer is ludicrous. Can you actually picture him sneaking poison into Francis' laudanum?"

"Mine is a lively imagination, madame. You would be surprised at what I can picture."

She was sitting on the opposite side of the room from the fire, and the draught from the windows behind her was a brisk one for early February. The warmth stealing over her face, therefore, could not be ascribed to climatic conditions. Certainly not to his words, either.

It was the cursedly *hinting* tone, the voice that could make "How do you do?" sound like a double entendre.

Or maybe it couldn't.

More likely the trouble was her own damnably active imagination.

"Very well," she said. "If you want to waste your time, that's your concern—or whoever's paying you. The government, I suppose."

"You are fond of Lord Avory, it would seem."

"He's an intelligent and agreeable young man."

"Not Monsieur Beaumont's customary type of companion."

"Not the average roué, if that's what you mean," she said. "But it wasn't at all unusual for Francis to take up with younger and less experienced people."

"And lead them astray?"

"Francis was hardly the sort to lead them in the opposite direction. Most of them came fresh from a Grand Tour of the Continent. He gave them a Grand Tour of the demimonde."

"Young men must sow their wild oats."

"Yes."

"But you wish this young man had not done so."

Really, what use was it to try to keep anything from him? And what was the point? Esmond was investigating a murder. He needed to know *everything*. He'd warned her yesterday: endless questions, some impertinent.

"I wish David had never met my husband," she said. "He's not like the others, not the typical idle aristocrat. And he does have the most dreadful parents. They haven't the least idea how to manage him. He was never meant to be the heir. I'm not sure he was ever meant to be born. There's a considerable gap between him and Anne, the next youngest," she explained.

"His birth came as a surprise to the parents, perhaps."

She nodded. "There are two more older sisters—I don't

remember their names. I never met them. Francis had met the older brother, Charles, ages ago."

"An older brother? Avory did not mention this."

"Charles died about three years ago," Leila said. "A hunting accident. Broke his neck. His mother still wears black."

"She does not accept her loss."

"The Duchess of Langford doesn't seem to accept or understand *anything*," Leila said. "The duke is even worse. A dukedom is a sizable burden, even for a young man reared to bear it. But his parents haven't helped David at all. They simply expected him to *become* Charles—adopt all of Charles' interests, friends, likes, and dislikes. Naturally, David rebelled. And, understandably, in the process of asserting his individuality, he went to extremes."

"Madame, you are most enlightening." Esmond rose. "You open some interesting avenues of speculation. The reasons for certain friendships, for example. Not always what they seem. How I wish I could remain to pursue this . . . and other matters. But I have promised to dine with the marquess, and I must not be late."

And afterward, will you go to a whore? Leila wanted to demand. *Your mistress?* For all she knew, he had one. It was none of her affair, she reminded herself. "Does that mean we're done for tonight?" she asked.

He crossed the room to her. "I could return afterward. But that, I think, would be most . . . unwise."

Leila told herself she heard no innuendo. "Undoubtedly," she said. "You and David won't be done much before dawn, I suppose."

"It is impossible to say."

"In any event, you'll be the worse for drink."

"It would appear that you also possess a lively imagination," he said.

The laughter she heard in his voice made her look up. Yet he wasn't smiling, and his unreadable blue eyes were focused on her hair. "A pin near your ear is falling," he said.

She reached up instantly—and an instant too late. He was already pushing the pin back into place. "Your hair is always so clean," he murmured, without withdrawing his hand.

She could have drawn back or pushed his hand away or protested in some way. But that would let him know how very much he disturbed her—ammunition he'd surely use.

"I couldn't abide it otherwise," she said.

"I wonder, sometimes, how long it is." His gaze slid to hers. "I want to see."

"I don't think—"

"It will be a week before I see you again. The question will plague me."

"I can *tell* you how long it—A week?" she asked, distracted.

"After Eloise and Gaspard arrive. Until they are here, my coming and going is fraught with inconvenience. Best to keep away meanwhile."

And while he spoke, he pulled out the pin he'd just pushed in, and drew a lock of her hair out between his fingers . . . and smiled. "Ah, to your waist."

"I could have told you," she said, her heart thudding.

"I wanted to see for myself." He toyed with the thick, tawny strand, his eyes still holding hers. "I like your hair. It is so wonderfully disorderly."

Francis, too, liked her mussed, she could have told him. But she couldn't keep Francis and his taunts in her mind. Esmond's soft voice and light touch drove everything else out.

"I-I couldn't abide to have servants fussing with me," she said. "I can't even sit still for a coiffeuse."

"You arrange your own hair and dress yourself." He glanced down. "That is why all your frocks fasten in front."

It took all her self-control to keep her hands from her bodice. It would be a futile gesture, anyhow, to shield garments he'd already analyzed in detail. She wondered if he'd surmised that her corset fastened in front as well. He'd probably worked out how many inches apart the hooks were, for all she knew. "How very *observant*," she said.

His smile widened. "The inquiring mind. That is one of the reasons I am so very good at what I do."

A lazy smile it was, sweet and utterly disarming. She fought to keep her guard up. "Perhaps you've forgotten that I'm not a suspect," she said.

"I cannot seem to forget that you are a woman." He was absently twisting the lock of hair round his finger.

"Which means you have to flirt, I see," she said, trying to keep her tone light. "That's not very considerate of David. A while ago—rather a *long* while—you were worried about being late for dinner with him."

He released a sigh, and the captive trees as well, and took up his hat. "Ah, yes, the tiresome suspects. I comfort myself that at least Lord Avory is interesting company. Too many of your husband's friends, I have noticed, are not shining lights of intellect. They can talk of nothing but sport and women—and women, to them, are merely sport, so it is all the same. But I must cultivate them all, if I hope to learn anything. With Avory as my guide, I shall meet them in their natural habitat and observe them when they are most themselves."

"I wonder what you'll see." She took up a pencil. "I wonder what they'll tell you unwittingly, and how you'll get them to tell you. I've never watched you at work as a detective. I almost wish I were a man, so that I could be there."

He laughed softly. "What you wish, I think, is to keep an eye on your young favorite."

That wasn't all she wished, but it was what she could admit. "Worse than that," she said. "If I could, I'd put David on a leash. But I can't."

"Ah." He bent nearer, and the familiar masculine scent wrapped about her like a net. "Shall I leash him for you, madame? Will that ease your anxieties?"

She focused on the pencil. "Why should you? Won't that impede your detecting?"

"Not if he wants to be reined in. From what you said a while ago, I received that impression. If the impression is correct, he will be grateful for a friend who leashes him—

and all the more inclined to trust me. You see?" he asked softly. "I listen carefully to what you say, and I am not altogether unwilling to be led. But now I must go to gather my clues." He drew back.

He bowed, and the unsteady light flickered over his pale gold hair, touching a thread here, another there. A fleeting, uncertain motion. In the same way, her hand moved, the fingers lifting from the table—as though they wanted to be the light, and touch, too. It was no more than a flicker of movement in no more than a pulsebeat of time. Her fingers were properly still by the time he straightened. Yet a part of her wished she dared to be as bold as he had been—to let her hand go where her eyes were drawn. Where her heart, too, was being drawn, she feared.

"Au revoir," he said. "Until next week, then. After Eloise and Gaspard arrive."

"Next week, then." She opened a sketchbook to avoid giving him her hand—because she wasn't sure she could trust herself to let go. "Good night, monsieur," she said politely.

ELOISE AND GASPARD appeared a week later.

Either one of them could have stormed the Bastille single-handed.

Eloise stood—and that was ramrod straight—five feet ten inches tall and was built along the lines of a public monument. Every inch of her was solid muscle. She was Michelangelo's ideal woman—if he bothered with women. One of Leila's painting *maîtres* had insisted Michelangelo's models had all been men. "One has only to study the musculature," he'd said. "Masculine, beyond doubt."

The painting master, clearly, had never met Eloise.

Her thick hair was dyed an uncompromising black and drawn back into a large, mercilessly tight knot—all as smooth and sleek as though lacquered over. Though she couldn't possibly dye her eyes, they were nearly as black as her hair, with the same steady sheen, so that they, too, seemed coated with varnish. They were enormous—or

would have been if the rest of her face hadn't boasted
equally powerful proportions: a great nose—beside which
Wellington's would have appeared dainty—broad cheekbones, a wide mouth filled with large white teeth, and a jaw
that made one think of nutcrackers.

Gaspard, too, was dark, large, and equally well muscled. Still, despite his two-inch advantage in height, he
seemed much the slighter of the pair. In the circumstances,
it was altogether strange to hear him call his monumental
wife *"ma petite"* or *"ma fille,"* or any of the other diminu-
tive endearments he treated her to.

Eloise scorned endearments. She addressed him by his
name. She referred to him as *"cet homme"*—that man. As
in "That man has not yet brought the coals? But what can
one expect? They are all the same. *Insensible.*"

After a mere twenty-four hours, Leila still found the
housekeeper rather overwhelming. She wasn't at all surprised that even Fiona was utterly bereft of speech for a
full two minutes after Eloise had left the parlor.

The housekeeper had brought tea—and enough sandwiches and pastries for two score ladies. Fiona stared at the
mountains of food, then at the door through which Eloise
had exited, then at Leila.

"I contacted an employment agency in Paris," Leila explained, as she'd rehearsed. She took up the teapot. "I've
never had much success with English servants, and in light
of recent events, I doubted I had a prayer of getting good
ones. English servants, generally, are exceedingly particular about their employers. I doubt one suspected of
murder—even if it was only for a day or two—would meet
their standards of respectability."

She filled Fiona's cup and handed it to her.

"Perhaps they misunderstood," Fiona said. "Perhaps
they thought you wanted a bodyguard. I daresay she
wouldn't experience any difficulty in keeping out
curiosity-seekers and undesirables. She has only to stand
there."

Clearly, Esmond had thought of that. He certainly
hadn't attempted to find someone unobtrusive.

"She doesn't seem to experience any difficulty with anything," Leila said. "She's been through the entire house, scrubbing and dusting and polishing every item out of its wits, yet somehow she also managed to cook—for a regiment, it would appear."

"It looks delicious, at any rate. And whether it tastes so or not, I expect we'd better make a good show of eating it."

They ate and talked and talked and ate, and the sandwiches and pastries disappeared at a startling rate. That is to say, Leila was as startled as Fiona when they finally stopped and discovered they'd left scarcely a crumb.

"Devil take her!" Fiona exclaimed, staring at the devastated tea tray. "I shall have to be carried to my carriage—by six burly guardsmen." She leaned back against the sofa cushions, her hand on her stomach. "Come to think of it, that's not such a bad idea."

Leila laughed. "Don't get your hopes up, my lady. Eloise can carry you. She won't even need Gaspard's help."

"Gaspard." Fiona's eyes twinkled. "I suppose he's even bigger than she is?"

"It's a matching set."

"How divine. I might have known you'd do something out of the ordinary. Parisian servants, and each of them built like a man o' war. To what end, may one ask? To keep your beaux out—or to keep the right one in?"

"To keep them out, of course," Leila answered lightly. "Haven't I always kept them out?"

"Even Esmond—the so-beautiful and charming Esmond? Surely he's called, and surely you didn't turn him away."

"Except for you, I haven't seen a visitor in days."

"But, my dear, he seems to be quite settled in dreary London. One can't help wondering why he prefers it to Paris. And one must bear in mind that he did set out in pursuit of you practically the moment he heard you'd left Norbury House. And he came directly here, did he not?"

"Certainly. He was all a-fever to have his pretty face immortalized," Leila said.

"Yes, he was consistent on that point. That was the excuse he gave me, and he stuck to it with the coroner. But then, Esmond is discreet. How silly of me to forget. Naturally, he wouldn't call so soon."

"He can't possibly be discreet to put that speculative look in your eyes."

Fiona laughed. "I think he's divine. Just perfect for you."

"I'm flattered to learn that a French debauchee is perfect for me."

"Come, you must admit that you'd like to do his portrait," Fiona said. "He's perfect in that way at least—a subject worthy of your talents."

"I've spent the last six years painting nothing but human faces. At present even a Royal commission couldn't tempt me."

"A pity you ended with Lady Sherburne." Fiona glanced up at the trio of oriental watercolors hanging over the mantel. "The portrait isn't in their drawing room, or anywhere that anyone can see. In fact, no one's ever seen it."

No one ever would, Leila thought, remembering Sherburne's last visit to her studio, when he'd destroyed the canvas with a stickpin. She hadn't told even Fiona about the episode. She hadn't told Esmond either, she realized. She'd written the earl's name, that was all. Well, she hadn't had time to talk about anything but David, had she?

"Not that one is surprised," Fiona went on. "Sherburne left all of London in no doubt he couldn't bear the sight of his wife—and, naturally, everyone soon deduced why. But then, he could hardly keep it a secret. He had to do *something*."

Leila looked at her friend. "I'm out of touch with town gossip. But I can guess what this is about. I've heard that tone and seen that expression in your eyes before. This has something to do with Francis, I assume. What happened? The usual? Was Lady Sherburne another of his conquests?"

"The evidence seems to point in that direction. Sherburne was one of his constant companions for months.

Then, suddenly, Sherburne would have nothing to do with him. Meanwhile, it was obvious the Sherburnes were at war—living in separate wings of that immense house—she, rarely going out and he, rarely going home."

And so the affair was public knowledge after all, Leila thought. Very likely Esmond had heard about it by now. "I'm sorry to hear it," she said. "I liked Lady Sherburne very much. A lovely girl, with golden curls and great blue eyes. All that innocence—and lonely besides. I can see how Francis wouldn't be able to resist. Still, you'd think even he would have known better. Sherburne wields considerable social power. If, as you say, he snubbed Francis—"

"He did, and a great many others promptly followed Sherburne's lead. About bloody time, too, that Francis got what he deserved."

Fiona had never made any secret of her dislike. Never before, however, had Leila heard such bitterness in her friend's voice.

The disquiet she felt must have shown in her face, because Fiona laughed. "You needn't look so amazed. You know I despised Francis. And I know you did."

"The way you spoke . . ." Leila hesitated. "I wondered if he'd offended you personally, that was all."

Fiona shrugged. "In Paris, I was mainly aware of his callous disregard for your feelings. Here, I watched him use and hurt others I cared for as well. Sherburne's a jackass in some ways, but he acted right in cutting Francis. He was a beast who should have been banned from Society ages ago. The demimonde was better equipped to handle him. Their feelings wouldn't be hurt, their marriages wouldn't be wrecked. Furthermore, the Cyprians get *paid* for their trouble."

"I wish he'd kept to the professionals, too," Leila said tightly. "But there was no way I could make him do so."

"I know that, love." Fiona's voice softened. "No one would dream of blaming you."

Leila rose and walked to the window. "Still, I can't help wishing I'd realized he was after Lady Sherburne." She gave a forced laugh. "I could have played the jealous wife. That might have frightened her off. She's younger than her years. But I couldn't have dreamed Francis would betray Sherburne, who was not only a boon companion, but also an influential one."

"A fatal mistake. It's as though Francis was *begging* for trouble."

Through the window, Leila watched a stooped, elderly woman's painfully slow progress toward the opposite corner of the square. "Deteriorating," she murmured. "He was only forty years old, but he was falling to pieces." She sighed. "And he left a shambles in his wake."

"The Sherburnes seem to be the only major shambles," Fiona said. "And tonight I get to view the damage for myself. Or the repair. They haven't been seen in company together since Christmas, you know."

Leila came away from the window. "I wouldn't know—about anybody. I wasn't about much, except with you, and even then I was . . . oblivious." On purpose, she thought. She had shut her eyes, not wanting to know, to see, even to guess.

"Yes, darling. That's one of your eccentric charms." Fiona's smile was affectionate. "And since you *haven't* been out and about, you won't have heard that Sherburne ordered a sapphire necklace from Rundell and Bridge, which he was to collect this very day. If his wife isn't wearing it tonight, one can safely assume there has been no reconciliation. In that case, I'll expect to see it adorning Helena Martin's snowy bosom at the theater tomorrow. Rumor has it Sherburne has beat out Malcolm Goodridge and the other rich tomcats vying for her favors."

"If he hadn't been competing with the other tomcats for a series of tarts, his wife wouldn't have fallen under Francis' claws," Leila said. "It's Sherburne's own dratted fault. It's unjust—*cruel*—to punish her."

"Perhaps I shall tell him so tonight." Fiona rose. "In that case, I shall want to appear my intimidating best—and Antoinette will want hours to accomplish that. All the same, she'll complain that I never give her time enough to dress me properly. You don't know how fortunate you are, my dear, to be allowed to dress yourself."

"And what a fine job I make of it," Leila said dryly. "If Antoinette could see me now, she'd go into palpitations— and this is one of my better efforts." She shoved a hairpin back into place.

"You look wonderfully artistic, as usual—but rather pale." Her expression concerned, Fiona took her hand. "I hope I didn't upset you, speaking of Francis in that way."

"Don't talk nonsense. If I'm pale, it's only from gluttony. My blood has been flooded out by tea."

"Are you sure you're all right?"

"The fussy mama role ill becomes you," Leila said. "When I'm truly ill, I shall tell you so—and make you nurse me."

Fiona answered with a look of horror so theatrical that Leila laughed. Melodramatically clutching her throat, Fiona ran from the room. Leila chased after. There was more laughter, and joking farewells, and by the time the door closed behind Fiona, Leila's niggling doubt about her was altogether forgotten.

Leila returned to her studio, took up a sketchbook and pencil, and focused on the untidy bookshelves. But they wouldn't take shape upon the page. She drew instead the elderly woman she'd seen making her slow way down the street, then the carriage that had entered the square just as the old lady turned the corner. A dashing carriage, sleek and assured.

So Francis had been once, long ago: sleek and assured and strong. She had been frightened, confused, and sick. A damsel in distress. And he had been her knight in shining armor, carrying her away to live happily ever after.

Only it wasn't for ever after, because he had changed. Paris, with its easy pleasures and easy vices, had corrupted him. Slowly, year by year, Paris had dragged him down.

Fiona didn't understand. She hadn't known him, the way he'd been at the beginning, when he'd first entered Leila's life.

"She doesn't understand," Leila said very softly, her

eyes filling. "You were good once. It's just so easy . . . to slip. So damnably easy."

A tear fell onto the page. "Oh, damn," she muttered. "Weeping—over Francis. How ludicrous."

But another tear fell, and then another, and she let herself weep, ludicrous as it was, beast that he'd been—because she had known him when he wasn't a beast, and if she didn't weep for him, no one would.

Chapter 7

THIS NIGHT, WHEN ISMAL ENTERED THE STU-
dio, Madame did not slam her sketchbook shut. She merely
looked up, her eyes changing focus slowly as she brought
herself from the inner world to the outer. Even when he
came to the worktable, she still seemed distant, a part of
her mind caught elsewhere. As he neared, he noticed the
rawness about her eyes, the drawn look of the fragile skin.
She had been weeping. His chest felt tight.

He looked over her shoulder at the drawing: the interior
of a carriage. "It was elegant once," he said, his voice betraying none of his dismay, "but it seems to have fallen
upon evil days. A hired carriage, I think, but not an English
one."

She glanced up, her tawny gaze sharpening. "You're
very good," she said. "It isn't English." She flipped to the
previous page. "There's an English one." She flipped back
to the second drawing. "Even while I was working on the
other, this came into my head."

"This held your mind more forcibly," he said. "The detail is more precise."

"Yes, it's rather vexing sometimes. I last saw that carriage ten years ago," she explained. "It took me out of Venice the day my father was killed. I was addled and ill—I'd been given laudanum—and yet I remember every last scratch, every stain on the cushions, the shading of the wood."

Ismal drew back half a pace, his heart hammering. "Ten years ago, and you remember so clearly? An extraordinary gift, madame."

"A curse, rather, sometimes. I hadn't thought of it in ages. It must be because of Francis. Images come into my head, as though his death had jarred them loose. As though they had been sitting in cupboards, and something knocked the doors open, and the contents spilled out."

"Old memories, indeed. If it was ten years ago, these must be your earliest associations with him."

"The carriage is where I met him. That's where I came to. It was Francis who rescued me. From my father's enemies." Her gaze reverted to the drawing. "I was remembering . . . that he wasn't always a swine. It's not precisely relevant to the case—yet it is. When we started this, you said justice was an abstraction—"

"I was tactless," he said tightly.

"Yet I do owe him something," she went on as though he hadn't spoken. "The fact is, ten years ago, Francis simply stumbled into someone else's nasty situation. He could have turned his back. I was nothing to him, and he didn't even know my father."

She went on to explain what had happened, and Ismal found nothing in her version that didn't fit his own memories of the circumstances.

First, Bridgeburton had given Ismal countless names, but not Beaumont's—which made it unlikely they'd had dealings together. Second, Ismal had gone off alone immediately after the encounter to sample the pleasures of Venice. Away from their master, Risto and Mehmet could have done just what Beaumont had described to her. To ensure the safety of the master he idolized, Risto would have wanted to do away with the girl as well as the father.

In short, Ismal must admit it was more than possible

that Beaumont *had* come to the defenseless girl's rescue. And so, thanks to Ismal, the pig had entered her life. He didn't want to hear more for which he could blame himself, but she was intent on proving how much she owed her husband, and Ismal, hearing echoes of his own native code of obligation, couldn't bring himself to change the subject.

She'd left Venice with nothing but the clothes on her back, she said. She'd known, though, that her allowance and school tuition had come from a Parisian banker. It was through the bank that Beaumont had—with no small difficulty—finally obtained the name of the man delegated to oversee Leila Bridgeburton's affairs. And it was Beaumont who sent for that man, Andrew Herriard.

Here again Ismal could discover no obvious wrongdoing on Beaumont's part. She'd been at his mercy, yet he had acted conscientiously on her behalf. Most telling of all was that he'd called her plight to Herriard's attention. Having looked carefully into the solicitor's background, Ismal was aware that Herriard was and always had been incorruptible. From the day he was born, apparently. A saint.

If Beaumont had been bent on evil, he wouldn't have given up to a known saint his power over a lonely adolescent girl. All the same, none of Beaumont's actions fit the man Ismal had known. Could his nature have changed so very much in ten years?

"Your father showed great wisdom in naming Mr. Herriard as your guardian," he said cautiously.

"I hope that's been marked to Papa's credit in the hereafter," she said. "He was a villain, yet an exceedingly protective father. For my sake, he did cultivate a few decent men—the banker, for instance, and Andrew. Everyone who dealt with my affairs was above reproach—and Papa saw to it they knew nothing of his actual activities. It was the police who told Andrew, when they questioned him—because he'd been named in Papa's will as my guardian."

She paused. "You can imagine the problem I represented for Andrew. He's a stickler for honesty. But revealing the truth—that I was alive—would very possibly prove fatal to me, and he strongly felt it was unjust for me to suffer for my father's crimes. And so, Leila Bridgeburton was permitted to be dead, and Leila Dupont was born."

"And he deemed Paris a safer place for you to live than London, no doubt. Less risk of being recognized, for instance, by a former schoolmate or friend of the family."

She didn't answer, didn't lift her gaze from the sketchbook.

Ismal perched on the stool near her. "The past is none of my affair," he said into the silence. "You only wished to clarify your sense of obligation to your husband. It is quite clear. I was unkind to mock your wish for justice."

"I fell in love with Francis." Her voice was low, taut. "He talked to me. Listened. He made me feel beautiful. Special. He *browbeat* one of the best painting masters in Paris to take me as a student. By the time Andrew came, wild horses couldn't have dragged me from Paris—from wherever Francis was. I let Andrew think it was all on account of my art studies, my need to earn my own way in the one profession for which I had talent. But the odds against a woman artist are daunting. I wouldn't have had the nerve to stay, to try, if not for Francis. I . . . needed him."

She looked up, her expression defensive. "To this very day, I don't truly understand why he bothered with me. He was handsome and charming and—oh, he might have had any woman he wanted. I don't know why he married me."

Ismal hadn't altogether understood, either. Until now. As his eyes locked with hers, he saw in those golden depths what Beaumont had seen. In his own heart he felt what Beaumont had felt.

Ismal had missed her, longed for the sight and sound and scent of her as an opium addict craved his drug. Desire, beyond doubt, was the drug to which Beaumont had succumbed. She'd intoxicated him from the beginning, and on through the ensuing years. She had loved and needed him at first, she'd said, and so she must have loved and needed passionately, as was her nature. Had Ismal been in

Beaumont's place a decade ago, he would have been intoxicated, too. He would have done anything to have her . . . and keep her.

It wasn't difficult to guess what Beaumont had done. So easy to seduce an infatuated adolescent girl and leave her no choice but to marry him. Ismal would have done it. He wished desperately he had. He had always despised Beaumont, but this comprehension made it far worse. Now Ismal hated him with a maddening, searing jealousy.

"You see so deeply into others," he said, keeping his voice calm. "You know what they are and paint the truth you perceive. You do not see yourself. That is why you cannot understand what he felt, why he wed you, and why he stayed—even after you denied him your bed. He was your first infatuation—a man who was like a prince to you. In time, you outgrew it, and your heart became free of him. But he, so much older and wiser than you . . ." Ismal looked away. "His fate was settled, sentence pronounced. He loved you and he could not stop, however much, however desperately he tried."

That was some comfort, he told himself. Undoubtedly Beaumont had suffered. He'd been caught in his own trap. As he deserved.

"You make it sound like a melodrama." A wash of pink tinged her cheekbones. "I told you more than a week ago that he recovered from this alleged 'love' very quickly."

He shrugged. "Monogamy was not in his nature. From all I hear, he cared for nobody, rarely bedded the same woman twice. Such men usually abandon their wives. I cannot tell you how many times his friends have remarked upon his baffling possessiveness regarding you. Given what you've told me, there can be no other possible answer but love. And that seems to answer a good deal about him."

"His *friends*?" Anger smoldered in her tawny eyes. "Is that what you've been doing this whole bloody time? Gossiping about me with his dissolute friends?" She sprang off the stool. "Good grief. And I've just told you—will you gossip about this, too?"

"Certainly not." Ismal fought a surge of outrage—that

she would think him so base. "You leap to the strangest conclusions. No one speaks ill of you. On the contrary—"

"It has nothing to do with me." Her voice rose. "He made enemies. You're supposed to find out what grudges they had against *him*. I didn't make him hateful. It wasn't—oh, for God's sake!" She hurried across the room, to the fire.

Ismal watched her warm her hands—for five seconds—then turn a small bust of Michelangelo to face right instead of left, only to turn it back. Then he saw her brush at her eyes and hastily drop her hand again. And that quick, angry movement tore at his heart.

She was wretched. He'd found her so, and for all he knew she'd been miserable for days. And alone, in whatever bitter sorrow it was. He doubted anyone, even her best friend, was trusted with the troubled secrets of her heart.

He knew that he of all people should not be trusted. Whatever he learned he'd be tempted to use to trap her. And that was unwise, on a hundred counts.

He told himself to remain where he was. He could change the subject, distract her. With business. The inquiry. That, after all, was his reason for being here. It was also his amends.

"No, of course you did not make him hateful," he said gently. "No one—"

"Don't humor me," she snapped. Turning to the sofa, she began rearranging, with some violence, the heap of decorative pillows. "You weren't gossiping, of course. Merely *eliciting information*. It's not my place to tell you how to conduct your investigation."

"The investigation, yes," he said. "I should have explained better—"

"Well, you couldn't, could you, with me maundering on about the past." She picked up a purple pillow and began untangling the fringe. She was blinking hard.

By Allah, how was he to keep his wits about him with her on the edge of tears?

He left his place and joined her at the sofa. "There was a purpose to what you told me," he said placatingly.

"You gave me perspective—as you had done some days ago regarding Lord Avory. The victim's character often offers important clues to the crime, and sometimes, to the perpetrator."

"And his home life? Does that offer clues, too?" She shoved the pillow back among the others. "You said Francis was desperate. Because of *love*."

"Because it was contrary to his nature to love." Ismal felt his patience slipping. "He was at war with himself."

"Which he wouldn't have been if he'd never met me," she said bitterly. "He would have gone merrily on his way. And never hurt anybody."

"You cannot believe that."

"Oh, can't I? I've done nothing but look, every way I could, this whole livelong day, and I don't see what else to believe. And you just confirmed it. You as much as said he got tangled with the wrong woman."

"Madame, that is insane."

"Is it?" Her eyes flashed. "*You* think I'm trouble, don't you? My father was a traitor. I covered up murder. I have temper fits and lose my mind and wreck my studio. I made my husband's life hell—drove him to drink and drugs and women. You didn't want to take this case, did you? Because the victim was a swine and his wife is a madwoman."

"You twist everything about," he snapped. "I said he loved you. This was trouble for him, yes, because his pride could not bear it. But his pride is not your fault, nor his vices. I cannot believe you make yourself wretched on his account. To weep—for *him*—"

"I wasn't—"

"You were weeping before I came, and the tears are waiting—for me to be gone, no doubt, so you can grieve all the night. For a *pig*!"

She retreated a pace.

"A *pig*," he repeated. "Do you think I did not know what he was? Do you think me so witless as to believe the excuses he made, blaming you? I said he loved you. Does this make the man—any man—a saint? Ali Pasha loved his wife, Emine. All the same, he roasted men on a spit or had them torn in pieces or shot from a cannon. More than once, Ali slaughtered all the men, women, and children of a town in revenge for an offense a few men had committed decades before."

He advanced on her as he spoke, and she edged away, her hand trailing along the sofa back.

"Deeply, passionately he loved her," Ismal went on, his voice rising. "All the same, he kept three hundred women in his harem. What miracle did love work upon his character?" he demanded. "What do you think this one woman could have done? Was it *her* fault he was a madman?"

"I couldn't say." She blinked up at him. "Who is Ali Pasha?"

It was then Ismal realized that she would not have been blinking *up* at him if he were not standing practically on top of her, glaring down into her baffled face. Almighty have mercy, what had he done? Lost his temper. Lost control.

And betrayed himself: the first lunatic who had come to mind was not some western European—Napoleon, for instance—but Ali Pasha. Of all the monsters in all the world and in all of history, Ismal had chosen an Albanian—his countryman, his own mentor and tormentor. He thought quickly.

"Do not tell me you never heard of Ali Pasha," he said, his tones instantly back to normal. "I thought your Lord Byron and his friend, Lord Broughton, had made the vizier famous in their writings."

"There's a great deal I haven't read." She was studying his face, searching. She had heard something, glimpsed a secret beneath the skin. Ismal was sure of that. Which secret she'd lit upon was the question—and he didn't want to know the answer.

"You sounded almost as though you knew him personally," she said, answering his silent question.

Cursing inwardly, Ismal retreated two paces . . . to keep from shaking her. "I met him, yes. I have traveled in the East, you know."

"I didn't know." Her head tipped to one side. Still searching. "Was it government business, then?"

"If you are not in a humor to discuss the case, madame, I shall be happy to bore you with tales of my travels," he said. "Only tell me what it is you wish, and I shall try to oblige."

"I wish you would not take that condescending tone with me," she said. "It's not as though you're in a perfectly equable humor yourself."

"How do you expect a man to remain tranquil when you snap at his every word and storm about the room? How am I to be orderly and logical amid the tempest you make? Almost, I think you do it on purpose."

"On purpose?" Her voice climbed. "Just what—"

"To distract me." His tone was dangerously low. "To make trouble. Is that what you wish? I can oblige, you know."

Run, he warned silently, as he closed the distance between them.

She wouldn't. She raised her chin and tried to stare him down.

"Perhaps that worked with him," he said. "But not with me."

He bent closer and saw her haughty confidence give way to alarm. Then she started to turn away. Too late, for he was quicker than she, trapping her in his arms and bringing her back . . . and in the next maddened instant, his mouth crashed to hers.

Trouble was there, and he claimed it, amid the shock waves of rage and jealousy and need pounding through his veins. Trouble was the soft ripeness of her mouth and its treacherous sweetness, stealing through his blood . . . the sweet poison of desire.

Aye, trouble was there, and she found it as well. She wasn't immune. He tasted her hunger in the first instinctive response of her mouth. Quick and hot it was, but only for a moment. One tantalizing taste—then she twisted away. He released her.

"I know what that was," she said, her voice choked. "*You're* the one who wants to distract. I'm to tell everything, but ask nothing, is that it?"

He couldn't believe his ears. He could scarcely think past the tumult of desire, and she—the curst woman—was *still* intent upon the clues she'd wrested from him.

"You went to Quentin for justice," he said. "He put it in my hands, and I will see to it, as I always do, *in my own way*. You can tell me everything or you can tell me nothing. It makes no difference. The murder is to be solved, and I will solve it, however I must. This is *my* business, madame. You play by my rules or you do not play at all."

She folded her hands tightly before her and, raising her chin, she answered, her voice low, level. "Then take your rules, monsieur, and go to blazes."

LEILA STOOD UNMOVING while he swung away and marched to the door. She didn't wince when the door slammed behind him. She remained arrogantly erect until his quick, angry footsteps had faded away. Then she walked to the cupboard, took out a fresh sketchbook, carried it to the worktable, and sat down.

She had cried for hours before he'd come, and she had more reason to weep now, but there weren't any tears left. He'd burned them up with one hot, punishing kiss.

Because she *had* asked for trouble. She'd done little else but vent her anger and hurt and guilt on him. As though it were his job to make it all better, to sort everything out and reassure her and fix all that troubled her. As though she were a child.

As, perhaps, she was. She looked about her, at the nursery she called a studio. Here she'd played with her toys and ignored what went on outside in the grownup world, where Francis had roamed like a monster at large.

She had shut him out with work, refusing to contemplate the destruction he wrought—until today, when Fiona had made her see what he'd done to the Sherburnes.

Because, perhaps, Francis' own marriage had made him callous and bitter.

Because, for years, he'd had nothing to come home to.

Because, after he'd betrayed her once too often, his wife had completely shut him out.

Because all she'd cared about was protecting herself, her pride. His infidelities were a convenient excuse to stay out of his bed . . . where she couldn't hide or pretend, but where she became what she truly was: worse than a whore—an animal, mindless, maddened, begging for more.

And Francis would laugh, and say she needed two men, or three, or perhaps a regiment.

In her humiliation, it had never occurred to her that he might have felt humiliated, too. He'd loved her and wanted her, yet he couldn't appease her.

And so he'd sought more normal women, who could give and take pleasure. And she'd punished him for it.

She'd driven him off, as far as she could. She'd driven him into the streets of Paris and their irresistible temptations. It was she who'd given him the first push down the treacherous slope to corruption. Never once had she tried to draw him back.

That was why she'd been weeping. For her selfishness and ingratitude toward the man who'd saved her life, and made her an artist. And loved her.

Esmond had found her sick with guilt, desperate for some excuse to deny responsibility. Alone, she'd gone back again and again, all the way to the beginning, to Venice, looking for an excuse and unable to find one. She'd been desperate enough to go back once more with Esmond—but he'd seen what she had seen, and said so. Though he'd camouflaged the truth in pretty, romantic words, it was there all the same, ugly and painful.

She'd struck out at him, like a temperamental child, because he wouldn't help her lie. He wouldn't pretend she was a damsel in distress and take her in his arms and promise to take care of her and never abandon her.

Yet all the while, she'd been aware that this was real

life, not a fairy tale. In real life, putting herself into his hands was asking to be his whore.

Under her restless pencil, the blank page was filling with line and shading: the outlines of the fireplace and the masculine figure before it. The figure was turned toward the sofa where she had stood. Or stormed about, rather, as he'd said. Ranting like the mad, wicked creature she was at heart . . . who wanted to be his whore, wanted his arms about her, wanted the hot assault of his mouth.

That first taste of fire had warned of the conflagration to come and how it would end—in the ashes of despair and shame. Despite the warning, she'd been almost mad enough to succumb. Only her pride had saved her. She had broken away because she couldn't bear to let him see the disgusting creature lust would turn her into.

And so she'd driven him off, and he would never come back, and she was safe.

She dropped the pencil and buried her face in her hands.

THE FOLLOWING MORNING, Fiona paid a brief visit. She stayed only long enough to report that Lady Sherburne had worn the sapphires at dinner and express vexation at having to leave London. Lettice, Fiona's youngest sister, had fallen ill while visiting an aunt in Dorset.

"It seems I shall have to play the nurse, after all," Fiona said. "Or, more likely, it's *relief* from nursing that Lettice wants. Aunt Maud is very attentive, but her manner is that of one attending a deathbed. If I do not go, my little sister may well expire of *gloom*."

"Poor girl," Leila said feelingly. "It's dreadful to be sick away from home. She may be eighteen, but I daresay she wants her mama."

"She does, indeed, and I am that to all intents and purposes. Mama, you know, lost all her enthusiasm for mothering by Baby Number Seven. What a pity she did not lose her enthusiasm for Papa at the same time. But then, I doubt she was ever altogether clear on where babies come from.

She was very much astonished each time she found herself enceinte. Papa was naughty not to explain to her."

"So that's where you inherited your naughtiness," Leila said with a smile.

Fiona smoothed her gloves. "Yes, I suppose I am terribly like him in many ways. Nine brothers and not a one of them seems to—Oh, what am I doing?" she exclaimed. "I meant to stop for only a minute. My coachman will be cross with me for keeping the horses waiting."

She gave Leila a quick hug. "I'll come back as soon as I can. Be sure to write every day, else I shall go mad with boredom."

Without waiting for a reply, she hurried out, unaware she was leaving her friend to go mad with boredom. And loneliness.

At Leila's urging, Andrew had resumed his interrupted business trip to France. She hadn't seen David in at least a week. No one else had visited since the funeral. Except Esmond.

She would *not* think about him.

She wouldn't think about anyone or anything. All she had to do was keep busy, and she could do that even if she couldn't produce anything of artistic value. She'd had dry spells before. She knew how to fill up the time.

She spent the afternoon building stretchers and the evening tacking canvas to them. The next day she prepared rabbit-skin glue and coated the canvases with it.

The next day she was preparing to apply the next layer—white lead paint mixed with turpentine—when the Earl of Sherburne called.

He was one of the very last people Leila expected—or wanted—to see. On the other hand, she'd seen no one else. Whether the visit boded good or ill, he would at least provide temporary distraction from a mind that refused, despite all the busy work, to stop thinking.

All the same, if the visit proved disagreeable, she would want an excuse to cut it short. Thus Leila's only effort toward making herself presentable was to remove her smock, wash her hands, and push a few loose pins back into the unruly mass of her hair. Sherburne would understand that he'd interrupted her work, and if she chose to get back to it quickly, he would have to understand that as well.

Gaspard having allowed him to wait in the parlor, Leila found His Lordship standing before the curio cabinet, his hands clasped behind him and a frown on his harshly handsome face. He hastily erased the frown, and they exchanged greetings. He offered his condolences. She made the suitable responses. She politely invited him to be seated. He politely declined.

"I do not mean to take up much of your time," he said. "I see that you have been working. I also understand that my presence cannot be altogether agreeable, given what passed the last time I had occasion to visit."

"There's no need to speak of that," she said.

"There is. I am aware that I behaved abominably, madam," he said. "The quarrel was with . . . others. It was wrong of me to bring you into it. I have long owed you an apology."

Leila had only to glance once into his countenance to comprehend that the words hadn't come easily to him. His expression was rigidly controlled. As it had been the day he'd mutilated his wife's portrait.

"You paid for the painting," she said. "It was yours to do with as you wished."

"I wish I had not done it," he said.

He wouldn't have, her conscience reminded, if she'd paid attention to what was going on about her.

"I rather wish you hadn't, either," she said. "It was one of my better efforts. But if it worries you so, I can always paint another."

He stared at her for a long moment. "That's . . . you are—you are very good . . . generous. I did not . . ." He put his hand to his forehead. "I fear it cannot be so easily mended. How . . . awkward. But you are very good. Truly. You have sent my wits begging."

She gestured at the decanter tray. "If you would be so

kind as to pour, I shall drink a glass of wine with you. Whether or not a new portrait is possible, we can make friends again, I hope."

She did not care for wine in the middle of the afternoon, but he clearly needed it. She owed him something. Some kind of help, even if it was simply giving him something to do while he recovered his composure.

It did seem to help. By the time he handed her the glass, he seemed fractionally more at ease. Yet she couldn't help wondering if ruining her painting was all that had troubled him. The way he had searched her face—what had he been looking for?

What would the *murderer* be looking for? she silently amended. Sherburne had by no means been obliged to come, and the visit was difficult for him.

Reasons . . . not what they seem.

She watched him take a long swallow of wine. "I didn't mean to imply you must make it up to me," she said carefully. "I had guessed you were angry with someone else. I often take out my vexations on inanimate objects."

"It was clear enough who I was angry with, thanks to the spectacle I made of myself that day. It couldn't have been difficult for you to put two and two together." He met her gaze. "I was not the only one who'd been betrayed by my spouse. I was a brute to heap insult upon injury."

"I've long been past that sort of injury," she said. "I wish you would put it behind you as well."

"I should like to know how that's done," he said tightly. "I should like to know how I am to look into my wife's face and pretend nothing has happened, nothing has changed."

She knew too well how it was done. She had done it, in the beginning. This man might not be standing here now if she'd continued to do it, instead of running away.

"You might try recalling the sort of man my husband was," she said. "I strongly doubt Lady Sherburne had any idea what she was getting into. Francis could be . . . unscrupulous."

He turned away, to the curio cabinet again. "So I

learned. The hard way." He paused, and Leila watched his fists clench and unclench.

"It was wrong, very wrong of me to bring you into it," he said. "My only excuse is that I was not altogether rational at the time. There was nothing I could do, you see. Having discovered what he was capable of, I dared take no action, because he might easily retaliate by publicizing the—the details of the episode. I should be made a laughingstock and Sarah should be ruined. Utterly. An intolerable situation. And so I relieved my feelings by destroying your work."

She knew he didn't, entirely, deserve her compassion. He'd betrayed his wife more than once. Yet Leila couldn't help understanding. She knew there rarely was anything anyone could do. Even she had been afraid to leave Francis, afraid of how he might retaliate. He'd not only humiliated this man, but made it impossible for Sherburne to call him to account. Intolerable, yes, it must have been, not to be able to avenge the injury in a duel. Intolerable enough, perhaps, to drive the earl to another sort of revenge.

"At least you paid for the portrait first," she said, crushing a surge of anxiety.

"Indeed, it seems we continue to pay." He turned back to her. "We have had a disagreeable few months. She weeps." He touched his forehead again, and Leila understood that it was a gesture of helplessness and, perhaps, incomprehension. "It is . . . not pleasant. I much dislike going home. Yesterday was our anniversary. I gave her sapphires. We had people to dinner. What a beastly farce it is."

"Lady Carroll mentioned the sapphires," Leila said gently. "She told me they were very fine and became your wife exceedingly."

"Sarah wept all the same. After the guests left. Again this morning. I wish she would not." He set down his glass. "I should not speak of it."

"Not to me, perhaps," she said, "but to your wife."

"We don't speak, except in company."

He was in pain, and Leila couldn't bear it. Whether or

not she could have changed or stopped Francis, damage had been done. It was a debt he'd left behind, and she must pay it, as she would have done financial debts.

"Were the sapphires a—a peace offering?" she asked.

His jaw hardened. "It was our anniversary. I could hardly give her nothing."

She put her own glass down and summoned her courage. "It's none of my affair, of course, but it seems to me that what she wants is forgiveness, not a lot of cold, blue stones. Haven't you both suffered enough? Will you let Francis' unkindness keep you apart forever?"

His mouth set in a thin line. He didn't want to listen. His *pride* didn't want to. Yet he remained and did not deliver the setdown Leila so richly deserved. He was a peer of the realm, she a mere bourgeois. He could not be standing there, stockstill, out of a politeness he by no means owed her.

Leila took heart. "Surely you must see that she's sorry for what she did. For your own peace of mind, can you not show her some affection?"

"Affection." His voice was expressionless.

"She's a lovely young woman, my lord. I don't see why that should be so very difficult." She took his hand. "Come, you are older and wiser than she is. Surely you can coax her round?"

He looked down at their clasped hands. Then a very reluctant smile softened his countenance. "I should like to know who's being 'coaxed round' at present," he said. "You possess talents of which I was altogether unaware, Mrs. Beaumont."

She released his hand. "It's not my place to offer advice. It's just that I'm sorry Francis caused so much trouble. I wish I could fix it. I shouldn't blame you for holding a grudge, but I'm greatly relieved that you do not."

"Not against you," he said. "I wanted you to know that."

She assured him she believed him, and they parted not long thereafter, to all appearances, as friends.

Not until he was safely out of the house did she allow

herself to sink to the sofa and pray she hadn't made a fatal
mistake.

She knew she'd let her feelings rule her intellect. Instead of keeping the conversation safely upon a social path,
she'd poked and prodded about the most sensitive area.
One needn't be an expert in murder inquiries to understand
that, if Sherburne had killed Francis to keep him from publicizing the ugly details of what had happened, he might
kill anyone else he feared possessed those facts.

Leila could only hope Sherburne believed she didn't
know the ugly details. She hoped he hadn't confided his
troubles and endured her unsolicited advice merely to pick
her brain. Yet every instinct told her he'd come for help,
likely because his pride wouldn't let him confide in friends
or relatives. Leila Beaumont, however, had survived countless episodes of infidelity. Who better than a survivor to
advise him?

Every instinct told her Sherburne had trusted her and
confided as much as he was capable of confiding to any human being. Yet that didn't mean he didn't have other secrets burdening his heart. Like murder.

He'd trusted her, and her heart had gone out to him—
and to his wife—and Leila must betray him all the same.
She'd asked for justice. She wanted to find her husband's
murderer. Sherburne had a motive. In justice, she couldn't
keep that secret. In justice, she had to tell . . . Esmond.

"Damn," she muttered, rubbing her throbbing temples.
"Damn you, Francis, to hell."

Chapter 8

A WEEK LATER, LEILA STILL HADN'T CONTACTED Esmond. She may never have brought herself to do it if David hadn't called.

After he'd finished apologizing for not visiting sooner, he let her know what had occupied him: his new bosom bow, the Comte d'Esmond.

David's idol, rather, for it soon became clear that Esmond had very quickly progressed in the marquess' estimation from casual acquaintance to some sort of demigod. David told her the count spoke at least twelve languages fluently, had been everywhere and done everything, was a scholar and philosopher, a brilliant judge of every subject under the sun, from literature to horseflesh, and an expert at everything, from chess to flirtation.

For nearly two hours he sang the count's praises while regaling Leila with details of where they'd gone, who had been there, what Esmond had said to this one and that, especially what he'd said to David. Every word, evidently, was a pearl of sublimest wisdom.

By the time he left, Leila's nerves were at the breaking point.

She had spent the last week in a torment of guilt and in-decision, aware it was her duty to tell Esmond about Sher-burne, but unwilling to open a door which could lead the earl to the gallows.

Instead, she'd dithered—making bad drawings, prepar-ing canvases she didn't want to paint, wishing some visitor would come to distract her, then feeling relieved and dis-traught at the same time when no one did. She'd gone for walks, to the burying ground, but even that didn't clear her head. Either Eloise or Gaspard went with her, because Leila was not permitted to go out unescorted. Though she was wise enough to appreciate the protection, she couldn't forget whose servants they were and whose orders they acted under. Which meant she couldn't keep Esmond out of the turmoil in her mind.

And while she'd been accomplishing nothing—except making herself more crazy—Esmond had been stalking David.

They had attended every rout, ball, card party, musicale, and play in London—where the count spent half his time playing the God of Perfection to David and the other half flirting with every female between the ages of eighteen and eighty.

He'd even taken David to Almacks'—that bastion of re-spectability to which Leila Beaumont never had, never would be admitted in a million years, because she was a mere peasant. Not that she *wanted* to enter those stuffy as-sembly halls. She had tried, though, every way she could, to get David to go—to meet respectable young ladies and associate with decent young men of his own class. David, however, had said he'd rather be buried alive. Neither his parents nor Leila had been able to persuade him to darken the portals of Society's marriage mart—but he'd gone at Esmond's bidding.

Esmond, whom he scarcely knew. Esmond, who was in-terested in him only as a murder suspect, who didn't give a damn about him, and who would drop David—and hurt him by doing so—the instant a more promising suspect came along.

And it was all her fault.

She stood at the parlor window, staring bleakly into the fog-shrouded square.

She'd said she wanted justice, wanted to know the truth, but she couldn't face truth if it was ugly, if it would hurt anyone she cared about. Esmond had been right. She wanted clean abstractions. Not dirty, painful reality.

Most of all, she didn't want the pain of seeing him again.

Shutting her eyes, she pressed her forehead to the cold glass.

Go. Stay. Keep away. Come back.

Come back.

Weakness.

Because she'd *let* him make her feel weak, she reproached herself. She'd never let Francis do it. She'd stood up to him, right to the very end. No matter how she felt, she'd behaved, always, as though she were strong.

She opened her eyes and turned away from the window, away from the haze and gloom outside.

She *was* strong. Cowardly and base in some ways, yes, but not in all. Sensual weaknesses weren't all she'd inherited from her father. He'd passed on his cleverness and toughness, too. If he'd been clever and ruthless enough to plot and get away with so many crimes, surely his daughter was clever and tough enough to face and *solve* one.

And surely, after ten years' dealing with Francis, she must be able to deal with Esmond. She knew how to close off her feelings, conceal her vulnerabilities. She'd amassed an arsenal of weapons against men. Somewhere in her armory there must be a weapon, a tactic, a defense that would preserve her.

HALF AN HOUR after Lord Avory departed, Madame Beaumont marched into the kitchen.

Gaspard thrust away the pot he'd been scouring and leapt to attention.

Eloise put aside her chopping knife, wiped her hands on

her apron, and gazed at her mistress with no expression whatsoever.

"I assume you have some discreet means of passing a message to the Comte d'Esmond," the mistress said haughtily.

"*Oui, madame,*" said Eloise.

"Then tell him, if you please, that I wish to speak with him at his earliest convenience."

"*Oui, madame.*"

"Thank you." She swept out of the kitchen.

Gaspard looked at his wife. She said nothing until the mistress' footsteps could no longer be heard.

Then, "I told you," said Eloise.

"He will not come, my little one," said Gaspard.

"He will not *wish* to come," his wife returned. "But this time, I think, the master cannot make matters exactly as he wishes. Well, why do you stand there like an imbecile? Go," she said, waving him off. She took up her knife once more. "Go tell him."

Gaspard went out, his face grim. Only when the door had closed behind him did Eloise smile. "How I wish I could see Monsieur's face when he's told," she murmured.

AT ELEVEN O'CLOCK that night, Ismal stood in Leila Beaumont's studio doorway. During the short walk down the hall, he had composed himself—or rather, the outer man. The inner man appeared to have no hope of composure.

Ten days he had kept away and kept himself busy, outwardly at ease and easily entertained. Inwardly he'd been wretched. To be with her made him edgy and irrational; to be away from her made him restless and lonely. The former was worse, yet it was the former he wanted, evidently, for she had only to beckon, and he had come running.

His willpower and wisdom hadn't held out more than a few hours. Her message had come at five o'clock, and here he was, will and wisdom crushed by longing. He had missed her. He'd even missed this disorderly room, because it was hers, where she worked, where her true self lived.

Nonetheless, he behaved as though he were exceedingly put out—as though she'd interrupted the most joyous day of his life.

She was sitting at the worktable, spine straight, chin high.

He imagined his lips against her smooth white throat. He gave her a curt nod. "Madame."

"Monsieur."

He would not go to her. A few steps closer, and her scent would come to him. He walked to the sofa and sat down.

There was a silence.

After a minute, perhaps two, he heard—for he wouldn't look—the rustle of fabric, the scrape of the stool upon the wood floor, then slippered footsteps approaching. When she reached the worn rug, the sound was further muffled, but it sounded as loud in his ears as drumbeats. So, too, did his heart drum, as her scent came to him, carried by the curst draught from the windows.

She paused only a few feet away. "I apologize," she said. "I humbly beg your pardon for offending your delicate sensibilities by trying to tell you how to do your job. Most thoughtless of me. You are a genius, after all, and everyone knows geniuses are exceedingly sensitive creatures."

Ismal looked up into her smoldering tawny eyes. How he wanted her—the insolence, the scorn, the heat . . . passion.

"It is true," he said. "I am very sensitive. But you apologize so sweetly that I cannot resist. I forgive you, madame."

"You relieve my mind. And I, of course, forgive *you*."

"I have not apologized."

She waved her hand dismissively. "I forgive you for that, too."

"You are a saint," he murmured.

"Possibly. You, regrettably, are not. But I'm prepared to overlook that, and help you. It's the Christian thing to do."

"Your generosity overwhelms me."

"I doubt anything overwhelms you." She moved away—to stand by the fire, he thought at first. Instead, she pushed a heap of canvas onto the rug, to reveal a shabby but comfortably cushioned footstool.

"If you wish to throw something at me, the bust of Michelangelo would be easier to lift," he said.

She shoved the footstool toward the sofa. "I'm not going to throw anything. I'm going to sit at your feet and humbly offer my pitiful bits of information and bask in your blinding brilliance."

Accordingly, she sat and folded her hands upon her knees. Her expression a perfect mockery of humble dutifulness, she asked, "Where should you like me to begin?"

Farther away, he thought. Her honey-gold head was just within reach. His fingers itched to tangle themselves in that tantalizing disorder.

"Wherever you wish," he said.

She nodded. "Sherburne, then. What do you know about him?"

He didn't want to know about Sherburne. Ismal wanted his hands in her hair, his mouth on hers. How was he to think about the inquiry when his head swam with her scent and his body ached to be near, enfolded with hers, as he had dreamed every curst night these last ten nights and all the nights before?

"He was a friend of your husband's," Ismal said. "Until, that is, Monsieur Beaumont offended. With Sherburne's wife, it would seem, for the friendship ceased, and the Sherburnes had some grave quarrel about the same time. I have also heard Sherburne visited you a week ago."

Her ripe mouth curled.

"You are amused that your husband debauched Lady Sherburne?" he asked.

"I am amused because this whole time you've behaved as though I didn't exist," she said. "You let me believe I couldn't be of any possible use to you—yet you've been spying on me all the while. I suppose Gaspard and Eloise provide daily reports."

"I am well aware you exist, madame. As aware as if you were a thorn in my foot."

"I'm amazed, then, that you didn't come the instant you'd heard. Weren't you in the least curious about what I might have found out?"

"You did not send for me."

"I am not in charge of this inquiry. You are," she said. "I'm the temperamental and irrational one, remember? You must have encountered difficult informants before and managed them. If you could get David to Almacks', you could surely get me to answer a few questions."

"You know very well that I cannot manage you," he said. "You make me stupid—as you make every man who deals with you. Even your husband was stupid where you were concerned. Knowing the secret about your father, he had the power to rule you, yet he could not."

"I should be in a fine predicament had I let Francis—"

"Even Quentin, one of the most powerful and clever men in England, could not manage you. It is no surprise, then, that Avory is enslaved—"

"Enslaved! What are you implying?"

"And Sherburne, too. I cannot believe it is a coincidence that he went home to his wife after visiting you, and remained with her all that night and all the following day and night—and that suddenly, since then, he is always wherever she is."

Her countenance lit. "Truly? Have they made up?"

Her triumphant expression told him all he needed to know: somehow, during that short visit a week ago, she had wrapped Sherburne round her finger.

"Yes," Ismal said, frustratedly aware that he was in a similar condition . . . and irrationally jealous, besides.

Her smile widened. "Then you've just proved yourself wrong. He wasn't stupid at all. On the contrary, he came to his senses."

Then she told him of her meeting with Sherburne. Ismal

tried to focus on the crucial aspects, but when she was done, his mind fixed on one issue, and that one ruled his tongue.

"You held his hand?" he asked tightly.

"To make him listen," she said. "It was instinctive, I suppose. Not ladylike, I'll admit. But it worked, and that's all that matters."

"It was not instinct," he told her. "Yours are disciplined hands." He nodded at them. "You exert your will through them, communicate. And I think you are conscious of their power. I hope you are," he added testily. "Otherwise, you were abominably incautious."

"Power?" she repeated, studying them, apparently oblivious to his irritation. Then her attention transferred to his right hand, resting upon the purple pillow. "You can do it too, can't you?" she said. "Exert your will. Communicate. Only you *know* what it is you're doing to the other person." She looked up. "Do you *ever* do anything without calculation?"

"Describe the stickpin," he said.

She stared at him for a moment. Then she bowed her head in a mockery of downcast humility. "Yes, sir. Certainly, sir."

He wanted to drag her off the footstool, onto the carpet. He leaned back and shut his eyes and made himself listen to her cool, concise description.

It was a man's stickpin, she told him, but Sherburne had not been wearing it. The one in his neckcloth was set with an emerald. The one with which he'd destroyed the painting had been plain gold, in some form she hadn't been near enough to distinguish precisely. She thought it was some sort of leaf or flower, but she wasn't sure. For all she knew, it might have been a face or a figure.

Ismal forced his unwilling mind to analyze. After a few minutes' reflection he asked, "What made you believe that all Lady Sherburne needed was forgiveness and affection?"

"She was obviously very much in love with her husband," she said. "He not only neglected her, but had flaunted his affairs. I'm sure she intended no more than a flirtation with Francis, doubtless in hopes of making Sherburne jealous or at least getting his attention. I doubt she had any idea what Francis was really like. Few women did. For some reason, they saw only what he wanted them to see—until it was too late."

"And so she was seduced, and discovered her mistake too late, you think."

"If she *was* seduced," she said. "Rather difficult to seduce a strictly reared, upper-class young lady who's desperately in love with her husband, don't you think? Not to mention Francis was forty, and looked sixty by then. Hardly an Adonis."

"What, then? What do you suspect?"

Her eyes darkened. "He got me drunk, you know. After the first time I rejected his advances. It worked. Once. Never again. But with Lady Sherburne, he would have needed only the once."

So that was why Madame drank so little, Ismal thought.

He said, "If this is the case, it is possible her husband found her intoxicated, in circumstances showing clearly that she had been with another man."

"Sherburne knew it was Francis, but I strongly doubt she told him." She considered. "I can only conclude the stickpin belonged to Francis . . . and he left it behind . . . and it was distinctive enough for Sherburne to know whose it was."

Ismal recollected a shop in Paris and an erotic pendant that had enchanted Beaumont. "I can make a guess why he recognized it," he said. "Your husband evidenced a taste for certain curiosities."

"There's no need to be delicate," she said. "I'm aware of his tastes. The oriental fertility deities in the curio cabinet are the mildest example. He also owned a set of lewd watches—and a collection of naughty snuffboxes. And the usual dirty books. Those items, unlike the oriental gods and goddesses, were not on public display. He kept them for his private amusement. And for selected friends, of course."

"I should like to examine them."

"You're more than welcome to them," she said. "I was tempted to throw them out, but some of the pieces probably belong in a museum—not that I can imagine what museum would wish to display them. They're still in his room. Shall I fetch them?"

Ismal shook his head. "I want you to give them to Lord Avory," he said. "I shall encourage him to visit again soon. When he does, you will ask him to take charge of these objects for you. He will do so to oblige you, though he will be most embarrassed. Then he will come to me for advice. While I examine them, perhaps he will reveal something useful."

"How clever," she said. "How *calculating*."

"I calculate upon Lord Avory's affection for you," he said.

"And his dependence upon your infallible wisdom," she returned.

He smiled. "I think you are jealous. I think you wish me to spend all my time with you instead."

"Clever, calculating, and *conceited*," she said.

"It is your own fault. If you had sent for me sooner, you should not have missed me so very much."

She lifted her chin. "You came promptly enough. Maybe you missed *me*."

"Yes," he said softly. "Very much."

"Because you need my help," she said. "Admit it. You wouldn't have known about the stickpin if I hadn't told you."

Ismal sighed. Then he came off the sofa to kneel beside her. She stiffened.

He bent nearer and grew drunk on the clean fragrance of her hair, mixed with the exotic combination of jasmine and myrrh and the elusive scent that was herself. He could not be wise and honorable. He'd given up fighting with himself the instant she'd come to him with her insolent apology and taunting golden eyes.

Effortlessly, without intention or guile, she'd shattered his resistance.

All that mattered to him now was wearing down hers.

"I need you," he said. "I admit this."

She stared straight ahead. A faint color washed over her high cheekbones. "I sent for you to discuss the case," she said. "To pass on information. That's *all*."

He said nothing. He waited, focusing every iota of his will on what he wanted.

THERE WAS A long, thrumming silence. Then Esmond leaned in closer, and her breath caught as his lips grazed her ear.

Don't. Her mouth shaped the word, but the only sound was her own too rapid breathing.

He brushed his cheek against hers, nuzzling, as a cat would. And *please don't*, she silently pleaded, while she fought to keep from reaching up to stroke his neck, to feel the silk of his hair against her fingers.

She'd had all her weapons ready, prepared for any assault, but this wasn't assault. His scent, the warmth emanating from him, and the teasing friction of his skin against hers worked some insidious spell, turning her weapons against her. All her muscles were taut and aching, fighting her, trying to break free of reason and self-control.

And he knew it. She saw that in the glance he slanted at her. He was waiting, aware of what he was doing to her. He didn't move, scarcely seemed to breathe, yet she could feel the pressure increasing.

Will. His against hers. And his was more potent. Dark, masculine, relentless. She strained against the pull, but it was useless.

She'd been born weak. Sin was in her nature.

He was strong and beautiful, and she wanted him.

His lips brushed her cheek, promising tenderness. And that promise opened a rift inside her, an emptiness she'd hidden from herself, successfully. Until now.

She lifted her hand to his sleeve, instinctively, to hold onto him, as though the aching loneliness were a treacherous sea, and his strong body a lifeline.

Then he caught her, as though she were, in truth, drowning, and swept her from the footstool, and drew her into the haven of his arms.

This time, when his lips met hers, there was no hot punishment. This time, as though aware of the emptiness she felt, he filled her with pleasure. His mouth played with slow sensuality over hers. A delicious game . . . so tender. No fire, but warmth and ease and languor.

All the world quieted and softened, and lulled, she was easily led, to part for him at the first light coax of his tongue and welcome him deeper. She'd tasted fire the last time, quick, fierce, and frightening enough to jolt her to reason. This time, no blaze burst through the darkness of desire. This time, the darkness was warm, rich with sweet sensation . . . the velvet stroke of his tongue, caressing, idly exploring, playing with her softness, stealing secrets and hinting of his own.

Beguiled, she wordlessly told too much, and soon, she asked too much. She wanted more warmth, and pressed closer. She wanted his strength and weight, to be crushed, overpowered. She answered his idly seeking tongue with demand: *More. Need me. Take me.*

And still he played, as though there were nothing else in the world, no other time but this, as though one deep, lazy kiss could go on forever. While she grew desperate, craving more, he toyed contentedly, as though he needed no more.

Except, perhaps, to make her beg, warned a voice at the edges of consciousness.

Then she realized what he'd done, that she'd been led, deliberately. She was still gently cradled in his arms like a child, yet somehow he'd brought her down to the carpet, and she was tangled with him, like a wanton, her body clinging to his. And she wasn't warm, but hot. Because he'd built the fire by slow, imperceptible degrees and she had never noticed until she was feverish with lust.

Poison, Francis had warned. *So sweet . . . just pleasure.* So it had been.

Like human laudanum, he'd said.

And she had been drugged.

She pulled away and, struggling against unwilling muscles, dragged herself up to a sitting position.

Slowly, he sat up and gazed at her. All blue-eyed innocence.

"You did . . . that . . . *on purpose*," she said, fighting for breath.

"Assuredly. You could not think I kissed you by accident."

"That's not what I mean. You wanted to make me witless."

"*Naturellement*," he said with maddening calm. "I strongly doubt you would make love with me if you were in full possession of your reason."

"Love?" she echoed. *"Make love?"*

"What other possible purpose could there be?"

"That's not what you wanted." Reminding herself that the "love" he referred to was generally called fornication, she staggered to her feet. "You wanted to—to prove something. Teach me a lesson."

"I cannot think what I would teach you. You were wed for ten years. One assumes you know how to make love. Certainly, you are adept with the preliminaries."

Then he smiled up at her, a boy's disarming smile. But it wasn't mischief she saw glinting in those midnight blue eyes. It was guile.

"Not half so adept as you, obviously," she said.

"*C'est vrai*. No one is, as it happens." He rose, graceful as a cat—unlike her. Even now, she felt weak and clumsy, her limbs rubbery, threatening to give way.

"Still, your will is formidable," he went on. "Very difficult to overcome. Most vexatious—so much work for one small kiss." He gazed at her thoughtfully. "It was easier when you were angry, but then I was angry, too, and it is impossible to be comfortable when one is in a rage. Next time, perhaps I must contrive to enrage you while remaining even-tempered myself."

Her eyes widened. The fiend was not only planning his next maneuver, but he had the audacity to *describe* it.

"There isn't going to be a *next time*," she said, with all

the icy command she could muster. But her heart was thumping anxiously all the same. What would she do if he persisted? How the devil could she stop him? She didn't understand how he did whatever it was he did.

"There shouldn't have been a first time," she added quickly. Straightening her posture, she moved a few steps away, toward the fireplace. "It's unprofessional. And inconsiderate of me—of my wishes. In case I didn't make it plain some time ago—which I'm sure I did—I don't want an affair, with you or anybody. In simple words, the answer is no. Not maybe, or sometime. *NO. Non. Absolument. Jamais.*"

He nodded. "I understand. There is a great resistance."

"There is a great *refusal*, confound you!"

"Ah, yes. That is what I meant. My English is not always so precise as I would wish, yet I comprehend very well."

She had no doubt whatsoever that he did comprehend, all too well. "I'm relieved to hear it," she said. "And now that we've settled that matter, and I've told you all I know regarding Sherburne, you'll want to be on your way."

"Yes, that would be best. You have given me a great deal to reflect upon." He gave her a considering, head-to-toe survey that made her skin prickle.

"Quite," she said. "Sherburne. The stickpin. You'll want to find out for sure whether it belonged to Francis."

"Avory should be able to settle that question," he said. "I shall arrange that he comes to you in about three days' time. It would look odd if he called again sooner than that. Does this suit?"

"My appointment calendar is not overcrowded at present," she said stiffly.

"I have engagements tomorrow night and the next," he said. "The night after, I must dine with His Majesty. I doubt I can escape him much before dawn, especially if he is in a talkative humor. In any event, I assume you prefer I do not return until we have something to discuss. Regarding the case."

She nodded. "Good night, then." She smoothed her skirts, to avoid giving him her hand.

He bowed. "*Au revoir, madame*. May your dreams be pleasant ones."

AS ISMAL HAD promised, Lord Avory called on Madame three days later. And as Ismal had predicted, the marquess came to him shortly thereafter. After a short discussion—apologetic and embarrassed on Avory's part—Nick was sent out to retrieve the box of Beaumont's belongings from the carriage. At present, the marquess was arranging the last of the items upon the library table.

"She was wise not to throw them out," Ismal said as he put down a watch he'd been examining. "Many of these are quite old and the workmanship is fine. A valuable collection."

Lord Avory did not seem to be listening. He was gazing at the now-empty box in puzzlement.

"Something is missing?" Ismal asked.

The marquess looked up in surprise. "Sometimes I do wonder if you can actually hear me thinking," he said.

"I merely observe your expression," Ismal said. "You had the look of one searching for something. When you were done, the look became one of dissatisfaction."

"It's not important. It may easily have been lost. A stickpin," the marquess explained. "Altogether vulgar."

"It does not matter," Ismal said. "What remains will bring in a good sum, I think. I am sure she could make use of the money at present, when she has no commissions."

What did she live on? he wondered, with a twinge of guilt. He made a mental note to look into her finances.

And Beaumont's, he reminded himself. The man had lived on the profits of *Vingt-Huit*, which Ismal had destroyed. If Beaumont had come to England with little money, he would surely have engaged in his specialty, blackmail, and he would have required more than one victim to maintain his costly habits.

"I only hope Mrs. Beaumont never saw it," Avory said. He took up a copy of *La Philosophie dans le boudoir*, flipped it open, and scowled. "I certainly wish she hadn't seen this. I scarcely knew where to look when she brought these out. Of all writers, the Marquis de Sade." He slammed the book shut and gestured at another. "There's *Justine*, as well. What a filthy hypocrite Francis was. And the whole time—two years—I had no idea what he was up to. I wonder who else knew."

"Of his liaisons with men, you mean?" Ismal shrugged. "Not many, I would think. I believe this was one of the few cases in which Beaumont exercised a degree of discretion."

The marquess got up and began to pace the carpet. "But *you* knew," he said. "Others might. Which means they surely wondered about me. I was his constant companion. You must have wondered, surely."

"I consider such matters irrelevant to our friendship," Ismal said. "Lately, all I observe is that you seem to have no interest in anyone, male or female. Except, perhaps, for a young lady I have never met."

The marquess abruptly halted.

"Lettice Woodleigh," Ismal said. "Lady Carroll's young sister. You have an interest there, perhaps, for when her name is mentioned, you become very attentive."

"I wasn't—that is, how did you—but you just said, didn't you? I—I hadn't realized I was so obvious." Avory's color rose. "Well, you're right, as usual. But it's no good. That is to say, I'm not deemed suitable. No, that's putting it too mildly. The instant I showed an interest, they sent her straight to that wretched aunt of hers in Dorset. Not that one is in the least amazed," he added, bitterness edging his tones. "Lady Carroll despised Francis, and I *was* his boon companion, wasn't I? And shockingly as she behaves, she's exceedingly protective of her sister."

"Indeed she must be, if she sent her away merely because you showed interest."

"I assure you, that was all I did. I hold Miss Woodleigh in high regard. Very high regard," the marquess said, dropping his voice. "But it's hopeless, I know. And I can't, honestly, blame it entirely on Francis. Or at all, perhaps. I'm not—I'm not fit—it . . . it's out of the question." He turned away, his head bowed. "I am so sorry," he said.

"The heart makes its own rules," Ismal said. "If it would only heed others' rules of what is wise and proper, it should never be broken. It should never ache at all."

"If I had been wise two years ago . . . but I wasn't." Avory's glance flicked to Ismal, then quickly away. "I met Francis shortly after I'd lost a close friend. He—he'd shot himself."

While he murmured some sympathetic reply, Ismal's mind fastened on connections: two years ago . . . a suicide . . . in Paris, for Avory had known Beaumont before the latter came to London. There were many suicides, every year, in Paris. But one young man, a patron of *Vingt-Huit*, had shot himself—because some government papers had been stolen from his keeping. Thanks to Beaumont.

Consequently, Ismal was not surprised when Avory spoke of a promising diplomatic career cut tragically short and named the unfortunate man: Edmund Carstairs.

"We were friends since our schooldays," the marquess went on. "I don't form many attachments. When I do, they seem to be very strong. I was much shaken by his death. I drank . . . more than I should have done. I met Francis in one of the places I'd frequented with Edmund."

Returning to the table, he took up a snuffbox. His mouth twisted. "My father would say that Francis led me down the path of vice. But I went willingly. And I can't blame it all on grief or drink or pretend I was out of my senses for two whole years. At any rate, what I've done is done. And what I've done . . ." He put down the snuffbox. "Sometimes I feel I was someone else all that time. Now I'm not sure who or what I really am, or what I want. It wouldn't be fair to marry—even to court—anyone, especially . . ." His voice caught. "Especially someone I hold in high regard."

High regard, indeed, Ismal thought. Avory's interest in the girl had been clear enough. The intensity of feeling, though, came as a surprise. The marquess possessed considerable self-control, yet he was at present perilously near tears.

"I agree that it would be unkind to attach a young woman when you are unsure," Ismal said.

"It's better she's away," the marquess said, more to himself than to his host. "While she was about, it was . . . difficult. To be sensible." He sank into the chair. "Merely calf love, of course—which one ought to know better than to take seriously. Even so, if Lady Carroll had been a fraction less hostile, I might have gone ahead and made an unforgivable mistake."

"I was unaware she disliked you," Ismal murmured.

Avory grimaced. "I didn't find out until early last December, at a ball. I made the mistake of dancing twice with Miss Woodleigh. Lady Carroll took me aside and threatened to take a horsewhip to me if I ever went near her sister again." He opened and closed a pocket watch. "She'd do it, too. She's more like her father than any of the others—and that includes her methods—and she does rule the family. In any event, in case I might be fool enough not to believe her, she sent her sister away."

Not merely for the reason Avory gave, Ismal felt certain. There had to be a more compelling reason than one unacceptable suitor. Just as there must be a stronger reason for Avory's accepting rejection, when he was obviously head over ears in love. Deeply, painfully so. Though the episode had occurred some two months ago, he was still utterly wretched.

"The young lady cannot be kept away forever," Ismal said. "I doubt Lady Carroll wishes to make a spinster of her. Miss Woodleigh is not very likely to meet an eligible *parti* in a small Dorset village."

Avory's fingers tightened on the pocket watch. "No, she'll be back for the Season, I daresay." He cleared his throat. "And wed before the year is out, undoubtedly. I wasn't the only one, you know, to—to admire her. She's beautiful—and clever—and when she laughs . . . Well, I was taken with her. Obviously."

Blinking hard, he set down the watch. "We might show the snuffboxes to Lord Linglay. He owns quite a collection. He's sure to find these titillating."

"A good suggestion."

The marquess' glance moved to the mantel clock. "It's getting late. I really ought to let you dress. One isn't asked to dine with His Majesty every day. You won't want to be late."

"No, I must leave the grand entrance to him," Ismal said. "And you, my friend—do you dine with Sellowby?"

"With Sellowby and a dozen other men, you mean. No, I think I'll spend a quiet night at home with a book."

Avory's countenance was composed, his voice normal again, but his grey eyes were bleak. He would return to his lonely townhouse and brood over his lost love—and whatever else tormented him, Ismal thought. And all would grow darker and more hopeless. To rescue him was common charity—not to mention that the more comfortable the marquess felt, the more he'd be inclined to confide.

"Spend it here, then," Ismal said. "Nick cannot come with me, and if he is occupied, impressing you with his culinary skills, he is less likely to get into mischief."

"Stay here?" Avory's glance darted about the luxurious, cozy library. "While you're out? But I couldn't impose. I've dozens of servants, paid to—"

"If it were an imposition, I would not offer. But this way, Nick will be happy and usefully occupied, and you will be not only well fed, but even amused, perhaps, for he can be most entertaining when he is in good humor. Then, when I return, I shall burn your ears with all the gossip I hear from His Majesty."

The King of England had a considerable affection for the Dowager Lady Norbury, Lettice Woodleigh's mother. Consequently, he took a keen interest in the family's affairs. The carrot Ismal held out, in short, was the prospect of news about Lettice.

Avory took it. "That does sound pleasanter than—Well, *yes*," he said, flushing. "How very good of you to offer."

Chapter 9

THE FOLLOWING NIGHT, ISMAL WAS SEMI-recumbent upon the studio sofa, watching Leila Beaumont through half-closed eyes. She was painting, and he knew he wasn't the subject. She was challenging her skill and torturing her vision with a disorderly array of glassware. Or had been, until about an hour after his arrival. At present, she appeared to be working up to a fit of temper.

"You *made* David stay last night?" she demanded. "You made him spend the night at your house—when he was so agitated? Hadn't you got enough out of him?"

"It is your fault," he said. "You are the one who makes me feel sorry for him."

"Sorry?" she echoed. *"Sorry?"*

"He was unhappy. You would think me hardhearted if I let him return to his lonely townhouse to grieve over Lettice Woodleigh, and all his terrible sins. One of which, I remind you, may well be murder. Which means he may have poisoned my coffee or cut my throat. Yet you do not say, 'Esmond, you are very brave.' Instead it is 'Esmond, you are a villain.'"

"Esmond," she said, "you are exceedingly provoking."

The faintest of smiles—not discernible at this distance—was the only indication that he'd noticed: not "monsieur," but "Esmond," she'd said. At last.

"You are vexed because you knew nothing of Lord Avory's *tendre* for Lettice Woodleigh," he said. "You are vexed because he confided this to me, not you. But you have not spent half your waking hours in his company. You knew something troubled him, but you had no opportunity to collect clues. Also, you are not so devious and manipulative as I."

She snatched up a rag and vigorously wiped the brush handle. "Very well, I am vexed," she said. "I cannot understand why Fiona never even hinted of the matter to me—of David's interest in her sister, of her own dislike of him, purely because he was Francis' friend. I can't believe that of her."

"She never told you why her sister was sent to Dorset?" he asked.

"I didn't know Lettice was *sent*. I assumed she wished to visit."

"With a widowed aunt, many miles away from her family and friends, at Christmastime?"

"I really didn't give it much thought."

"It is interesting that so much occurred during this time," he said meditatively. "The Sherburnes' marital difficulties, Miss Woodleigh's banishment to Dorset, your husband becoming persona non grata to Sherburne and his followers." He paused briefly. "Your decision to stop painting portraits."

"That last is obvious enough, I should think," she said. "Self-preservation. When matters reached the point where Francis' enemies started taking out their frustrations on me, I made a strategic retreat."

"Indeed, matters did reach a point," he said. "Some kind of crisis, it would seem."

She took up another brush and started cleaning the daylights out of that.

"What do you think?" he asked.

Her brow knit. "I think it was a crisis," she said. "When

Sherburne wrecked the painting, I knew that Francis had crossed some dangerous line. There's a code about these things. Married ladies may indulge in discreet affairs—but *after* they've produced at least one heir to secure the line. Lady Sherburne hadn't done so yet. According to the rules, the gentlemen must consider her out of bounds. To cross that boundary is bad enough. To cross it with the wife of a highly influential friend sounds like self-destruction."

She began scraping her palette clean. Ismal waited, curious whether she'd make more connections.

After a minute, she spoke again. "It's possible that Fiona sent Lettice to Dorset to keep her out of harm's way. Francis did bear Fiona a grudge. The day he died, he ordered me to stay away from her."

"What reason did he give?"

"Don't act stupid," she said. "He thought she was trying to forward an affair between you and me. Which she was. Which you know perfectly well."

"Indeed, I am exceedingly fond of her."

"She's been trying to get me to have an affair for years," she said crossly. "Just to upset Francis. But you were the only one who did upset him. Naturally, she was delighted."

"And I was delighted to accommodate her," he said.

"Esmond."

"Madame."

"Don't be tiresome. I'm trying to *think*." She flung the palette down, and began to pace before the heavily draped windows.

Watching her pace was far more interesting than watching Avory, Ismal reflected. To and fro she swept, skirts rustling, hairpins scattering.

"Fiona does tend to shield those she cares about," she said after a few tumultuous turns. "Including me. She never mentioned her suspicions about Francis and Lady Sherburne until a fortnight ago. Until then, I didn't know Sherburne had actually snubbed Francis publicly. But now that I think of it, she was constantly pressing me to go away to this house party or that—wherever Francis wouldn't be—and nagging me to leave him and live with her instead. At the time, I simply put it down to her dislike of him. But now it seems more likely she was worried about my living with a man who was, apparently, becoming more irrational and dangerous by the day."

"From all I have heard, this seems to have been the case," Ismal said.

"Then it makes sense she'd send Lettice away," she said. "Fiona wouldn't want her within fifty miles of Francis."

"You said he bore a grudge against Lady Carroll. You think she feared he would try to hurt her through her sister?"

"That's about the only way he *could* hurt Fiona."

"Then you think Miss Woodleigh's exile had nothing to do with Lord Avory's interest in her?"

She mulled over the question, pacing again. "Damn. I don't know. Fiona's fiercely protective of Lettice. And David did stick with Francis, after all the others had turned their backs, evidently. Even I have to wonder what was wrong with David. If he truly wished to wed Lettice, you'd think he'd go out of his way to earn her family's approval: drop undesirable companions, change his ways—offer some evidence of reforming, in other words."

"He seems to view his situation as hopeless," Ismal said. "Apparently, he has believed this for some time. Certainly, whatever troubles him is so distressing that he will not confide it even to me."

"But you must have some theory," she said. "Some inkling what the terrible sin might be."

"Murder is one possibility."

She stopped short and threw him an exasperated look. "Murder wouldn't have been troubling David back in early December. Unless you think he's been going about killing people for months."

"That is possible. He may be insane." Ismal arranged the pillows more comfortably under his head, and sank back. "Or maybe it is a sexual matter," he murmured.

There was a long, pulsing silence.

Then she plunked herself upon a stool and took up her sketchbook and pencil.

"What do you think?" he asked.

"If David can't bring himself to speak of that sort of thing even to you, it must be truly appalling," she said caustically. "And if *you* can't deduce what it is, it's obviously far beyond the bounds of my paltry expertise."

"Sometimes a man will confide to a woman what he would not to another man."

"I assure you, David and I were never on terms even approaching that degree of intimacy."

"Perhaps he confided in a mistress, then? Perhaps you know the names of them?"

"None. Not a one. Never heard a word about it."

"Nor I," he said. "Not even in Paris. Strange."

"Not strange at all," she said. "Some men are very discreet."

Not *that* discreet, Ismal thought, closing his eyes. Avory had gone to Helena Martin's after all. Half the Beau Monde's male population had been there, along with London's most famous courtesans. It was hardly the place to seek a *discreet* liaison, for these were women who sought the limelight. They were the social leaders of the demimonde.

It was far more likely that Avory attended such events to keep up appearances. But to conceal what?

"You aren't going to sleep, are you?" his hostess tartly inquired.

"I am thinking," he said. "You and Lord Avory pace. I lie quietly."

"Yes. Well. *Do* make yourself perfectly at home, monsieur."

"This sofa is very comfortable. You keep it here for models?"

"I haven't done a life study since I came to London. Can't have naked people lying about. It disconcerts the servants."

"For your own rest, then."

"For reading," she said. "Sometimes I do read."

"Yes, this is a good place to read and to think," he said. "Comfortable. Close to the fire. You have arranged your studio well. One area for working, by the windows, where you have the best light. And one area for relaxation."

"I'm so relieved you approve."

"Indeed, it is an intriguing topic—the way you arrange your life—but I should be thinking of the inquiry. You are distracting me," he chided gently.

There was a small flurry at the other end of the studio, then silence, but for the whisper of pencil upon paper. Though the room became quiet, it was not tranquil. The atmosphere continued to pulse for a while, like an unquiet sea, until at last she became absorbed in her work.

Ismal tried to absorb himself in his own, in puzzling out the riddle of Lord Avory. He was not doing very well. He would concentrate better at home, he knew.

But he didn't want to concentrate better. Here, he was surrounded by her, by what she was: the rows of art books, the clutter of artistic materials, their distinctive odors mixed with the occasional whiff of smoke from the fire, and now and again, the teasing hint of her own scent, carried by the mischievous draught.

Here, Ismal could listen to—and feel—her working, making her magic with such humble implements: pencil, brush, paint, canvas, paper. He possessed many gifts, but this had been denied him. Her talent intrigued and excited him—the mind, the hands . . . those beautiful, restless hands.

They were working now, making their mysterious artist's love to pencil and paper.

He wondered if he'd become her subject again. He hoped so. He wanted her to attend only to him, and fix on him . . . and come to him. He wanted her to come and caress him with the honey of her eyes . . . and with her passionate artist's hands . . . and bring her mouth to his as she had done the other night.

She'd done so against her will, because it could not withstand his. This time, however, Ismal knew he must work harder. This time, she must believe it was all her own doing. And so, once more he concentrated his will upon her, but with more dangerous cunning, for he let his breathing become steady and even, as in sleep.

LEILA GLANCED AT the clock. He had lain there more than an hour without moving a muscle. He must be asleep. She looked down at the sketch she'd made. She drew what she saw, and this was a body in repose, a face of almost childlike innocence. So the adult countenance often appeared, in sleep.

It was past two o'clock in the morning. She had to wake him. And send him home.

She shouldn't have to. He had no business falling asleep on her sofa. If he wanted to think—or sleep—he should do it in his own house. Really, his audacity was beyond anything. *He* was beyond anything.

Her glance flicked from the drawing to the subject and back again.

He was very strange, even for a Frenchman.

One should not generalize, she knew . . . but that countenance was *not* French. Somewhere in that noble bloodline some past Delavenne had mixed his blood with something . . . exotic.

She advanced a few steps, her head tilted to one side. But he did not *look* exotic—not in the dark, mysterious way one associated with the Orient, for instance. Perhaps not so far east, then. Perhaps no farther east than one of the Italian states. Certainly Botticelli had found his like centuries ago in Florence.

At the moment, the count seemed even more fragile than a Botticelli creation. But he often gave that impression even when awake, she thought as she neared the sofa. She knew he was about as delicate as a jungle cat. And just as dangerous. She'd seen them in menageries. They looked like big versions of house cats, some of them like kittens. They would look up at you with those big sleepy eyes, and you'd want to stroke them. Until they moved. Until you watched them prowl their cages, muscles rippling under the sleek coats.

Her face grew very warm, recalling: a dance, when she had stumbled . . . that moment, at Francis' door, when she'd fallen apart . . . strong arms wrapped around her . . . the confusion and the dangerous warmth. And the other night . . . *I need you*, he'd said. And in an instant he'd made her need him, desperately.

Though she had reached the sofa, she only stood there, gazing at his hands. His left arm lay across his flat stomach. His right, angled upon the pillows, partly framed his head, and the hand—that poor broken and mended hand—was curled as though it lightly clasped some invisible object.

She wanted to slide her fingers into the beckoning curve.

Into danger.

Her gaze slid lower, to the pale gold hair, slightly tousled now.

She wanted to slide her fingers into that silken disorder and muss it more.

Two silken strands had fallen over his eyebrow. She ached to smooth them back. Ached unbearably.

Don't, she told herself, even as her hand lifted to his face.

She brushed the hair from his forehead . . . and his eyes opened, and before she could snatch her hand away, his long fingers closed round her wrist.

"No," she gasped.

"Please."

He simply held her, exerting no pressure at all. She might have withdrawn, knew she ought, but she couldn't. It was as though the blue depths into which she gazed were some vast sea, and she were caught in the undertow. Heart hammering, she brought her mouth to his.

She met a too familiar tenderness and a sigh like welcome. He slid his fingers into her hair—to hold her, but so gently, as though he'd lured a bird into his hands and the touch were meant only to quiet and reassure, not to imprison. He'd held her so the other night, and still she didn't know how to resist. She could no more fight the light clasp than she could the tender claim of his mouth.

This time, she'd come of her own volition, drawn not by guile or art, but by her own wicked desire . . . for more of what he'd given her before, though she knew it was a lure to ruin. He'd made no secret of his intentions. Now, he'd know that her rejection had been a lie. But right now, she didn't care. All she wanted was his lazily tender kiss, the caress of his fingers, trailing over her scalp so languidly that he might have been asleep still.

For this moment, she could almost pretend he was asleep, and she was in his dream. She gave herself up to the dream, and to the intoxication of his kiss, and the churning emotion inside her eased and curled into simple pleasure.

So the hand he still so lightly clasped curled in pleasure against the slippery fabric of the pillow. So, by slow degrees, did her taut muscles ease. The sensuous touch upon her scalp seeped under the skin and made slow trails of warmth through her neck and shoulders and on to the very ends of her fingers. In the same way, his lazily tender kiss sent shimmering trails of sweetness through her, to steal deep into her troubled, wanton heart.

She knew he wasn't asleep, that intent and calculation informed his idlest caress. She knew this was seduction, a beguiling prelude to her undoing. But the awareness was Reason's voice. Faint and far away, it warned in vain, because she was lost in him, beyond heeding anything but his coaxing mouth and tongue, his sinfully seductive hands.

He drew her down, and she went without a struggle . . . and tasted the first spark of fire as he drove deep into her mouth. Then his arms lashed about her, and in one surging movement he pulled her off balance and onto the narrow sofa. His powerful body closed about her, a human trap of steely muscle, weight, and heat. The languorous pleasure vanished like any dream. In its place throbbed the reality of six feet of potent male animal, stirring now, restless . . . and dangerous.

She told herself to break away—now, before the restlessness blazed to masculine impatience. But already his hands were dragging over her, searing her flesh through layers of bombazine, cambric, and silk. She knew how to fight—she'd done it often enough—but she didn't know how to fight herself and him at the same time. She didn't know how *not* to want him—his scent, his heat, his hard, powerful body.

His hand, too sure, too knowing, closed over her breast in brazen possession, and she couldn't raise her own hand to push him away. Her aching flesh strained against the confining fabric, and her fingers itched to rip the cloth and bare herself to him. And while she fought not to betray herself, he was ravishing her mouth with slow, sensuous strokes. It was a sinful promise, a bold mimicry of the act of love, yet it ravished her needy heart, and made her ache to be loved, sin or no. To be his, however he wanted. Even to be wanted, for this moment, was enough. She was burning. She couldn't bear to burn alone. And so she urged him on, sinking into the hot liquor of his kiss, while she gave her body over to the simmering command of his hands.

She heard the low moan, deep in his throat, felt the shudder that ran through his frame and left it taut with tension. If sense or reason or will had remained to her she would have fled then, in that last remaining moment before his control slipped. But she wanted him to ache and shudder and grow savage . . . for her.

He raked his hands down and, roughly cupping her hips, dragged her against his groin. He pushed against her, and through the frustrating barriers of silk and wool she felt the thrust of hot male arousal. He could have had her then, in a moment. He had only to drag up her skirts and tear away the flimsy garments beneath and drive into her. She was ready, hot and damp. But his devilish control wouldn't break. He held her where he wanted her, his fingers kneading the ripe curves he'd captured, while slowly, rhythmically, he moved against her, a tormenting promise that turned her mind black with lust.

She wanted sin. She wanted to rip away the curst garments and touch that throbbing heat, and make it hers, make *him* hers. She wanted him inside her, driving deep, overpowering, possessing. She wanted to drown in the hot, drunken rapture he promised.

Wanted. Wanted. *Wanted.*

So very eager . . . insatiable . . .

She saw then, and couldn't drive the image away . . . herself, writhing in Francis' arms . . . his laughter . . . her helplessness . . . and after . . . sick and ashamed.

A sob caught in her throat, and she wrenched away, and scrambled up from the sofa.

She was fighting for breath and her limbs were like India rubber, unwilling to support her. All the same, she made herself move—and not look back. She couldn't look him in the eye and see her shame reflected there.

It was her shame. She couldn't blame anyone but herself. She was fully aware of the demoralizing effect her harlot's body had on men, and Esmond had told her plainly enough he wanted that body. She knew he was treacherous. She knew she should have kept away.

Instead, she'd let beauty lure her, and pleasure hold her, then slipped almost instantly to wanting sin, *thinking* sin. She pressed her fist to her temples and wished she could tear her brain out.

She heard his voice, and knocked the stool aside. It crashed to the floor, drowning him out.

She swept her arm over the worktable. Brushes, charcoal, paints, pencils, jars, sketchbooks, clattered to the floor.

"Madame."

No. She wouldn't look, wouldn't listen. She grabbed the easel and flung it down, and knocked over the glassware. Then she fled the room, slamming the door behind her.

ISMAL GAZED ABOUT him at the wreckage and waited for his heart to slow down. Then he left the studio and headed up the stairs to her bedroom. He knocked on the door.

"Madame," he said.

"Go away. Go to the Devil."

He tried the handle. It wouldn't move. "Madame, please unlock the door."

"Go *away!*"

It took mere seconds to locate a stray hairpin near the head of the stairs. He bent it and returned to the door.

"This lock is worthless," he said, inserting the pin. "A child can pick it."

"You are *not* to—Esmond—Don't you even think of—"

The door shuddered as she hurled her weight against it. But he'd already released the lock. He pushed the door open, and she backed away.

"You *bastard.*"

"Yes, I know you are vexed," he said. "I am not so tranquil myself." Gently he shut the door behind him. "That is a very bad lock. I will tell Gaspard to install a better one."

"If you don't leave this instant, I shall tell Gaspard to *throw* you out." She snatched up a poker. "I'm warning you, Esmond."

"I advise you not to strike me with the poker," he said. "There will be much blood, and it will make you sick. Also, if you kill me, there will be no one to help you deal with the police. There will be another inquest, more disagreeable than the last one."

He approached, extracted the poker from her stiff fingers, and returned it to the stand.

"I cannot believe you have the effrontery to come in here—to *break* into my room," she said in a choked voice. "I don't want to talk to you. I don't even want to *look* at you. I cannot believe you can be so—so *insensitive.*"

"I am not insensitive," he said. "I have feelings, and you have hurt them. What did I do that you thrust me from you, as though I were some filthy dog?"

"That's not what I did. I left."

"In a rage. What did I do that was so abominable?"

"It wasn't you!" She retreated, pressing her hands to her

temples. "It's—I'm sorry. I know I gave you every reason to believe—Gad."

She stared at the carpet, her face crimson. "I know I behaved in a—I made an *advance*. I know it wasn't you. I'd told you no—and then I . . . succumbed. As they all do. Crawling over you like—like the rest of them. As he said. Like maggots. The same as every other wh-whore." Her voice broke.

"You are so crazy." He scooped her up in his arms and swiftly deposited her upon the bed. While she was still trying to catch her breath, he propped up the pillows behind her and nudged her back against them.

"You are *not* spending the night," she said shakily.

"That has become obvious," he said. "I am here because I wish to know how I distressed you. I do not know what I have done—whether I alarmed you or disgusted you—or how I did this."

She rubbed her eyes. "It has nothing to do with your curst *technique*."

"So I am discovering." He gave her his handkerchief. "This appears to be a question of character."

"And *morals*. Mine, that is. Since you haven't any."

He seated himself on the bed near her feet, and leaned against the bedpost. "I do have rules, though," he told her. "One of them is not to become romantically entangled during a delicate investigation. It is distracting, and distraction at best impedes efficiency. At worst, it is dangerous. The trouble, in your case, is that the effort to resist becomes a worse distraction."

She pushed her hair out of her face. "To resist? You've shown no signs of resisting. On the contrary—"

"Yes, I leave it to you and, worse, I try to make resisting as difficult for you as I can." He smiled. "I know. But I cannot *resist*, you see?"

She scowled down at the handkerchief. "It hardly matters what you resist or don't. I started it—and took my damned time about ending it."

"That does not make you a whore. And certainly not a maggot—'crawling' over me, you said."

"Well, I did throw myself at you, didn't I?"

" 'Crawling . . . like maggots . . . as he said.' Those were your words a moment ago. As who said? Your husband?"

She began to fold the handkerchief. "In Paris, before we left, Francis told me the tarts swarmed over you like maggots on a ripe cheese."

"A vivid image." He considered. "Calculated, very likely. It is an image you would find especially repellent, *non*? And one which I should have the greatest difficulty eradicating. It appears he made it so that any attraction you might feel for me would give you great self-disgust, for you would see yourself as another maggot. Very clever," he added softly, "the way in which he poisoned your mind against me." He wondered what other kinds of poison Beaumont had fed her, and whether it was simply the one revolting image which had driven her away.

"*Was* it poison?" she asked without looking up. She was folding the handkerchief into smaller and smaller squares. "Was he lying?"

"When could he have observed such a thing?" he returned. "At orgies, perhaps? Is that how you imagine I spend my time? Lying in some brothel or opium den, with naked females by the dozens, writhing in lust about me?"

Her rising color told him he'd guessed accurately.

"Why not?" she said. "I've certainly noted the debilitating effect you have on apparently respectable women at reputable gatherings."

"I have noticed you have a similar effect on men," he said. "Yet I do not imagine hosts of them crawling over your beautiful body. Only one. Me. And the image does not repel in any way. *Au contraire*," he said softly. "I find it most appealing."

She looked up. "Because you're a man. You've nothing to lose. As long as you keep within certain very wide boundaries, every conquest is marked to your credit."

By heaven, could she think nothing but ill of him? But this wasn't her fault, Ismal reminded himself. Her husband had poisoned her mind.

"Only if I flaunt them," he said, striving for patience.

"And as to conquest—that is a matter of perspective. I told you my rules. And so, in our case, who has conquered whom, do you think?"

"I never cast lures!" she cried. "Even tonight. I only came to wake you up. And then . . ." She pressed the heel of her hand to her temple.

It was as she had done earlier, Ismal recalled. She'd made the same gesture a moment before she'd had the tantrum. Warily, he came off the bed. "Your head aches?" he asked.

Her eyes ominously bright with unshed tears, she turned away.

And Ismal cursed himself for what he'd done, whatever it was. Many people had such vulnerable spots, he knew: places where all forms of trouble—shock, grief, guilt, fear—settled and became a chronic physical ailment. His own troubles sometimes settled upon the scar in his side. Though the wound had healed years ago, it could throb as though freshly opened.

So her head must throb, because he'd opened a wound, made trouble. Because he *was* trouble to her, he amended unhappily. Years before, he'd opened the door that let Beaumont into her life, to wound and scar her, and now Ismal, the cause, reaped the results. A fitting punishment, he thought as he moved to the head of the bed.

"I can make it go away," he said gently.

"Don't touch me."

The words hurt more than he could have imagined. He wanted to take her in his arms, kiss and caress, and drive all the trouble away with sweet pleasure. He wanted to hold her, shield her from all that caused her pain. Yet he knew shame hurt her most at this moment, and he was the cause. The only way to ease her pain was to tell the truth.

"It was not your doing," he said. "I was a villain to let you think so. I pretended to be asleep, so that you would come to wake me."

Still she wouldn't look at him. "I didn't have to touch you."

The self-loathing he heard in her voice twisted like a blade in his heart.

"I invited it," he said. "I know very well how to invite— in ways you cannot begin to imagine. And whether you had touched me or not, it would have made no difference. All I needed was to have you within reach. The rest was . . . seduction. For which I have no small talent. And, since you are strongly opposed to being seduced, I exerted this talent to the utmost."

She turned a wary golden gaze upon him. "Talent," she said. "You're telling me it was all *guile*—planned, from the start?"

"I could not help it," he said. "I want you very much. I have wanted you . . . for a very long time. I do not know how to make it stop. It is unmanageable, this desire. And so, *I* am unmanageable. I cannot even apologize. I am not sorry, except that I have distressed you. But even that is selfish. The truth is, I am sorry because you were distressed enough to leave my arms." He paused. "The truth is, I came to lure you back."

"To soften my heart," she said.

"Yes." He stepped back from the bed. "And in another moment, I shall be on my knees, begging you to take pity. I am abominable. A great problem."

"Yes," she said. "Yes, you are. Go away, Esmond. *Now*."

He went promptly because, though he'd spoken as truthfully as he could—more truthfully than he'd done in years—he could not overcome the habits of a lifetime. He had missed nothing—the way her eyes softened while he spoke, the way her posture eased and her body shifted ever so slightly, inclining toward him—and every instinct had urged him to take advantage. He *would* have fallen to his knees and begged, conscienceless beast that he was. Because he hadn't lied. He didn't know how to stop wanting her. And so nothing—honor, wisdom, caution, even pride—could keep him from trying.

Chapter 10

ON THE STROKE OF NOON, NICK ENTERED IS-mal's bedroom to announce Lord Avory's arrival. Ismal was still in his dressing gown.

"Shall I let him cool his heels in the library?" Nick asked.

"What sort of mood is he in?"

"About as beastly as yours." Nick slammed shaving materials onto the washstand. "I daresay you'll expect to get shaved in thirty seconds."

"You should not have let me oversleep."

"When I *tried* to wake you, you offered to relieve me of my private parts. In painfully explicit terms." Nick commenced to stropping the razor with vicious energy.

"I think I prefer to shave myself today," Ismal said. "Send His Lordship up."

Nick stalked out.

Ismal had lain awake a long time, pondering Leila Beaumont's aching temples and the self-loathing that seemed to be part of it—a shame Ismal had little doubt her husband had planted. Beaumont, clearly, had possessed a gift for poisoning minds.

Undoubtedly, Sherburne's mind had been poisoned, to cause such a bitter and painful estrangement from an adoring wife who'd erred but once—and then mainly thanks to her husband's provocation. Then there was Lady Carroll, who'd conceived such an intense hatred of Lord Avory . . . and Avory himself, with the terrible secret that prevented his wooing the girl he loved.

Unfit, Avory had called himself. He had also pinpointed the time his problems had begun. Two years ago, right after Edmund Carstairs' suicide.

During his sleepless hours, Ismal had begun to formulate a theory. Now, as he began lathering his face, he prepared himself to test it. He wasn't looking forward to the procedure. He had become rather fond of Lord Avory . . . who was attached to him, trusted him, looked up to him as though Ismal were an infinitely heroic and admirable older brother.

Avory couldn't know Ismal was a vulture, waiting to pluck out his secrets.

Just as Ismal finished lathering his face, the marquess entered.

"Please forgive me," Ismal said as he took up the razor. "I overslept."

"I wish I had done." Avory plunked himself down on the window seat. "Instead, I spent the morning reviewing my accounts with Mama."

Ismal gave him a sympathetic glance. "Your expression tells me the experience was not agreeable." He began shaving, his mind working with the same brisk sureness as his hand.

"It is thoroughly *mortifying* to have to account—with receipts—for every curst ha'penny," his guest said. "Today I learned receipts aren't enough. I'm now expected to provide all the whys and wherefores as well. So we quarreled." He bent to brush a speck of dust from his boots. "I told her that if she disapproved of how I spent my paltry allowance, she needn't give me any. She threatened to oblige me. I recommended that she and Father make a proper job of it and disown me entirely," he said, straightening.

The vulture began to circle and descend.

"It is no use, you know," Ismal told him. "If you do not wish to inherit, you will have to hang yourself. They cannot disown you. You are all they have—the last male of your line."

"Not *all* they have. There are other branches of the family tree." Avory gave a short laugh. "Still, I most certainly am the very last of the *direct* line. Father's so proud of the fact that the title's gone straight from father to son since the time of the first Duke of Langford—unlike the convoluted genealogy of the Royal Family. As though that were anything to boast of, when it's just a matter of luck."

His face hardening, he rose and moved to the dressing table. "It seems our luck has run out." He sank down into the chair and began arranging Ismal's toiletries in rows in order of size.

"So that is the problem," Ismal murmured as he angled the shaving glass for a better view of the marquess' countenance. "You believe you will fail to produce the necessary heir." He saw the muscle leap in Avory's jaw. "Or do I misunderstand?"

There was a very long silence. Ismal continued shaving.

"I shouldn't have quarreled with Mama," Avory said at last in a low voice. He was staring at the orderly arrangement he'd made. "I simply should have told her. But it's not the sort of thing one tells anybody. I didn't mean to tell you. But I seem to have dropped a broad enough hint. I'm always complaining to you. Sorry."

"It is necessary to speak to someone," Ismal said. "You refer to impotence, yes?"

SEVERAL HOURS LATER, Ismal sent Avory home with a list of dietary instructions, a recipe for an herbal tisane, and the promise that Nick would prepare and deliver some pills before nightfall. The pills were no more necessary than the diet and tisane, for the cure was already taking effect. The problem was all in Avory's head, where Beaumont had maliciously put it with a few well-chosen words. Ismal had simply excised it with a few very different well-chosen words. But being English, the marquess was more likely to believe in the efficacy of bad-tasting medicines than mere speech.

After instructing Nick to make the harmless pills as foul-tasting as possible, Ismal set out for a walk. The last few hours had proved emotionally wearying. Since the fatigue was mental rather than physical, exercise was a preferable remedy to lying about brooding.

He was striding briskly through Pall Mall when he spied a familiar black-garbed feminine figure entering the door of number fifty-two—the British Institution. Madame Beaumont was accompanied by a gentleman. And neither Gaspard nor Eloise was anywhere in sight.

Within minutes, Ismal had gained admittance. Moments later, he found her in a chamber where a handful of artists labored before an assortment of old master works. She was speaking to one of the artists—a young woman—and the fellow with her turned out to be Lord Sellowby. Who turned out to be standing much too close.

Ismal simply stood in the entryway, looking idly about while he focused all his furious concentration on Leila Beaumont. Finally, after two interminable minutes, her posture stiffened and her gaze shot to him.

Arranging a polite smile on his face, Ismal approached.

"The British Institution is exceedingly popular today," said Sellowby, after greetings had been exchanged and the young artist introduced as Miss Greenlaw.

"I misunderstood," Ismal said. "When I saw Madame Beaumont enter, I assumed some of her works were on display."

"They might be," said she icily, "if I'd been dead a couple of centuries."

"And if she were a man," said Miss Greenlaw. "You shan't find a woman artist's work in *this* lot." She informed Ismal that she was entering the annual competition to create a companion piece to one of the works on display. The three best works would win prizes of one hundred, sixty, and forty pounds, respectively.

"Miss Greenlaw did me the honor of requesting a critique," said Madame. "Which I am sure she would prefer *not* be done before a crowd."

"I do not believe two onlookers constitute a crowd," Sellowby said with a faint smile.

"Two bored and fidgety men do," she said. "I know you'll fidget—first, because the discussion isn't about you and second, because you won't understand what it *is* about." She waved her hand dismissively. "Go talk among yourselves—or look at the pictures. Perhaps you'll absorb some culture by accident."

"I shouldn't dream of taking such a risk," said Sellowby. "I shall await you outside, Mrs. Beaumont. Esmond, care to join me?"

By the time they reached the pavement, Ismal was apprised of the fact that Mrs. Beaumont had consented to dine with Sellowby and his sister, Lady Charlotte, at what Sellowby deemed the ungodly hour of six o'clock.

"One encounters fewer strictures when dining with the King," Sellowby said as they ambled down the street. "My sister must have an early dinner. Mrs. Beaumont must speak to Miss Greenlaw first, for she promised. But before she could do that, we had to wait for Mrs. Beaumont's womanservant to finish whatever it was she was doing, so that she could accompany us."

Eloise, it turned out, was waiting in His Lordship's carriage. This news allayed Ismal's agitation not a whit.

Sellowby was a large, dark, well-built man with a sleepy gaze and sardonic manner certain women found irresistibly intriguing. Ismal imagined one certain woman intrigued across a dinner table set for two. Thence his imagination moved through a dimly lit hallway, up a set of stairs, through a bedroom door and on, with bloodcurdling clarity, to a bed.

"It would have been a good deal simpler if Fiona were about," Sellowby went on. "But if she had been, we shouldn't have this problem in the first place."

Despite the thundering in his ears, Ismal did understand the words and somehow amid the turmoil, his brain managed to operate.

"I am sorry to hear this," he said. "Madame Beaumont has had problems enough, I should think."

"I mean Charlotte, my sister," Sellowby clarified. "She's in a dither because Fiona hasn't answered any of her letters—or anybody's, it seems. Charlotte's heard from most of the Woodleigh family, *all* in a dither because they haven't had a word from Dorset—not even a note from their pestilential Aunt Maud. If Mrs. Beaumont can't quiet this tempest in a teapot, I know just what will happen. I shall be ordered to Dorset to demand an explanation—from a woman who can't bear the sight of me—for the benefit of *her* family and my busybody sister."

"But there are nine brothers," Ismal pointed out, his detective instincts stirring.

"And every last one of them dances to her tune. Fiona ordered them to keep away, and they wouldn't dream of disobeying. Have you ever heard anything so idiotic?"

"It is odd that Lady Carroll would write to no one," Ismal said. "Surely she realizes they are anxious about her sister's health."

Sellowby paused to frown into a printshop window. "Odd isn't the word for Fiona. I'm not sure what the word is. 'Inconsiderate' will do for the moment. Because of her, we are obliged to plague Mrs. Beaumont. And wouldn't you know it? Not a one of them thought to invite her out until they needed something from her. Even then, they must do it by proxy. My only consolation is that Charlotte has ordered an excellent dinner and I shall supply my very best wines. Mrs. Beaumont will be lavishly fed, at any rate."

"You make her sound like a lamb led to the slaughter."

Sellowby turned away from the window and gave a short laugh. "Quite. I begin to sound just as theatrical as the others. But she knows what she's getting into. I did warn her about our ulterior motives."

And naturally, she would jump at the chance to go out,

to do some detecting of her own, Ismal unhappily realized.
Or perhaps she simply wanted to spend a few hours in the
company of a more manageable man, a normal English
rake.

Finding he liked neither proposition, Ismal tried to persuade himself she simply wanted to help, as she'd wanted
to help Sherburne. Yet she had held Sherburne's hand . . .
and she *had* been detecting. And so, Ismal couldn't like the
way she "helped," either. His gut was in knots and he had
the irrational urge to dash Sellowby's brains out on the
pavement.

Still, he remained outwardly his usual ingratiating self.
When at last Madame exited the building, Ismal bid her
and Sellowby a courteous *adieu* and casually sauntered
away.

LEILA CAME HOME at half-past nine. At nine thirty-
seven, she was quarreling in the studio with Esmond.

"*Asked* you?" she repeated indignantly. "I don't ask
your or anyone's *permission* to dine out."

She stood, stiff with outrage, in the center of the carpet.
She wanted to throw something. That *he* of all men—lying,
manipulative snake that he was—should dictate to her—in
her own house. And look at him. He couldn't even pace
like a normal man. Instead he prowled the room, like a
surly jungle cat, closing in for an attack. She wasn't afraid.
She had some attacking of her own to do.

"You were not dining," he snapped. "You were detecting. Which is not your business, but mine."

"It's not your business to tell me what my business is,"
she said crisply. "You do *not* dictate my social activities—
such as they are. Do you think I've nothing better to do
than sit about all evening, waiting for you? If, that is,
you're in a humor to turn up. Not that you've turned up
lately to much purpose other than immorality."

"You try to turn the subject," he said, stalking past the
draped windows. "That has nothing to do with the issue at
hand."

"It *is* the issue," she said, summoning her control. "I have learned virtually nothing from you but how extremely talented a seducer you are. And I begin to suspect you want it that way. You don't want me to know *anything* about this case. You especially don't want me to suspect there's more to it than meets the eye."

His restless motion slowed fractionally, telling Leila she'd aimed accurately.

"That's why you don't want me out with others," she went on, her confidence building. "You're afraid I'll hear something. Well, it's too bloody late." She marched straight into his path, bringing him to a sharp halt. She looked him square in the eye. He tried to stare her down, his eyes shooting fierce blue sparks. She refused to be cowed. She was getting used to being singed.

"I went out, Esmond," she said. "I heard something. Do you care to hear about it—or do you prefer to waste your valuable time in an idiotic row?"

"I am not idiotic! You put yourself in danger. You do not even consult with me first."

"So you can tell me what to do?" She swung away from him. "Because I'm too *stupid* to figure it out for myself? Because it's so easy for you to play havoc with my morals, you think I'm brainless, don't you? Because you've pulled the wool over my eyes from the start, you think I'm an imbecile."

"That is nonsense," he said, storming after her, toward the fire. "What is between us has nothing to do—"

"It has *everything* to do with everything! There's nothing between us. Never has been. You only pretend it to keep me distracted—and you're good at that, aren't you?" she demanded. "At pretending. Distracting. You drove Francis distracted. With jealousy. Do you actually believe I'm too stupid to see the flaw in that picture?"

He drew back sharply.

Ah, yes. He hadn't been prepared for that.

There was a short, deadly silence.

Then, with a patently false, patronizing smile, he asked, "What flaw?"

"If you want to seduce another man's wife," she said, her voice low and level, "it is counterproductive to arouse the husband's suspicions. You are far too clever and calculating to let that happen. *Ergo*, your main interest was *not* seduction."

She moved to the sofa and perched on the arm and watched the words sink in. Now that she'd commenced what she'd braced herself to begin and finish, she felt wonderfully calm. Outrage and hurt rolled away, like a spent storm, leaving crystal clarity behind. "I have a theory of what you did want," she said. "Thanks to something Sellowby mentioned."

"A theory." He turned away to the mantel and took up the small bust of Michelangelo, then put it down again.

"It begins with Edmund Carstairs," she said.

He went very, very still.

"That friend of David's who shot himself after some important papers were stolen from him," she amplified. "According to Sellowby—who was in Paris at the time, having an affair with a diplomat's wife—the papers were confidential letters from the tsar. Your friend, the Tsar of Russia."

The light played fitfully upon his pale gold hair, but that was the only sign of motion.

"The tsar demanded someone get to the bottom of it," she said. "According to Sellowby, no one could. And so I found myself wondering, Esmond, just who might be called in to solve a riddle no one else could. Then I asked myself why the tsar's good friend, the Comte d'Esmond—who also turns out to be friends with British and French royalty—should choose, out of all the men in Paris, a sodden nobody like Francis Beaumont as boon companion."

He turned then, very slowly, as though drawn in spite of himself. The lines at the corners of his eyes were sharply etched.

"'The reasons for certain friendships,'" she softly quoted. "'Not always what they seem.' I pay attention, you know. I do treasure your little gems of wisdom."

His blue gaze grew clouded.

"It was a slow ride home," she said. "The streets were busy this evening. I had ample time to ponder a number of puzzling matters. Why, for instance, the great Lord Quentin bothered with the suspicious death of a nobody like Francis. Why His Lordship had no trouble believing my astonishing announcement that my husband had been murdered. Why His Lordship was so very obliging about conducting a covert inquiry into the murder. And why, of course, he sent for *you*."

"In the carriage," he said very softly. "You formulated this theory of yours during the ride home."

"I believe I see the outlines," she said. "I do see a *discreet* inquiry regarding those Russian letters that began some time ago. And Francis must have been the primary suspect, since you devoted nearly all your time to him. Since it was so very discreet, since he was never prosecuted, I assume there must have been potential for some nasty scandal. What I can't decide is whether the papers alone held the potential for scandal or whether Francis was involved in some larger crime, and the papers were merely a part."

Shaking his head, he looked away. "This is bad," he said. "You cannot—You should not—Ah, Leila, you make me so unhappy."

She heard the unhappiness in his tones, and something more in the sound of her own name. Not the crisp English *Lie-la* nor yet *Lay-la*, but something uniquely, caressingly, his. The sound echoed achingly inside her, and she understood then that he was genuinely troubled on her account.

"That's your conscience," she said, striving to keep her tones cool. "Telling you how unfair and sneaky and disrespectful you've been. If I were you, I should make a clean breast of it. You'll feel better, and so shall I. I should like to have it all clear and settled, so we can put it behind us and get down to our present business. We'll never make proper progress with this—this—whatever it is—hanging between us."

He wanted to. She saw that in his taut stance and in the

rigid planes of his perfectly sculpted profile. More important, she could feel it.

"Oh, come, Esmond," she said. "Be reasonable, will you? Just tell me the story. A report, if you will. As though we were colleagues. I've already figured out it's going to be nasty. But I have a very strong stomach. Obviously. No woman of delicate sensibilities could have survived ten years with Francis."

"I should have killed him." His voice was low, tight with remorse. "I should not have brought you into it. A stupid mistake."

She believed the remorse she heard was genuine, too. He had used her, as she'd guessed. But not altogether cold-bloodedly, as she'd feared.

"Yes, but your mind was clouded by lust," she said. "It happens to the best of men. Nobody's perfect."

She waited through a long, unhappy silence. Then, finally, he came to the sofa, and without looking at her, sat down.

Then, still without looking at her, he told her about a place called *Vingt-Huit*.

ISMAL DIDN'T TELL her everything. He limited himself to a few of the milder examples of *Vingt-Huit*'s activities. And his concise summary of what he'd done to destroy it and Francis Beaumont's sanity didn't include Beaumont's infatuation with himself. This wasn't to spare her the news that Ismal had deliberately misled the man, but because he didn't want her to know her husband had for years been betraying her with his own sex as well as with women. She was English, like Avory. And if Avory could regard one drunken episode with Carstairs as an unforgivable, beastly and unnatural crime, Ismal had little doubt Leila Beaumont would be sick with horror that she'd ever let her husband touch her.

Even now, though she heard him out quietly, Ismal had no idea of her state of mind. When he finished, he braced himself for the bitter recriminations that were sure to follow and, worse, the tears he knew he couldn't bear.

After an interminably long moment, she let out a sigh. "Oh, Lord," she said softly. "I had no idea. But then, I couldn't, could I? Even professionals—even you—had a devil of a time getting to the bottom of it."

She laid her hand on his shoulder. "Thank you, Esmond. You have relieved my mind. There *wasn't* anything I could do. Francis wasn't just weak. He was *evil*. Even Papa's crimes seem small compared to this. Papa was greedy and conscienceless, I'm sure. But Francis was *cruel*. I can see why you wish you had killed him. I can also see why you wouldn't want to dirty your hands."

She had not taken her hand away, and it took all his self-control to keep from pressing his cheek against it and begging forgiveness. "I am not an assassin," he said.

"No, of course not." She squeezed his shoulder. "Are all your missions so horrid and complicated? How the devil do you bear it?—dealing with the lowest of vermin, and having to walk on eggs the whole time. No wonder the Royals think so highly of you." She laughed softly. "Francis said you weren't quite human—and he didn't know the half of it."

That affectionate squeeze, the compassion he heard in her voice, bewildered him. Her laughter left him utterly at sea.

"You are laughing," he said stupidly.

"I'm not a saint," she said. "I'm not above enjoying a bit of vengeance. Francis deserved to suffer. And you, apparently, were the only one who could make him do so. I wish you'd told me sooner. It appalls me to think of the tears I wasted on that filthy, despicable—Gad, I don't know any words bad enough."

She got up from the sofa arm. "But you do, I daresay. You've twelve languages at your disposal, Avory says. Would you like some champagne?"

He couldn't make sense of her. He rubbed his head. "Yes, yes. I should like something."

"Lady Charlotte and Sellowby gave me a few bottles,"

she said, moving toward the door. "At first, I was sufficiently vexed with you to consider breaking them, one
by one, over your head. But you've risen above yourself
tonight, Esmond. And I think one ought to reward good
behavior."

Numbly he watched her leave the studio.

She wasn't angry, hurt, disgusted. She thought he'd
been *good*.

She had actually thanked him a moment before and said
he'd relieved her mind. And she had touched him, all on
her own, unbidden. In affection. And sympathy. "Horrid
and complicated" she'd called his work—as it was. And
she'd wondered how he bore it—as he wondered sometimes, late at night, alone.

She could have turned away and hated him, for using
her, for leaving her to deal with the maddened wretch he'd
made of her husband.

Instead, Leila Beaumont had turned to him, and touched
him, as though *he* were the one who had suffered and
needed comforting.

He realized then how very much he'd wanted comforting. Because the task had been vile, and he had resented it
and the demands the curst Royals made upon him. And he
had grieved for Beaumont's victims, just as he'd grieved
today for Avory's lonely misery.

And, yes, Ismal had wanted her compassionate voice
and the touch of her strong, beautiful hand, because he was
almost human, and he wished, like any mortal, for someone to turn to.

Which was a risk he couldn't afford.

ISMAL WAS STANDING at the worktable when she returned with the champagne.

Moving to her work area had helped him bring his
mind and heart back to objectivity. He had collected his
composure and his wits, and had sunk his unsettling
emotions back into the quagmire that passed for his
heart.

After he'd filled their glasses and given her hers, she said, "I shall propose the first toast. To you." She touched her glass to his. "For your clever handling of a thorny problem—and for showing a proper respect for my intelligence. For once."

"I am in awe of your intelligence," he said. "I knew you were perceptive. I did not realize, though, how diabolically quick your mind was."

Or how generous your heart was, he added silently.

"Flattery," she said, and sipped her wine.

"Truth," he said. "Your mind *is* diabolical. It goes with your body. I should have realized."

"You were bound to say something like that." She brought her glass to his. "Very well, Esmond. To my confounded body, then."

She took a longer sip this time, then settled onto one of the stools at the table and proposed they get down to business.

"I've already relayed my most momentous discovery," she said. "My hosts believe or pretend to believe Lettice chose to go away for a change of scenery and rest. They are aware of David's interest in Lettice and of Fiona's disapproval. Lady Charlotte is on Fiona's side. Sellowby is square on David's. That was how I learned about Carstairs. Sellowby was pointing out to his sister that David had lost a brother, then, a year later—in shocking circumstances—a close friend. Sellowby feels David is fundamentally a model of propriety who went a bit wild on account of confusion. Furthermore, being young, David needed a good bit of time to sort things out."

"Sellowby is closer to the mark than he can know," Ismal told her. "Avory *is* confused, and Carstairs' death was the start of his problems. We spent half the day together. I learned his terrible secret."

Her fingers tightened about the glass stem. "How terrible?"

"Actually, it is not so bad. He is impotent and—"

"Oh, God." Her face white, she set down the glass with shaking hands.

Ismal hadn't expected her to take it so hard. Hadn't she listened to the tale of *Vingt-Huit* and her husband's perfidies as calmly as though it had been a lecture on galvanic currents? But she'd despised her husband. Avory she cared for very much. Ismal should have understood the difference.

Inwardly cursing his tactlessness, he took her hand. "Do not upset yourself. It is not permanent. A simple case to remedy. You do not think I would leave your favorite to suffer, do you?"

He released her hand and gave her back the glass of champagne, and ordered her to drink. She did.

"Avory's ailment can be easily corrected," he assured her. "When I tell you the story, you will understand. He was out debauching with Carstairs the night the papers were stolen. The next day, Carstairs shot himself. The shock of his friend's death, along with some needless guilt and too much liquor, caused Avory a common, but temporary malfunction. Unfortunately, shortly thereafter, he met up with your husband, to whom he confided his problem during some drunken evening. Your husband told him it was an incurable disease—worse than the pox—contracted through certain intimate activities."

"Don't tell me," she said. "I can guess. There isn't any such disease, is there?"

Ismal shook his head. "But Avory believed the lie, and his mind, deeply affected, affected his body. If he had told a doctor what he told your husband, he might have been healed long since. But Beaumont made Avory so sick and ashamed that he could tell no one else. And so he has lived two years with the loss of his manhood. Also, in recent months, I am sure he lived with the anxiety that your increasingly irrational husband would expose the hideous secret."

She drew a long, steadying breath. "Cruel," she said. "Unspeakably cruel. Poor David." She emptied the champagne glass. "Is that why you were so unreasonable when I came home? You had a delicate job, I collect, to get the details out of him. It must have been beastly for you. If I'd had to investigate a friend—Fiona, for instance—in such a way, and hear of such cruelty and misery, I should be wretched." She stroked his coat sleeve. "Oh, Esmond, I *am* sorry."

The emotions he'd so ruthlessly buried began struggling to surface. Shoving them down, he said, "If you feel sorry for me, I can only conclude you are drunk."

She shook her head. "It takes more than two glasses of wine—with a large dinner—and one glass of champagne. And it's no use trying to persuade me you don't feel anything—especially regarding David. I know you're upset because he's got a strong motive for murder."

"He does, certainly. Now he also has a strong motive to kill *me*."

"You're upset because you like him," she persisted. "You always call him my favorite, but he's your favorite, too, isn't he?"

"I am *not* upset," he said, edgily aware of her hand still upon his coat sleeve. "Even if he did the murder, it does not follow that he must be punished. My ideas of justice are not English. And all Quentin wants is to satisfy his curiosity. He likes to know all the answers. He is like *you*."

She was absently stroking the sleeve, her countenance thoughtful.

"You don't want me to believe you have a heart," she said. "Or a conscience."

"Leila."

"You might have a *little* bit of a heart." She lifted her hand and brought thumb and forefinger nearly together. "Since you're almost human, you might have a tiny little piece of a heart," she went on, squinting at the narrow space between her fingers. "And a tiny, tiny sliver of a conscience." She shot him a glance from under her lashes. "And I never gave you leave to use my Christian name. You normally manage to observe certain formal proprieties of address, even when you're behaving most improperly. But tonight I've got you so upset that you say—"

"*Leila.*"

"That's three times now. Very upset, indeed."

"Because you provoke me," he said, grabbing her hand. "Because you probe. But I am not Avory. I do not tell my every thought and feeling to everyone who shows me a small kindness."

"*Kindness*?" she echoed. "Is that what I'm accused of? For heaven's sake, do you think every time a human being tries to deal with another *as* a human being—as a friend— there's some ulterior motive?" She pulled her hand away. "Because I haven't taken fits and broken things over your head and made an unprofessional fuss about a professional matter, you think I'm engaging in some sort of cold-blooded *manipulation*?"

"You were *probing*," he said. "I could *feel* it."

"I wasn't *detecting*! I was trying to understand—to see matters from your point of view."

"As a friend, you said."

"And what's wrong with that?" she demanded. "Aren't you friends with some of your colleagues—accomplices— whatever they are?" She paused to study his face. Then, her voice dropping almost to a whisper, she said, "Don't you *have* a friend, Esmond?"

It was truth, and it stabbed deep. He had colleagues and countless accomplices and acquaintances and even de-voted companions, like Avory. But Avory looked up to and confided in him. There was no equal give and take. There was no friend with whom Ismal shared himself as an equal.

For one terrible moment, gazing into her golden eyes, Ismal wanted, with a loneliness as sharp as physical pain, to share himself with her. His buried secrets struggled, as though they were living things, up—toward her compas-sionate voice, the soft warmth of her body, the promised welcome and shelter of her generous heart.

One moment of unbearable temptation . . . Then he saw there could be no welcome for him. Every secret was tan-gled in lies. He could not extract even one harmless secret, for it might carry a hint of some damning truth that could turn her against him forever. To share with her anything at all was to open the door to more probing, for she wouldn't be satisfied until she knew everything. That was both her nature and her calling, as an artist who sought the truth beneath the skin. Already, she had reached too deep.

"You are probing still," he reproached, drawing nearer. "Stop it. Now, Leila."

"I only wanted to—"

"Now." He continued to advance, until her knees were pressed against his thighs. Then he leaned in close.

"Don't," she said. "Stop it."

"You stop it."

"Unfair tactics, Esmond," she said edgily. "You are not to—"

He crushed the rest with his kiss and, holding her fast, tenderly punished her mouth until she gave him entrance to its sweet, dark depths. And, in an instant, the ache of loneliness fled on a bolt of pleasure that made his limbs tremble. Then came another bolt, stunning him, when she reached up and caught hold of his shoulders, her fingers digging into his coat.

His mouth still locked with hers, he lifted her up onto the edge of the table and, sweeping the clutter aside, eased her back while he nudged himself between her legs.

She gasped and started to pull away.

"No," he said softly. "Now I interrogate *you*. Let us see who discovers the most."

He took her mouth again, and she answered swiftly, hotly. He slid his hands over her bodice, and she shivered, and arched into his urgent touch, pressing the delicious weight of her breasts against his hands.

"Ah, yes," he murmured against her lips. "Tell me more, Leila."

"You already know, damn you," she answered breathlessly.

"Not enough." He drew another long, deep kiss from her while he reached down for the fastenings of her bodice. Then, keeping her distracted with feather kisses along her cheek, her jaw, her neck, he quickly freed one hook, then another. He continued unfastening hooks and buttons while he brushed his mouth over her ear and teased with his tongue and grew dizzy with wicked delight when she shivered and twisted against him. Finally, impatient, she caught his hair and brought his mouth back to hers and pressed and coaxed until he surrendered, and answered with the passionate plunder she wanted.

Under his deft hands, her armaments surrendered, too: the twilled wool and silk of her bodice and, beneath, the soft cambric and, beneath . . . heaven . . . the warm silk of her lush breasts, rich with her scent . . . taut under his soft, wondering caress.

"Ah, Leila." His voice was soft and wondering, too, as he brushed his thumb over a hard, trembling bud. She answered with a moan, and drew his head down, and let him worship with his mouth, because there was no choice, for her, for him. No choice at all once they came together. They were strong-willed, both, but this desire made a mockery of will. Just as it did of honor. For him. For her.

And for this moment, for him, there was no will or honor or anything but her . . . welcome and warmth . . . creamy flesh under his lips, his tongue . . . and the intoxication of desire he heard in her low moan, when he took one tawny rose peak into his mouth and tenderly suckled.

At this moment, all the world was one woman and the need she stirred in him, fathoms deep, to the very bottom of his black, false heart. Lost in need, he could not keep himself from restlessly seeking more of her, pushing back every barrier in his way until her lavish bosom was fully exposed, and he could bury his face in that creamy softness.

Her caressing hands and aching sighs told him, as her trembling frame told him, that she was lost, too, for this moment. And lost beyond conscience, he pushed the moment on, with long, drugging kisses, while his too-quick hands were busy as well, dragging up her skirt, stealing under the petticoat, sliding swiftly over the silken drawers to the feminine secrets the fragile fabric so inadequately shielded.

The instant he touched the thin barrier, she recoiled, as though she'd been burned. But he was burned, too, for her damp heat was a fiery current that darted through his fingertips and raced through his veins. She was hot and ready for him, and he was on fire, mad to possess.

With one arm lashed against her back, he trapped her in a deep, plunging kiss while he found the silken drawstring. Swiftly untying it, he slid his hand under the fabric.

He was aware of her body stiffening, aware of her withdrawal even before she broke from his desperate mouth, but he couldn't draw his hand from that rapturous womanly warmth. He couldn't keep his fingers from tangling in the silken curls and closing over her moist heat in mindless possession.

"No," she gasped. "For God's sake—no."

"Please," he whispered, blind, besotted, needy. "Let me touch you, Leila. Let me kiss you." Even while he begged, he was sinking, ready to fall to his knees. He would die if he could not put his mouth to her sweet, damp heat.

She grasped a fistful of his hair and jerked him upright. "Stop it, curse you." Digging her nails into his wrist, she wrenched his hand away.

He stood panting like an animal, his loins aching, and watched in furious despair while she retied the drawstring, shoved her skirts down over her long, shapely legs, yanked up her chemise, and hastily refastened her bodice.

"On the table," she said, her voice throbbing. "You would have had me on the be-damned *worktable*. I wish I had been drunk. That at least would have constituted some sort of excuse. But I wasn't drunk. I wasn't flirting, making advances. My only fatal error, it seems, was trying to— Lord, how am I to explain?" She pushed herself off the worktable and gazed at him exasperatedly. "Don't you understand? I want to *do* something. Instead of waiting about, all the day. When we began this inquiry, you said you needed my help," she continued quickly, before he could answer. "You called me a 'partner.' But you're doing it all by yourself, and you don't even want to *tell* me anything. You'd never have told me about *Vingt-Huit* if I hadn't worked half of it out for myself—then nagged you for the rest. How was I to help when you wouldn't even tell me the basic facts about Francis? How was I to know what to look for?"

His conscience gnawed. He had kept her in the dark about *Vingt-Huit* only to protect himself, because he'd feared she'd never forgive him for using her.

"Why do you bother coming here at all, when you don't trust me?" she asked, her eyes still pleading with him. "Is it just to seduce me? Is that all I am? A challenge to your powers of seduction? An amusing problem to solve in your leisure time?"

"You are the worst problem of my life," he said bitterly. "And it is not amusing. This night I have trusted you with more than any one other person knows. But that is not enough for you. You want *everything*."

"So do you," she said. "But you don't want to give anything. You don't know how to be friends with a woman. Which shouldn't surprise me, since you don't know how to be friends with anybody. You don't know how to have a conversation that isn't manipulative, or—"

"You were trying to manipulate *me*!"

"Which is intolerable, obviously, since you took swift measures to put a stop to it." She reached up to smooth his rumpled neckcloth. "God forbid you should have to regard me as an equal, and play fair."

Though he suspected she was manipulating now, his heart responded to the physical gesture—with its hint of forgiveness, and more important, possessiveness—and softened accordingly. "You are not playing fair now, Leila. You are trying to confuse my mind. I do not know what you want."

"I'm trying to be patient," she said. "Because maybe if I'm patient and reasonable, you'll believe I can keep a cool head when need be. And maybe, in time, you'll actually let me help you."

He smiled. "I can think of several ways you can help—"

"With the inquiry," she said. She gazed up at him, her golden eyes lit with something startlingly like admiration. "I want to be *part* of it, knowingly, this time."

Then it finally dawned on him what had happened. She

thought he was a hero. *"Vingt-Huit,"* he said dazedly. "You were not distressed at all. You were . . . fascinated."

"Yes." She smiled, too. "I think it was a fascinating case, and you were brilliant. And this time, I want to be your *partner*."

Chapter 11

THOUGH WELL AWARE ISMAL HAD COME HOME after three o'clock in the morning, Nick mercilessly roused him at seven-thirty.

"Guess where the Duchess of Langford went yesterday," he said as he set the breakfast tray on Ismal's lap.

"I am not in a humor for riddles," Ismal said.

"Mount Eden."

Ismal had just raised the coffee cup to his lips. He set it down. One of Nick's tasks was to cultivate the servants of all those connected with the inquiry. Among these "new friends" was the Langfords' cook.

"She left about an hour after quarreling with Avory," Nick amplified. "It's speculated that she went to cry on the Dowager Lady Brentmor's shoulder—as I'm informed she's in the habit of doing."

The dowager was Jason's mother. She was also grandmother of Esme, now Lady Edenmont—the young woman Ismal had tried to steal ten years ago. According to Jason, Lady Brentmor was a formidable businesswoman who struck terror into the granite hearts of London's most powerful financiers. Her own heart was about as soft as a paving stone. Ismal doubted her shoulder was any more accommodating.

"Lady Langford's been going to her for years," Nick was saying. "Ever since she was a new bride and got into some money troubles. You said the duchess and Avory had a row about money. Maybe she's gone to Lady Brentmor because he's in deeper than he lets on."

"I do not like this," Ismal said.

"Well, you can't keep *everyone* confined to quarters." Nick moved away to open the drapes. "Can't stop them from going out, can't control who sees them and who doesn't. Can't arrange *everyone's* household to suit your convenience."

"I assume there is some point to these not so subtle remarks," Ismal said coldly. "You find fault with my methods?"

"I wouldn't dream of questioning your methods," Nick said. "But then, no one would, would they? Even Quentin must assume you're seriously trying to solve Beaumont's murder with your usual cold-blooded efficiency. So I couldn't possibly wonder why, considering her talents, you don't encourage Mrs. Beaumont to interact with as many people as possible. She practically had Sherburne eating out of her hand, you said."

"I do not want murder suspects eating out of her hand," Ismal said sharply. "She is not a professional. It is too dangerous."

Nick stared at him for a moment. "Oh. Yes, certainly. Shall I let Quentin know about the Duchess of Langford?" he asked in more mollifying tones. "He may want to go to Mount Eden and find out what that was all about."

"Yes. Go tell him. *Now.*"

HAVING EXPERIENCED DIFFICULTY running Quentin to ground, Nick didn't return until two hours later. By then, Ismal had washed, shaved, and dressed, and retired to the library to brood upon the sofa.

At eleven o'clock, Nick entered the library to inform his master that the Dowager Lady Brentmor was standing in the vestibule, insisting she knew perfectly well that the Comte d'Esmond was at home, and she had no intention of leaving until she'd spoken to him.

"She won't go away," Nick said. "I don't know what to do—short of picking her up and chucking her out the door."

Ismal was already on his feet, shrugging into his coat. He'd heard the noise, and all his instincts were on the alert. Now the old scar in his side twinged as well. Though he'd never met the woman, he'd heard enough about her from Jason to understand that being thrown bodily from the house wouldn't daunt her in the least.

"Send her up," he said.

Moments later, the door swung open and a small, fierce old lady marched into the room. She was scowling like a thunderhead and thumping a cane which must be intended primarily for use as a weapon, for she was in no need of its support. In her other hand she carried a purse nearly as big as she was.

Ismal had already arranged his countenance into a politely smiling welcome. Now he bowed—though he rather expected she'd take the opportunity to rap the cane upon his skull—and murmured that this was an unexpected and most pleasurable surprise.

"Unexpected it may be," she said with a sniff. "The pleasure I strongly doubt, but you was born a liar, I collect."

She stalked about the room, punctuating her steps with thumps of the cane.

"Read, do you?" she asked, eyeing the bookshelves.

"Yes, my lady. I can write as well."

Shrewd hazel eyes fixed on him. "I know that well enough. You're a dab hand with a pen, as I recall. Brilliant forgery that was, of Mrs. Stockwell-Hume's hand."

Ismal winced inwardly. Ten years ago he'd forged a provoking letter in Mrs. Stockwell-Hume's hand to lure the dowager and her granddaughter to London. "Your memory is excellent," he said, betraying not a glimmer of uneasiness.

"I didn't come to reminisce about old times," she said. "I come to have a look at you." She did so, eyeing him up and down, not once but three times.

"Handsome is as handsome does," she grumbled. Selecting the hardest chair in the room, she sat. "The question is, what've you been doing?"

"I believe Lord Quentin told you of my present task."

"Don't be tiresome. Sit down," she ordered. "I'd rather look a man in the eye without getting a crick in my neck."

Ismal drew up the next hardest chair and perched upon it.

She opened the immense purse and took out a document. "Lady Langford come to see me yesterday," she said, handing it over. "In a fever about that, among other things."

Ismal quickly perused the paper. "In December, Lord Avory bought one thousand pounds worth of shares in Fenderhill Imports," he said. "An unwise investment, you think?"

"Depends on your point of view," she replied. "Fenderhill Imports don't exist. Never did."

"Then he was deceived."

"What he was, was blackmailed." She scrutinized his face. "You ain't surprised. I know you've come across this sort of thing before."

"I first discovered the technique ten years ago," he said. "Bridgeburton provided similar 'receipts' to his blackmail victims, to help them account for the loss of large sums of money. He told me your son, Sir Gerald, had taught him the method."

"So he did," she said, not in the least disconcerted by the mention of her blackguard son. "And you come across the same sort of thing in that *Vingt-Huit* business Quentin told me about. So I guess it ain't hard to figure out who was blackmailing Avory."

"This would appear to be Francis Beaumont's handiwork," Ismal cautiously agreed. "I trust you did not tell Lady Langford so?"

She snorted. "What sort of halfwit do you take me for? I told her Avory bought worthless stock, and he ain't the first and won't be the last, and she should thank her lucky stars it was only a thousand quid. She spends as much on a Season's bonnets. It weren't the money that put her in such a taking, anyhow, but his impertinence, she claimed. Impertinence, my foot! He's a grown man, and it ain't any of her business what he does with his allowance, so long as he keeps within it and don't pester his ma and pa for more. Which he don't. Which ought to settle it, I should think." She thumped the cane impatiently. "Now, what's this she tells me about Avory being besotted with Leila Beaumont?"

"It is absurd," he said coldly. "What do you think—that scarcely is Madame Beaumont's husband buried before she begins hunting for a rich and titled replacement?"

"No need to get your innards in an uproar," she said. "I'm only passing on what his mama told me. Thought you ought to know she ain't happy about his calling on Beaumont's widow twice in one week—and staying far too long for propriety. I won't ask how long *you* been staying," she added scornfully. "I've met her. It don't take a genius to figure out why you're still dawdling about London on this plaguey business."

"Beaumont has been dead not even six weeks." Ismal kept his voice level. "Most of my investigations take months. Some, years. Surely you understand the delicacy and complexity of the problem. One does not assault it with a battering ram. That, apparently, is your technique. It is not mine."

"It certainly ain't my technique to confuse my breeding organs with my thinking one," she retorted. "I'll wager you ain't even looked into Beaumont's finances—though you know he come back to England next to bankrupt—and all the world knows he couldn't get a farthing of his wife's funds, not with Herriard minding 'em. Or do you think the finances of a man who lived on blackmail money ain't important? Not as important as sniffing about his widow's skirts, certainly."

Reining in his temper, Ismal pointed out that the man's wife was a crucial source of information. He explained about Sherburne and the stickpin—and how he'd learned more about Lord Avory's problems while trying to find out more about the stickpin. "And it was with Avory, I admit, that I became preoccupied," he said. "The marquess has some problems I am not at liberty to discuss. They are of a nature which would make him vulnerable to blackmail, which you have just confirmed."

Her shrewd gaze sharpened. "You sure Avory paid Beaumont to keep quiet about his own problem—or someone else's?" she asked.

Ismal knew this woman was no fool. If she asked the question, she had good reason. He thought it over. There was small advantage in publicizing another man's impotence. Coming from a drunkard and opium addict, the news was likely to be disregarded. Even if believed, it would be more likely to elicit pity than to cause disgrace.

"What 'someone else' do you have in mind?" he asked.

"Mebbe you didn't know that Avory's brother, Charles, didn't fancy women," she said. "Mebbe you didn't know it was Charles got that Carstairs boy the diplomatic post. That is to say, Charles talked his pa into using his influence. Not that I'd expect you to know. Lady Langford tells me a good deal she don't tell anybody else. And she didn't tell me about what Charles liked better than gels because she don't know, or don't want to. I figured that matter out for myself. I see a lot more than some people—mebbe because I ain't afraid to look."

Leaning toward him, she lowered her grating voice a fraction. "If I was you, I'd find out what Avory bought for his thousand quid. I'll wager you fifty it weren't Beaumont's worthless promise to keep quiet about his 'problem.' "

If what she said was true, Charles must have been romantically involved with Edmund Carstairs. Who had killed himself. Why? Ismal wondered, not for the first time. Why not simply resign? Unless something else had happened. Perhaps more than government documents had been stolen. Carstairs must have agreed and planned for that, and must have been prepared to deal with the consequences. Something else must have been taken, then, which he hadn't been prepared for.

"Letters," Ismal guessed. "Avory paid to get back his late brother's letters to Edmund Carstairs."

The dowager gave a disdainful sniff. "It appears you do have a brain, after all—so long as it ain't a buxom young widow you're talking to."

Ismal summoned his patience. "I am grateful for this valuable information, my lady. You have answered a question which has vexed Madame Beaumont and me very much. For, whether you wish to believe it or not, she and I talk of little else but the case. In truth, she cannot take her mind *off* it. She is like a dog, worrying a bone."

"What do you expect?" she demanded. "It ain't as though she's got much else to think about. From what I've heard, she's scarcely set foot out of the house in weeks."

"I do not keep her under lock and key," Ismal said, wondering if there was some sort of conspiracy afoot. First Leila, then Nick, now this old witch. "She is free to come and go as she pleases."

"Where the devil's she to go when she ain't *asked*?" the old witch demanded. "Why ain't you using your influence to get her out where she can do some good? If she's as quick and noticing and clever as you say—"

"It is *dangerous*."

"Then look out for her."

He stared at her. "I beg your pardon?"

"You heard me. You're good at not getting killed, ain't you? At not being dead when any normal person would be. According to Jason, you been poisoned, bashed in the head, shot at, drowned, stabbed, and Lord only knows what else. Watching out for a mere female should be child's play."

"I cannot be with her every moment," Ismal pointed out

irritably. "Even if I could, it would look very strange. People would talk."

"Don't be such a sapskull," she said. "Not every moment. I'll look after her while she's with me."

A feeling of cold dread settled into Ismal's gut. "But you are returning to Mount Eden."

"No, I ain't."

"But Lady Edenmont is expecting her babe any day, Quentin told me."

"Had it last night. A gel. Finally."

"You will want to be with her."

"No, I won't. I aim to be in London—since it's obvious you ain't getting anywhere on your own." She left the chair to yank upon the bell pull. "Might as well have that black-eyed rogue of yours bring us something fit to drink. You got the same look on your face Jason gets when he don't want to see reason."

AT NINE O'CLOCK that evening, Leila stood before her easel, pretending to paint while she wondered whether infatuation was playing tricks on her reason. Or at least her hearing.

Last night, Esmond had responded to her request by trying every way he could to change the subject. When that had failed, he'd pleaded exhaustion and decamped. Now, if her ears weren't deceiving her, he had actually just announced that he wanted her out sleuthing among Francis' enemies. Not only wanted it, but had arranged this very day to make it happen.

One of the upper class' most formidable women, the Dowager Lady Brentmor, was coming tomorrow to begin the process of getting Leila established in London Society.

According to Esmond, the old lady was even now telling her friends that her primary reason for coming to London was to visit Mrs. Beaumont and congratulate her on her triumphant handling of the Home Office imbeciles.

Leila was well aware that Lady Brentmor was notorious for her low opinion of men in general and her contempt for those in authority in particular. The dowager was also quick to defend women who, like herself, made their own way in the world despite the masculine forces arrayed against them.

It was, therefore, as Esmond explained, perfectly in character for Lady Brentmor to take under her wing a woman who had shown the authorities for what they were: a "lot of bullying ignoramuses." Those, according to him, were the dowager's exact words. Having met her months before, Leila was certain these were among the mildest of the old lady's choice stock of descriptives. She could make even Fiona blush.

It was also perfectly in character, Leila thought, for Esmond to choose a sponsor whom few in Society would dare contradict.

"If Lady Brentmor told the prime minister to jump off a bridge," Fiona had once remarked, "Wellington would meekly ask, 'Which one?' "

Leila had no doubt that Esmond had found the ideal chaperon. She couldn't help wondering about his abrupt change of mind, however. He'd just said that her talents were being wasted, that she would be of greater use out in the world gathering information—all of which was very flattering, and precisely what she wanted, desperately. Yet he didn't behave as though he was happy about it. Though she had kept on trying to paint while he talked, she could hardly fail to notice his restlessness.

He had scarcely sat down on the sofa before he got up to walk to the fire. Then he moved to the bookshelves and studied them. Then he went to the cupboards and opened and shut every single door. Then he went to the windows and studied the closed drapes. He went on to unstack and restack the canvases leaning against the wall. He ended his circuit of the studio at the worktable. Having made a neat pile of her sketchbooks, he was at present putting all the pencils into one jar and all the brushes into another.

"It sounds like an excellent plan," Leila said cautiously into the silence. "I assume she understands what I'll be doing—or have you persuaded her to sponsor me out of the goodness of her heart?"

"I have told her about the inquiry." He perched on the stool and, taking up a knife, began sharpening a pencil with quick, sure strokes. "I know she can be trusted. Quentin himself often consults her on financial matters. She has a vast network of informants in the world of commerce, here and abroad. In fact, it was she who called on me today. She had previously provided some information during the *Vingt-Huit* case. Yesterday, she obtained a document she believed I would be interested in."

He paused briefly. "I might as well tell you. Your husband was blackmailing Lord Avory. But it was not for the reason one might expect. We did not know—and Lady Brentmor was one of a very few who did, it seems—that Avory's elder brother was . . . attached to Edmund Carstairs."

"Attached?" Leila repeated uneasily.

Esmond explained.

She stared at him.

He shrugged. "Indeed, it vexes me. Charles was unforgivably careless. For him, an Englishman, to write indiscreet letters to another Englishman—in the diplomatic service, no less—is the height of stupidity. Worse, his younger brother—who *already* has problems because of this same young diplomat—must pay for the elder's mistake. Worse still is that Avory paid, most likely, to shield his parents—the same parents who cannot forgive him because he is not the model of perfection they think his brother was. Still, it is some comfort to know our affections are not misplaced. Avory may be confused, but he is not base or evil. Instead, it appears that he has been caught in a trap of others' making."

Leila realized her mouth had been hanging open for some time. She shut it and commenced to cleaning her brushes. Charles had been guilty of an unspeakable crime against nature and Esmond dismissed this monstrosity as *carelessness*. All that annoyed the count—and annoyance seemed to be his sole emotion—was that Charles had been *indiscreet*. Which shouldn't surprise her, given the cool way he'd described *Vingt-Huit*'s trade in sordid secrets and perversion.

She wondered whether there was any vice, any sin, any crime Esmond wasn't familiar with and equally casual about. A vivid image appeared in her mind's eye of herself, entangled with him upon the worktable, crazed with lust like an animal—and mere inches away from discovering what, precisely, he liked to do with a woman. She felt the blood draining from her face.

Who are you? she wanted to shriek. *What are you?*

"I have shocked you," he said.

She picked up her palette knife and began viciously scraping the palette. "I'm simply not quite adjusted to the fact that pursuing these sorts of puzzles is like putting one's hand in a nest of venomous snakes," she said. "The closer you get to the bottom of the matter, the more tangled it becomes with complications—and they all turn out to have *fangs*. But I suppose that's only because I'm not used to poking into other people's nasty secrets," she quickly added. "I daresay in time, I'll develop an immunity. Like yours."

"I was born in a viper's nest," he said, examining the deadly point he'd made. "I have lived among serpents. But so have you. The difference between us is one of degree—and of awareness, assuredly. You were kept in ignorance. But from my earliest consciousness, I knew what was about me. If I had not, I should have been dead long since."

She watched numbly while he returned the pencil to the jar and selected another. "If you are to go out into the world seeking a murderer, Leila, you had better understand what is about you. I shall be vastly annoyed if you get yourself killed."

A chill slithered down her spine.

"I shan't be altogether pleased myself," she managed to choke out. "If you're trying to terrify me, you're doing an excellent job. Do you want me out sleuthing or not?"

"I would prefer to keep you where you will be safe."

With you? she asked silently, while she watched the knife flick steadily, transforming her pencil to a needlelike shaft.

"But it is too late," he said. "You are fascinated, obsessed with this mystery, and you probe at me and plague me because there is no one else. *Tiens*, I must turn you loose to plague others—and hope, meanwhile, that your survival instincts are as strong as your inquisitive ones."

"There's only one killer," she said.

"And a host of people with secrets they might kill to protect." He tucked the pencil back among its fellows. "Please do not forget this, even for a moment. You must consider every one you deal with a venomous serpent and deal with each as the snake charmer deals with the cobra. *Everyone*, Leila. No exceptions. Trust no one."

Trust no one. Born in a viper's nest. Lived among serpents. Yes, that fit, she thought, turning toward her canvas—fireplace, footstool before it, a corner of the sofa. Simple interior. Unlike his. She had sensed early on that there was darkness behind his fair, angelic exterior. Darkness in his past and in his heart.

And he was right. She was fascinated and obsessed . . . with every thread of the case that connected to him and told her something about him and what he was. She did plague him, because he plagued her. She hardly cared any more who had killed her swine of a husband. It was the man who'd charmed and tormented Francis who fascinated her. A dangerous fascination, as Francis had learned to his cost. He'd compared Esmond to laudanum, but Esmond put it better: a snake charmer. Truth again.

Once he turned the charm upon you, you couldn't look away. He didn't have to beckon. His physical beauty and some innate magnetism drew effortlessly. When he did beckon—and all he needed were a few artfully chosen words, the right tone of voice—you were done for.

"Leila."

There. Soft, questioning, the faintest hint of anxiety. Just right. Perfect.

Slowly she brought her gaze to his and felt the tug, palpable, of that aching blue.

"Are you listening to me?" he asked. "It is important." He came off the stool.

"You want me to be careful," she said. "And discreet. I understand." She edged to the other side of the easel.

"I do not want you in danger," he said. "I would keep you safe, but all I do is make a prison, it seems. I trap you with me. It is not fair. I know this. I cannot help it." Moving nearer, he touched her hair. "I weary you with demands—your mind, your feelings, your body. It is not fair, as you said. With others, even though you will be working, there will be some amusement, stimulation, *non*? If not rest, a change at least. And the satisfaction of discovering your own way. You will like this, will you not?"

"Yes." That was the truth, too. To have something, some small part of her life, under her control. He understood that. But then, it was his business to understand others.

"I have pleased you, then?" he asked softly, taking her hand.

"Is that what you want?" she asked. "To please me?"

"Since the plan displeases me greatly, it must be for you," he said, playing with her fingers. "Fortunately, it is also sensible and efficient—which is what I shall tell myself a thousand times while I go crazy with worry."

"You can't expect me to believe you'll be sitting—or lying about—fretting, while I do all the work." She wondered despairingly how so light a touch, upon her fingers only, could flood every inch of her body with tingling sensation.

"I do not see what else I can do. All I seem to be good for lately is looking after one confused marquess and devising ways to lure one too-clever woman into my arms." He took her other hand. "I did not sleep so well last night, Leila. You cut up my peace."

"Knowing you hasn't been exactly tranquilizing for me, either," she said, her gaze dropping to their twined hands. Even now she felt the tug, though he wasn't pulling. Her body ached to be closer . . . to what? Physical beauty and fatal charm. Exteriors. She should be trembling to contemplate what lay within.

"It is true. I am a problem, I know." He released her hands and wandered away to the sofa.

Watching him subside into his usual oriental potentate pose, she wondered how much time he had spent in the East. Few western European aristocrats could have overcome years of breeding to loll about in that careless way. Fewer still could make it look so natural. If he beckoned with his hand and a crowd of dancing girls whirled into the room at the summons, Leila wouldn't have been in the least taken aback.

Mechanically, she reached for her sketchbook.

"Nay, Leila," he said. "Come, talk to me."

"I think we'll converse more productively at a distance," she said.

"I know you think I am unreasonable," he said. "But I am not altogether a brute. I wish to make amends." He laughed softly. "Come, I will teach you a trick—to manage me."

She gave him a look of patent skepticism.

"Well, then, what will you do?" he asked. "I am not like your husband. You have tried saying 'no' and I answer with coaxing. Or faulty hearing. The locked door is useless. You have tried taking a poker to me. Also useless. Do you wish to try something else—and risk failure? Or will you take advantage of my present remorseful mood and learn what I shall regret telling you later, when I recover?"

She supposed she had nothing to lose. If he was lying, she was done for. But she would be done for in any case. She tossed the sketchbook onto the worktable and crossed the room to him.

He shifted back and patted the exceedingly small space he'd made for her, near his waist. Cursing under her breath, Leila sat.

"There. Already I am quieting," he said. "Because you are near, where I want you to be, and I can feel your warmth."

She, too, was aware of warmth, and of the scent pulsing

in it, exotic, male. Like invisible smoke, it mingled with
her own, a thread of myrrh coiling through it—hers or his,
she couldn't tell.

"Now, the trick is to lull my mind," he said. "You do not
want me to think, because I am devious. You want to make
the male instincts sleepy, dull. You make a bargain with
me. Instead of the pleasure I seek, you will give me one
more acceptable to you." He brought her hands to his face.
"Weave me a dream with your hands. Make a beautiful
painting in my mind," he told her, guiding her hands to his
temples.

She didn't believe it was possible to lull or dull him in
any way. On the other hand, she couldn't pretend she
didn't want to touch him. The woman wanted to stroke and
caress. The artist wanted to study the angles and curves of
his intriguing face. She couldn't resist any more than the
sculptor, Phidias, could have resisted, had Apollo appeared
in his studio and, placing himself under the mortal artist's
hands, given him leave to study immortal beauty.

She slid her hands free. "Don't tell me any more," she
said. "Let me work it out on my own."

Reminding herself that he wanted to be lulled and
soothed—not examined—she began as she would have
wanted someone to begin on her. Lightly placing her fingers at the center of his forehead, she brushed outward.
Very gently. Not oil brushstrokes, but watercolor.

He closed his eyes and let out a whisper of a sigh.

She went on with feather-light strokes from the center
outward to the silken hairline. The faint lines on his
forehead—indiscernible until now, when she concentrated
there—eased under her rhythmic touch. She sensed, as
well, the slight relaxation in his breathing.

Encouraged, she moved on to the bridge of his nose and
stroked out over his eyebrows, noticing that they were
shades darker than his hair, and only a tint lighter than his
long, thick lashes. Then, down and outward she brushed
her fingers, from the patrician nose out along the high angle of his cheekbones. She found the tiny lines she'd noticed weeks ago, which tightened when he was disturbed.

She discovered as well something she hadn't noticed before. Just below his right ear near the jawbone was an irregular line of minute scars.

Whatever he was, whatever he'd done, he'd suffered more damage than she'd guessed. The awareness hurt, gentled her inwardly, and in an instinctive act of comforting, she stroked his hair back.

"Ah, yes," he murmured, turning his head into the strokes.

Like a cat, she thought, biting back what must surely be an idiotish smile. He wanted to be petted, wicked creature, and like any cat unself-consciously sought more.

But she liked it, too: the silken hair sliding over her fingers, the warmth of his scalp, the supple muscles of his neck, moving sinuously in response to her hand.

At this moment, he was a beautiful cat, delicious to stroke. She enjoyed the power, even the uncertainty of it—the awareness that he was dangerous and could turn upon her at any moment. The sense of imminent danger stirred its own dark species of pleasure.

At any rate, he seemed to like this best, and his breathing was slowing, deepening. Remembering the magic he'd worked on her, she focused on stroking and kneading his scalp and neck in the same hypnotic way.

The action lulled her as well. Her mind wandered through dreamy images—of shimmering golden cats prowling silk-draped rooms . . . deep blue midnight through an open window . . . the mingled scents of flowers and herbs and smoke . . . a faint melody, the aching wail of a woodwind . . . a summer breeze whispering in fir trees.

Entranced, she lost track of time and might have gone on petting her purring jungle cat all night, but even her strong hands had their limits. Aching muscles brought her back to the waking world . . . and to the realization that the purr she heard was the deep, steady breathing of a man sunk in slumber.

He seemed truly asleep this time, for when she took her hands away, he didn't move a muscle. Experimentally, she shifted away a bit. No response. She got up from the sofa. He was oblivious.

She padded quietly out of the studio and carefully closed the door behind her. Then, erasing the triumphant smile from her face, she headed downstairs. She found Eloise in the dining room, polishing the china cupboard.

"Monsieur has fallen asleep," Leila told her.

Eloise's sleek eyebrows went up.

"I don't know whether to wake him or not," Leila said. "The fact is, I'm rather tired myself, and he's arranged for me to meet with an important caller tomorrow. The Dowager Lady Brentmor. I want to be at my best."

Eloise nodded. "If he wakes, he will wish you to go back to work with him—for he is a man, and *insensible*. But you wish to make an early bedtime, which is wise. Go to bed, madame, and enjoy your respite. Be assured he will be roused and out of the house before daylight."

"Yes. Thank you. And—and if he wakes before then—"

"He shall go home, madame." She gave Leila a conspiratorial smile. "You need your rest. It will not be disturbed, I promise you."

Chapter 12

THREE WEEKS LATER, LEILA WAS BEGINNING TO wonder whether she really *was* being left to do all the work.

Esmond hadn't sneaked into her house since the night she'd put him to sleep. He had said something then about her finding her own way. Evidently, he'd meant it, because the following day, during her first meeting with Lady Brentmor, the dowager had relayed a message to that effect: when Mrs. Beaumont discovered something of importance, she was to summon the count. Until then, he'd keep out of her way. With which proposal Lady Brentmor heartily agreed.

"You ain't never done Society proper before," she had said. "It's *work*, my gel, and make no mistake. The last thing you'll need is him pestering you in the middle of the night when you're dead on your feet and your head's pounding like a steam engine. It's going to be talk, talk, talk, dinning in your ears until you wish you was born deaf."

As it turned out, the dowager hadn't exaggerated.

In accordance with proper mourning etiquette, the gentlemen could not ask Leila to dance or indulge in even the

mildest flirtation. That left her most often in the company
of women and limited her exercise to talking and listening.
Thanks to Lady Brentmor's inexhaustible energy, Leila
had been talking and listening for nearly every minute of
her waking hours.

At the moment, she was pretending to be listening to
and watching a somewhat inept comedy being enacted
upon the stage beneath the dowager's theater box. In reality, Leila was wrestling with a pair of riddles while trying
very hard not to let her eyes stray to a box nearby. Lord
Avory's box, to be precise, which he and Esmond occupied
at present.

Leila didn't want to look that way. She had seen Esmond many times in these last three weeks at the various
entertainments she attended. She had found that if she
wanted to speak privately with him about the case, she was
the one who'd have to make it happen. She had resisted
that temptation. She meant to continue resisting until she
had something of value to share. She wanted to present
him with solutions or at least solid clues, not questions.
And only if her information would advance the inquiry.
She wasn't sure that her two riddles would. But they
nagged at her.

First, there was Sherburne. Ever since she'd learned that
he had led Society in snubbing her husband, Leila had assumed it was the only revenge he dared for Francis' debauching Lady Sherburne. According to the dowager's
gossipy friends, though, Sherburne had first cut Francis at
Lady Seales' rout. That had taken place more than a week
before Sherburne destroyed his wife's portrait. Had he
waited all that time after discovering Francis' treachery to
take out his frustrations on the painting? Or had Francis
previously offended him in some other way? If so, how?

The second problem sat beside her: Fiona. She had returned to London yesterday—without Lettice—and something clearly was wrong. She had hardly mentioned her
sister at all, except in the most vague and evasive way.
Leila doubted her friend would have returned if the girl
were gravely ill. On the other hand, Fiona seemed far more

troubled now than she had been when she left for Dorset. Her eyes were dull, her color poor, and she had been unusually subdued since yesterday.

"Ain't asleep, are you?" The dowager's sharp inquiry jolted Leila from her meditations and to the realization that the curtain had fallen for the interval. While assuring the dowager she was fully awake, Leila darted a glance at Avory's box. Empty now.

She turned to Fiona, who was watching her with a faintly amused expression.

"He was trying very hard not to look this way," Fiona said. "With mixed success."

"I collect you refer to Lord Linglay," Leila said coolly. "I'm told that jerking motion of his head is the result of a palsy." She addressed the dowager. "Is that not so, Lady Brentmor?"

"He's a decrepit old goat," the old lady answered. "Ogles everybody, especially the servant gels." The box door opened then, and she glanced over her shoulder. "Well, look what the cat drug in."

Leila didn't have to look. She felt the air change and pulse even before she caught the faint, familiar scent. Turning slightly in her chair, she directed her forced smile at David, just as though every iota of her consciousness wasn't concentrated on the man with him.

She directed her chattily bright words to David, too, while pretending not to notice that Esmond, who had advanced to pay his respects to Lady Brentmor, was standing two vibrating inches away.

Several agonizing minutes later, the two men left, and Leila found she couldn't for the life of her remember a word of what had been said. All she could remember was scent . . . the brush of a coat against the sleeve of her gown . . . and the stabbing blue of his eyes.

Even while desperately hoping her delirium had gone unnoticed, Leila braced herself for a dose of Fiona's teasing.

The attack came from the other side, however, and the artillery wasn't aimed at her.

"Plague take you, Fiona Elizabeth!" the dowager cried. "What's that boy done to you to be treated so shabby?"

Fiona went rigid. Leila was too stunned to open her mouth.

"He asked after your sister," Lady Brentmor went on, leaning over Leila's lap to scowl at Fiona. "You know he's worried to death about her. And you look at him like he just crawled out of a rathole. Think Letty's going to do better than him? A royal duke, mebbe? If I was you, I'd be thanking Providence the boy *bothered* to ask, after the scene you made last winter."

Lady Brentmor drew back. "Threatened to horsewhip him, she did," she told Leila. "Fine manners for a lady, don't you think? Fine way to show her gratitude. Horsewhip *him*—Langford's heir. Mebbe she forgot how Langford and her pa was bosom bows. Mebbe she forgot it was Langford found places for all them brothers of hers after her pa died."

Fiona had not moved a muscle through this diatribe, but sat woodenly staring at the stage. Now she sprang up. Without a word, she swept out of the box, slamming the door behind her.

Leila leapt up, too, but the dowager grabbed her arm. "Go careful," she said, dropping her voice. "Watch what you say. But don't let her off 'til she tells you. Not only about Avory, but about what Beaumont done. I'll lay you any odds he got his hands on Letty."

Leila glared at her. "That is my *friend* you—"

"You can't afford friends this minute, my gel. This is business. You got a job to do. I primed her. Now you best set your mind to finishing it."

Leila shot a glance at Avory's box. The two men were talking, their heads bent close, but she was sure Esmond hadn't missed Fiona's exit. He'd expect answers.

"Goddamn," she muttered, and hurried out of the box.

A short while later, after a frantic search, she stormed into the ladies' retiring room. She dug into her reticule, thrust a coin in the attending servant's hand, and ordered her out.

When the door had closed behind the attendant, Leila marched up to the screen. "I know you're not there on nature's call," she said. "Shall I join you or will you come out and give me the explanation you should have done months ago, Fiona? What did Francis do to your sister, and why do you blame David? And what in blazes do you think to accomplish by hiding her away in Dorset?"

Fiona came out from behind the screen, her eyes bright with unshed tears. "Oh, Leila." Her voice caught. "She's breaking her heart over him. What the devil am I to do?"

Leila held out her arms. With a choked sob, Fiona went into them. The tears flowed then, and soon, she was stammering out the story.

It had happened at the Linglays' anniversary ball, in early December. Lettice had danced twice with David, despite Fiona's warnings to keep a safe distance from Francis' friends. Since Lettice had proved incapable of behaving wisely, Fiona had gone after David and warned him off. He left the party immediately after. But Francis stayed to plague Fiona. He had mockingly told her that everyone in the room could see Lettice was besotted. And all would agree she'd make Langford's heir the ideal wife: she was excellent breeding material, wasn't she? The Woodleighs did breed like rabbits. Beyond doubt she'd have David's heir in her belly when she stood at the altar, saying, not "I do," but "I did."

Just as enraged as he'd intended to make her, Fiona had responded by enraging him. She'd taunted him about Esmond.

"Forgive me, Leila," she said, drawing away. "But it was the only way I could think of to upset him."

Leila led her to a chair and nudged her down. "I understand," she said. She found her handkerchief and pressed it into Fiona's hands. "Francis had a gift for finding sore spots and he adored twisting the knife. So you went after *his* sore spot. Which is only natural. Though usually a mistake. Because, being Francis, he was bound to get even. Which he did, I suppose, by going after Lettice."

Fiona wiped her eyes and blew her nose. "It was hours

later when she went missing. I wasn't terribly alarmed. I'd thought Francis had been long gone, that he'd left right after our row. I learned my mistake when I finally found Lettice. In the conservatory. Dead drunk on the floor." She gave a shaky laugh. "She was a sight—half in, half out of her gown. Her hair—" She hiccupped. "But he hadn't r-ravished her. He wasn't *that* reckless. All he t-took were her g-garters."

"To humiliate her. And you, of course." Leila moved to the washstand. Her hands trembling a little, she poured water into the basin.

"You can guess why he stole them," said Fiona.

Leila kept her back to her friend, while her mind worked feverishly. "A trophy," she said, keeping her voice even. "To show off to his friends."

If he had shown David, she thought as she dampened a dainty linen towel, David would have killed him. Yet the timing was wrong. David would have done it right away, in the first heat of outrage—and not sneakily. David wasn't sneaky. And Francis wouldn't have waited until January—a month and more later—to show those garters. He would have done it within hours, or a day or two at most. And he'd want to show them off to someone he'd believe would applaud his daring. A more experienced rakehell than David. Someone to share a private joke. It would have to stay private, because Lettice was not just a virgin, but one of good family, a member of the nobility. Out of bounds, in short. If word got out, Francis would be . . . persona non grata. Which he had become. Thanks to . . .

Leila swung abruptly toward her friend, the damp towel clutched in her hand. "Sherburne," she said.

Fiona stared at her.

"Lord love you, Fiona." Leila shook her head. "I'll wager David knows nothing about the garters business. It was *Sherburne* Francis showed them to." She shoved the towel into her friend's hands. "Wash your face. And tell me what's so unspeakably wrong with David."

* * *

THE ANSWER FIONA gave proved to be the most venomous serpent of all. And the venom sped through Leila's system, leaving her shaken and sickened. She couldn't afford the luxury of indulging her emotions, however. This was business, as Lady Brentmor had reminded, and Leila was determined to handle it with all the brisk dispatch Esmond would have employed. Not with his infernal tact, though. That was beyond her capabilities at present.

"You asked me before what you were to do," she told Fiona. "You are the man of the family, are you not? David wants to wed Lettice. What would your father have done, in the circumstances?"

"Bid him to blazes, as I did," Fiona said. But there was a trace of doubt in her voice.

"Your father would have told him *why*," Leila said. "Your father would agree that a man has a right to face his accuser. And that man should be given a chance to defend himself if he can."

"Are you mad?" Fiona bolted up from the chair. "I cannot—"

"If you cannot, then you're a coward," Leila said calmly.

Fiona stared at her.

"Well?" Leila asked. "Are you or are you not?"

"Blast you."

That was all the answer Leila needed.

Moments later, the retiring room attendant—enriched by an additional coin—carried Leila's message to Lord Avory. Within minutes, he and Esmond were hurrying toward the main entrance of the theater.

Leila was standing there with a crimson-faced Fiona.

"Lady Carroll is unwell," she told David. "Would you be kind enough to take her home?"

David's countenance promptly assumed an equally vivid shade of red. But aristocratic breeding swiftly took over. With resolute courtesy he pronounced himself honored to oblige. The words were hardly out of his mouth before he briskly signaled for a lackey and ordered his carriage.

"I believe Lady Carroll would prefer to wait *outside* for

the carriage," Leila told him as the lackey bustled away. "She needs air. Do you not, Fiona?" she asked sweetly while bending a threatening look upon her friend.

"Above all things," Fiona replied, adding under her breath, "Confound you."

David dutifully advanced and offered his arm. Fiona grimly accepted it.

Leila waited until the two were safely out the door and upon the pavement before daring to meet Esmond's bemused gaze.

"I hope to heaven you're well on your way to curing him," she said. "I hope his male disability is *all* that's wrong with him. Because if it isn't, there'll be the devil to pay tomorrow."

His gaze slid away. "The play is nearly ended," he said in polite, carrying tones. "I understand you will be supping with Lady Brentmor after."

"I've lost my appetite." Leila turned away and left him.

ISMAL ENTERED LEILA'S kitchen in time to hear Lady Brentmor's carriage clatter away from the front door. He reached the ground floor hall just as Leila was heading up the stairs.

He called softly to her. She stopped short at the landing and swung round.

"I'm *tired*," she said. "Go home."

He continued up the stairs after her. "You are not tired. You are running away. I understood what you said to me before. I have a strong suspicion what the trouble is."

"Oh, no, it's no trouble at all." Her voice was caustic. "Merely the usual thing. Merely catching you out in a few more falsehoods, that's all. Or should I say *discretions*—because you seldom actually lie outright. You just sneak ever so cautiously about the truth."

She marched on up the stairs. "Every time I manage to drag one of your pestilential secrets out of you, I'm fool enough to think that's the end of it, and the picture's clear at last. But it never is, because you aren't. You're a god-damned Proteus. Every time I turn around, you turn into someone else, something else. No wonder Francis said you weren't human. The mastermind of *Vingt-Huit*, the genius at figuring out what people wanted and making them pay for it—even *he* couldn't figure out what you wanted. Who you wanted. Me . . . or *him*."

She had reached the first floor and was continuing up, Ismal trailing after her. The last bitter utterance did not take him by surprise. He remembered what she'd said about Avory: *I hope his male disability is all that's wrong with him.* Ismal had a good idea of what Lady Carroll had told her.

"It was my business to make certain he did *not* know what I wanted," he said mildly. "The success of my mission—even my life, perhaps—depended on this. Come, you must understand. You should not be so agitated."

"I am *tired*," she said. "I'm tired of having to wrench the truth out of you—and having it come down on my head like the club in a Punch and Judy show. I'm tired of being struck down and having to bounce up again, pretending I feel nothing."

She reached her bedroom door. "You could have warned me, Esmond. You could have prepared me. Instead, I had to stand there and listen to Fiona tell me my husband was a *sodomite*. That David was one of his—his *boys*. And that it was *you* Francis was jealous about, not me. That he made the fuss about you because he wanted you for himself. And while she treated me to these stunning revelations, I had to pretend I wasn't in the least affected."

She pushed the door open. "My bedroom," she said. "Please make yourself at home, monsieur. I'm well aware you can't be kept out. What you might want here is another matter altogether. I haven't the least idea. But I collect I'll find out. And I suppose I'll survive. I'm good at that. At bouncing back. Surviving."

She stormed into the room, tearing her bonnet off and hurling it aside. Ismal followed and gently closed the door behind him.

"I'm good at a lot of things," she raged on. "At falling in

love with the Devil's spawn, certainly. I have a genius for it, don't you think? And for leaping out of the pan, straight into the flames. From Papa to Francis to *you*."

He leaned back against the door, a sledgehammer driving at his heart with slow, fierce blows. "In love?" he repeated, his mouth dry. "With me, Leila?"

"No, with the Bishop of Durham." She fumbled at her cloak fastenings. "For all I know, you'll be *him* next. And do as brilliant a job as you did disguised as a constable." She ripped off the coat. "What else have you been, I wonder? How long have you been a French count? How long have you been *French*?"

He stiffened.

She swept to the dressing table, flung herself onto the chair, and began pulling pins from her hair. "Alexis Delavenne, Comte d'Esmond, is it? Where did they find your title, I wonder? One of the unfortunate families decimated during the Terror? Were you the infant Delavenne—sent away and hidden—until it was safe to return and claim your birthright? Is that the story you and your colleagues fabricated?"

He stood unmoving, outwardly calm: a normal, civilized man patiently absorbing the outpourings of an overwrought woman. Yet the barbarian inside him believed the Devil must be whispering these secrets in her ear. It was surely the Devil who made Ismal choke on the smooth denials and evasions ready to spill from his tongue. It must be the Devil who held him helpless, transfixed on one treacherous word: love.

It was that word which tangled his brain and tongue, which opened the rift in his proud, well-guarded heart, leaving a place that ached, needing tending. Needy, he could only ask, like a foolish, besotted boy, "Do you love me, Leila?"

"If you can call anything so monstrous *love*. I'll be damned if I know what else to call it." She snatched up her hairbrush. "But names don't signify, do they? I don't even know yours. There's the hell of it," she said, dragging the brush through her thick, tangled hair. "That I should care for and want the respect of a man who's utterly false."

His conscience stabbed deep. "You must know I care for you." He came away from the door to stand behind her. "As to respect—do you not understand? Do you think I would seek your help—send you on your own to work—if I did not respect your intellect, your character? Never have I relied upon and trusted a woman as I have you. What better proof could you want than what I did this night? I did not interfere. I trusted you to deal with your friend. I trusted that you judged aright in sending her away with Avory."

She met his gaze in the mirror. "Does that mean it wasn't a mistake? Does that mean David isn't what Fiona said he was? Was she wrong about him? About Francis—and the rest?"

The rest. It was himself she meant. Ismal stared incredulously into her accusing tawny eyes. "Allah grant me patience," he whispered, stunned. "Do you truly believe I was your husband's lover? Is *that* what has upset you?"

She set down the brush. "I don't know who you are," she said. "I don't know *what* you are. I don't know anything about you." She rose to push past him to the nightstand. Yanking the drawer open, she pulled out a sketchbook.

"Look at that," she said, thrusting it at him. "I draw what I see, what I sense. Tell me what I've seen and sensed, Esmond."

He opened the sketchbook and began leafing through the pages. It was filled with sketches of him—standing before the fire, at the worktable. He turned the page and paused. On the sofa. Lying in state, like a pasha. He turned to the next page. Again. Pages later, her clever pencil was transforming him. The cushions about his head became a turban. The well-tailored English coat had softened into a loose tunic. The trousers were full, the fabric falling in silken folds.

The old scar in his side was throbbing ominously. This was the Devil's work, he told himself. The Devil whispered his secrets in her ear and guided her mind, her fiendish hand.

"You just said 'Allah.'" Her voice was low, troubled. "You call yourself *Esmond*. Es . . . mond. 'East of the world,' one might translate. Is that where you really come from? Another world, to the east? I've heard it's different. Altogether."

He closed the book and laid it down on the nightstand. "You have a curious image of me," he said.

"Esmond."

"I do not lie with men," he said. "It is not to my taste. I did not tell you about your husband's tastes because I knew you would make yourself crazy and sick. I was unaware Lady Carroll knew of the matter. In Paris, your husband was discreet. Evidently, in England he became reckless about this, along with everything else. Suicidal, perhaps, for it is a hanging offense in this intolerant country."

"Intolerant? Do you—"

"What does it matter what one human being does in private with a willing partner—or ten partners, for that matter? What should it matter what I have done or not done? Or what *you* have done or not done?" he demanded—and silently cursed himself when she backed away, to the foot of the bed.

He caught the shreds of his self-control. "How am I to know what tastes your husband cultivated in you?" he asked more gently. "Or fears? Or revulsions? Do you not think both of us must have some trust? Never have I wanted a woman as I want you, Leila. Do you truly believe I would wish to distress you, shock you?"

She was rubbing her thumb against the bedpost, her brow furrowed.

He started cautiously toward her. "Leila—"

"Tell me your name," she said.

He stopped short. Curse her. To hell with her. No woman was worth—

"You don't have to," she said, still frowning at the bedpost. "We both know you can lure me straight into this bed with some lie or evasion or other. And I know that learning your name won't change anything. I'll still be a whore. And you'll know everything about me. It can't be helped. I'm . . . besotted." She swallowed. "I'm so tired of fighting with myself, trying to be what I'm not. I just want this one thing, you see. Your name. That's all."

He would have given her the world. If she asked, he would gladly abandon everything and take her away and shower her with his treasures. Anything she wanted.

She wanted his name.

He stood, fists clenched, heart pounding.

He saw a tear glisten at the corner of her eye. He watched her blink it back.

The rift inside widened.

Shpirti im, his soul called to hers. My heart.

He turned his back and left the room.

TO HELL WITH him, then, Leila told herself as she prepared for bed.

To hell with him, she told herself hours later, when she woke sweating from a dream, which she angrily banished to the deepest recesses of her mind.

Whatever Esmond felt for and wanted from her, it wasn't important enough to make him yield one small point: his curst name.

He expected trust. He was incapable of giving it, even to a woman who'd offered all hers, and her pride as well. She'd told him she loved him—as though that would matter. Women, men—and wild beasts, for all she knew—had been falling in love with him all his life. He thought no more of it than he did of breathing.

At least she wasn't the only idiot, she consoled herself hours later, when she rose and dressed and went downstairs, determined to eat her breakfast. She would not starve on Esmond's account. She'd refused to let Francis make a wreck of her, hadn't she? She was damned if she'd let Esmond affect her appetite.

Leila had scarcely sat down before Gaspard entered the

dining room to announce that Lady Carroll was at the door. Moments later, Fiona was at the breakfast table, slathering butter and preserves on one of Eloise's enormous muffins.

"I thought you'd want to be the first to know," she was saying. "David leaves this afternoon for Surrey, to seek Norbury's permission to court Lettice."

The permission was merely a formality. If Fiona had pronounced David acceptable, the others must. Leila filled her friend's coffee cup. "Then I may conclude you're satisfied he's not a monster of depravity."

"Not a monster, no. But he didn't pretend to be a model of innocence, either, and so one must give him credit for honesty. And for poise," Fiona added as she dropped a lump of sugar into the coffee. "For I did set my teeth and tell him direct that Francis claimed an intimate knowledge of his hindquarters. 'Well, he was lying, as usual,' says His Lordship, quiet and polite as you please. So I got just as quiet and polite and asked if anyone else had such a knowledge, because I wouldn't put my sister in the hands of a mollying dog. Marriage is difficult enough, I told him, without those sorts of complications."

"Complications," Leila repeated expressionlessly, while she wondered whether murder would fall into the same category.

"Well, I know what goes on at public school, don't I? Or if not there, then at some point during the Grand Tour." Fiona bit into her muffin and chewed thoughtfully. "Forbidden fruit. Boys will be boys, Papa would say. But one must draw the line when it becomes a habit. Bad enough to catch your husband with the chambermaid, but when it's the groom or the pot boy—"

"I quite understand," Leila said. Grooms, serving lads, boys on the streets, for all one knew, she thought, sickened.

Her Ladyship went on talking between mouthfuls. "Anyhow, he bravely admitted to one drunken episode, a few years ago. He gave me his word of honor that was the first and only time. Then, still polite as ever, he wanted to know if there was anything else troubling me. 'Should I know of anything else?' I asked him. 'Can you promise that my sister will be safe and happy in your hands?' Then he became rather maudlin. I shan't repeat his effusions. Suffice to say, he is wretchedly in love with Letty, and she thinks the sun exists solely to shine on him. It's thoroughly disgusting. Is there sausage in that covered platter, love?"

"Bacon." Leila handed it over. "Did you mention the garter business?"

"I treated him to the whole story." Fiona dropped three rashers of bacon onto her plate. "It was obvious he hadn't known. He went white as a sheet. When he finally collected himself, however, he did it thoroughly. No more dramatics. He simply said, 'No one shall ever distress her again, Lady Carroll. You have my word. I shall take care of her, I promise you.' Well, what was I to say? I told him he might call me Fiona, and recommended he speak to Norbury as soon as may be—and get to Dorset before Letty murders my aunt."

Leila mustered a smile while she watched her friend make short work of the bacon. "And they all lived happily ever after," she murmured.

"Perhaps he'll ask Esmond to stand as groomsman," said Fiona. "Speaking of whom—"

"We weren't."

"What *has* been going on while I've been away?" Fiona attacked another muffin. "Something terribly discreet, no doubt, for I haven't heard a whisper."

"You've heard nothing because there *is* nothing."

"You were looking at each other in the same famished way David and Letty gaped at each other during the Fatal Ball. It was quite painful to watch."

"To imagine, you mean," Leila said stiffly. "Just as you imagined David was some evil pervert longing to do unspeakable things to your little sister."

"Actually, it was the promiscuity that bothered me. Neglect, disease—the sorts of things a wife has virtually no control over. As to unspeakable acts—Letty is no milk and water miss, you know. If she doesn't like it, she won't put up with it."

Fiona swallowed the last of the muffin. "Or am I naive?

Is there something you know and I don't? Was Francis a brute in bed as well as out of it?"

"David is not Francis, as I told you several times last night," Leila said. "As I hope you discovered for yourself. From what you tell me, David answered in a frank, gentle-manly way—which is more than most of the men we know would do in like circumstances. To have his masculinity impugned—and with Francis, of all men—a filthy, sodden lecher—"

"Oh, I knew I was risking my neck, to accuse him of a hanging offense." Fiona wiped crumbs from her mouth. "Indeed, it's a wonder His Lordship didn't throw me from the carriage. But that's why I could believe him, you see. He took it like a man and answered me straight, man to man—without turning into the maddened animal most men become when you touch a sore spot. Except for the few, like Francis, who answer with a stab at *your* sore spot. Francis was good at that, laughing and mocking at what troubled you, and making a cruel joke of it. Gad, he was a swine." Her voice deepened and darkened. "He's dead—and the brute is still troubling us, still poisoning our minds and lives. He fouled everything he touched. Because of him, I nearly ruined my sister's chance for happiness. I listened to his filth, and believed it—when I of all people should have known better. When I'd spent years watching what he did to others—and worst of all, to you."

"It's over," Leila said, uneasy. "You've mended it."

"It isn't over for you, though, is it?"

"Of course it is," Leila said. "I've helped fix what I could. The Sherburnes are living in each other's pockets. David and Letty will be betrothed before the week is out, I daresay. And—"

"And you're still not cured of Francis Beaumont."

"I do not—"

"Francis didn't want you to know even a moment of happiness with any man," Fiona interrupted. "Especially not Esmond." She got up and came round the table to crouch beside Leila's chair. "Recollect what your husband did to my sister after I taunted him about Esmond," she said, her eyes searching Leila's. "Recollect the poison he dropped in my ear about David. I know Francis poisoned your mind about love—and lovemaking, no doubt—long ago. Don't tell me he didn't increase the dose when it came to Esmond."

"You're obsessed with Esmond," Leila said tightly. "You know far less of him than you do of David, yet you've been urging me to an affair practically from the moment you clapped eyes on that curst Frenchman. You invited him to Norbury House, you sent him after me when I fled, and you seem unable to spend an hour in my company without mentioning him. Yet you know no more of his character than you do of the man in the moon's. I half suspect it's sheer spite. Francis is dead, and you *still* want to spite him."

"I shouldn't mind in the least if it added to his eternal sufferings." Fiona took Leila's hand and pressed it to her cheek. "I shouldn't mind anything that added to his punishments for what he did to you—to anyone I hold dear," she said softly. "When I have trouble sleeping, or feel in the least agitated, I imagine him in his death agonies, or enduring the hideous torments of hell. It is wonderfully soothing." She smiled. "Do I shock you, love?"

Deeply. Chillingly. A question was forming in Leila's mind: Where had Fiona been the night before Francis died?—the night she'd been so late reaching Norbury House?

"You might," she said, "if I didn't know you never mean half what you say. All the same, it isn't soothing to *my* sensibilities to be urged to ruin just to satisfy your hunger for revenge."

"I said I shouldn't *mind*," Fiona corrected gently. "I assure you I am not so demented as to actively seek revenge on a dead man. He poisoned everything he touched—and died of his favorite poison. Poetic justice, don't you think? I'm satisfied with that. His afterlife I am content to leave in the hands of Providence." Releasing Leila's hand, she rose.

"Likewise, I should be content to see you in proper hands. Because you're right about one thing: from the moment I clapped eyes on Esmond, I was positive he was the one for you. I can't explain. It just looked like, felt like . . . Fate."

Chapter 13

THAT NIGHT, LEILA LEFT MRS. STOCKWELL-Hume's card party early, claiming a headache. While the carriage maneuvered through the evening traffic, she was recalling Esmond's sarcastic comments the first night they'd met privately: a cold trail . . . a host of suspects to be dealt with cautiously . . . a case that could occupy the rest of his life. She wished now that she'd heeded the warning.

She certainly wished she had never left Norbury House that fatal day in January. She wished she'd stayed and minded her own damned business.

As Francis' killer had expected her to do.

As Fiona had cajoled and begged her to do.

"Damn," Leila muttered to the empty carriage. "And damn again."

Between callers and dressmaker appointments, it had not been very difficult to keep the nagging suspicion at the back of her mind. But now there was no distraction, only the chilling recollection of the venomous hatred glittering in Fiona's eyes when she'd spoken of Francis and poetic justice.

Fiona certainly had a motive, every bit as powerful as

Sherburne's or David's. She had, moreover, the character, brains, and guts to avenge her sister's honor.

The evidence was circumstantial, but damning.

Plenty of people had known of Leila's plans to spend at least a week at Norbury House with Fiona and her family. The arrangements had been made well in advance—a few weeks after the Fatal Ball, as it happened. Any of Francis' enemies—and their name was legion—could have known and taken advantage of Leila's absence from home.

It might have been anyone.

But it was Fiona who'd arranged for Leila's absence. It was Fiona who'd been delayed at the last minute and bundled Leila off to Surrey with a cousin. It was Fiona who'd arrived, very late, on the night someone had put poison in Francis' laudanum.

Fiona, who'd never had a headache in her life, had blamed her tardiness on a headache. She'd had to take laudanum and lie down. The ailment having cleared by mid-evening, she'd left London and raced to Norbury House. That was her story. Her alibi, Leila amended.

It didn't matter, she told herself. If one meant to excuse David for murder, one had bloody well better be prepared to excuse Fiona—to excuse everybody, in fact, because Francis was a swine who should have been hanged long since. It didn't matter who killed him or why. Justice had already been done.

So much for English justice, she thought bleakly as the carriage turned into the square. So much for her morals. So much for Andrew's efforts to make a decent human being of her. All she'd learned was how to pretend to be decent. Under the skin, she was Jonas Bridgeburton's daughter. The instant morality inconvenienced her, she knocked it down and ground it under her heel.

She doubted, in fact, that she'd truly wanted to solve the murder in the first place. It wasn't her conscience that had driven her to Quentin, but Esmond. She'd confessed the smaller crime so that he'd believe she hadn't committed the greater one. Very likely her intuition had told her Quentin would send for Esmond.

At any rate, common sense surely must have told her that Esmond could solve the murder without her help. She could have refused to become involved, or at least so deeply involved. Instead, for every inch Esmond had offered her, she'd demanded a mile. From helping to partnership . . . to possession.

Because it was Esmond she was obsessed with solving. It was his heart she'd been trying to unlock with her clumsy pick.

Last night she'd actually begged. What next? she wondered, turning away from the carriage window and the steady drizzle outside.

Groveling, she answered herself. Sinking lower and lower. That was all that could happen. Esmond knew what she was doing and he'd told her loud and clear last night that she was doomed to failure. She'd begged, nearly wept—and he had turned his back and walked out.

She clenched her hands.

She would never, *never* humiliate herself so again. She would rather be hanged, shot, burned at the stake.

He'd only broken her heart. She'd recover. She had merely to shut the door on him, then pick up the pieces, put them back together, and get on with her life. She'd done it before. She'd shut Francis out, even though she was bound to him. This would be simpler.

Quentin hadn't been enthusiastic about the inquiry in the first place. She was the one who'd browbeaten him into taking it up. She could certainly persuade him to drop it— and dismiss the chief investigator. If Providence would be merciful for once, she wouldn't even have to say a word to Esmond about it. He would simply . . . vanish. To wherever he'd come from. Wherever that was.

The carriage rumbled to a halt, ending her gloomy reflections. She disembarked and hurried through the drizzle to her front door. Gaspard opened it with a welcoming smile.

She would miss her temporary servants, of course. But life would go on after they left. She'd do well enough. Her house was comfortable, the studio large and well lit, and she had ample funds to live on. Furthermore—

"Monsieur is in the studio," Gaspard said, taking her cloak and bonnet.

So much for counting on Providence to be merciful.

Setting her jaw, Leila marched down the hall and up the stairs, hastily composing her farewell speech as she went. Short, simple, to the point.

You win, Esmond. You didn't want to do this in the first place. You warned me and I wouldn't listen. Very well. You were right and I was wrong. I certainly don't possess the necessary patience for sleuthing. I most certainly do not want to spend the rest of my life on this case. I do not want to spend another minute on it. I'm not cut out to be your partner, and the last thing in the world I want is to be the equal of such a man. You win. I give up. Now go away and leave me in peace.

She swept through the study door. "Very well," she said. "You win, Esmond. You didn't want—"

The rest of her speech tumbled away to some distant nothingness.

There was no speech, no thought, nothing else in all the world but the picture before her.

Esmond sat cross-legged upon the carpet before the fire. He had made a nest of cushions and pillows about him. Her sketchbook lay open on his knee. A small pan of coffee stood in a warmer at his elbow. A plate of pastries lay beside it.

He was draped in shimmering silks. He wore a loose, buttonless gold shirt, like a short robe, with a sash of sapphire blue. The trousers were the same jewel blue—the color of his eyes, she saw, as he lifted them to hers.

A golden prince.

Out of a fairy tale. Or a dream.

She wanted to rub her eyes. She was afraid he'd vanish if she did. She took a cautious step closer. He didn't vanish, didn't move, only watched her. She dared another step, to the edge of the carpet.

"You wanted to know who I am," he said. "This is who
am—as you sensed, as you drew."

Even his voice was different, the slight French accen
gone. In its place were the unmistakable accents of the En
glish privileged classes . . . and a trace of something else
unidentifiable.

She couldn't find her voice. He didn't seem to notice
She *must* be dreaming.

"You were not altogether correct," he said, glancing
down at the sketchbook. "I never wore the turban. It makes
too tempting a nest for vermin. Cleanliness is a problem ir
my country, you see. A bath requires several hours' hare
work—and the time is not easily spared when one is constantly battling enemies."

If she wasn't dreaming, she must be drunk. He hadn'
come. He wasn't there, speaking so casually of turbans and
baths. It was wishful thinking, delirium.

She took another step nearer.

"But I was spoiled," he went on, his eyes still on the
sketchbook. "I was treated to luxuries my poorer countrymen could scarcely imagine. I would not wear the turban
and I dressed in my own way. Yet no one dared mock or
chide me, because I was born strange and my mother was
believed to be a sorceress. My cousin, Ali Pasha, believed
it. He even believed her prediction that I would become another Alexander, destined to lead my countrymen out of
bondage and restore Illyria to greatness."

Mesmerized, even while disbelieving her own eyes and
ears, Leila had been creeping ever closer while he spoke.
Now she sank onto the carpet opposite him.

"Illyria," she repeated breathlessly.

"That was its ancient name," he said. "A part of it is
known to your people as Albania. I am an Albanian by
birth and blood." He paused briefly. "You wanted to know
my name. My mother, who was a Christian, wished to
name me Alexander—*Skander*, in my own tongue. My father, a Moslem, chose Ismal. I am Ismal Delvina. I take my
surname from the region of his family."

Alexis Delavenne, Comte d'Esmond.

In reality, he was Ismal Delvina, whose mother had wanted to name him Alexander. His name, she thought, her heart aching. What she'd begged for—and more. He had a mother and father, and a place of birth, Albania. And even his countrymen thought him strange.

"Ismal," she whispered. "Your name is Ismal."

He watched her for a moment, as though waiting for something, but she could only wait, too, for whatever else he meant to tell her.

"It is a common Moslem name," he said expressionlessly. "My father was an unpretentious man. A warrior. From him I inherited my height and my strength. It was strength, perhaps, that assisted the growth of superstitions about me. They began, however, when I was born, at the height of the full moon. My hair was white. That was the first omen. The second omen was that, as a babe, I could not be kept swaddled. Always I worked myself free, for even in infancy I could not be confined. The third omen was observed when I was three years old. While I played in the garden, a viper crawled into my lap. I strangled it and draped it about my neck, and strutted about to show my elders."

"When you were three?" she asked weakly.

"It is significant," he said. "Three years old, the third omen. My people believe three is a number of great power and importance. They are superstitious. They believe witches and vampires live among them. They believe in magic, in the Evil Eye and curses, and in charms to ward off ills and evils. After these three mysterious events— which my mother made sure everyone knew of—it was easy for them to believe I was not altogether human." His smile was mocking.

As though he were embarrassed, Leila thought, surprised. "The Albanians sound rather like the Irish," she said. "Imaginative. Poetic. They made you special."

"With some help from my mother." He darted her a veiled glance. "It was from her I inherited my guile. If not for guile, I should not be what I am today."

After another pause, he went on. "When Ali heard of

this strange little boy, his curiosity overcame him. He came
to look at me, and while he looked, my mother told him the
dream she'd had of my destiny. I doubt she had such a
dream. She was a skilled liar and deceived him because she
wanted to live in luxury. She succeeded, for Ali took my
family back with him to his court. He was the greatest
miser in all the Ottoman Empire, but because of her lies, he
paid to send me abroad, to be educated among westerners.
In Italy, France, and England. Here I attended Westminster
and Oxford."

That explained the public school accent.

"It was only for a few years," he continued, "because I
learned quickly, and soon outpaced my masters."

There was another silence, a very long one. Leila was
afraid to break it.

The lines at the corners of his eyes tightened when he
spoke again. "As I said, the future my mother predicted
was a lie. But I grew up believing it. When I reached my
young manhood, I determined that the first step toward
achieving my destiny was to overthrow Ali."

He cast her another glance from under his lashes. "You
must believe that by this time I owed him nothing. Every
coin he'd spent had been paid back threefold in service. I
brought him considerable wealth. It was my people I
owed—or so I believed in my youthful arrogance. I set out
to destroy the tyrant. I failed. He repaid my treachery by
having me poisoned. By slow degrees."

The hairs on the back of her neck lifted.

He laughed softly, mockingly. "But I am very hard to
kill, as others besides Ali have learned to their annoyance.
Two loyal servants rescued me. In time, after a few other
ill-fated enterprises, Fate led me to Lord Quentin. It was he
who found a productive—and profitable—use for my pe-
culiar assortment of talents. What I have done since then I
am not at liberty to reveal, even to you. Suffice to say the
Vingt-Huit matter was typical."

He set the sketchbook aside. "Except for you, that is. I
have worked with women before. I do not become entangled with them. I do not let them cut up my peace. I am

careful not to disturb theirs, either, for an agitated woman can be very troublesome. Last night you troubled me very much. I vowed I would go back to Paris."

Her enchantment with the story swiftly ebbed under a wave of mortification. "You're rather troublesome your-self," she said. "As a matter of fact, I came in here ready to tell you I was quitting the inquiry and never wanted to see you again."

"Tsk." He gave a sharp nod. "You do not truly wish to quit the case. You will never rest easy not knowing the an-swer. You could not even rest easy not knowing my name. I have told you all you asked and more because I knew I could not keep away, and so, you would pry the truth from me sooner or later, one way or another."

"You're telling me you just wanted to get it *over* with?" she asked, nettled.

"Yes."

"So I'd stop nagging and making scenes. So I wouldn't be *troublesome*."

"Ali Pasha had three hundred women in his harem," he said. "All three hundred at once could not make me as crazy as you do. All three hundred, using all their wiles, could not have coaxed even my name from me."

She blinked. Harems. He had told her his life story and not once had it occurred to her that he might have a wife— a dozen of them—hundreds.

"How many?" she choked out. "How many did you—*do* you have?"

He toyed with the ends of his sash. "Women? Wives, concubines, you mean?"

"Yes."

"I forget."

"Ismal."

He smiled down at the sash.

"It isn't amusing," she said. "One doesn't forget wives."

"How easily it falls from your lips," he said softly. "My name."

"Don't tell me, then," she said. "I suppose it's none of my business." And it wasn't, she guiltily realized. He'd al-

ready told her more than she had any right to know. She
had asked for his name only.

She had an abrupt and painfully vivid recollection of
the circumstances under which she'd asked. She'd as much
as offered to go to bed with him if he told her his name.
Worse, she'd offered to do so whether he told her or not.
Heat stung her neck and swarmed over her face.

"You were very good to tell me as much as you have,"
she added hastily. "Even if it was only to shut me up.
Which I ought to do. Because you weren't lying this time,
I'm sure. Maybe you left some things out, but a person's
entitled to some privacy. I suppose you should be allowed
more than most. Obviously your work is dangerous," she
babbled on. "Your life has been dangerous, since the day
you were born, it seems. People have tried to kill you. For
all I know, some might still want to. But you needn't worry
about me. You trusted me—and I'm honored, really. I
shan't give you away. I promise. Word of honor. Wild
horses couldn't—"

"Leila."

She stared very hard at the pillow near her knee. "It
looks as though you found every pillow and cushion in the
house," she said. "Including the garret."

"Leila." His voice was soft, coaxing. "There is something
between us to settle, I think."

There was a rustle of silk, gold and blue, shimmering in
the firelight, as he moved, graceful as a cat, to close the
small distance between them. The loose shirt had fallen
open slightly, revealing the hollows at his neck and the
bare expanse of one marble-smooth shoulder. Even where
it covered him, the silken robe hid nothing. It outlined the
whipcord muscles of his arms . . . the hard planes and contours of his chest. He was pure, male animal . . . and he
was closing in.

She couldn't move, could scarcely breathe. Already,
wanton heat coiled through her body to throb in the pit of
her belly . . . the heat of animal hunger.

Her eyes lifted to his, to blue guile. Seduction.

"Last night," he said.

"Yes." A breath of a word, barely audible.

"You said you wanted me."

Run, some inner voice cried, while the images rose in her mind: herself writhing in feverish need, Francis' mocking laughter . . . shame.

But it was too late to run. She was lost. Trapped, as she'd been countless times before. Tangled in the Devil's nets, in desire. She had wanted this man from the beginning. She wanted him now—this beautiful, exotic creature—beyond bearing.

"Yes," she said helplessly, drowning in the fathomless blue depths of his eyes. "Still. More."

"More," he repeated very softly.

He leaned in close, flooding her senses. Glistening blue and gold . . . silk whispering over rippling muscle . . . warmth . . . and scent. She quivered under it, like any animal, caught by the scent of its mate. But there was fear, too, trembling at the core of desire. Fear of the mad desperation that, once triggered, she couldn't control, and of the humiliation, when it was over.

He trailed his finger down her cheek, and she trembled. With desire. With fear.

"Leila," he whispered. "In Persian, it means 'night.' You are all my nights. I dream of you."

"I dream of you," she said shakily. "Wicked dreams." She wanted to tell him, warn him. "I'm not . . . good."

"Nor am I."

He dragged his hand through her hair and held her while he brushed his cheek against hers. "I cannot be good tonight." His breath was warm on her ear.

She shivered.

"I need you too much," he said. His mouth grazed her ear, and fluid heat washed through her to tingle in her fingertips. She clutched his sleeve, and the muscles bunched under the silk. Leashed power pulsed under her hand and through her.

She was growing feverish already, squirming inside, trying to keep still while he teased her ear with his warm breath, his sensuous mouth. She gripped his arm hard. She

wanted him to hurry. She was afraid she'd beg. Her fingers
dug into unyielding muscle.

"Nay, do not fight yourself, Leila," he murmured.

"You don't know . . ." She couldn't finish, couldn't tell
him the truth.

"I gave you trust this night. Give me the same."

He had told her who he was and what he was, and she
knew it had not been easy for him. She knew that he, too,
had felt some deep shame. He had risked more than his
pride. And he'd done it for her.

And so, she had to give trust, too. She turned and
brought his mouth to hers, and kissed him as she'd wanted,
deeply, desperately. Because she wanted him and loved
him, whatever he was or had been or would become. She
clung to him, and boldly asked with her mouth and tongue.
And he gave her what she sought, a hot fierce answer, his
tongue plunging inside, bold and wicked, as she wanted.

She wanted him to ravish her, body and soul. She
wanted to be possessed, burned, consumed.

She slid her hands under the silken shirt to trace the
hard planes and contours with her fingers. She dragged her
mouth from his and kissed his neck, the hollow of his
throat, the marble smooth skin of his shoulder. "I want
you," she said, past shame. "So much."

"Ah, Leila." He pulled her down with him onto the pillows, and rolled onto her. She wrapped her legs about him,
relishing his weight, his heat, the hard arousal pushing
against her skirts, while he possessed her mouth and ravished it, in hot rhythmic strokes that pulsed in her muscles
and pounded in her blood.

She slid her hands over his back, over silk that hissed
under her touch, whispering sin, and down that sleek
length, relishing the masculine beauty of his form . . . narrow waist and hips and lean buttocks.

He groaned and eased away. "I think you like me." His
voice was thick.

"Oh, yes. God help me." And, God help her, she showed
him what she felt, bringing her hand brazenly down over
her bodice, to the buttons. He had seen her before. She had

nothing to hide. She didn't want to hide. She wanted his hands, his mouth, on her. She tugged a button free.

He made a choked sound, then pushed her hands away, and swiftly unfastened the bodice. She lay still, her breath coming faster, her mind dark and thick with heat. She made herself clay in his hands and, moving at a nudge here, a tug there, let him strip her. If he'd torn the clothes from her, she wouldn't have cared. She wanted to be his. She wanted him to do what he wanted with her.

He worked quickly, with an impatience that made her heart race in anticipation. He stripped her garments away, his hands rough and gentle at once, his blue eyes fiercely intent. And at last, only she was left, naked, needy, and trembling.

He sat back on his haunches and she watched his gaze trail slowly down the length of her body. "Tell me what you want," he said unsteadily.

"Anything. Anything you want."

He skimmed his fingers down along her jawline, her throat, over her breast. "Like this?"

"Yes." His touch seemed the idlest of caresses, but the naked hunger in his eyes told her otherwise. "I love your hands," she told him. "Your mouth. Your eyes. Your voice. Your beautiful body. I want you to crawl all over me, the way you imagined. I want to be your night, your dreams, Ismal. That's all I want: everything."

With a flick of his hand, he undid the sash. The robe fell open, and she caught her breath.

"Are you afraid?" His voice was low, throbbing.

"Yes. But I don't care." She didn't care. He was a god. Blindingly, stunningly, beautiful. Michelangelo would have wept, and taken a sledgehammer to his own David, could he but see what she did: broad, straight shoulders and a leanly muscled torso tapering to a slim, taut waist. He was hard and marble smooth . . . fine golden hair glinting on his chest, his forearms . . . an arrow of darker gold below his waist . . .

She struggled up, needing to touch. "You're beautiful," she whispered as she stroked down his chest.

His breath hissed out between his teeth. "You make me crazy, Leila." He pushed her hand away. "Have a care. I am not so tame."

He quickly slid out of the loose trousers and, pushing her back down, knelt between her legs.

Cupping her face, he kissed her, then began stroking down in slow possession . . . her shoulders, arms, her taut breasts, and down over her belly. So slowly, achingly so.

He leashed himself, she knew. She could have told him he didn't need to, that he might tear her to pieces if he wished. Yet she wanted him to take her in any way he chose. At this moment, he wanted control, and she was happy, this moment, to be controlled, to let him build the fire slowly.

He kissed her again, and it was a deep, slow, erotic eternity of a kiss. She lifted her hands to his shoulders, to stroke down over his lean frame as he'd done to her, savoring, possessing. He cupped her breasts and sensuously kneaded, his palms warm against the hard peaks. She sighed and arched up to fill his hands with herself, to let him enjoy her, because the pleasure was rich, beyond anything she'd ever known or dreamt. And for the first time, she was glad of her too-lavish harlot's body, of the pleasure he took from and gave it.

When he bent to tease her breast with his tongue, the touch rippled through her, a delicious stream of sensation. She slid her fingers into his silky hair, and let herself float on the rippling stream, until he took the sensitive bud in his mouth, and the first tender tug sent crackling currents racing over her skin. *Don't stop*, she begged silently. *Don't ever stop*. Her heart was aching, as though it were there he tugged, but the ache was sweet and fiery at once. He made it last and, moving over her to the other peak, made it begin and end again.

He lifted his head to look at her. "I cannot get enough of you," he said.

"Nor I of you."

She drew her hands down over his torso, pausing an instant as her fingers touched the thickened skin of a scar.

But only for an instant, because she couldn't stop herself. Down she stroked, to the golden hair at the base of his hard belly, the curls soft against her fingertips . . . and on still, to his maleness. "Dear God," she breathed. "I'm so wicked." Her fingers trembling, she touched him.

She heard him suck in his breath. She snatched her hand away and looked up, her face blazing. "I want to love you," she said helplessly.

His gaze locked with hers, he brought her hand back. "Yes, touch me," he said. "I am yours, Leila." He guided her fingers over the throbbing heat. "Yours." His voice was deepening, roughening. "And you are mine."

He pulled her hand away and did to her what she'd done to him. He raked his hands down over her tingling skin then, more gently, through the soft mound of curls between her legs. His fingers stroked the tender flesh and slid to the core of her heat and the liquid evidence of her desire. Then, lightly, his thumb brushed the sensitive bud, and she uttered a choked cry. Then another, as he slid his fingers inside her.

Then she was lost. He stroked the tender folds, found secret places she didn't know were there, and triggered bolts of sensations she couldn't name. His fingers, so gentle, drove her to frenzy. She quivered and shuddered and strained against his hands. Will, reason, control vanished, and she swept into some dark torrent and tossed there, helplessly.

Low, terrible sounds tore from deep in her throat, futile cries against the hot tide surging through her. The waves rose and crashed, thundering in her ears, and rose and crashed again, hurling her higher still. And still he urged her on, beyond what she'd ever known or imagined, to a black delirium . . . until the light burst—startling, blinding . . . release.

She hung there, stunned, while pleasure cascaded over her. She heard, outside herself, his low, ragged voice. "Come to me, Leila. Come and love me."

"Yes." Her voice was a sob. "Yes."

With one sure thrust, he sheathed himself inside her,

and she arched up in yearning welcome, desperate to take him deep, to fill herself with him. He took her fiercely, with hard, relentless strokes. He was pure power, demanding. She wanted it so, the passionate rage that threatened to tear her to pieces. It was fury and joy at once, and she gloried in it.

She pulled him down to her and branded him with her mouth, her greedy hands. She was surging high on the tide, more thunderous now, and sweeter, because he was with her, and because she was his, possessed, possessing.

"I love you," she gasped. "I love you, Ismal."

"Leila." A low, ragged cry, and with it, the power thrust deep, bolting through her. It blasted the darkness, fierce and white as a lightning shaft, and shattered her.

ABOVE THE GRADUALLY slowing beat of their hearts, Ismal could hear the tick of the clock, the crackle of the fire and, beyond, outside, the hiss of the rain. Cautiously, he eased his body from hers. She winced.

He brushed a kiss against her swollen lips and, moving onto his side, gently gathered her into his arms. She was warm and soft, limp with exhaustion, her silken skin damp in passion's aftermath.

She was his at last.

She loved him, she'd said. He feared it was a costly possession, her love.

He had, perhaps, a superstitious fear, barbarian that he was. He had, often enough, accepted the love others offered. He had done so without letting it touch him, because he'd understood long ago that love was a treacherous thing to give and receive. It could turn the world from heaven to hell in an instant and back again, again and again.

So had his world changed moment to moment since last night, when she had made the gash in his heart with her small, despairing plea for his name. It was not a mortal wound, perhaps, but near enough—deep and searing as the hole Lord Edenmont's bullet had torn into his side a de-

cade ago. This time, however, even Esme's salves could
not have eased the hurt.

The remedy Ismal needed was in the keeping of the
woman who'd done the damage. She'd offered love, and
made a terrible magic with that gift. When he'd come
this night, he'd known that her love was a serpent that
could turn upon him in an instant, spitting revulsion,
fear, contempt.

Yet he had given her what she wanted because there was
no choice, and stoically he had waited for the serpent to
strike. Rejection would not kill him, he'd told himself. It
would release him at last, after a year and more, and he'd
be free of her. The need, in time, would fade like any other.

But Fate had not written it so.

Fate had given her into his keeping. And all his peace,
he saw with a terrible clarity, was now in hers. It was too
late to fear the treacherous magic of this woman's love. All
he truly dreaded now was losing her.

He drew her close and nuzzled the soft tangle of her
hair. She stirred sleepily. Then she tensed, drawing her
head back to look at him in bewilderment.

"You fell asleep," he chided, smiling because he
couldn't help it. "The tigress at last is sated—and falls
asleep. Selfish cat."

Color flooded her cheeks. "I couldn't help it. I was—
that was—you are—"

"Very demanding," he supplied. He kissed her eyebrow.

"Yes. But . . ." She bit her lip.

"Tell me."

"I don't know, exactly."

"Tell me *approximately*, then." He stroked down her
smooth, supple back.

She let out a small sigh. "That never happened before."
With her thumb, she traced small circles in the center of
his chest. "I don't know whether it's you . . . or whether I
had it completely wrong. Lovemaking," she explained,
darting him an embarrassed glance. "I thought it was
like—like a rash."

"A rash." His voice was expressionless.

"The more you scratch, the more you itch."

In other words, her husband had failed to satisfy her, Ismal interpreted, not altogether surprised. Opiates and drink took their toll on a man's stamina. Furthermore, being Beaumont, he must have made it out to be her fault.

"This is what happens with Englishmen," he said. "They are not properly trained regarding women. A strange delusion is bred into them that women are weak and inferior, consequently, unworthy of the trouble of understanding. Albanian men are not so ignorant. From the cradle we learn that women are powerful and dangerous."

"Are they, indeed?" An uncertain smile tugged at the corners of her mouth. "Is that why you keep them locked in harems?"

He grinned down at her. "Aye—and to keep other men from stealing them. Women are like cats. Independent. Unpredictable. You give a woman all she asks—you die to please her. Then, one day, another man passes her window and calls to her, 'Ah, my beautiful one. Your burning eyes make roast meat of my heart. *Hajde, shpirti im.* Come to me, my soul,' he beckons. And so your woman goes, forgetting you, just as the cat forgets the carcass of the poor sparrow she ate the day before."

She laughed, and the sound was delicious, tickling his skin, warming his heart. "Roast meat," she said. "Sparrow carcasses. How romantic."

"It is true. A woman cannot be controlled. Only appeased. Temporarily."

"I see. You told me your story to shut me up—"

"And to entertain," he said. "As I would amuse a cat with a ball of string."

"But you succeeded," she said. "I was utterly captivated, enthralled. And *appeased.*"

"Ah, no," he said sadly. "For you wanted me, still, and I saw my fate. 'It must be done, Ismal,' I told myself. 'Recall your father, the mighty warrior. He would not shrink, even from certain death. Be strong like him. Take courage. The goddess demands a sacrifice. Lay yourself upon her altar, and pray she will be merciful.' And so I did." He licked her ear. "Though my heart drummed with terror."

She squirmed and pulled away. "Don't. That makes me *demented*."

"I know." He was growing aroused again, though his body had scarcely quieted from the first tempest. Gently he released her and shifted himself up onto one elbow.

"You fire up in an instant," he said as he lightly caressed her breast. Smooth and white as alabaster. Full and firm. So beautiful she was, and passionate. Made to make a man weep. "It is frightening," he added. "Luckily, I am Albanian, the son of a strong warrior."

"And the son of a sorceress." Her tawny gaze was darkening. "I suppose there's some comfort in that. At least I haven't disgraced myself with someone ordinary."

He clicked his tongue. "It is not disgrace. We care for each other. Neither of us belongs to another. We—"

"Neither of us?" she interrupted. "Aren't you forgetting your wives?"

With his index finger, he wrote his name over the smooth curve of her breast. "This matter of wives plagues you excessively," he said.

"I can understand a man having trouble cleaving only to one," she said. "But when he's allowed scores of them, it's very difficult to understand what the problem is. Obviously, it's too late for me to object, but I am curious. Purely for intellectual enlightenment, I wish you'd explain. Why should a man of your cultural background stray? Or was it the circumstances? Were you obliged to leave them in Albania?"

He let out a sigh. "I vowed to myself that I would not respond to any more interrogations, at least for this night." He moved over her and eased himself between her thighs. "Perhaps I should distract you," he added, skimming his fingers down over her belly.

Her eyes widened. "Oh, no. I shan't survive another— Oh-h-h," she moaned, as his fingers grazed her tender woman's flesh.

"*Méchant*," he murmured while he caressed the sensitive peak with feather-light strokes. "Wicked, curious cat. I give you everything you want, and it is not enough, ungrateful creature."

Her eyes were glazing over. "Dear God. Oh. Don't. *Oh-h-h-h.*"

He bent and feathered a trail of kisses over her breast, then lightly took its trembling crest between his teeth. A low, surrendering moan answered, and she slid her fingers into his hair.

Smiling, he trailed down slowly, teasing her silken skin with his lips, his tongue, his teeth.

She gasped, and tugged at his hair as he stole lower, to the center of her heat. She was damp already with wanting. Ready, vulnerable to delicious torment. He wanted to make it long and delicious. He had claimed her like a savage. Now he would enjoy his conquest at his leisure. He flicked his tongue over the delicate bud. This time, her moan pulsed through her muscles and on through him, to vibrate in his heart like the strings of a lute.

She was the night, and the night was dark, hot honey, thick with pleasure. She was his, hot and helpless under his tongue, and her soft, tremulous cries were for him. He toyed and tantalized, savoring the desire he drew from her, the moist warmth of her feminine secrets. Again and again he coaxed her to the crest of pleasure, and grew drunk with power as each climactic shudder pulsed through him.

"Please. *Ismal.*" She fisted her hands in his hair. "Please," she gasped. "I need you *inside me.*"

He rose to her, smiling his triumph and happiness while his swollen rod throbbed against her heat.

"Like this, my heart?" he asked huskily as he eased into her slick core.

"Oh. *Yes.*"

Slowly, this time. Lovingly. She was his now, sweet and hot . . . and needing him . . . inside her. Her body welcomed, opening gladly to him . . . surrounding him, taking him deep, and tightening, to hold him in the most intimate of embraces while she moved to the sensuous rhythm he set, and joined with him in lovers' dance.

She was the night, and the night sang in his heart, low and aching as the music of his homeland. She was the Ionian wind, singing in the pines. She was the rain streaming into his parched and lonely exile's heart to nourish his soul. She was the sea and the mountains, the soaring eagles and the rushing rivers . . . all that he had lost. In her he found himself. Ismal. Hers.

She reached for him, and he sank gladly into her welcoming embrace, and drank the heady brew of simmering kisses. Her passion was *raki*, a potent whiskey racing through his blood, inflaming him.

The music of desire grew louder, their rhythm stronger and faster, driving to *appassionato*.

She was desire, and desire was a mad dance, a wild *vallë* with the night. She clung, surging with him in stormy harmony. She was lost, as he was, to feverish need, yet she was with him, holding him, even as they raced to *crescendo*.

Then she was eternity, and eternity was the vast night heavens where the stars blazed. His needy soul reached for her, into the void. *Leila. With me. Keep me.*

She was there, her mouth claiming his, her strong, beautiful hands holding him fast. She was there, a burning star, his, and rapture was a searing burst of gold fire. He blazed for an instant . . . then fell . . . into the void, consumed.

Chapter 14

DESPITE ORDERS TO THE CONTRARY, NICK WAS waiting up when Ismal returned near daybreak. "Herriard's back," Nick said as he took his master's hat and coat. "He—What the devil have you done to your neckcloth?" He scowled at the linen dangling limply from Ismal's neck. "I hope to heaven no one saw you like that. And where are your other things? You didn't *leave* them there, did you?"

Ismal remembered Leila in his silk robe, the sash draped about her head like a turban, the trousers clinging to her lush hips and long, slender legs. "They were stolen," he said. "How did you learn about Herriard? I thought he planned to be away until the first of April."

"Lady Brentmor came looking for you not ten minutes after you left. Bursting with news for you. Only you weren't here and she had to collect Mrs. Beaumont from Lady Carroll's and take her to a card party."

Ismal headed up the stairs. "I trust her news can wait until morning."

"It *is* morning, in case you haven't noticed," Nick said, trailing after him.

"Tell me after I sleep, then. I am rather weary."

"Well, so am I. Only I had to stay up, didn't I, because you won't let me write things down, and if I fell asleep I might forget an important detail."

Ismal ambled into his bedroom and, pulling off his cravat, sat on the edge of the mattress. "Tell me then." He began to tug off his boots.

"Evidently, the old lady got some reports from her informants late in the afternoon," Nick said. "Item one: Late in December, the Duke of Langford paid two thousand quid for shares of a company that doesn't exist."

"Ah." Ismal set his right boot down. "This makes sense. Lord Avory is kept on a relatively modest allowance. It was more profitable for Beaumont to bleed the father. Also, much more dangerous."

"Suicidal, I'd say. Because—and this is item two—the Duke of Langford has some interesting friends in the demimonde. Some burly fellows you wouldn't want to meet in a dark alley. And a talented courtesan by the name of Helena Martin. He's her landlord."

"This is *very* interesting." Ismal placed the left boot beside its mate. "According to Quentin, Helena in her youth had a brief but highly successful career as a thief." He had not considered it unusual or significant. Hundreds of children in London's slums stole and whored to survive. Helena Martin was one of the very rare cases of upward mobility. A skilled—and discreet—thief could prove quite useful at times. Certainly Beaumont had employed such in Paris.

"That's item three," Nick said. "But I told her you already knew. Item four is a reminder that Quentin's men didn't find a single document in Beaumont's house that could be used to blackmail anybody."

Ismal nodded. "Either none were left or someone stole them." He looked up at Nick. "So it is possible Helena stole them—for Langford."

"An experienced thief would know where to look, wouldn't she? Not to mention it's possible Helena had been in the house before. Beaumont did take tarts home when his wife was away."

"The trouble is, once the papers were stolen, it was unnecessary to kill the blackmailer." Ismal pulled off his shirt and tossed it to Nick.

"Maybe Helena had reasons of her own—or Langford felt it was safer to be rid of Beaumont once and for all."

"An interesting theory. But no more than that. We need something more substantial than speculations."

Nick was frowning down at the wrinkled shirt. It took him a moment to respond. "Yes. Well. Speculations."

"Is that all? May I rest now?"

Nick shook his head. "Item five."

"No wonder you were afraid to sleep. The old witch came with a very long list, it seems."

"The old witch has been busy," said Nick. "Unlike some people I could mention."

"It is a tiresome case." Ismal yawned. "I prefer to let you and her do all the boring work. Perhaps you would be so kind as to proceed more concisely with the rest of your items, and keep the editorial comments to yourself."

Nick's jaw clenched. "Very well. *Sir*. Item five: Lady Brentmor—by means she doesn't choose to explain—has obtained information regarding Mrs. Beaumont's finances. Thanks to the financial acumen of her man of business, Mr. Andrew Herriard—"

"I know his name," said Ismal.

"The dowager says every last ha'penny is accounted for. Mrs. Beaumont has an ample income, thanks to a series of sound but canny investments. A few risks that paid off very well. No oddities or discrepancies. No skirting the bounds of ethics."

"Just as we already knew."

"Indeed, all was in order. Except for one thing."

Ismal waited through the obligatory dramatic pause.

"Mrs. Beaumont started out with only a thousand pounds," said Nick.

"That is not so surprising." Ismal's stomach was a bit queasy, though he was certain the dowager would not have breathed a word to Nick about the secrets of a decade ago. "It was my understanding that her father was bankrupt."

"Apparently, Lady Brentmor thinks there should have been a lot more money, not less. I'm to inform you—this is item six—that she intends to contact sources at a bank in Paris. She seems to think Beaumont got his hands on the money before Herriard turned up to take charge."

"I do not see what Her Ladyship hopes to accomplish," Ismal said with a trace of irritation. "It was ten years ago—and stealing from an orphaned girl would fit Beaumont's character. It would be but one in a long list of injuries he did her. However, since she did not kill him, it is irrelevant to the inquiry."

"I did point that out to Lady Brentmor. She told me it wasn't my business to think, but to listen. Item seven," Nick began.

"Heaven grant me patience!" Ismal fell back on the pillows and shut his eyes. "When will you be done with your accursed items? I shall be an old man before you finish, I think."

"Next time, I'll make the old lady wait," said Nick. "I'd like to see you make *her* stifle editorial comments. I haven't told you the half of what she—"

"Item seven," Ismal coldly reminded.

"Christ. Item seven," Nick grated out. "News from abroad. From Turkey."

Ismal's eyes flew open.

"Jason Brentmor left Constantinople three months ago," Nick said. "He's on his way home. She thought you'd want to know." He left, slamming the door behind him.

LEILA WAS ACUTELY conscious of the fine thread of moisture stealing down between her breasts. Fortunately, several layers of clothing concealed this fact from nearby onlookers.

At Lady Seales' soiree at present, only two onlookers stood nearby, discussing the political situation in France. One was Andrew Herriard, the picture of quiet gentlemanly elegance as he hovered protectively at her shoulder. The other, unquietly stunning in a midnight blue coat and

blinding white linen, was the cause of Andrew's reversion
to guardian role: the so-called Comte d'Esmond.

Her former guardian's behavior was making Leila wonder whether the spurious count was also Andrew's reason
for returning to London two weeks ahead of schedule. Earlier in the day, when he'd called, Andrew had in his mild
way given her to understand that he was concerned. Oh, he
had approved of Gaspard and Eloise. After all, they were
quiet, well-mannered, and obviously diligent—as the terri-
fyingly clean house practically screamed. Even in her studio, not a trace of the previous night's profligacy
remained—no forgotten bit of clothing, no spilled cognac,
not a strand of hair clinging to carpet or sofa pillows, not a
speck of dust, a piece of lint. Just as though nothing had
happened.

Only it had, and Leila had been burningly conscious of
the fact throughout her previous conversation with Andrew.
Her stomach had knotted with guilt, just as it had when she
was a girl, listening to one of his gentle lectures. He hadn't
precisely lectured today. But even while applauding her
choice of staff, he had managed to drop more than one subtle hint about her finding a live-in companion. She had met
those mild hints with evasive incomprehension. Luckily
for her, he hadn't pressed.

Today, evasion, she thought. Tomorrow, black falsehoods, no doubt. She had failed Andrew and fallen, but she
was wicked at heart and didn't care. All she cared about—
like any hardened sinner—was not getting caught. She was
Jonas Bridgeburton's daughter, truly.

Ismal—*Esmond*, she reminded herself—was not helping. He remained talking to Andrew as though the man
were his dearest friend. He was cultivating Andrew, which
the latter, being nobody's fool, must surely comprehend.
Meanwhile, Leila sweated with the strain of driving away
simmering recollections of the previous night.

"King Charles could do with a better advisor," Andrew
was saying.

"I agree. It is not wise to antagonize the bourgeoisie. It
was they who bore the costs of the Law of Indemnity. Then

he alienated them further with the Law of Sacrilege. Then he dissolved the national guard. And to appoint Martignac as minister was most incautious." Esmond shook his head. "The world has changed. Even the King of France cannot turn back time to the old days. He cannot restore the *ancien regime*."

"Still, one can't altogether blame the French nobility for wanting to be restored," Andrew said. "Your family, for instance, lost a great deal. The Delavennes were believed decimated during the Terror, I understood."

Sympathetically as he'd uttered the words, Leila perceived the probe. Beyond doubt, Esmond did, too.

"To all intents and purposes, they were wiped out," he answered smoothly. "It is as though the Delavenne family was a great tree struck by lightning. Only one obscure shoot survived—like one of the sucker shoots the wise arborist normally prunes and discards. I am certain that if the king had not been so desperate to rebuild the ranks of the nobility, I should have remained in deserved obscurity."

"You couldn't have believed you deserved obscurity," said Andrew. "You did assume the title."

"I had little choice, monsieur. More than one monarch told me in no uncertain terms that it was my duty to be the Comte d'Esmond."

He was, truly, a marvelous liar, Leila reflected. Or rather, a genius at arranging truth to suit his purposes. He had not, for instance, claimed to *be* that "sucker shoot" of the Delavenne tree, merely arranged his sentences to make it seem so.

Aloud she said, "Naturally, you could not disregard Royal commands."

He sighed. "Perhaps I am a great coward, but in truth, Tsar Nicholas in particular is exceedingly difficult to disregard. As both Wellington and the Sultan have discovered."

Very neat, the way he shifted the subject, Leila silently observed.

"Certainly the tsar has placed England between the rock and the hard place," said Andrew. "Because of the atrocities against the Greeks, the British public wants an end to

Turkish power. The politicians, on the other hand, aren't eager to see Russia controlling access to eastern ports. If one is coldly practical, one must prefer the weaker power in control," he explained to Leila.

"Oh, I understand," she said. "Lady Brentmor has explained the Turkish business to me. Her son, Jason, has been in Constantinople this last year, playing the thankless role of go-between—and greatly discouraged, according to his last letter, she says. According to her, the problem boils down to man's innate inability to keep his hands off what his intellect is unequipped to manage."

"I daresay she has the proper solution," said Esmond.

Leila shook her head. "Her Ladyship says there is no hope of solving anything so long as a man is involved."

Andrew smiled. "Her Ladyship is known to entertain an exceedingly low opinion of our gender."

"But she is correct," Esmond said. "Men are the inferior sex. Adam was made first, and the first effort is always the simpler and cruder one, *non*? With the second, one refines." His blue glance flickered ever so briefly to Leila—one sizzling instant's reminder—then back, all limpid innocence, to Andrew.

"An intriguing theory," said Andrew. "I collect you can account for the serpent in the Garden, then?"

"But of course. Temptation. To make life interesting, *n'est-ce pas*?"

"Of course, we must keep in mind that the story of Creation was written down by *men*," Leila put in.

"That sounds like more of Lady Brentmor," Andrew said. "A most extraordinary woman. But then, the entire family is. Fascinating character studies, Leila."

"As painting subjects, you mean."

"Yes—if you can get any of them to sit still long enough. The Brentmors, that is. Edenmont is another matter. He's always struck me as the serene island in the midst of a seething sea. Are you acquainted with him, monsieur?"

"We have met." Esmond's gaze strayed past Andrew.

"Ah, Lady Brentmor comes—to scold us, no doubt, for monopolizing her charge."

Leila had an instant to wonder why the lines at Esmond's eyes had tightened. Then the dowager was upon them.

She cast a baleful glance over the trio. "I was beginning to wonder if you was putting down roots."

"Actually, we were having a fascinating discussion about islands," Leila said smoothly. "Andrew views Lord Edenmont as a serene one."

"He's lazy enough, if that's what you mean."

"With all due respect, my lady," said Andrew, "he is most diligent in his Parliamentary duties. I daresay we shall see him back in London soon. I realize Lady Edenmont may not be up to the Season's exertions at present, but London is within reasonable riding distance for His Lordship."

"Far as I can see, it won't be any time soon. Mebbe not this century," the dowager grumbled, half to herself.

The lines at Esmond's eyes grew tauter. "Sometimes, the duties to the estate and family must come first. That is our loss. I am sure they will be much missed. I hope you will convey my good wishes, my lady. *Maintenant*, I must excuse myself. I shall be late for an engagement."

He took Leila's hand and barely touched his lips to her knuckles. An erratic current skittered through her nerve endings. *"Enchanté, madame,"* he murmured. With a courtly bow for Lady Brentmor and a friendly nod to Andrew, he walked away.

"To be sure, he's a pretty enough rascal," the dowager said, watching him go. "You could do worse, Leila."

Leila hastily collected her composure and manufactured an indulgent smile. "Lady Brentmor can be shocking at times," she told Andrew. "She provides a detailed assessment of every man who looks my way."

"Don't see what's so shocking about it. Beaumont's dead. You ain't, as Esmond can see plain enough. And the man wouldn't back off for all Herriard's clucking over you like a hen with a new-hatched chick. Am I right or ain't I, Herriard?" the dowager demanded.

Andrew colored a bit, but managed a smile. "I had hoped I wasn't so obvious as that."

"Well, you was, and you ought to know better. People see *you* making such a fuss, they're bound to talk."

Leila wished she knew what the old lady was about. "Andrew was not fussing," she said. "He and the count were discussing politics, and it was most interesting."

He patted her shoulder. "No, my dear, Lady Brentmor has the right of it. I *was* fussing and it was very bad of me. Your position is delicate enough—"

"It ain't," the dowager declared. "If mine ain't, hers ain't."

"I do beg your pardon," Andrew said. "I did not mean to insult you, my lady. It's just that Leila is—well, she was my ward, once, and old habits are hard to break."

In other words, he doubted her ability to resist Esmond—the personification of Temptation. But it was too late for Andrew to help her. She didn't want to be protected from herself or Esmond and, in any case, Andrew's hovering about her would prove inconvenient to the inquiry. That must be what Lady Brentmor had decided. One could only hope she'd chosen the right tactics. Nonetheless, it was very difficult for Leila to stifle a nagging sense of guilt.

"It's your generous habit to be kind," she told Andrew. "You're both very kind to me. I'm exceedingly fortunate in my friends."

"You'd be more fortunate if they'd keep to what they know best," the dowager retorted. "See here, Herriard. This is just the sort of thing where a man's bound to do harm for all he means to do good. You leave her beaux to me, my lad, and you tend to her business affairs."

"I beg you will not give Andrew the notion that I'm collecting beaux, Lady Brentmor."

"I don't need to give him notions. He gets 'em all by himself." The dowager fastened her shrewd gaze upon Andrew. "I collect you checked on him in Paris."

"In light of certain rumors, I believed it my duty," he said stiffly.

"Oh, Andrew—"

"Well, it was, wasn't it?" said the dowager. "To make sure Esmond wasn't out at pocket or had a wife tucked away somewhere."

Leila stiffened. "I suppose it's no use reminding either of you that you're putting the cart before the horse—and I've been widowed only two months—"

"My dear, no one is accusing you of behaving improperly," Andrew said soothingly. "It's simply that the count showed a marked interest in you in Paris, and he did admit—to a jury, no less—that he'd sought you out—and he does linger in London. While I cannot be certain he remains solely on your account, I felt it was best to err on the side of caution. I do regret, however, that this night I behaved, apparently, with far less discretion than Esmond. Lady Brentmor was correct to set me down, and I am much obliged." He quirked a smile at the dowager. "If a trifle abashed."

Her ladyship nodded. "There, I knew you was a reasonable fellow, Herriard. And you may be sure that when it comes to the marriage settlements, I'll leave the field to you." She and Andrew exchanged conspiratorial smiles.

Swallowing an oath, Leila looked from one to the other in disbelief. "You are shocking, both of you," she said.

They laughed at her.

ISMAL WAS WAITING at the top of the stairs when Leila returned. She scowled up at him when she reached the landing.

He leaned on the banister. "No, do not tell me. I can guess. After I left, the party became insupportable, and you died of loneliness and boredom."

"I died of *mortification*," she said.

"Then you must punish me. It cannot be helped."

Slowly she ascended the stairs, dangling her bonnet by

the strings. The soft hall light glimmered in her hair, picking out threads of copper, bronze, and gold. Straightening, he moved to meet her. He took the bonnet and tossed it aside, then folded her in his arms.

"I missed you very much," he whispered against her hair. "All the time I stood before you and could not touch you and all the time I waited for you to come home."

"You shouldn't have gone to the soiree," she muttered. "You made it very difficult for me. You're an expert at deception. I'm not."

He drew back and looked at her. "But you did very well. You did not tear off my clothes and throw me to the floor and ravish me."

"Ismal."

"You did not make me scream and beg for mercy."

"Ismal."

"How terrible it was to wait, trembling with fear. Any moment, I thought. Any moment, the fire will blaze in her eyes and she will leap upon me and plunder and despoil my innocent body. I was aquake with . . . anticipation."

"You evil man. You found it all *exciting*, didn't you?"

"Yes. Also very frustrating." He took her hand. "Come to bed."

"We need to talk," she said.

He kissed her nose. "Later. After I have calmed down."

He tugged her along, on up the next flight of stairs and into her bedroom. By the time he closed the door, his heart was drumming with impatience.

"Calm me down," he said.

"You've ruined me," she said. "You've *decimated* my morals."

"Aye, they are gone. Forget them."

"Or maybe I only imagined I had them." With a small sigh, she reached up and loosened his neckcloth. Then, slowly, she drew it away. "Tear off your clothes, indeed," she said as she let the linen drop from her hand. "Wishful thinking."

She began to unfasten her bodice. "I'm not that desperate."

"I am." He watched while, one by one, the jet buttons sprang from their moorings, slowly baring an expanse of creamy flesh and embroidered black cambric.

A dark snake of heat coiled in his loins. He wanted to reach for her. He curled his fingers tightly into his palms.

She stepped behind him and eased him out of his coat as smoothly as the most practiced of valets. "Throw you to the floor, will I?" she said. "You're living in a dream world."

"A beautiful dream."

She unfastened her skirt in the same unhurried way. The black dress rustled to the floor, revealing a black demi corset and short petticoat.

She relieved him of his waistcoat, his shirt.

She surveyed his rigid torso. When he saw her gaze settle on the ugly scar in his side, he tensed, but she didn't touch it. "Guess what you're going to explain later," she said.

"Never." He managed a smile.

"We'll see." She untied the petticoat, and he watched it slither down over black silk drawers to pool at her feet.

He sucked in his breath.

"You're going to explain a lot of things," she said.

He shook his head.

Sitting down on the bed, she untied her kid slippers and lazily removed them. "Come here." She patted the mattress.

He sat. She knelt, and took off his evening slippers. Then she rose and, while the blood thundered in his ears, methodically unlaced her corset. It fell to the floor. Then the chemise. Then the silken drawers. Then the stockings.

No trace of black remained. There was only creamy, supple flesh . . . the tawny rose peaks of her lush breasts . . . the triangle of dark gold between her long legs.

"I like you very much," he said hoarsely.

"I know."

She found his trouser buttons. Clutching at the bedclothes, his eyes shut, he let her strip away the last of his garments.

"You said something about begging for mercy," she whispered. "About screaming."

He shuddered as her fingers stroked his thickened manhood. He didn't have to open his eyes to know where she was. Kneeling, between his legs. The awareness made him delirious. No. Yes. No.

Her tongue flicked over the hot flesh and searing pleasure tore through him. *Yes*.

He clamped an iron will upon his maddened body, and only a small groan escaped him.

And he endured, while she put him on a rack of erotic torture, toying with him, tantalizing, caressing with her ripe, wicked mouth.

He held himself in check, denying his body the release it screamed for until at last the iron bands of his will began to give way.

"Enough," he gasped. He pulled her away and up onto his lap to straddle him. *"Méchant."* He quickly found the center of her heat—slick, ready for him.

"I'm wicked. All day long I wanted you." Her voice was thick, dazed, her eyes dark with desire.

She gave a low moan as he smoothly eased into her. "Wicked," she repeated, wrapping her legs about his waist.

He crushed her softness to him, and she clung, her body answering the urgent rhythm of his possession. She was his. He had waited all this long day and half the night for the door to close on the outside world and shut him in with her. He had waited all these endless hours to hold her, be with her, part of her. No woman in all of creation loved as she did.

"Love me, Leila," he groaned against her mouth.

"I love you."

He took her love in a deep, searing kiss, and carried her with him to the last pleasure . . . and sweet release.

WEARING NOTHING BUT the silk robe Leila had laid claim to the night before—and wearing it only at her insistence—Ismal had crept down to the kitchen. He returned bearing a tray that held a small decanter of wine, wineglasses, and plates heaped with bread, cheese, and olives.

Sitting tailor fashion opposite each other amid the tumbled bedclothes, they ate and drank. She told him about Andrew's Parisian investigations, and how the dowager had handled the hapless solicitor, and he told her what the dowager had learned about the Duke of Langford.

Leila did feel that as a murder suspect, His Grace was vastly preferable to David or Fiona. On the other hand, she wasn't pleased by certain implications of the theory.

"I assume this means you'll be cultivating Helena Martin next," she said.

"You overestimate my stamina," he said. "Or perhaps you taunt. For you must be well aware that after you are done with me, there is nothing left for another woman."

"Oh, certainly I believe that," she said. "I also believe in gnomes, pixies, and goblins. How did you get that scar?"

"I thought we were speaking of Helena Martin."

There they were, the tight lines at his eyes.

"I'm tired of Helena Martin," she said. "Was it a bullet or a knife?"

"A bullet."

She winced inwardly.

He looked down at the scar and wrinkled his nose. "I am sorry it offends you."

"Not a fraction so much as it offends you, I collect. Who did it, then? One of your jealous wives? Or someone's outraged husband?"

"I have no wives," he said.

"At present, you mean. Nearby."

Sighing, he picked up an olive. "None. I never wed. Now what shall I tease you with instead, I wonder?" He popped the olive into his mouth.

No wives. The beast. She eyed him balefully. "Don't you think it was a trifle unkind to let me think you were married?"

"You were not obliged to think it."

"I wish Eloise had not pitted those olives," she said. "I wish there were a stone and you choked on it."

He grinned. "No, you do not. You love me very much."

"Really, you are so gullible," she said. "I *always* say that when I'm heated. Cats howl. I say, 'I love you.' "

"You howl also. You make strange little cries."

She leaned toward him. "You make some strange ones yourself." Drawing back, she added, "Are you going to tell me the story behind that scar or do I have to figure it out on my own, as usual? I've already got an intriguing theory, you know."

"You also had the intriguing idea that I had a hundred wives." He set the tray upon the nightstand. "Me, I have some intriguing thoughts regarding dessert." He stroked her knee.

"Why were you so upset when Andrew mentioned Lord Edenmont?" she asked.

"I must find some way to get even for what you did to me before," he murmured, trailing his fingers along the inside of her thigh.

She caught his teasing hand and brought it to her mouth. Lightly she bit the knuckle of his index finger. "Jason Brentmor spent more than two decades in Albania," she said gently. "That's common knowledge. He married an Albanian woman and produced one daughter, Esme. Edenmont married her in Corfu ten years ago. Fiona once mentioned that Lord Lackliffe told a romantic—and probably highly imaginative—story about it. He and Sellowby had been in Greece at the time. Lackliffe was at the soiree tonight."

She was aware of the muscles tensing in Ismal's hand. "It's very easy to get him to talk about his adventure ten years ago," she went on. "About taking Edenmont and his new bride back to England in a mad race across the Mediterranean. Apparently, it was the most exciting thing that's ever happened to Lackliffe. He said he has a poem written by a Greek about the two handsome princes who fought for the hand of the Red Lion's daughter. One prince was a black-haired Englishman. The other was a golden-haired Albanian whose name was Ismal."

She released the stiff hand to touch the scar. "It's an old scar," she said. "Is it ten years old?"

He had turned away while she spoke. He was gazing steadily at the window, the telltale lines at his eyes deeper than she'd ever seen them.

"The sun will rise in less than two hours," he said. "We have so little time. We could be making love, my heart."

The words made her ache. "I just want to know where I stand," she said. "I know ours is merely an affair. I know what I've got myself into. But I can't help being a woman, and I can't help wanting to know if you love her still—if that's why you never wed."

"Oh, Leila." He moved closer and brushed her hair back from her face. "You have no rivals, *ma belle*. I was two and twenty, and I can scarcely remember what I felt. A youthful infatuation, and like other youths, I was arrogant and rash."

"Then it's true. I guessed aright." She let out a sigh. "I wish you wouldn't make me guess and drag things out of you. I wish you'd tell me something on your own once in a while. Like about youthful infatuations. Not but what I'll probably want to scratch her eyes out if she so much as blinks at you," she added irritably. "Lud, I am so jealous."

"And I am truly frightened." He tilted her chin up to study her eyes. "How in the name of heaven did you connect my scar with Edenmont?"

"Woman's intuition."

"You said I was upset about him," he persisted, still holding her gaze. "How did you know? You must tell me, Leila. If I betray myself to you, I might to another. You do not wish me to endanger myself unwittingly, I hope."

The words chilled her, reminding her that his life depended upon deceit, concealment. The scar was old, its cause in the past. But it was vivid testimony that he was human . . . that she could lose him.

She didn't have to look at the scar, because the image of the gnarled flesh was vivid in her mind. She'd noticed it last night—and how he winced when she touched it. The scar had given her nightmares after he left. A huge brute leaping out at him from a shadowy hallway . . . a blade gleaming in flickering candlelight . . . a small, wiry man with feral eyes who dripped poison into the gash the knife had made.

She had bolted up from her pillows in a cold sweat, and remained trembling in her lonely bed a long while after, despite the reassuring sunlight of morning. She shuddered now, recalling.

"Your eyes," she said, touching her finger to the tiny network of lines. "When you're at ease, the lines are indiscernible. When you're upset, they become tight, sharp. I think of them as little arrows pointing out sore spots. My intuition must have connected the sore spots."

He muttered in what she guessed was his native tongue—a series of curses, judging by the tone. Then he was off the bed and across the room to peer into the cheval glass. "Come, show me," he said. "Bring the other lamp. I cannot see by this one."

She could see well enough: a stunning view of about six feet of leanly muscled, gleaming, naked male. They had so little time left this night, and they might be making love. Instead, they would spend the precious moments examining his eyes.

By gad, she was a hopeless case. Utterly depraved. She dragged herself from the bed, took up the lamp, and joined him at the mirror.

Chapter 15

FROM THE TIME SHE'D DISCOVERED THE SCAR, it had taken Leila less than twenty-four hours to light upon the names associated with it. It took Ismal less than a minute to understand that Fate had just tightened the screws another painful notch.

He was already well aware that it didn't matter whether Bridgeburton had fallen or been pushed into the canal that night long ago. If he'd been pushed, it didn't matter who'd done it—whether it had been Ismal's servants, an enemy of Bridgeburton's, or a treacherous friend. Beaumont, for instance. Those details didn't matter. What mattered was that when Ismal left that Venice palazzo, he'd set events in motion that had ruined a young girl's life. Every hour of unhappiness Leila had endured since then was a stain on his soul.

He was prepared to devote himself to her happiness, to make up for every minute of grief his actions had caused her. But he needed time. If she discovered his infamy too soon, he might never get the chance to make amends. She would shut her heart to him just as she had to Beaumont.

He was miserably aware that he should have told her the

truth at the beginning. Then at least, whatever she thought of him, she would not think him false. He should have let her know precisely what he was and let her choose with full knowledge whether to love him. Instead, he'd won her love unfairly.

Now he couldn't bear to lose it.

While he stood in front of the mirror and studied the lines at his eyes—a betrayal as clear to her as Avory's twitching jaw muscle had been to him—Ismal was plotting against her, playing for time.

She must be occupied, her mind fixed elsewhere. And so he began by fixing it on helping him overcome the involuntary reaction of the tiny facial muscles. Then he fixed it on lovemaking, so that when he left shortly before dawn, she was too exhausted to think.

The following day he carefully prepared their work for the weeks to come, and planned how to present her time-consuming assignments.

That night, instead of leading her straight to the bedroom, Ismal took her to the studio and sat her down at the worktable. He handed her a sheet of paper containing, among other scribblings, a column titled "Prime Suspects" under which were five names: Avory, Sherburne, Langford, Martin . . . and Carroll.

She stared at the scrawled notes for a full two minutes without uttering a sound. When at last she found her voice, it was harsh. "Where did you get this?" she demanded. "This is Francis' handwriting. What the devil was he doing making notes about prime suspects and alibis?"

Ismal opened an inkwell, took up a pen, dipped it into the ink, and wrote: *Monday, 12 January, Account for whereabouts.*

She inhaled sharply. "I see. Your talents include forgery."

"One should always be prepared for the possibility that notes or letters may fall into the wrong hands." He nodded at the list. "As Avory and his father learned, such materials may prove costly, even years later."

"It would appear you've kept something else from me."

She did not look up. "How long have you suspected Fiona of murder?"

"Leila, neither of us is stupid or blind," he said. "We cannot go on pretending forever that we do not see what is under our noses. Lady Carroll hated your husband. For years she hated him because he behaved shamefully toward you, whom she views as a sister. Not many weeks before his death, he shamed her actual sister. The night on which the poison must have been administered, she was in London. We both recognize that her alibi is somewhat suspicious."

He drew up a stool and sat close beside her. "Still, she is one of several to whom our attention has been drawn," he said. "Nearly everyone your husband knew could have reason to kill him. We have made ourselves dizzy with motives, and we have been distracted with Avory's romantic problems. What I propose is that we take a new tack and attempt to narrow our list. I suggest we begin by accounting for the whereabouts of these people on the night in question."

She said nothing, only kept her eyes upon the piece of paper.

Ismal went on explaining. Of the five prime suspects, only Lady Carroll had been in a situation requiring her to explain her whereabouts to anybody. None, including her, could be interrogated directly.

"We must find out by devious means," he said. "It will not be easy, but I see no alternative, if we hope to solve the problem in this century."

"I suppose you never said anything about Fiona because you knew I'd make a much worse fuss than I ever did about David," she said at last. Her voice was low, level. "Very unprofessional of me."

"Very silly, also." He tweaked a curl at her temple. "You know I dote upon Lady Carroll. She has been my staunchest ally. Frankly, she would be my preferred choice for murderer, because she at least would never harm you—even to save her own skin."

She looked up at him. "It had better not come to that."

"I shall take care it does not," he said.

Her troubled expression eased.

"Also, I shall understand if you do not wish to snoop behind your good friend's back," he said. "Perhaps you prefer to leave this disagreeable business to me?"

She returned her attention to the paper, and considered. "No, I'll take Fiona." Her voice was businesslike now. "If I were you, I'd leave Langford to Lady Brentmor, since she's his wife's confidante. But you ought to take David, obviously."

"He left with Norbury yesterday for Dorset," he said. "That may serve us well. While he is away, Nick and I—in disguise, of course—may be able to learn something from the servants."

"That leaves Sherburne and Helena Martin." She frowned.

"I shall leave Sherburne to you," he said magnanimously.

"You jolly well won't," she said. "I'll take Helena."

"Most certainly not. You will have plenty to do with Sherburne and Lady Carroll."

"I'll take the women. You handle the men."

He made himself speak calmly. "This is not rational. Your friend is one matter. Helena is an altogether different problem. In the first place, you cannot cultivate the friendship of a prostitute without risking scandal. In the second, I ask you to recollect that she has dangerous friends—not to mention a past that will not bear close scrutiny. If she—"

"According to Lady Brentmor, Helena is in Malcolm Goodridge's keeping at present." Gold fire flashed in her eyes. "If you expect to be given private audiences with Helena, you'll have to make it worth her while. I greatly doubt she'll risk a comfortable berth with Goodridge merely for the privilege of gazing into your lovely blue eyes. And if you think I'll tolerate your acquiring an English harem, I strongly advise you to think again."

"Leila, it is most unprofessional to allow jealousy to supersede caution."

"Unprofessional I may be," she said. "But most certainly not incautious." She stood up. "If you begin hovering about La Martin, you'll make two deadly enemies. Malcolm Goodridge—" She smiled. "And guess who else?"

He should have realized that matters with her would never go precisely as he wished. Ismal had been prepared to let her deal with Sherburne. He was at least a gentlemen. Also, he wasn't the cleverest of men, and Leila had managed him well enough before—had him eating out of her hand, as Nick had said. Helena Martin, however, was a far more dangerous species.

"I know you have a wonderful mind," he said. "But in certain cases, that will not make up for experience. With Helena Martin, you will be out of your depth. She grew up in the thieves' kitchen, and she did not achieve her success by chance or luck."

"I lived ten years with Francis Beaumont," she said, moving away. "My father was Jonas Bridgeburton. I believe I am up to her weight." She headed for the door. "All I need is a pretext for speaking to her. Do you want to help, or do you prefer to let me stumble about in my own amateurish way?"

FIVE DAYS LATER, Leila stood in the front hall of Helena Martin's house. She had come without Ismal's permission or knowledge. She had devised her plan without him, because he had done everything but help. Instead, over the last five days, he'd tried every way he could to distract her. He was very good at it, Leila had to admit. With a less obstinate subject, he might have succeeded.

He distracted her in bed—not to mention on the floor, in a chair, on the window seat, against the armoire, and on the garret stairs. Lest that not be sufficient to occupy her, he exerted himself to addle her in company. He sent sultry silent messages across dinner tables, drawing rooms, and ballrooms. He tried her composure and her wits with his unique brand of double entendre. It didn't matter that no one else discerned his wicked meanings.

Leila did, and it took all her concentrated will not to betray herself.

She didn't waste her breath berating him afterwards, when they were alone. Obviously, if she couldn't handle a bit of teasing, he'd never believe she could handle the likes of Helena Martin. Besides, Leila couldn't pretend she objected to the imaginative locations or positions for lovemaking, any more than she could complain about his stamina. As to the teasing—she found it rather exciting to play secret games with her lover in public.

Bridgeburton's daughter, apparently, was in her true element at last. She was living a life of sin and secrets, and she was wicked enough to enjoy it.

Which wasn't to say her pleasure was unadulterated. Fiona's possible guilt cast its shadow. David was another, albeit not so heavy, shadow. And there was the nightmare, regular as clockwork.

Every morning it jerked Leila from a dead sleep. The same gloomy hallway. The same two men—one massive brute and one dark, small one with Cassius' "lean and hungry look." And trapped between them, Ismal, murmuring words in a foreign language. He would turn his head, and the light would shimmer over pale gold . . . then the glint of the blade . . . a gash, blood red, and blue poison dripping into it. Then came the buzzing . . . and the suffocating blackness. And at last she'd wake, shivering and sick with dread.

Helena Martin's French maid returned to the hall, and Leila quickly jerked her mind to the present.

The servant apologized for keeping Madame waiting, and led her to the parlor. Eloise, who'd insisted upon coming, did not—thank heaven—insist upon following, but remained straight, silent, and coolly expressionless by the front door. Just before entering the parlor, Leila threw her bodyguard a grateful smile. Ismal had told the two servants that Madame Beaumont was *not* to be allowed within a mile of Helena Martin. Eloise's loyalty, however, inclined to the mistress of the house.

Leila was still smiling as the door closed behind her. She met Helena's wary gaze.

"It is rude to scold a guest," Helena said, "but really, Mrs. Beaumont, you ought to know better. If word of this gets out, your reputation will be in tatters."

"Then I shall have to return to Paris," Leila said. "Fortunately, I know the language and can work there as well as I do here. Our professional requirements, you see, are not entirely unlike."

"Shocking thing to say." Helena gestured at a richly upholstered sofa, and Leila obediently sat. Her hostess perched stiffly on a chair opposite. "Next, I suppose, you'll be offering to do my portrait."

"I should like that, very much," Leila said. "*If* I could think how to manage it without sending Mr. Herriard into an apoplexy. That, however, is not my present errand."

She opened her reticule and withdrew a ruby and diamond ear drop. "This is rather awkward, but the thing's been plaguing me since I found it, and I'm sure whoever it belongs to would like to have it back."

She handed it to Helena, who said nothing.

"I've begun rearranging the—my late husband's room," Leila lied. "My servant found the earring wedged in a crack under his bed. I suppose that's why the police never found it, though they tore the house apart, looking for heaven knows what. But Eloise, you see, is obsessively thorough—"

"It isn't mine, Mrs. Beaumont." Helena's face was a cool blank. "I'm partial to rubies, but this definitely isn't mine."

"I do beg your pardon." Leila let out a sigh. "It's deuced awkward but—well, I might as well be straightforward. I'm aware Francis brought women home from time to time when I was away. And I did recollect—that is, you and I have stood near each other at the theater once or twice, and I noticed your perfume. A distinctive blend, I must say. And—to blunder on—I had occasion to notice it on Francis—or in his room—I'm not sure when exactly. But not long ago, or it shouldn't have stuck in my mind. It must have been the last time I noticed such a thing before he died."

Helena's dark eyebrows rose very slightly. "Another woman's perfume. How odd."

"I have an abominably keen sense of smell," Leila explained. "Like a hound, Francis used to say. But I'm obviously not a good detective." She was aware of Helena's expression sharpening several degrees. "I'm sure you wouldn't be so missishly impractical as to deny owning such an expensive item. It's not as though I'd be shocked, and it's been years since his infidelities troubled me."

"If it were mine, I wouldn't deny it, Mrs. Beaumont. I'm certainly not missish."

"Yes, of course. Well, my deductive powers seem to have failed me this time." Leila shook her head. "How disappointing. I had hoped—that is, whoever it does belong to had to work hard enough for it, I daresay. And I strongly doubt that whatever Francis paid her would make up for the loss."

Helena looked down at the earring in her hand. "If she was careless enough to leave it behind, she deserves to lose it. It's very bad manners to leave evidence for the wife to find. I wouldn't trouble myself about this particular whore's loss if I were you, Mrs. Beaumont. She's obviously not worth your trouble."

She gave the earring back. Her fingers barely touched Leila's hand, but that fleeting contact was icy. "I've heard you've been busy with good deeds," Helena added with the smallest of smiles. "Sherburne. Avory. Patching up Beaumont's damage, people say. You are quite the talk of London. Still, correcting the mistakes of stupid little tarts is carrying it too far. Not worth the risk—to your reputation, that is—to consort with the likes of us. If the earring troubles you, I suggest you leave it in the nearest poor box, for the deserving needy."

* * *

ISMAL RESISTED THE urge to peer out the window of
the hackney. The exterior of Helena Martin's house would
tell him nothing, and he must not risk being observed. The
sky was rapidly darkening with an approaching storm, but
was not nearly dark enough. He took out his pocket watch
and studied that instead.

Leila had been inside twenty minutes at least. He'd arrived too late to prevent her—which was his own fault. He
should have suspected trouble the instant she stopped
plaguing him about Helena.

There was, unfortunately, a good deal he should have
done these last few days and hadn't. Leaving Avory's servants to Nick, he'd turned his attention to Sherburne—who
had, with a few jocular remarks, succeeded in riveting Ismal's mind elsewhere.

Thanks to Herriard's small fit of overprotectiveness at
the soiree, most of Society seemed to be growing
fiendishly curious about the Comte d'Esmond's intentions
regarding Mrs. Beaumont. Being one of the Beau Monde's
leaders, Sherburne had appointed himself spokesman.

Now that Mrs. Beaumont was out and about again,
Sherburne had said a few nights ago, it was hoped she
wouldn't remain a widow much longer. Still, it would be a
great pity if London lost her altogether—to Paris, for instance, he'd added with a knowing smile.

That and a few more equally unsubtle comments had
succeeded in unsettling Ismal's mind, if not his outward
composure. It became very clear then that—despite Mrs.
Beaumont's being widowed little more than two months
and the Comte d'Esmond's being a foreigner with a reputation as a ladykiller—they were expected to wed. Soon.

If they did not—if, in fact, Ismal didn't soon start giving clear signals of honorable intentions, the current
friendly rumors would turn hostile, and Leila would pay
with her reputation.

The trouble was, he could not hurry her into marriage, whatever Society thought. Ismal could not stand
before a man of God and utter solemn vows while his

soul was stained with her unhappiness. To bind Leila to him while she remained in ignorance of the past was dishonorable. Cowardly. He needed time to prove himself, time to prepare her for the confession he should have made weeks ago.

Unfortunately, he might have already deprived himself of time. They had been lovers for a week. He had not once taken precautions, and she hadn't suggested any. She probably assumed she was barren because she hadn't borne Beaumont a child.

Ismal knew better than to make such assumptions. He knew it would be exactly like Fate to give the screws another twist, in the form of a babe. Then what would he do? Confess?—when it was already too late? Leave her to choose between marrying her nemesis and bearing a bastard?

He dragged his hand through his hair. "Imbecile," he muttered. "Coward. Pig."

At that moment, he noticed movement outside. He sank back against the seat. The door swung open. An instant later, Leila stepped in—then froze.

"Madame?" came Eloise's voice from behind her.

Ismal pulled Leila onto the seat beside him, told Eloise to find Nick, gave the driver a few brisk commands, and yanked the door shut. The carriage promptly jolted into motion.

"It's starting to *rain*," Leila said. "You will not leave her in the street." She reached for the rope, but Ismal grabbed her hand.

"Nick is watching the house from a carriage near the corner," he said. "Eloise will not melt before she reaches him. It is *you* I should leave in the street—and tell the driver to trample you down. I am not pleased with you, Leila."

"The feeling's mutual," she said. "In case you haven't noticed, it's broad day. What if someone sees us?"

"What difference does it make who sees us if one of us ends up dead by morning?"

As though to punctuate his prediction of doom, thunder crashed.

"There is no need to be theatrical," she said, lifting her chin. "If someone attempts murder in the dead of night, it's most likely he—or she—will have to contend with us both. Plus Gaspard and Eloise. And even though you have been utterly unreasonable—and just threatened to have me trampled—I shall do my utmost to protect you." She patted his arm. "Come, don't be cross. I think I've found something."

"You have put my stomach in knots." He frowned into her beautiful face. "You make me frantic with worry, Leila. You said you would deal with Lady Carroll. Since she is your friend, one would think you would prefer to settle that first. Instead—"

"Instead I trusted woman's intuition," she said. "Lady Brentmor was the one who called our attention to Helena, and she doesn't make idle suggestions. My instincts don't usually make idle suggestions, either. Ever since I studied that list of yours, I've had a feeling."

"A feeling." He sighed.

"A very strong one," she said. "That Helena's the key. It was the same kind of feeling I had about that scar of yours. That it connected to something important."

He knew better than to question her instincts. "The tigress has caught the scent, I perceive." He leaned back against the squabs. "I was ten times a fool to think I could stop you from hunting. Tell me, then."

She told him about her ploy with her earring. It was not the most brilliant strategem, but she had used the opportunity well. She hadn't missed the smallest change in Helena's face, posture, gestures. By Allah, she'd even taken note of the woman's temperature. And Leila had analyzed these minutiae just as Ismal would have done, and reached the same conclusions.

Beyond doubt, Helena had been deeply disturbed by the hint that she'd been with Beaumont. Yet he was dead, and all the world knew his wife had no illusions about his fidelity. If Helena was worried, it must be because she'd committed a greater crime than prostitution.

"I knew I'd struck a nerve with that business I made up about its being the last time I noticed perfume," Leila was saying. "But her reaction made me remember something connected. On New Year's Eve, I spent the night with Fiona at her brother Philip's house. I came home to the usual disorder, the usual signs that Francis had entertained at home."

She took Ismal's hand and squeezed it. "Now isn't the timing *interesting*?" she said. "If Helena was with him that night, she had a perfect opportunity to scout the house. Then, the next time I was away—not two weeks later—she could make a very quick, neat job of whatever she had to do: find and steal the letters for Langford, and maybe poison Francis' laudanum for her own satisfaction."

"Yes, madame, it is very interesting." Ismal closed his eyes. "If your theory is correct, you have now given Helena Martin an excellent reason to kill you. She has only to report your visit to Langford, and there will be *two* people wishing to kill you. Perhaps *I* shall kill you and spare them the trouble—and myself a painful period of suspense."

"I'm *counting* on her reporting my visit to Langford," she said. "If all goes as I hope, I expect he'll call on me soon. Then, I think, we'll get some clues, if not answers."

He cocked one eye open. She was watching him with ill-concealed excitement. "I am listening," he said.

"Lady Brentmor told me this morning that the Langfords received a note from Dorset," she said. "David and Lettice are betrothed. Langford is tickled to death. Recollect, Lettice's father was his dearest friend. Also, thanks to Lady Brentmor and Fiona, the Duke of Langford thinks he owes it all to *me*."

Ismal had both eyes open now. "It is true. You instigated everything, ordered everyone about."

"The point is, my alleged good deed may nearly balance my poking my nose into certain delicate matters," she said. "Langford won't be so quick to crush me. When he calls, he'll probably just try to pick my brains. And I'll let him, because I've got a lovely explanation."

"But of course."

"It *is* lovely," she said. "I shall tell him I found out Francis had some damaging documents, which I fear have fallen into the wrong hands."

"Helena's, for instance."

She nodded. "I shall ask for Langford's help. And he'll believe me, because half of London has this notion I've been doing good deeds. Even Helena had heard about David and Sherburne. She claims people are saying I was patching up Francis' damage. So this will fit the pattern. Don't you see? This is the perfect time, while Langford's prepared to think kindly of me."

Ismal didn't answer. Her words were beginning to take hold in his mind. Timing. Patterns. And inconsistencies.

Both Avory and his father had paid blackmail money in December. The garter episode had occurred early in the same month. Sherburne had evidently known about the garters, yet he'd said nothing to Avory. Shortly thereafter, Beaumont had debauched Lady Sherburne, and all the husband had done was destroy a portrait.

Sherburne and Avory were definite problems. Neither man possessed the character for weeks of cool, patient plotting—especially for a crime so underhand as poisoning. The timing and crime might fit Lady Carroll's character, but she was no Helena Martin. How could she—without help—have entered, unnoticed, an empty, locked house? And if it weren't empty, would she have been brazen enough to enter while Francis Beaumont was there alone? Was it possible she had swallowed her revulsion and gone to bed with him just for a chance to poison his laudanum? Would she have left so much to chance?

And suppose she had. What, then, of the missing letters? Admittedly, there may have been no more letters after the ones Beaumont sold to Avory and his father. But all Ismal's instincts told him there had been more, that it was as Leila had surmised: Helena had been at the house twice because Langford had hired her to steal.

It was very doubtful he had hired her to kill as well. It

was one thing to take back his son's letters, which rightfully belonged to the family. Even the courts must agree though the law might nitpick about the methods employed. But to conspire murder with a prostitute who, if caught, would assuredly incriminate him was foolish beyond permission.

Nor could Ismal believe Helena would be so reckless as to commit the greater crime while employed by Langford to commit the lesser, and relatively safe one. Yet if she'd committed only the one, safe crime, why had she been so worried?

"Ismal." Madame shook his arm. "We're home. If you want to talk about this, I can cancel my engagement for tonight. It's just a gathering of Lady Brentmor's gossipy friends. They won't miss me."

He studied her animated countenance. She was very pleased with herself. Perhaps she was entitled. He knew to his own cost that her hunter instincts were excellent. Perhaps she was closing in on her quarry. Whatever happened, he had better be in on the kill.

"I am not sure I wish to speak to you," he said. "You have been very disobedient."

"I'll make it up to you." She tugged at his neckcloth, bringing his face close to hers. "We can have dinner together. I'll tell Eloise to make your favorites. And then . . ." She lightly brushed her lips against his. "You can practice your favorite perversions on me."

"Aye, you think you can wrap me about your finger," he said. "With food and lovemaking. As though I were an animal. As though I had no higher, spiritual needs." He wrapped his arms about her. "You are not altogether correct. But close enough. I shall come after nightfall."

Taking her into his arms was a fatal error. Once he held her, it was very difficult to let go. It was very difficult not to bring his mouth to hers again. Then it was impossible to make do with one quick, chaste kiss.

He lingered. The kiss deepened. The warmth swirled through him, and the sweetness. He'd just brought his hands to her cloak fastenings when the carriage door swung open. Wet wind gusted in, and a large umbrella appeared at the door.

"If you don't hurry, Leila," called a feminine voice, "this curst gale will blow me to kingdom come."

Ismal jerked his hands away from the cloak, just as Lady Carroll poked her head through the door.

In the midst of the storm, as in the eye of a hurricane, there was a short, sharp silence.

"My lady," Ismal said politely. "What a delightful surprise."

"*Monsieur,*" said Lady Carroll, green eyes gleaming. "My sentiments exactly."

SOME HOURS LATER, Leila sat at the dinner table, watching Ismal crack nuts while she tried to formulate a tactful response to the issue he'd just raised with her. This would have been difficult in any case. It was rendered doubly so by the complication he'd added: in the course of escorting Fiona home, he'd let her know just where he'd met up with Leila. He had also given Fiona the same explanation for Leila's being at Helena Martin's that Leila had planned to give Langford.

She decided to deal with the complication first and hope he'd forget the other issue . . . for about a year.

"It never occurred to me to explain our encounter that way," Leila said carefully. "That was clever of you. And as usual, it was at least partly true. I certainly didn't plan to meet you there."

He dropped a nutmeat onto her plate. "That is not why I told her. You had spoken of connections and timing. I think there are more connections than we have perceived. I believe this may be why we have fixed on these five people, of all the hundreds who might wish to kill your husband. Our instincts tell us something, but we do not yet understand what it is."

He glanced down at her plate. She shook her head. "I've had enough. I want to hear about our instincts."

"Today you told me you had a feeling Helena Martin

was the key," he said. "That gave me some ideas. So I tried your technique with Lady Carroll. I mentioned Helena as a test and watched the reaction. She is not so hardened a character as Helena. Her Ladyship was most disturbed, then quickly tried to cover her discomposure by putting me on the defensive. She knows very well there is no preventing your doing whatever you set your obstinate mind to. Yet she insisted to me that you would not be getting yourself into scrapes if I were not so lackadaisical about courting you."

So much for hoping he'd forget about *that* issue.

"She was talking utter rot," Leila said. "One doesn't even consider courting a widow until she's out of full mourning."

He cracked another nut and popped the meat into his mouth.

"A year," she explained. "Fiona knows that perfectly well."

"A year," he said. "That is a very long time."

"I think it's one of the few sensible rules," she said, squirming inwardly. "It would be very easy for a woman to make a great mistake when her mind is disordered by grief."

After a moment's sober consideration, he nodded. "Even if she is not grief-stricken, she might be lonely, and so, vulnerable. It would be unfair to exploit her feelings during this time. There is the matter of freedom to consider as well. A widow is permitted more latitude than a maiden, and she does not answer to a husband. It does not seem unreasonable to grant a woman at least twelve months of such freedom."

"All of which Fiona ought to understand," Leila said, frowning down at her plate. "*She's* certainly been in no hurry to give up her freedom. She's had six years."

"I agree she was unreasonable. But she was alarmed, as I said. Still, I am glad we have discussed this. If she presses the matter, I shall explain that you and I have discussed it, and I shall repeat what you have told me. So I will inform everyone who questions me about my intentions."

She looked up, her heart thudding. "Everyone? Who else would—"

"Better ask who else has *already* questioned me. In addition to Nick, Eloise, and Gaspard, there is Sherburne—who speaks for multitudes, apparently. Next it will be Langford, I think." He rose. "Unless I miss my guess, he will have heard from two women by tomorrow: Helena Martin and Lady Carroll."

She stared dumbly at him, unable to collect her thoughts. They darted from Sherburne to Fiona, from Intentions to Connections.

"It is complicated," he said as he drew her up from the chair. "But we can sort it out more comfortably upstairs. Tonight we shall have plenty of time for conversation." He smiled. "Also, I believe there was some mention earlier of *perversions.*"

Chapter 16

WHILE HE TRAILED LEILA UP THE STAIRS, ISMAL was pondering perversions. He wondered whether Beaumont had deliberately denied his wife pleasure or had simply been incapable of satisfying her. Whatever the man's motives, it was clear by now that Beaumont had restricted his marital intimacies to a few basic acts and satisfied his less prosaic tastes elsewhere.

Ismal wondered what service, for instance, Helena Martin had been obliged to provide Beaumont. The images conjured up drew his gaze to the master bedroom door. He paused, his hand on the banister.

"Ismal?"

He frowned. "There are no secret compartments in this house," he said, moving to the door. "No false drawers or hiding places in the furnishings. Quentin's men are very thorough and know what to look for. I also looked." He opened the door and entered the dark room. "But the papers must have been in the house, and that must have been why Helena came. Assuredly she did not need your husband as a customer. She had richer and more attractive ones with simpler tastes. But she would not have come only to kill him, for she could have arranged to do this elsewhere, without having to bed him."

While he talked, he found a candle and lit it.

"Shall I fetch a lamp?" Leila's voice came from the doorway.

"No, no. She would not have had more light than this. Less, perhaps. I—" He looked round and gave her an abashed smile. "Forgive me."

"That's all right. You've got an idea." Ismal recognized her "investigative" voice, crisp and businesslike.

"A riddle," he said. "How and where did she find the letters, if there were letters?"

"You want to see with her eyes, is that it?" She advanced into the room. "I can tell you that Francis generally conducted our marital relations in near darkness. He may have been different with others, but I doubt it. He was subject to headaches."

He nodded. "That is what I thought. Since he drank and used opiates to excess, his eyes would be sensitive."

"What else were you thinking?"

"That your giving Helena the earring did not trouble her nearly so much as the mention of your keen sense of smell." He sat on the edge of the bed. "You said you noticed the usual disorder when you returned on New Year's Day. Did you come into this room?"

"Yes. Francis was shouting for Mrs. Dempton and storming about. I had to remind him she'd taken the holiday."

Ismal patted the mattress. Obediently, she sat beside him.

"Close your eyes," he said. "Make a picture in your mind. What did you observe?"

She told him where various garments had been strewn. She described the disorder of the dressing table . . . the drawers of the wardrobe, which had been partly open . . . fresh wine stains on the rug . . . his neckcloth, tied to the bedpost . . .

Her eyes flew open. "And the curtain there was torn— pulled right off the rod." She got up and moved to the foot

of the bed. Drawing the hanging out, she showed the place
where Mrs. Dempton had mended it. "A large tear," she
said. "You'd have to yank hard to do that."

"And it is near the bedpost the cravat was tied to," he
said. "If he tied her to the bedpost, and she was in
discomfort—or pretending to be—she might have
clawed at—"

"In *discomfort*?"

He saw her fingers tighten on the fabric. "Your husband
took pleasure in others' emotional pain," he said. "It is reasonable to suppose he would also take pleasure in their
physical pain. Being a professional, Helena would surely
give him a dramatic show."

Leila let go of the hanging and moved to the opposite
side of the bed. "Well, then, I was luckier than I knew. Poor
Helena."

"Helena knew well enough what to expect and how to
deal with it," he said. "She did not come up from the sink-
holes of London by magic, you know. Not many with such
low beginnings manage to live past adolescence, let alone
rise to the heights she has. That is a formidable woman,
Leila."

"I understand. It's just the—the irony. If Francis hadn't
married me, I should have learned firsthand what Helena
knows." She gave a short laugh. "How exasperating. No
matter how you look at it, he truly was my knight in shining armor. I might have ended on the Venice streets, or the
Paris ones, if not for him. Certainly he saved me from the
more immediate danger. Those men who killed my father
might have . . ." She shivered.

The reminder stung deep and sharp as a viper's fangs,
and Ismal lashed out reflexively, his voice harsh. "Aye, he
was like the prince in the fairy tale. He stole your innocence, and for once—perhaps the only time—in his life did
the honorable thing and gave you his name. Then he gave
you so agreeable a view of wedded life that you will risk
your reputation and career before you will even *consider*
trying it again."

He heard her sharply indrawn breath, and cursed himself. Wrenching back his self-control, he stood up. "I talk like an ignorant brute," he said. "Please forgive me. To think of you upon the streets—a young girl . . . It upset me. Yet it is just as I deserve, for I thoughtlessly distressed you about Helena. Even for her, you feel compassion."

If he had inflicted hurt, she concealed it well. She stood a bit more arrogantly erect, but that was all. "Compassion is one thing," she said. "Maundering on about the past is another. It's probably this damned room. I always found it . . . oppressive. Everything so heavy and ornate. The air was always stale, because he'd never open a window. After his little soirees, it would reek of wine and smoke."

"It is an oppressive room, I agree," he said.

"I always said his tarts had to have strong stomachs. Not to mention that he created a prime environment for vermin. You could not have got me into this bed, even if the entire mattress were stuffed with strong repellent herbs like tansy. As it was . . ."

Frowning, she stepped back a few paces from the bed, her gaze lifting to the rectangular canopy.

"The bags," she said after a long pause. "The bags of herbs."

He looked up, too, and his brain promptly went to work. "To discourage the insects, you mean."

She drew back the fabric. "There, you see? In all four corners—those small balloonlike decorations with the tassles. He had them made to match. That's why they look like part of the draperies. But they aren't. They tie to the supports. Every few months, you take them down and put in a fresh supply of herbs."

Ismal was already pulling off his boots.

"He did that himself," she said. "His sole domestic chore."

He understood. In the next moment, he was standing on the bed, squeezing the fabric bags as Helena had probably done. He found what he was looking for in the right-hand corner at the head: paper crackled under his hand.

Balancing himself with one foot on the nightstand, he

untied the bag. Then he dropped down to a sitting position. Leila climbed onto the mattress and sat beside him.

He gave her the bag. "You made the deduction, madame. You must do the honors."

She loosened the drawstrings and emptied the contents onto the mattress. The resulting heap comprised a handful of tansy and one carefully rolled-up sheet of lavender-tinted stationery. It took but an instant to open it. It was blank.

She turned gleaming eyes upon him. "She did it. She got the letters. I'll wager fifty quid this is her own writing paper." She held it up to his nose, though Ismal already recognized the paper as well as the scent.

"Perfumed," Leila said. "Helena's scent. Very distinctive. She left it on purpose, so Francis would know who'd done it—just as he had left that stickpin for Sherburne to find."

That was all it took. The one sentence. After weeks of collecting bits of information and doing precious little with them, Ismal's mind finally began assembling the pieces.

He took the sheet of paper from her. "Evidently, Helena did not realize your husband had no sense of smell," he said. "Still, the paper is also distinctive. All in all, a broad enough hint. Do you not find this odd?"

She looked at him, then at the paper. "Goddamn. Yes. It's obvious, isn't it? She wouldn't have left a message if she'd poisoned the laudanum. You don't hide messages for a man you know will be dead within twenty-four hours. Also, you don't *deliberately* leave incriminating evidence behind."

He nodded. "Even if we supposed she stole the papers on New Year's Eve, and came back weeks later to poison him—"

"Which is highly improbable—"

"She would have remembered to remove the evidence implicating her."

"So someone else poisoned him," Leila said. "And Helena didn't know. That would explain her being so upset about my sense of smell. Francis' death and the inquest must have come as a shock to her. And probably to Lang-ford, if he'd hired her to steal."

"Timing," he said. "We have both been puzzled by the timing. It seems that the theft and poisoning did not occur at the same time—most likely, not even the same day. So we must theorize that Helena stole the papers either on New Year's Eve or the next time she was sure you were safely away. That leaves the first night you were at Norbury House. Sunday, the eleventh of January."

"Either way, I think we have to eliminate Langford, too. Why risk a scandal at best—a nasty murder trial at worst—when Francis couldn't bother him any more?"

"That leaves us with Avory, Sherburne, and Lady Car-roll." He was beginning to see just what was left—timing, personalities, connections. He should have put it together weeks ago. A week ago at least.

"Yes, yes, I know." She rubbed her head. "But it doesn't—there has to be something. Helena. I know she's the key. Damn. I need to see it in black and white." She stuffed the paper back into the bag and got off the bed. "I need to get out of this beastly room, too. As soon as we've solved this pestilential murder, I'm going to strip this whole damned chamber down to bare walls and floors, I vow."

"Actually, I would prefer we found another house."

She halted halfway to the door.

"After we are wed," he said. "A larger house. So that you might have one full floor for your work area."

The air began to pulse. She marched to the door. "We can talk about that later," she said. "I'm having enough trouble keeping things straight in my head as it is. I need to write it down. I'm going to the studio."

He could have told her she didn't need to write any-thing down. He could explain what had happened, or most of it. But it would give her more satisfaction to work it out on her own. And so he held his tongue and followed her to the studio.

* * *

IT TOOK LEILA about ten minutes to realize Ismal was humoring her. He sat beside her at the worktable, his attention seemingly riveted on the sheet of foolscap she was covering with notes and arrows. He seemed to be listening attentively to every syllable she uttered.

And he was bored.

She put down the pencil and folded her hands. "Go ahead, tell me," she said.

"I am listening," he said. "It is very interesting what you say of Sherburne. I myself saw him with Helena Martin on that night I encountered Avory. Indeed, it is possible Sherburne confided his troubles—or part, at least—to her."

"You may be listening, but you're not thinking."

He treated her to his most seraphically innocent expression. "What makes you believe I am not thinking?"

"Your eyes. Your thinking color is several degrees more intense. You don't need to think because you've worked it all out."

He let out a sigh. "I thought you would prefer to assemble the pieces yourself."

"I prefer to observe the genius at work," she said.

"It is not genius. You have pointed out some pertinent issues. I have merely connected them."

"I'm well aware that we make a good team," she said.

With a faint smile, he took up the pencil. "It is true. For instance, you did say a short while ago that Helena did to your husband as your husband had done to Sherburne. That made me wonder how much she knew of the Sherburne episode, and whether she had purposely adopted your husband's spiteful style."

He turned the sheet over. At the top, he wrote Helena's name, then Sherburne's, connecting the two with a line.

"This afternoon, you reminded me that Langford and Lady Carroll's father were close friends," he said. "Lady Carroll is considered head of her family. Everyone turns to her. I asked myself, if she found herself in an impossible situation, to whom would she turn?"

He wrote Fiona's name below Sherburne's, and Langford's under Helena's, then drew connecting lines—Langford to Fiona, Langford to Helena.

"We believe Langford also had a large problem with your husband—blackmail. This bothered me, not simply because the duke is so powerful, but because it did not fit your husband's pattern. Customarily, Beaumont lured one into his nets, *then* exploited or attacked. So I considered the timing."

On the lower half of the paper he drew a grid. "The month of December," he explained as he filled in the dates.

"On the second of December is the Fatal Ball. Letty's garters are stolen, and we assume Lady Carroll goes to the Duke of Langford for help. To Langford, your husband is a worthless cur, a pernicious influence on his son. At this point, however, he realizes that the cur is rabid."

Leila was beginning to see, too. "It's one thing to corrupt a grown man," she said. "Another to abuse a gently bred virgin—especially the youngest daughter of his best friend."

"So I theorize that Langford confronted your husband. Perhaps he threatened destruction if the rabid dog did not leave England immediately. Your husband, cornered, responded by producing one of Charles' letters—and evidence that there were more. The duke found himself not only two thousand pounds poorer but at the mercy of the mad dog."

"Intolerable," she said. "So Langford went to Helena."

"And they made their plans. I have little doubt these included having Lady Carroll deal with you—to get you out of the way so that Helena could do her work."

Leila looked up from the rough calendar. "So you think that's *all* Fiona did? But why was she so late coming to Norbury House? You don't think she was helping Helena, do you?"

"I think—" He turned toward the windows. "I think a carriage has stopped in front of this house. A coach and four." He was off the stool and at the windows in the next instant. He peered through the slit between the drapes. "A gentleman emerges."

"At this hour? It's past eleven." Her heart hastened to double time. "You've got to get out. Hide. You can't—"

"Certainly not." He came back and patted her on the shoulder. "It is only the Duke of Langford. You wait here. I will go down and calm Gaspard. He will be alarmed."

She couldn't believe her ears. "Are you mad? You can't go . . ." But he was already across the room and out the door. Gone.

Leila stared at the open doorway. Langford. At this hour. And Ismal, cool as you please, going down—to *her* front door—to what? *Greet* the duke? At eleven o'clock at night—in the house of his *mistress*?

She got up from the stool, then sat down again. Ismal had told her to wait. He was the professional. He knew what he was doing. Beyond doubt he'd been in far more awkward situations before. More dangerous ones. Gaspard and Eloise were downstairs. Langford wouldn't commit mayhem in a respectable neighborhood, before witnesses.

But what in blazes was he doing here at this hour? He was supposed to come tomorrow. She'd planned for that. She hadn't planned for this—tonight. What would she have done if Ismal hadn't been here? *Esmond*, she corrected. She must think of him as Esmond for the moment. She mustn't forget that. No slips. He wouldn't make any. He was discreet. He'd have a brilliant excuse for being here.

At least they were fully dressed. Or were they? She tried frantically to recollect. Had she taken off his neckcloth? Had he? She checked her buttons and hooks. All fastened. Her hair was a mess, but then, it always was.

She heard footsteps, voices. She snatched up the piece of foolscap, folded it, and thrust it into the sketchbook. She leapt off the stool just as the Duke of Langford entered, Ismal close behind.

Then, too late, she noticed the herb bag hanging from the easel.

Swallowing an oath, she lifted her chin and marched to

her guests. She sketched the duke a curtsy, received a sketchy bow in return and icily polite greetings.

"This is an unlooked for honor," she said.

He directed a steely grey gaze down his nose at her. If the look was meant to be intimidating, it failed. All that impressed Leila was his strong resemblance to David. It was very evident when one stood so near. She focused on that, to keep her mind—and eyes—off the telltale bag.

His blond hair was a shade darker than his son's, but without a hint of grey. His countenance was harder and colder, his eyes more cynical and arrogant. His was a stronger-willed, far more ruthless character than David's, clearly. But then, the duke had carried the weight of his title, with all its attendant burdens, since adolescence. Those responsibilities included a family.

She remembered then, that he was a father as well as a powerful nobleman, that he'd suffered his share of parental grief. And shame: Charles' indiscreet letters, in the hands of a mentally unbalanced degenerate . . . David's dangerous friendship with the same degenerate.

With a twinge of guilt, Leila realized that the poor man had been allowed not twenty-four hours to rejoice over David's betrothal before she had cut up his peace.

Instinctively, she took his hand. "By gad, how vexed you must be with me," she said. "I can guess what you're thinking—that I am a meddlesome—"

"What I am thinking, madam, is that you ought to be kept on a leash," he said, frowning down at her hand. "It's a good thing Esmond here has some concern for your safety. Obviously, *you* haven't. What in blazes were you thinking of, to visit that woman—in broad day, no less, when all the world might see? Did it never occur to you, the sort of persons who might be about? You might have been robbed or assaulted. Or followed, as Esmond feared. At the very least, you might have been subjected to insult and indignity. I vow, I am strongly tempted to take you over my knee, young lady."

Before she could respond, Eloise entered with a tray,

which she silently placed on the worktable. She left just as quietly, closing the door behind her.

Esmond moved to the tray. "I would recommend you not let Madame Beaumont hold your hand overlong, Your Grace," he said as he picked up the brandy decanter. "The effect often proves debilitating to a gentleman's intellect."

Leila hastily released the duke. "I beg your pardon," she said, retreating to the worktable. "My manners are abominable."

"Your brain, on the other hand, appears to be in excellent working order." Langford stepped up to the easel and studied the bag. "I see you found it, as Helena feared. Sniffed her out, did you?" He absently accepted the glass Esmond offered him and tasted the brandy in the same preoccupied way.

Leila glanced at Esmond as he handed her a glass. His expression was not enlightening.

"I take it Miss Martin has confessed to Your Grace," Leila said carefully. "In which case, I assume you've taken the proper steps, and the documents will trouble nobody."

"I should like to know how you learned there were documents," the duke said, turning back to her. "Is that what your quarrel with your husband was about? Is that why you refused to describe the quarrel to the coroner? Am I to believe you've been searching for *papers* these last two months?"

As she met his penetrating gaze, Leila saw plainly that he wasn't going to believe anything like it. "Not exactly," she said.

His smile was thin. "Quite. I am not a fool, madam. Just because I repose confidence in Quentin's judgment doesn't mean I'm oblivious to his charades. That inquest was a well-orchestrated one. Not one genuine poison expert in the lot. I also found Esmond's role in the proceedings most intriguing. Couldn't shake off the feeling he was the orchestra leader." He lifted his glass to Esmond, then sipped.

"As you have apparently deduced, Your Grace, Lord Quentin felt the negative consequences of a murder investigation greatly outweighed the positive effects of technical justice," Esmond said.

"Knowing what I do about Beaumont, I couldn't agree more. I only regret I didn't know until rather late. Had I taken steps sooner, I might have spared someone the revolting task of killing him." Langford's gaze moved to Leila. "That's what you're looking for, isn't it? The killer."

She hesitated.

"Fiona said you told her a man had a right to confront his accuser. Haven't I that right, Mrs. Beaumont?"

"You would," she said. "But I can't accuse you." She gestured at the bag. "That pretty much proves neither you nor Helena helped Francis to his Maker."

"I am inexpressibly relieved to hear it."

She straightened her spine. "Still, you said you took steps. Is it impertinent of me to ask what those steps were? Merely in the interests of enlightenment."

"Madame is abominably curious," Esmond murmured.

"Not at all," said His Grace. "I came on purpose to put her mind at ease regarding these troublesome documents. I had intended to omit the disagreeable details, but if Mrs. Beaumont has the stomach to contemplate murder, I doubt my poor crimes will send her into fainting fits."

His cool grey gaze swept the studio. "All the same, I've had enough experience of women to know they're unpredictable. I should feel vastly more at ease, madam, if you were safely seated upon that well-padded sofa."

Leila opened her mouth to announce that her sensibilities weren't at all delicate. She shut it, and headed for the sofa. If the man was willing to talk, she told herself, the least she could do was accommodate a chivalrous request.

Esmond wandered over to the bookshelves behind her. Langford positioned himself at the near end of the fireplace and clasped his hands behind his back.

His story began as she and Ismal had surmised, with the garter episode, and Fiona going to the duke for help. He'd already begun putting his plan into action when Sherburne came to him.

"He was appalled by the nasty scene he'd made in your studio," Langford told her. "He said that if something weren't done soon, Beaumont would surely drive someone to worse, and you didn't deserve to be the scapegoat. He also pointed out that Avory was in a similar position, being the man's bosom bow. By that time, I hardly needed the warning. I simply apprised Sherburne of my plans and promised he'd have a chance to settle his own score, as long as he followed orders."

Fiona was ordered to get Leila out of the way at the critical times, he explained. Sherburne was to do the same with Avory. The next part fit Leila and Esmond's theory: New Year's Eve, Helena scouting the house—and finding the herb bag. She duly reported to Langford, and final plans were laid. Fiona arranged a weeklong visit for Leila, to allow for possible failure on the first attempt to get the papers.

"Helena set out on the very first night you were gone," Langford said. "The Sabbath, I'm sorry to say. Which brings me to the more distasteful aspects. But I think you understand strong measures were required."

Leila assured him she understood.

"I had Sherburne with me, and two sturdy fellows whom I trust implicitly. Helena lured Beaumont into our ambush. While we took Beaumont off for a private discussion, she went on to do her work at the house. We kept Beaumont until nearly dawn—to give her plenty of time— and meanwhile taught him a lesson."

"Your sturdy fellows were professionals, it seems," Esmond said. "There were no recent bruises on the body."

"We shan't discuss the details," the duke said. "Enough to say Beaumont was made to understand *his* orders. He was to settle his affairs forthwith and leave England permanently. He was not to take his wife with him. Fiona had insisted upon that, and we all agreed. We certainly weren't going to let him relieve his spite on you," he told Leila. "I made it very plain that he must be gone before you returned from Surrey."

"No wonder he was so incensed when I came home early," Leila said, recollecting. "But it wasn't altogether rage, I see now. Panic, more likely."

"I can tell you Fiona was in a panic when you left Surrey on Tuesday," Langford said. "Unfortunately, by the time I received her message, Beaumont was dead, and your house was overrun with law officers."

That did explain why Fiona had plagued her to stay at Norbury House. And it was just possible Fiona had encouraged Esmond to follow for the same reason: she'd been frightened for Leila's safety.

"Indeed, the timing of his death was most inconvenient for you," Esmond said from somewhere behind her.

"Not his death, but that infernal woman servant's howling about murder," the duke answered. "We knew the house would be searched. That's why I attended the inquest. Wanted to know what they'd found. Wanted to be prepared, you see, to do the right thing by Helena. After all, I made the plan and gave the orders. The rest of us were safe enough. Alibis, that is, for the entire night. Until half-past five o'clock, the night before his death, the servants had been in the house. No visitors, they testified. From half-past five to eight, my troops were with me at Helena's, celebrating. We burned the letters and didn't spare the champagne. Sherburne and I saw Fiona home right after. Her servants can vouch for her whereabouts from then on. Sherburne went on to the Dunhams' and I stopped in at my club for a while, then went home."

He took his neglected brandy glass from the mantel. "Does that satisfy your curiosity, Mrs. Beaumont? Are you sufficiently enlightened?"

She was so relieved she wanted to hug him. She clasped her hands tightly together. "Yes, certainly. Thank you. Indeed, you have been very kind, very patient, Your Grace."

He looked at her for a long time, his expression unreadable. "Helena said you were a piece of work. I quite
agree. Mending marriages. Matchmaking. Hunting
thieves and murderers." He frowned at the empty glass in
his hand. "I don't think the last is wise. But one must assume Quentin knows what he's about, and one knows better than to interfere with his delicate contrivances. I
should be content with what small enlightenment I have
received—and, of course, to offer my paltry services,
should the need arise."

"That is exceedingly kind of you," Leila said.

"Most generous," said Esmond.

"Least I can do." The duke stalked back to the worktable, set his glass upon the tray, and bid Leila good night.

Surprised at the abrupt leave-taking, she bolted up, and
managed a creditable curtsy. "Good night, Your Grace.
And thank you."

He was already heading for the door. "Esmond, I want a
word with you," he said. Without a glance back, Langford
strode out.

LEILA STOOD IN the hall waiting until the front door
shut. Then she hurried down to the landing. "What did he
say?" she whispered.

Ismal paused at the foot of the stairs and glanced over
his shoulder toward the door. His silken hair glimmered in
the light from the wall sconce. Something glimmered in
Leila's mind: a thread of a thought, a memory, but it vanished the instant he turned and looked up and smiled.

"Ah, nothing," he said softly as he began to ascend.
"The usual thing. I am not to trifle with your affections. I
am not to make a scandal. I am to protect you with my
life—a task he tells me would be much simpler if we were
wed."

Damnation. He was going to persist. "Very well," she
said. "If you want to talk about it now—"

"Also, I am not to waste my valuable time checking

Avory's alibi. Those two sturdy fellows watched him, day and night, from the time the duke made his plans with Helena until the day your husband died. The duke saw to his heir's protection, you see. Avory was nowhere near your house, neither on the Sunday nor the Monday."

He joined her on the landing. "We have worked two months, only to learn we must discard all five of our prime suspects."

"Maybe I'm not such a good partner after all," she said.

He took her hand and led her up the stairs. "You are an excellent partner. Did I not tell you at the start that these matters require patience? This is not the first time I have traveled in circles and had to begin again."

"Do you really think we'll spend the rest of our lives on this case?"

"The prospect does not dismay me." He led her on up to the second floor and into her bedroom. As he shut the door, he said, "At the very least, it will keep me occupied these next interminable ten months. And during that time, I shall prove to you what an agreeable husband I will make."

"You might also learn what a disagreeable wife *I'll* make," she said. "You've never been married before. You don't know what it's like."

"Neither do you. You were married to Francis Beaumont." He began to unfasten her bodice. "At least you are aware I am a more entertaining companion *dans le boudoir*."

"That isn't everything."

"I am much tidier."

"Oh, well, that settles it."

"Nay, we have not discussed my flaws." His hand closed over her breast. "I am bad tempered sometimes. Moody." He kissed her neck. "Also, I am very old fashioned. My tastes do not incline to perversions."

"But you know all about them. About tying people to bedposts."

He drew back. "I see. I have made you curious."

She fixed her embarrassed gaze on his neckcloth. "I thought . . . perhaps . . . it needn't be *uncomfortable*."

He considered for a moment. Then, with a low chuckle he took off his neckcloth. "As you wish, *ma belle*," he said softly. "Only tell me, is it to be you—or me?"

Chapter 17

TWO WEEKS LATER, ISMAL WAS STILL BROODING over the events of that day and night.

There was no question that, *dans le boudoir* at least, Leila trusted Ismal not to hurt her. Still, as she had said, lovemaking wasn't everything. In marriage, there were many other ways to hurt one's partner, as she had learned the hard way. He couldn't blame her for being cautious. He knew well enough he hadn't earned her full trust. If one expected trust, one must be willing to give it. And he was not ready. He, too, had a fear he couldn't reason away: that in trusting her with the truth, he would lose her.

He stood beside her in a corner of the Langfords' crowded ballroom. While he watched Avory dance with his betrothed, Ismal wondered how the marquess had endured those long months of believing his beloved was lost to him. Beyond doubt, he had more than paid for his present joy in suffering. Ismal was glad for his joy, yet it hurt to watch. Unlike Ismal, Avory might hold his woman in his arms, for all the world to see.

"I wish we could dance," he muttered. "It has been months since we waltzed together."

"Later," she said. "When we get home. You can hum in
my ear and whirl me about the studio."

Home. He wished it were, truly: that they could sleep
together and wake together and share breakfast. He hated
his predawn departures. He hated them more lately, because Eloise had reported that Madame suffered bad
dreams. Twice in the fortnight since Langford's visit,
Eloise had been working on the second floor and heard her
mistress's cries of distress. Leila had cried Ismal's
name . . . and he had not been there for her.

"I think instead I shall put you straight to bed," he said.
"You are not getting enough rest lately. Eloise says you
wake screaming—"

"I do *not* scream, and everyone has bad dreams," she interrupted. "It's just because of this provoking mystery. I
didn't mind any of our five favorite suspects running loose.
But now our villain has become a faceless monster. I need
the face of a real person, and we haven't got a one."

He knew she was evading the issue, but he didn't press.
She would not discuss her dreams. He suspected it was because she'd rather be shot than admit she was frightened.
She wouldn't want to give him any excuse to keep her out
of the inquiry—not that they'd accomplished much lately.

Since Langford's visit, Ismal and Leila had reviewed
the list of Beaumont's acquaintances several times, but no
one stirred their interest. They attended at least one, usually more, social affairs each evening, and talked and listened until they were dizzy. Each night, they returned to
her house, put their heads together, and produced nothing.

They tried making love first and handling business after.
They tried the reverse. They tried business-love-business and
love-business-love. It made no difference. Their intellects
simply whirled uselessly, like spinning wheels with no wool.

Though he was beginning to wonder whether they were
wasting their time, he wasn't ready to give up. The notion
that anyone could outsmart him was intolerable. Never in
his career had his prey been able to elude him for long. In
any case, he felt sure that the cleverness of their prey
wasn't the real problem.

From the start, his mind had not been working with its usual cool efficiency. He knew why. The reason stood beside him. Until matters were fully settled between them, he couldn't attend properly to this case or any other.

He watched her tawny gaze move restlessly from guest to guest.

"I can't believe that not one name has even jiggled my intuition," she said. "Most of the Beau Monde is here, and not a single face stirs anything. I feel nothing."

She turned back to him. "I even wonder if we stuck to those five because we sensed they were 'safe' somehow. Don't you find it odd that we persisted, even though something didn't fit in each case: circumstances, character, means."

"You will give yourself a headache," he said. "Leave it alone for tonight. This is a joyous occasion, celebrating a betrothal. Assuredly, their happiness will continue. They are admirably well suited, are they not? Miss Woodleigh fully appreciates Avory's many superior qualities, and he hers. Also, the strengths of one character neatly balance the weaknesses of the other. But you were aware of this, I think, the instant I told you he was in love with her."

She rewarded him with a smile. "I shouldn't have browbeaten poor Fiona otherwise," she said.

"Poor Fiona" at the moment was detaching herself from a small crowd of admirers. She made directly for Leila and Ismal.

"I count half a dozen hearts crashing to the floor and splintering into pieces," Ismal said as she joined them.

"They recover quickly," she said. "The instant they discovered Leila was out of bounds, they latched onto me. I daresay they'll latch onto someone else soon enough."

"I do not think Lord Sellowby will," he said. "That one looks like a man whose mind is made up."

Leila followed his gaze. "Most observant, Esmond," she said.

"Don't be tiresome," said her friend. "Sellowby is a rattle, and a confirmed bachelor. Not to mention I've known him this age—lud, since the nursery, I think. He might as well be another brother."

Ismal gave his partner a conspiratorial look. "Madame, it has been weeks since you made a match," he said. "You will not wish your skills to rust through want of practice."

"I certainly don't."

"Leila, you will not—" her friend began.

"Yes, I will. I owe you this, Fiona."

Leila had but to look Sellowby's way to catch his eye. Then she lifted her fan and beckoned.

Remembering a certain night in Paris when Lady Carroll had summoned him, Ismal watched Sellowby respond in the same unhesitating way. This man, too, knew what he wanted, judging by the intent expression in his dark eyes as he joined them. Clearly, Lady Carroll's days of freedom were numbered.

"I'm sorry to trouble you," Leila told Sellowby. "But I was telling Esmond about your race across the Mediterranean. Lackliffe described it to me, and I do recall that it was amazingly swift—but I can't remember exactly how long he said it took."

"Gad, ancient history," Fiona muttered.

"Indeed it is—a decade ago," Sellowby said. "One of the follies of my youth. A month—six weeks—perhaps more. Frankly, all I recollect with any clarity is beating Lackliffe by a hairsbreadth and finding London perishing cold."

"I collect you were drunk most of the time," said Lady Carroll. "Time passed in a pleasant haze, no doubt."

"At any rate, time passed," he said. "You must not twit me with the foibles of my youth, Fiona. You were hardly a paragon of decorum then. When you were Letty's age—"

"It's exceedingly ill-mannered to call attention to a lady's age." She briskly fanned herself.

"Ah, well, you're not so old as that," he said. "Not quite decrepit yet."

She turned to Ismal. "As you see, Esmond, chivalry is stone dead in England. I vow, directly after Letty is shackled, I shall take the first packet to France."

"That would be just like you," said Sellowby. "To hare off to a country on the brink of revolution."

"You'll never intimidate her with threats of riot," said Leila. "On the contrary, you've only made the prospect more exciting."

"Riot, indeed," Her Ladyship said scornfully. "You are not to take his side, Leila. You know as well as I there's no imminent danger. If there were a hint of it, Herriard would never have left Paris without his clients."

"What the devil has Herriard to say to anything?" Sellowby asked. "Has he been made ambassador while I wasn't looking?"

"He does have the confidence of several members of the diplomatic corps," she said. "He would know if there were immediate peril, and if he knew such a thing, Andrew Herriard would haul his crew of English exiles home by main force if necessary. What do you say, Leila? Who knows Herriard better than you?"

"It's true," Leila said. "He wouldn't leave until he'd done his duty—until every last one of his charges was safe away."

"And all their affairs tied up neatly," said Lady Carroll. "Every 'i' dotted. Every 't' crossed."

"Precision," Ismal murmured. "The hallmark of a superior legal mind."

"Everyone knows how Herriard is," said Lady Carroll. "Even you, Sellowby. Come, admit your error like a man."

"I shall do better than that," he said, his dark eyes glinting. "I shall spare you the filthy packet and take you to France on my yacht."

The fan went into violent motion. "Will you indeed? Drunk or sober?"

"I shall want all my wits," he said. "Sober, of course. But you may be as drunk as you please, my dear."

A SHORT WHILE later, Sellowby was whirling a flustered Fiona about the dance floor. Leila wasn't looking at them, but at Ismal. She didn't want to think what she was thinking. She certainly didn't want to say it. To her dismay, she saw she didn't need to. She recognized the predatory glint in Ismal's blue eyes. She had seen that look before, the first time she'd met him, in Paris.

"Every 'i' dotted. Every 't' crossed," he said, confirming her fears. "All neatly tied up, in perfect order."

"It's not the same," she said.

"Your house was in perfect order when you returned, you told me. I examined the bedroom myself. Even upon the dressing table, the objects were arranged with military precision. Avory does this—but only when his mind is troubled and he tries to sort out his thoughts. It is not a personal habit, for his servants do everything for him."

"We haven't a motive," she said, while her heart told her they'd soon discover it.

"We have the character," he said. "The precise legal mind. Cool-headed, quick to note detail and use it to his advantage. Discretion, too, is the hallmark of the superior lawyer. He is the keeper of family secrets."

"He couldn't have been in two places at once. He'd already left for Dover, and he was on the first packet to Calais. Otherwise he would have received my message."

"If you truly believed that, you would not be so agitated," he said gently. "But your mind has leapt just as mine has, because the way is clear for the leap. The others' problems, the obvious problems, are out of our way. We fixed on them for a reason, as you said. I believe, in some way, we sensed their difficulties were connected. Perhaps that puzzle solution itself is a clue. But first, we should examine the alibi."

"No," she said. "I can't stop your doing what you want. But I shan't help. There's no 'we' in this. I won't be a party to it."

He stepped closer. "Leila, you have trusted me to deal kindly with your friends. Surely you can trust me with this."

She shook her head. "No. I never *owed* them. I owe him. I won't—" Her throat was tight, and her eyes were stinging. She couldn't trust herself to utter another word.

"Leila, look at me," he softly urged. "Listen to me."

She wouldn't. Dared not. In another moment, she'd disgrace herself. She was already moving away as quickly as she could without attracting notice. She needed to be alone, for just one minute, to collect herself.

Scarcely able to see past the welling tears, she made for the nearest door.

She hurried on through and down the corridor and down another. She didn't know where she was going. It didn't matter. One minute's privacy. That was all she wanted.

"Leila."

His anxious voice came from behind her.

No. Please. Leave me alone. Just one minute, she told herself. That was all she needed. There were stairs ahead. She hurried up them to the landing.

"Leila, please."

She paused and turned, just as a footman emerged into the hall. She saw Ismal move to the servant to say something. She saw the light shimmer in his hair, heard the easy, friendly murmur . . . smooth and soft as silk. There was a strange buzzing in her ears, a flash of color.

She sank down onto the nearest stair and held her head and took deep breaths. The dizziness passed swiftly, but the chilling dread remained. For a moment, she'd experienced the dream, yet it wasn't the same. Not the same hall. There was only one man with him, not two, and this one was English, while the ones in the dream were foreigners.

She was dimly aware of footsteps, voices.

"Madame."

A hand covering hers. His hand.

She raised her head. Ismal crouched before her. The servant stood behind him.

"You are ill," Ismal said.

Though she wasn't, she nodded for the footman's benefit.

Ismal swept her up into his arms and carried her up the stairs, the servant leading the way.

He took them to a small sitting room. Ismal gently deposited Leila on the chaise longue while the servant poured her a glass of water.

While she dutifully sipped, he had another whispered consultation with Ismal, then left.

"I have ordered a carriage," Ismal said when he returned to her. "One of the maidservants will accompany you home."

She looked up, confused. "Aren't you coming?"

"I think I have done enough damage for one night." His voice was harsh. "I drove you from the ballroom in tears. You nearly collapsed on the stairs. I think I might at least stop short of making scandal. I shall remain and make soothing excuses for you. A combination of a rich dinner, champagne, and an overcrowded room made you ill, I shall tell your friends. Meanwhile, I shall pray you did not swoon because you are with child."

He turned away, raking his fingers through his hair. "Only tell me, Leila, if it is so."

"Is *which* so?" she asked dazedly. "You didn't—" She gave herself an inward shake and quickly sorted reason from emotion.

"I was overset," she said steadily. "I didn't want to make a spectacle of myself in company. I'm sorry I upset you. I assure you I'm not breeding—can't be."

He let out a shaky sigh, then came back to her. "When you turn away, terrible things happen inside me," he said. "I am sorry, my heart. I have been most unkind, thoughtless. In too many ways."

"Terrible things," she said. "Inside you."

His eyes were bleak. "You are dear to me."

She didn't know what was wrong, only that something was—something apart from alarm that she might be enceinte, something more troubling even than Andrew. She doubted she could bear it, whatever it was. Already her world was falling to pieces. If Andrew was false, nothing, nobody was true.

All she had left was this man, whom she loved with all her heart.

Don't, she begged silently. *Don't be false. Leave me something.*

She heard footsteps approaching. "Don't keep away tonight," she said softly. "I need you. Come as soon as you can. Please."

HE CAME A few hours later.

She had donned her nightgown and sat propped up against the pillows, the sketchbook in her lap, the pencil in her hand. Even after he entered the bedroom, it took her a moment to tear her gaze from the page.

Ismal wanted to know what had captivated her quick mind, but even more, he wanted to get his ordeal over with.

"There is something I must tell you," he said.

"I want to explain," she said at the same time.

"Leila."

"Please," she said. "I need your help. I can't—I don't know what to do. I can't bear to fail you."

His conscience stabbed deep. "Leila, you would never fail me. It is I—"

"I understand," she said. "You just want things settled. You don't *want* to hurt anybody. I know you wish as much as I do that we could find a villain. Someone we could loathe. Someone we could want to punish. The trouble is, Francis was so horrible that one can't imagine anyone worse. So we won't get what we want. Instead, we get people we care about, sympathize with. I *know* you don't want to harm Andrew—if he's the one. I love you, and I want to be your partner—and I'd follow you to the ends of the earth. But—"

"I do not ask it," he said. "I have no right to ask such a thing, to ask anything."

"Yes, you do. I just need you to understand." She patted the mattress.

"Leila, please. Before you say anything more, I must—"

"I know," she said. "You've some ghastly confession to make."

His heart pounded. "Yes."

"Are you going to break my heart?" Her eyes burned too brightly. "Shall I go to pieces, do you think? And who shall pick me up, I wonder, and help put me back together? That's the trouble with Andrew, you see. One relies on him. Whenever I had a problem, I knew I could turn to him, and he'd help me set everything right. He set *me* right when I was a girl. He taught me how to be strong and as good as I was capable of being. And now I'm to view him as a cold-blooded murderer. Now I can't *help* viewing him so."

She rubbed her temple. "I wish you'd come sooner. I've had such horrible thoughts. I think I'm becoming hysterical. It was the near-fainting. And the buzzing in my ears. The last time that happened was the night Papa was killed, and Papa turned out to be false, too. So now it's all mixed up. Papa and Francis and that gloomy hallway. I keep dreaming about it," she went on hurriedly. "I thought I was dreaming tonight. I saw you turn your head to speak to the servant, and I was so frightened. It wasn't the same hall or the same servant, but I was frightened for you all the same. Only this time I didn't wake up, because I wasn't asleep."

He moved to the bed and took the sketchbook from her. On the page was one of her rougher drawings. Nonetheless, he recognized Mehmet and Risto and guessed who the vague figure between them was. The view was from above, the artist looking down on her subjects . . . as she must have done that night a decade ago.

"This is what you dream," he said, his gut in icy knots. "Do you know what it is?"

"The light's always the same," she said. "Coming from that open door. The same two men, and you between them."

He sat down on the bed. "I was between them." He kept his eyes on the page. "Ten years ago. In a palazzo in Venice. There was a girl upstairs, Risto told me." He forced the words past the constriction in his throat. "I did not trouble to look. I assumed she was a child."

The air about him throbbed ominously.

"You?" Her voice was low, hard. "That was *you?*"

He nodded.

"You lying, false—you *bastard.*"

He felt the movement, heard the rush of air, but he

moved a heartbeat too slowly. Something slammed against his head, and he fell forward, onto the floor. The world spun perilously toward darkness. There was a terrible clanging, like hammer blows, vibrating through his skull. He grabbed blindly and something crashed beside him.

There was a tumult—cries, pounding footsteps—but he couldn't make sense of it. All his will was fixed on resisting the darkness, unconsciousness. He heaved himself onto his knees just as the door opened.

"Monsieur!"

"Madame!"

He dragged his head up and made himself focus. A toppled nightstand next to him . . . Gaspard . . . Eloise.

He found his voice. *"De rien,"* he gritted out. *"Allez-vous-en!"*

"Get him out of here!" Leila cried. "Take him away before I kill him! Get him—make him—" The rest was a sob.

Eloise pulled her husband back through the door. It shut.

Silence, but for Leila's weeping.

Ismal's own eyes scalded. He turned toward her. She sat on the edge of the bed, her face buried in her hands.

He couldn't ask a forgiveness that was impossible to give. He couldn't utter apologies for what could never be excused. All he could offer was the one true thing in his false, breaking heart.

"Je t'aime," he said helplessly. "I love you, Leila."

SHE GAZED DOWN despairingly at him. She didn't want to understand. She didn't want to cope with him, with anything, anyone, any more.

Papa. Francis. Andrew.

And this man, this beautiful, impossible man to whom she'd given everything—honor, pride, trust. She'd held nothing back. Body and soul she'd given herself to him. Gladly.

And he had made her glad, her heart reminded.

He'd given, too.

He was, after all, almost human. She saw the hurt in his eyes, and her heart reminded her that the monstrous admission he'd just made, he'd made on his own.

"You're all I've got," she said unsteadily. "There's only you. Give me something, please. I love you. You've made me so happy. Please, let's be fair with each other." She held out her hand.

He stared at it for a long moment, his face taut. Then he put out his own hand, and she took it and joined him on the floor.

"I know I should have told you long ago, but I was afraid," he said, his eyes upon their joined hands. "You are dear to me. I could not bear to lose you. But tonight, I could not bear what *was*. I could not comfort you. I could not take you home. Just as I could not be there for you when the dreams frightened you. I could not take care of my own woman, because she was not my wife. And I could not prevail upon you to be my wife. I could not even ask properly. Only in joke, making light of what was most important to me, because it was dishonorable to urge or coax until I could offer with a clean heart."

"Is it clean now?" she asked. "Was that all? That night in Venice—you were the one with Papa, and those were your men?"

"It is not all of my past," he said. "Not even the worst, perhaps. I injured others. Yet those debts have been paid long since. Even to your country I have made amends. I have served your king nearly ten years." He looked up, his eyes dark. "But to you I have not made amends. Instead, I only compound my sins."

Ten years, she thought. A decade serving a foreign king, making amends by dealing with the worst and lowest of villains, the most complicated and delicate of problems. Whatever was too much, too dirty, or too disagreeable for His Majesty's government was thrust into Ismal's elegant hands.

"If His Majesty is satisfied," she said carefully, "then I ought to be. Even if—even if you killed Papa, it sounds as though you've paid."

"I did not kill him," he said. "Please believe this."

"I believe you," she said. "But I should like . . . just to know. What happened."

"It is not pleasant," he said.

"I rather expected it wouldn't be."

His expression eased a fraction, and he arranged himself in storytelling mode, his legs curled up tailor fashion.

Then he told her, all of it, from the time he'd begun buying stolen weaponry from her father's partner, whose name Ismal said he wasn't at liberty to mention. He told her how his planned revolution in Albania had gone awry because he'd tangled with the wrong men and become besotted with Jason Brentmor's daughter. He told her how Ali Pasha had poisoned him, and how Ismal had escaped with the help of his two servants, and gone on to Venice, where he'd terrified Jonas Bridgeburton into providing incriminating information against the anonymous partner. Ismal described how he'd used the unseen Leila to hasten the negotiations, and how he'd had her drugged.

He told her about racing on to England—against his servants' advice—to get revenge on everyone he imagined had thwarted him: the anonymous arms dealer as well as Esme's lover, Edenmont—and, of course, Esme herself. He told her of the bloody climax in Newhaven and how Esme had saved his life and how he had paid the family— in precious jewels, no less—for his crimes.

He told her of the voyage to New South Wales and the shipwreck that he'd used to his advantage, and of his encounter with Quentin, who decided that Ismal could be more useful in Europe than among transported felons.

When he concluded, Ismal bowed his head—as though inviting her to whack him again.

"It would appear that eighteen hundred nineteen was an eventful year for you," she said. "Small wonder being knocked on the head hardly fazed you. I'm amazed, in the circumstances, that you remembered Bridgeburton's daughter at all."

"I remembered," he said grimly. "The instant you said your father's name. Even then, I was troubled. When you told me of Beaumont and how he took you away, I knew he stole your innocence, and this was why you wed him—and I thought I would die of shame. Ten years of wretchedness you endured, and all because of me."

She bridled. "I was not wretched. You are not to make me out as a pathetic victim of that sodden pig. He was obnoxious, I'll admit—"

"Obnoxious? He was faithless, and he did not even compensate by pleasing you in bed. He was a drunkard, a drug addict, a peddler of flesh, a traitor—"

"He made me an *artist*," she snapped. "He respected that at least—and long before anyone else did. He recognized my talent and sent me to school. He *made* my first master accept a female student. He brought me my first patrons. And he had to live with the consequences—of my career and ambition, and of all his infidelities. He may have crushed others and ruined other lives, but not me, not my life. I am my father's own daughter, and I gave back as good as I got. I nearly knocked you unconscious with the bed-warming pan a while ago. I promise you that's not the first time the man in my life has felt the brunt of my temper. Don't you *dare* feel sorry for me."

She snatched her hand from his and bolted up, to pace angrily before the fireplace.

"Pity," she muttered. "You say you love me, and all it turns out to be is pity—and some mad notion of making amends. When you, of all men, ought to know better. You know everything—more than Francis ever did: all my failings, all my unladylike ways. No secrets from you, not a one—and yet you make me out to be some pitiable little martyr."

"Leila."

"It's that curst male superiority is what it is," she stormed on. "Just as Lady Brentmor says. Just because they're physically stronger—or *think* they are—they think they're the lords of creation."

"Leila."

"Because they can't bear to admit they need us. Adam

needed someone, to be sure. He never would have had the courage to eat that apple on his own. Eve should have just eaten it herself and let him wander about Eden knowing nothing, and no better than the dumb brutes about him. The idiot didn't even know he was naked. And who sewed those fig leaf aprons, I ask you? Not him, you may be sure. He wouldn't have—"

The door slammed.

She whipped round.

He was gone.

She hurried to the door, pulled it open, and crashed into him. His arms lashed about her, holding her fast.

"I *am* stronger," he said. "And my head is harder. But I am not a dumb brute. I made a mistake. I am sorry. I did not mean to insult you. I know you are strong and brave and dangerous. I love you for this, and for your devilish mind and your passionate heart and, of course, your beautiful body. Now, my tigress, may we make peace?"

WHEN ISMAL AWOKE, a warm feminine backside was pressed to his groin. He slid his hand over the luscious curve of Leila's breast and dreamily contemplated love-making in the morning.

Morning?

His eyes shot open—to sunlight. Quelling his panic, he was gently disentangling himself when she turned and murmured and nestled her head in the hollow of his shoulder.

Then he could only smile down at her in idiotic plea-sure, and stroke her back while he thought how well they fit together, and how sweet it was to wake to a sunny morn with the woman he loved in his arms.

She moved under his caressing hand and in a little while raised her head to smile sleepily up at him. "What's so amusing?"

"I am happy," he said. "Stupid but happy."

She blinked as she, too, noticed. "By gad, it's morning."

"So it is."

"You're still here."

"So I am. Stupid, as I said. I seem to have fallen asleep."

She made a face. "I suppose it was the blow to the head."

"Nay, it was my conscience. So many weeks of guilty worry had exhausted me. You wiped away the agitation and I slept like an innocent babe."

"Well, I suppose it's wicked and incautious, but I'm glad." She rubbed his beard-roughened jaw.

"It would not be wicked and incautious if we were wed," he said. "Will you marry me, Leila?"

She put her hand over his mouth. "I shall pretend didn't hear that, and we'll start with a clean slate—on both sides. I have to tell you something, because you seem to have the wrong idea. I wasn't as clear as I might have been last night, and it wouldn't be fair—" Taking a deep breath she hurried on. "I can't have children. I've tried. I went to doctors and tried different diets and regimens. I shan't bore you with the details. I'm barren." She took her hand away from his mouth.

He looked down into her anxious eyes. "There are plenty of orphans," he said. "If you wish to have children we may acquire as many as you like. If you had rather not then we shall be a family of two. Will you marry me Leila?"

"Orphans? Would you really? *Adopt* children?"

"There are advantages. If they turn out badly, we can blame their natural parents. We can also choose our own assortment of ages and genders. We can even get them ready-grown, if we wish. Also, strays can be most interesting. Nick is a stray, you know. But that was not so difficult even for a bachelor to manage. He at least was an adolescent when I found him. I did not have to mix pap and wipe his bottom. Will you marry me, Leila?"

She hugged him. "Yes. Oh, yes. You are a truly remarkable man."

"Indeed, I am a prince."

"Noble to the core."

He grinned. "At the core I am very bad. A big problem. But only you see the core. My pedigree is enough for the others. It should be—I worked very hard to earn my title."

She drew back. "To *earn* it? You are not telling me your title is *legitimate*?"

"King Charles himself bestowed it upon me."

"But you're not Alexis Delavenne."

"By French law, I am."

He explained that finding the missing "sucker shoot" of the Delavenne family had been one of his earliest missions. He finally located Pierre Delavenne in the West Indies and was obliged to kidnap him to bring him back to France.

"He was very angry," Ismal said. "He had taken a black woman as his mistress and fathered half a dozen children and liked his life just as it was. He hated France in general and the Bourbons in particular. Eventually, it occurred to some of us to make intelligent use of his hostility. I needed an identity; he didn't want his. The similarity of surnames, as you can imagine, struck my superstitious nature. I legally adopted the name, which pleased King Charles, and he bestowed the title upon me, which pleased my English slave drivers."

She laughed. "And so you really are the Comte d'Esmond, after all."

"And you shall be my comtesse."

"How absurd. I—an aristocrat."

"It is not absurd. You are haughty as a duchess." He tangled his fingers in her hair. "You do not mind, I hope?"

"I shall try to ignore my consequence as much as possible," she said. "And I shall continue to call you Ismal in private. If it slips out in public, we shall say it's a pet name."

"You may pet me all you like, wherever you like." He guided her hand downward. "Let me help you find some places."

Chapter 18

THE DOWAGER ARRIVED JUST AS LEILA AND IS-
mal were enjoying a second cup of coffee.

She followed close upon a harassed-looking Gaspard's
heels, and pushed her way into the dining room before he
could announce her, let alone ascertain his employers'
wishes.

Ismal calmly greeted her and pulled out a chair. She
swept the room and its occupants one withering glare, then
sat and opened her mammoth purse.

"You'd better marry her," Lady Brentmor told Ismal as
she slammed a sheaf of papers onto the table.

"I am happy to report that Madame has perceived the
error of her ways. She has agreed to let me make an honest
woman of her."

"It was the charitable thing to do," Leila said. "He's utterly useless without me."

"That's true enough," her ladyship muttered. She
handed two documents to Ismal. "I hope you've told her a
few things. Otherwise, you've got a devilish lot to explain."

"I have confessed all my black past—all but the secret

that was not mine to reveal." He frowned down at the documents. "This is Jason's hand."

"He come in late last night. He's still sleeping, and I wasn't about to wait all day for him to wake up." She turned to Leila. "Would've been here weeks ago, but he got my letter finally, and stopped in Paris to look into the problem himself. The money," she added in response to Leila's baffled look. "I thought there was something wrong about your money—that bank account. I was sure Jason had told me, ages ago, that your pa had set aside ten thousand pounds for your dowry."

"Ten thousand?" Leila repeated blankly.

"Jason did go looking for you—after he'd settled other pressing matters here, that is," the dowager said with a scowl at Ismal. "But by the time he got to it, you was wed, and Herriard seemed to be looking after your affairs well enough. So Jason never gave it no more thought."

"Ten thousand pounds," Leila said, her mind whirling.

"Jason had a lot of cleaning up to do after his fool brother," Lady Brentmor went on. "Your pa's partner in crime. That's the name Esmond here was too delicate to mention. My son Gerald. You might as well know. We're in the same boat, ain't we?"

"Your son was my father's partner," Leila said slowly, trying to take it in. "And I had a dowry of . . . ten thousand pounds. That does . . . explain . . . a good deal."

"It certainly do explain why Andrew Herriard took such good care of a little nobody orphan gel, protecting her funds from her philandering sot of a husband. It was one thing in the beginning, when Herriard was just starting his practice. But even after he got important, he looked after you like you was the Royal Family. But then, he wouldn't want anyone else looking after you. Someone else might start asking embarrassing questions."

Leila turned to Ismal. "That would explain why Andrew was so disturbed about your interest in me."

"I assuredly mean to ask embarrassing questions." Ismal handed the two documents to Leila. "These are Jason's copies of the instructions your father supposedly wrote to the bank, the day before he disappeared. I suggest you pay close attention to the language."

Leila needed to read only the first letter to understand.

"The style is familiar, is it not?" he asked. "You have received countless business letters from your solicitor over the years."

"In other words, Andrew forged these letters to the bank."

"Also your father's will, I have little doubt. A trip to Doctors' Commons will settle that question easily enough." His smile was grim. "A forger to catch a forger, you see."

"He stole my dowry," Leila said. "Nine thousand pounds. From an orphan. And all the world thinks him a saint. I certainly did. He could tie my insides into knots with just a few words, ever so kindly uttered. That manipulative *hypocrite*."

"I am sorry, Leila. I know I must not say it was all my fault—"

"Not unless you wish to persuade me you're the Prince of Darkness," she said crisply. "You didn't *make* Andrew do it, any more than you made Francis take me away and seduce me."

"All the same, they took advantage of a situation I created: your father crazy with fear and drink—the servants drugged or incapacitated—and you unconscious, unable even to scream for help."

"They didn't *have* to take advantage. Decent men wouldn't. Can't you see?" She flung the papers down and got up to pace the room. "It was *planned*. I'm sure of it. They already knew about the ten thousand pounds. Had to. That's not the sort of thing you find out in a matter of minutes from a raving drunk. And they knew about me. They didn't just wander in off the street. That carriage was *packed*. Those letters were written ahead of time, I'll stake my life. Andrew couldn't do that on the spur of the moment."

"Unless you have the gift, it requires repeated attempts."

She scarcely heard him. She was trying to remember. "The servants, too. That was wrong. The little kitchen maid . . . when it should have been Gabriela who brought my tea. Something was wrong before you came." She closed her eyes. "In the hall. Papa. You. The big man and the small, dark one with you—and Papa was annoyed."

She opened her eyes to stare at the doorway. "Because Antonio wasn't there. Papa had to answer the door himself."

"It is true. I wondered why he had so few servants. Risto had no trouble. He did not even need Mehmet's help."

"Because Andrew and Francis had already lured away or driven off the servants who would have caused difficulties. All they had to do was wait until Papa's unexpected visitors had left, then move in to carry out their plan." She turned to him.

"Your mind has leapt, as mine has, I think," he said. "When you came to in the carriage, Beaumont told you your father was dead. I wondered how he knew, for Jason said the body was not found for two days."

"He said your men carried Papa away. But that doesn't make sense, does it? Even if they disregarded your orders, even if they had made off with Papa, they wouldn't have left me—an eyewitness—behind. It was Francis and Andrew who carried or led Papa off and dropped—or pushed—him into the canal."

"And so we have our motive," Ismal said.

"We have a villain," Leila said.

"I wish Jason was here," the dowager muttered. "He wouldn't believe me when I said you was made for each other."

MR. ANDREW HERRIARD, returning from his midday meal, paused before the front door of his office to gaze at the man he'd just passed. He wasn't the only one to stare, though there were others who preferred to look the other way when the shabbily clad man with the lantern, cage, and dog passed. While a necessity in London, the ratcatcher was not the most agreeable of figures to contemplate. He was certainly not agreeable to contemplate directly after luncheon.

Mr. Herriard was still frowning when he entered the ground floor office. His senior clerk, Gleever, looked up at him with some concern. "I do hope the pies weren't overcooked again, sir," he said.

Mr. Herriard explained that the pies had been satisfactory, but seeing a ratcatcher was not. "I do hope our neighbors aren't experiencing problems again," he said. "If one becomes infested, we all soon do, and it makes a singularly poor impression upon clients—as I've told my colleagues repeatedly."

"No danger of infestation, sir, I promise you. The fellow did come here, but it was a mistake, as it turns out. He'd got the wrong street altogether, you see. We'd been in the cellar but a few minutes before he realized his error. He did apologize, sir. And took the trouble—since he was here, as he said—to look at the places we'd closed up after the last time. Said they were nice and tight."

"I'm relieved to hear it."

"Said we might get a mouse now and again, but no worse."

"I'd rather no vermin of any kind," said Mr. Herriard. "Let us go down and see what may be done."

Half an hour later, Mr. Herriard stood at his office window, gazing down at the street below, and chillingly aware that something had already been done. The small, dusty jar of prussic acid his landlord kept in the cellar was gone.

The lawyer told himself it might have disappeared weeks ago. The landlord might have removed it, convinced the rat problem was solved.

Mr. Herriard returned to his desk, signed the papers Gleever had prepared for him, ticked those items off his schedule, and left the office to attend to the next.

His errand took him to Great-Knight-Rider Street, to the south of St. Paul's. It was there, in Doctors' Commons, that he received the second shock.

"I *am* sorry, Mr. Herriard," said the clerk. "I did promise to have the documents ready for you, but we've been at sixes and sevens. Lord Quentin was here with the Comte d'Esmond, and it took nearly an hour to find what they wanted. And we were fortunate indeed it was only an hour—for a will ten years old and misfiled in the bargain."

"How very odd," said Mr. Herriard.

"I didn't see why they must come pester us about it," the clerk said. "But then, they should have pestered you instead, I don't doubt. I hope we spared you that inconvenience at least."

"One of my clients' wills, I take it," said Mr. Herriard. "Of ten years ago, you said."

"Bridgeburton was the name, sir. I haven't put it back yet. Perhaps you'd like to look at it, refresh your memory—for they may bother you all the same."

"That won't be necessary," said Mr. Herriard. "I remember."

AFTER HE LEFT Doctors' Commons, Mr. Herriard walked through the busy streets of the City, and on westward. He walked steadily, shoulders straight, his face its customary mask of quiet amiability.

He walked to a burial ground, and through its gates, and made his way along the narrow paths until he reached a three-month-old grave.

He stood a long while studying the simple monument Leila Beaumont had ordered. No cherubs or weeping willows. No poetic inscriptions. No mention of beloved spouse of anybody. Just the simplest bare facts of name, date of birth, date of death: 13 January 1829.

"You bastard," he said.

Then he bowed his head and wept.

THE AFTERNOON WANED, and the shadows about him lengthened. He remained in the same rigid pose, weeping still, oblivious to the law officers scattered about the graveyard, blocking all escape routes. He didn't notice that their leader stood with a man and a woman not many yards away.

"They're all in place," Quentin said. "Best take him while there's still light. Mrs. Beaumont, I think you ought to return to the carriage. If he won't come quietly, matters could become unpleasant."

"Matters *are* unpleasant," she said. "I want to speak to him." She started to move away.

Ismal clasped her arm. "Do not be foolish," he said. "Even villains weep. He cries for what he has lost, not remorse."

"I need to understand," she said. "And he won't tell me with the lot of you about."

"He stole from you," Ismal said. "He taught you to mistrust yourself, so that he could control you. What more is there to understand?"

"I don't know—but if there is, he deserves a chance to explain. As Sherburne did. As David and Fiona did. As you did," she added in lower tones.

Ismal let go of her. "I shall be but a few feet away," he whispered. "If he raises a hand to you, I shall cut out his heart."

"I should hope so," she said, and briskly walked on down the path to Andrew.

Even when she stood beside him, he didn't so much as turn his head. "Andrew," she said.

He stiffened, and looked about, then hastily drew out a handkerchief and wiped his face. "Have they come for me?" he asked.

Perhaps she was a gullible fool, but her heart went out to him. She had to clench her fists to keep from taking his hand. "Yes," she said.

"I'm sorry," he said. "A nasty murder trial. Just what nobody wants, I'm sure. I thought of hanging myself. A bullet through the brain. A dose of prussic acid would be easiest—and appropriate. But Esmond took it, didn't he? And I never thought to stop at the chemist's first. I just . . . walked . . . here." He put the handkerchief away. "Beaumont was insane, you know. I hadn't any choice."

"Francis was mad and desperate and he was forced to leave England," she said. "He must have needed money. He must have threatened to expose you unless you helped him. Is that it?"

"I didn't know what he'd been up to until he told me. About Langford and the letters. Sherburne and his wife. Lettice Woodleigh. Avory. I had no idea. I didn't even know about that filthy brothel of his until he told me. He was waiting outside the office the morning after they gave him what he deserved. I didn't want to be seen talking to him. I took him down to the cellar. And I listened to him raving, and wanted to throttle him. Then I spotted the bottle of prussic acid. I wasn't sure then how I would do it, but I knew I must. I hadn't any choice. They poison mad dogs, you know. That's what he was."

"You had no idea what your partner had been up to all these years?" she asked. "Am I to believe you two only came together to kill my father and steal my dowry? Then you went your separate ways?"

"We did what we had to ten years ago," he said. "Your father ruined us. I invested in good faith. It wasn't until he'd lost all my money that I found out the kinds of criminal enterprises he'd put my funds into. The authorities were closing in on him, and I'd be dragged down with him. There wasn't any choice. We had to get rid of him and destroy everything that could link us to him."

"You didn't have to steal my dowry," she said.

"It wasn't stolen. Your dowry went to your husband."

"I see. And he gave half to you—for services rendered, I collect."

He winced. "I tried to make it right," he said stiffly. "I told Francis at the start that we couldn't take your money unless one of us married you. I told him we couldn't abandon a seventeen-year-old girl—leave her fatherless, with a paltry thousand pounds and no one to take care of her." He met her gaze. "Even after Beaumont ruined you, I would have married you, Leila. I would not have abandoned you.

Perhaps I should have wed you, regardless. As it is, I shall never forgive myself for not watching you more carefully—or him, rather."

"You let me believe it was my fault he seduced me," she said. "All these years I've believed I was . . . a whore. By nature. Weak-willed and inclined to wickedness, like Papa. All these years I've felt ashamed of who I was and what I was."

He inhaled sharply, as though she'd struck him. "Dear God—I—my dear, I never meant *that*."

"That's what I believed," she said.

His shoulders sagged. "I only wanted to make you strong. You were so naive. You hadn't an inkling of your effect on men. I was afraid Beaumont would neglect you, leaving you prey to others like him. I wanted to put you on your guard, that was all—so that no one else would use and hurt you and destroy your self-respect. The last thing I would have wanted was to destroy it myself. I think the world of you, Leila. Always have."

As she looked up into Andrew's pale, tautly composed countenance, her conscience urged her to put herself in his place—a thirty-two-year-old bachelor confronting a despoiled adolescent girl—and ask whether she could have dealt with it any better than he had.

And looking into her own heart, she had to admit that she *had* been abominably naive, even in adulthood—about men, about love, about normal human desire, as Ismal had taught her. Perhaps she would have soon put Andrew's long-ago lecture into more rational perspective if Francis hadn't made her believe something was wrong with her. Just as he'd made David believe something was irreparably wrong with *him*.

"I believe you," she said gently. "I should have realized. It's not your nature to be cruel or manipulative. That was Francis' talent. Simply because you had the misfortune to be tangled with him doesn't mean you were like him."

"I didn't know what he was like," he said. "If I had . . . well, there's no point in 'if onlys.' I didn't know. Not a fraction."

She brushed a twig from the tombstone. "I didn't realize more than a fraction either, until very recently."

"With Esmond's help, apparently." He glanced back. "There he is, like some damned nemesis. And Quentin with him." With a weary shrug, he turned back to her. "I had a feeling something was wrong when I heard Lady Brentmor had taken you up. I knew that her son, Jason, had been in Venice ten years ago, on your father's trail. Then there was Esmond, in Paris a year ago. And within a month, it appears, Beaumont's disgusting empire fell to pieces. I suppose Esmond saw to that."

"Yes."

"Yes, of course, for there he was again and again. In the house right after Beaumont died. And at the inquest, testifying. And still in London, week after week. All the same, I tried to believe these were coincidences. Just as I convinced myself all he wanted was an affair with you. I waited, telling myself he'd give up sooner or later, because you'd never consent."

"He doesn't give up," she said.

Andrew smiled bleakly. "I misjudged him. Wishful thinking, perhaps. I thought, in time, you'd turn to me, and we would wed—as we should have done ten years ago, in Paris. I wanted to take care of you. I wanted to make things right. I never meant you harm, Leila. You know that, else you wouldn't have come to me today."

She blinked back tears. She couldn't help grieving for him. He was a good man who'd had the misfortune to become tangled with the worst of villains. Her father. Francis.

"And you ought to know better than to tell me as much as you have," she said, her throat tight. "You know you needn't confess, even to me. You must be aware how little proof we have."

"It doesn't matter. You know the truth."

"That isn't evidence." They hadn't any. A bottle of prussic acid, which one might find in countless houses. A forged will, and no way to prove it was forged, because no sample of her father's handwriting existed. Esmond could explain how Andrew had gone to the house, poisoned the laudanum, and still managed to be on the Dover mail coach he was supposed to be on. But they hadn't found the coachman, and even when they did, he might not remember Andrew, especially after three months and countless passengers. Or if he did remember, he might not be willing to admit to taking up a passenger where he wasn't supposed to.

"Circumstantial evidence will do," he said. "And he's clever enough to put together a case, eventually. I'd rather not wait. I've never been hunted before. It's a horrible feeling. I don't want him hunting me. I'd rather get it over with." He cleared his throat. "You're not to worry, and your friends aren't to worry. I know how to hold my tongue. I'm a lawyer, recollect. The only public scandal will be my own."

"Oh, Andrew." Her eyes filled.

"I shouldn't have let Beaumont marry you," he said. "But I did and can't undo it. He's done enough damage. I shan't add to it." He smoothed his gloves and straightened his spine. "You'd best let them off their leashes, my dear. It's growing late, and they'll be missing their tea."

ISMAL STOOD AT the window in Quentin's office while Mr. Herriard wrote his confession. When the solicitor was finished, he reviewed it twice, made a few minor corrections, then handed it to Quentin, who gave the pages but one quick glance before handing them to Ismal.

The circumstances of the crime were clearly described, from the moment Beaumont had accosted Herriard on the morning of 12 January. Beaumont had threatened to reveal the lawyer's part, ten years earlier, in a "criminal conspiracy involving weapons stolen from the British military." In exchange for silence, Herriard had agreed to take his former partner to the Continent and provide him with ten thousand pounds.

Just after six o'clock that evening, Herriard had arrived to collect Beaumont and found him in an advanced state of intoxication, raving that he would not leave England without his wife. Herriard dragged him upstairs and urged him to hurry with his packing. Beaumont only fell upon the bed, and continued drinking, while Herriard, concerned they'd miss the mail coach, began packing for him. Before he finished, Beaumont passed out.

Having already made up his mind to kill Beaumont at some point on the journey, Herriard altered his plans. While his victim slept, he dropped into the laudanum bottle a few grains of the prussic acid he'd brought with him, unpacked, and tidied the room. He then went downstairs, packed up the dinner Beaumont had scarcely touched, tidied up there and in the kitchen, and left by the back entrance—the same way he'd come.

Some blocks from the house he hailed a hackney and ordered the driver to take him post haste to the coaching inn in Piccadilly. They'd arrived seconds before the Dover mail coach was to depart. Fortunately, Herriard's place hadn't been taken. He ate Beaumont's dinner en route.

His confession contained nothing about Leila's father, no hint of what Beaumont had told him about the five people who'd taken their carefully planned revenge, and no mention of *Vingt-Huit*. It dealt only with the murder, with means, motive, and opportunity. It was neatly and concisely explained, every "i" dotted, every "t" crossed. The confession was guaranteed to result in a speedy trial and prompt condemnation to the gallows.

"I am sorry, Monsieur Herriard, but we cannot hang you," said Ismal. "If you force us to go to trial, you will assuredly be condemned, and we shall be obliged to seek the Crown's mercy. Madame will insist upon a pardon, and I cannot get one without explaining the mitigating circumstances. Several people will be obliged to support my petition: Lord Quentin, the Duke of Langford, Lord Avory, Lord Sherburne, Lady Carroll—and Madame Beaumont, of course. All that we have tried to keep quiet will be revealed, along with all that Quentin and I had previously tried to suppress."

"That *Vingt-Huit* business, you mean," said Herriard. "But there is no need—"

"I worked very hard to keep Beaumont's crimes from being known, you see, because the exposure would hurt his victims. I should have killed him, but I have an unconquerable aversion to assassination. If I had it to do over, I still would not kill him. Yet I would have managed matters differently. I fear I erred in letting him return to England. The consequences of that error fell upon you. For this reason, I feel some responsibility. If not for me, you would not have been placed in so distressing a predicament."

"My predicament was a consequence of what I did ten years ago," said Herriard.

"Madame believes you have made amends for that," Ismal said. "For ten years, as all the world knows, you have served your clients conscientiously, often above and beyond duty. You care for them as though they were your children. Never, since Jonas Bridgeburton betrayed your trust, have you allowed any other to betray the trust of those in your charge. That, to me, seems very like amends."

"I wasn't looking for her pity," said Herriard. "I only wanted her to understand I wasn't like Beaumont, that I wasn't his partner in crime all these years."

"She understands. Her heart is generous, monsieur. And just. She said that because of you, she became as good as she was capable of being. She told me how your lectures, your care, your unwavering support made her strong. Because of you, she strove to achieve great things. And because of you, she had both the means and the courage to prevent her husband's making a victim of her."

Ismal came away from the window and held the confession out to Herriard. "I know it relieved your heart to write this, monsieur. I ask you, for her sake, to destroy it."

White-lipped, Herriard stared at the page. "You hunted me. You had a score of men there to take me up. Isn't this what you wanted?"

"We took you into custody as a precaution," said Quentin. "No telling what your state of mind was."

The lawyer met Ismal's gaze. "You thought I'd hurt her."

"She is dear to me," Ismal said. "I, too, prefer to err on the side of caution."

"Dear to you. I see." Herriard took the confession then and, his face rigidly composed, tore the sheets into neat halves. Then he halved them again, and once again. He laid the pieces on the desk.

"What am I to do now?" he asked. "I can't—you can't expect me to take up my life as it was."

"I believe Lord Quentin has some ideas," said Ismal. "He has dealt with such thorny problems before." He stepped away from the desk. "Now, gentlemen, if you will excuse me, I have some private matters to attend."

HE FOUND LEILA in the studio trying to occupy her mind by occupying her hands. She was tacking canvas to a stretcher. She set the hammer down when he entered.

"Is it all right?" she asked.

"Did you not tell me to make it right?" he returned. "Do I not obey your smallest command? Am I not your slave?"

She threw herself into his arms. "You are a *wonderful* man," she said. "You are the most understanding, wise, clever, compassionate—"

"Slave," he said. "I am your slave. It is very, very sad."

"It isn't. You know it was the right thing to do. You knew just how Andrew felt. He'd paid for ten years, tried to make up for what he'd done, clear his conscience. Then to have Francis threaten to destroy everything he'd worked for and built—it wasn't *fair*. It would be criminal to hang him for what he did. It would be the most horrible kind of justice. A hideously cruel joke—another of Francis' cruel jokes."

"Do not upset yourself." He held her close, stroking her hair. "Quentin will find some way to make Herriard useful. He will make a new life, as I did, and cleanse his soul with disgusting work. Who knows? Perhaps the Almighty will show mercy to him as well and lead him to a brave and loving woman. Who will make him her slave."

"I shall pray for that," she said. "I never understood why he didn't wed. There were lots of women who would have jumped at the chance. But he said it today. One of them had to marry me. I suppose staying unwed was part of Andrew's 'amends'—so he could be there for me if anything happened to Francis."

"Now you have me, and no Herriard to fall back upon," he said. "You had better take very good care of me."

She drew back a bit. "I'm not very good at taking care of husbands. An artist is not the most attentive sort of wife."

"Fortunately, I do not require very much attention. I am well able to amuse myself." He glanced at the stretcher. "Perhaps I shall learn some new skills."

"You want to be a *painter*?"

"Nay. One in the family is enough. But you must show me all your secret arts and preparations, and I shall exert my mind to devise improvements. Also, I can cultivate clients. Perhaps, in time, you will receive Royal commissions. Now that I am retiring from Quentin's employment—"

"You're not serious." Her tawny eyes widened. "You'll be bored to distraction."

"You will not drop your work to traipse about the globe with me, and I would not take you on such missions. Nor would I go away without you. Naturally, I must retire. Besides, you forget that I will also be busy acquiring strays."

He took her hand and led her to the door. "I think that between furthering your career and accumulating children—oh, and matchmaking, beyond doubt—I shall have my hands more than full."

"I hope not," she said. "I was rather looking forward to continuing our partnership—as sleuths, I mean. It's been very interesting. Stimulating. Perhaps . . ." She paused as they reached the foot of the stairs. "Perhaps Quentin might let us look into the occasional problem. You wouldn't want your skills to rust from lack of use, would you?"

"The occasional problem. Theft. Blackmail. Murder, I suppose."

She continued up the stairs. "People have all sorts of terrible secrets that lead to problems. Only look what we've accomplished in three months: the Sherburnes. David and Lettice. David and his father, too. You know Langford's proud of David's effort to protect his brother's secret."

"Good deeds," he said. "You have resolved to become a saint, it seems."

They had reached her bedroom door. Her mouth slowly curved. "Not altogether. We could be saintly in public and wicked in private. We seem to be good at that."

"We." He opened the door.

"Oh, yes." She stepped inside. He followed and shut the door.

"*We*, certainly," she said. "As in 'made for each other,' as Lady Brentmor remarked. And Jason Brentmor agreed with her. He stopped by while you were with Quentin. He brought Mrs. Brentmor with him."

"Ah, the divine Arabella." He pulled off his neckcloth.

"They decided they approved your choice of countess." She sat on the bed and took off her slippers. "Apparently, I am sufficiently willful, bad-tempered, and just reckless enough to keep you alert."

"I see. You told them about hitting me with the bed-warming pan." He shrugged out of his coat.

"I'm glad I did tell them. I'd felt rather guilty." She began unfastening the jet buttons. "But Jason explained that it was simple amends. You'd abused my trust. I exacted payment on your skull. He agreed, too, that it was proper for me to give Andrew a chance to admit his wrongs and for me to offer forgiveness as I saw fit."

"Naturally, Jason would agree. You acted just as he would have done. I told you how he helped me make peace with his family ten years ago."

He watched the dress slip down over her shoulders, then her hips. "Like him, you want to understand fully before you judge. Like him, you will change your mind if facts warrant it. Like him, you have a wisdom distinct from intellectual quickness. Fortunately, yours is also a woman's wisdom."

While he spoke, the dress had dropped to the floor, followed by the chemise.

"And it inhabits a woman's body," he murmured. Swiftly, he rid himself of his own few garments and bent to unlace her corset.

"You like the body very much, I know," she said.

The corset fell away, revealing creamy curves. Swallowing a groan, he untied the petticoat and eased it down.

"Ah, well, I am almost human," he said hoarsely.

"Yes. You were born strange."

He drew the silk drawers down over her lush hips. They slid down her shapely legs and sank with a rustling whisper to the floor. He unfastened the garters, tossed them aside, and drew the black stockings off.

She slid back to the center of the bed. He crept toward her and knelt between her legs. "I was born for *you*," he said.

He bent and kissed her, deeply and lingeringly, while slowly driving her down onto the pillows. She wrapped her arms tightly about him.

"Yes, hold me," he said. "Keep me, Leila. You are the night. All my nights. And all my days. All my happiness. You know this." He stroked longingly, lovingly, down her silken skin. "*Je t'aime.*"

"I know," she said. "But tell me. Again. And again."

He told her in all his twelve languages, and with his hands, his mouth. He told her freely, and happily, for his heart was light. There were no secrets left between them. This night, he could love her fully, give of himself entirely, as she had given of herself to him. And that, he found, as she welcomed him inside her, was the way to paradise.

LATER, AS ISMAL held her in his arms, and their hearts slowed to quiet contentment, he told her what paradise was to him.

"I loved my homeland," he said softly. "I have dreamed of it as good men dream of heaven."

"In Paris, I told Fiona you were like Lucifer," she said.

"Cast out from Paradise. You sensed this."

"I wasn't aware of that at the time. I simply suspected

you were a devil with the face of an angel. But I always did have a soft spot in my heart for Lucifer. I should have given him another chance. I'm sure there were extenuating circumstances."

"Only you would look for them." He smiled. "Only you could see what I truly was. If I had been Lucifer, you would have knocked me about, and dragged me hither and yon doing good deeds. And then you should have pounded on heaven's gate and demanded I be let back in."

"I should do my best." She trailed her fingers through his hair. "I should like to go there with you."

"To heaven?"

"To Albania. To share it with you."

"Perhaps, one day. But it is not necessary. I only wanted to explain, to you and to myself, that this was all I knew of love—to love my homeland. I think this is why I had so much dread of love. I grieved ten years for what I had lost."

"I love you," she said. "I wish I could give everything back."

"You have," he said. "It is in your soul, I think. Perhaps the Almighty put it there, that you might keep it safe for me until I was ready. I hear it, see it, smell it when I am with you: the Ionian wind singing in the fir trees, the rushing rivers, the sea, the mountains, the soaring eagles. I see my homeland, my people in you, in the way you move, in your nature. Proud and fierce and brave. I think you were Albanian in another life, and my soul sensed this when I met you in Paris. I looked into your burning eyes, and my soul called to yours. *Shpirti im*, it called."

"*Shpirti im*," she repeated.

He drew her closer. "How easily it falls from your lips. Surely it is your soul's own language."

"It must be. Teach me more."

"In our tongue—"

"*Ours.* Yes."

"It is not Albania, but *Shqiperi*. And I, your husband-to-be, am a *Shqiptar*."

"*Shqiperi. Shqiptar.* And I, your wife-to-be—"

"You are *Madame*," he said. "My lady. Always. So it is written."

"*Kismet*," she whispered.

"Yes. *Kismet*." He brought his mouth to hers.

"My lady. My Leila. My beautiful Fate."

Turn the page for a special preview of
Loretta Chase's brand-new novel

LORD PERFECT

Available now from Berkley Sensation!

Egyptian Hall, Piccadilly, London, September 1821

HE LEANT AGAINST THE WINDOW FRAME, offering those within the exhibition hall a fine rear view of a long, well-proportioned frame, expensively garbed. He seemed to have his arms folded and his attention upon the window, though the thick glass could show him no more than a blurred image of Piccadilly.

It was clear in any case that the exhibition within—of the marvels Giovanni Belzoni had discovered in Egypt—had failed to hold his interest.

The woman surreptitiously studying him decided he would make the perfect model of the bored aristocrat.

Supremely assured. Perfectly poised. Immaculately dressed. Tall. Dark.

He turned his head, presenting the expected patrician profile.

It wasn't what she expected.

She couldn't breathe.

* * *

BENEDICT CARSINGTON, VISCOUNT Rathbourne, turned away from the thick-paned window and the distorted view it offered of the lively scene outside—of horses, vehicles, and pedestrians in Piccadilly. With an inner sigh, he directed his dark gaze into the exhibition hall, where Death was on display.

Belzoni's "Tomb," exhibiting the explorer's discoveries in Egypt a few years ago, had proved a rousing success since its debut on the first of May. Against his better judgment, Benedict had formed one of the nineteen hundred attendees on opening day. This was his third visit, and once again, he had much rather be elsewhere.

Ancient Egypt did not exert over him the hold it did over so many of his relatives. Even his numskull brother Rupert had fallen under its spell, perhaps because the present-day place offered so many opportunities for head-breaking and hairsbreadth escapes from death. But Rupert was most certainly not the reason for Lord Rathbourne's spending another long afternoon in the Egyptian Hall.

The reason sat at the far end of the room: Benedict's thirteen-year-old nephew and godson Peregrine Dalmay, Earl of Lisle. The boy was diligently copying Belzoni's model of the interior of the famous Second pyramid, whose entrance the explorer had discovered three years ago.

Diligence, Peregrine's schoolmasters would have told anyone—and had told his father, repeatedly—was not one of Lord Lisle's more noticeable character traits.

When it came to things Egyptian, however, Peregrine was persevering to a fault. They had arrived two hours ago, and his interest showed no signs of flagging. Any other boy would have been wild to be out and engaging in physical activity one and three-quarters of an hour ago.

But then, had this been any other boy, Benedict would not have had to come himself to the Egyptian Hall. He would have sent a servant to play nursemaid.

Peregrine wasn't any other boy.

He looked like an angel. A fair, open countenance. Flaxen hair. Clear, grey, utterly guileless eyes.

A group of boxers under "Gentleman" Jackson's super-vision had been employed to keep Queen Caroline and her sympathizers out of the king's coronation in July. These fellows, if they stuck together, might have contrived to keep the peace while the Marquess of Atherton's heir was about.

Other than these—or a large military force—the only mortal with any real influence over the young Lord Lisle was Atherton's brother-in-law Benedict—the only one, that is, except for Benedict's father, the Earl of Hargate. But Lord Hargate could intimidate anybody, excepting his wife, and he certainly would not stoop to looking after troublesome boys.

I should have brought a book, Benedict thought. Stifling a yawn, he directed his gaze to Belzoni's reproduction of a bas-relief from a pharaoh's tomb and tried to understand what Peregrine, along with so many other people, found so stimulating.

Benedict saw three rows of primitively drawn figures. A line of men whose beards curled up at the end, all leaning forward, arms pressed together. Lone hieroglyphic signs between the figures. Columns of hieroglyphs above their heads.

In the middle row, four figures towed a boat bearing three other figures. Some very long snakes played a part in the scene. More columns of hieroglyphs over the heads. Perhaps these figures were all talking? Were the signs the Egyptian version of the bubbles over caricatures' heads in today's satirical prints?

On the bottom, another line of figures marched under columns of hieroglyphs. These had different features and hair styles. They must be foreigners. At the end of the line was a god Benedict recognized: Thoth, the ibis-headed one, the god of learning. Even Rupert, upon whom an expensive education had been utterly wasted—Lord Hargate might have fed the money to goats with the same result—could recognize Thoth.

What the rest of it meant was work for the imagination, and Benedict kept his imagination, along with a great deal else, under rigorous control.

He turned his attention to the opposite side of the room.

He had an unobstructed view. For most of the Beau Monde, the exhibition's novelty had worn off. Even their inferiors would rather spend this fine afternoon outdoors than among the contents of ancient tombs.

Benedict saw her clearly.

Too clearly.

For a moment he was blinded by the clarity, like one stepping out of a cave into a blazing noonday.

She stood in profile, like the figures on the wall behind her. She was studying a statue.

Benedict saw black curls under the rim of a pale blue bonnet. Long black lashes against pearly skin. A ripe plum of a mouth.

His gaze skimmed down.

A weight pressed on his chest.

He couldn't breathe.

Rule: The ill-bred, the vulgar, and the ignorant stare.

He made himself look away.